About the Author

Tom Keya is an award-winning lawyer, founder and entrepreneur with a passion for history, culture, and in particular, big urban cities. Having lived in the middle east, London, and spent a great deal of time in New York, his inspiration comes from traditional noir and neo noir fiction as well as actual ancient historical events. With his passion for mental health awareness, his works focus on normalising mental health problems and bringing them out of the taboo and towards open and clear treatment.

The Third House

Tom Keya

The Third House

Olympia Publishers
London

Dedication

To my mother, Afsar. My brothers, Kevin, Alex, and Phil. My forever found sister, Sara, and my niece, Soraya. For Sofia, for whom I owe myself breathing today. And for Tarlan and the journeys, the excitement, and the adventures that await us. For my friends, Bas, Ian, Claudio, Karim and Marc – who lifted me up whenever I needed them the most. Finally for my dad, Amir. May he be laughing now as he forever did in my never fading memory.

Acknowledgements

A very special thank you to London and New York City – and everyone who lived, passed through, or even stopped over in them. Your small, creative spark drives me.

Part I

Chapter 1

Bishops Avenue, Hampstead, London

Detective Mulligan had been in the job for twenty-three years. He'd seen all there was to see. Nothing surprised him any more. He learned a long time ago not to be shocked by human nature —how violent, low, twisted, and sick it could be. He was the lead detective in the Bolívar case, which involved far too many chainsaws, even for a Colombian drug cartel. He had led the investigation on Stephen McLafferty, the cheeky performance artist with a rather peculiar passion for needles and eyes. But this case was different.

Granted, the scene was unsurprising and unimaginative. Brains and flesh were splattered on the floor; the vic's body was slumped forward and at an angle over his knees, a gaping hole to the back of the head—your standard assassination. But the deceased represented the culmination of the detective's lifework. His Magnum Opus. His great achievement. His ticket to retirement. All of it fucked. Like the bloody remains scattered across the hardwood floor, the detective was exactly where he was twelve years ago—in a very sticky situation.

Then again, in some ways, the ultimate fate of this operation, this final coup de gras, was Mulligan's own doing. It had been a matter of *when* to pull the plug, not *if,* and he'd waited too long.

He had all he needed months ago, but for someone all too aware of the inherent complications of human nature, the detective had given in to the most basic flaw of all—greed.

"So what do we fink, sir? Robbery gone wrong?"

That was Michael Anderson. He was new. It showed.

"Tell me, Anderson. If a thief was here, why the fuck would he leave the fuck-off big gold ring and chain with enough ice to fill the North Pole on the desk right next to the corpse, you fly-fucking moron?"

"Well, I fou…'old on. Is that who I fink it is?" Anderson's hefty jowls dropped in dismay.

"Yes, Anderson. Think of it like a jigsaw puzzle. Take the eyes here." Mulligan bent down and pointed at the face of the corpse, its eyes bulging and seeping around the exit wound between his eyebrows. "Plus that piece of the skull there."

He gestured towards a white fragment, dyed pink with blood, which was sitting at the corner of the plush living room rug.

"And some of that hair off the wall." A thick, dark, matted lock was glued to the hideous ochre paint by congealed brain matter. "And you'll get him. Terry Hunter."

"Arsenal ain't gonna win no cup anytime soon, that's for sure. They spent at least forty mil on him."

Who would be crowned champion that season was the last thing on the detective's mind. He couldn't care less if one of the best football players in the world was now lying somewhat headless beside a couch in the living room of a luxury mansion in Hampstead with some hooker face-up on the floor next to him; her face smashed to shambles and with half a dozen stab wounds to her gut, a steak knife still protruding from her large intestine. If anything, given Mulligan's distaste for football, he'd have been delighted to see many players receive such an admirable, albeit graphic, ending. But while the world would mourn Terry the Tiger—the Arsenal striker and FIFA football player of the year—the detective would be grieving the loss of a leading mole in one of the biggest investigations ever carried out on a criminal organisation. Hunter hadn't just been a mole, though. He was a witness. He was the sole proprietor of a cache of evidence hidden away, even from Mulligan. Everything Hunter had or knew or could testify about was gone, shot to shit, sprayed across the walls and across the body of his co-decedent.

Suddenly, Mulligan's eyes lost focus, and everything went blurry. He needed to sit down, but the nearest seat available—an ottoman that looked cheap and handmade, but likely cost a fortune—had too many fleshy fragments decorating its iridescent fabric. He ran towards the doorway, nearly losing himself in the seemingly enormous expanse between the living room and cavernous, sterile kitchen. He collapsed on a stool at the island worktop, already taking a glass from the dish-drying rack and reaching for the faucet. A nice glass of tap water would set him just right. A nice glass of tap water, fresh from a filtered, chilled, luxury water dispenser. A nice glass of tap water assisted by two tiny, loving pills of valium.

There. That calmed the shakes.

He'd played his hand right. It had all been within reach. Three of London's leading Mob Houses were all about to fall at the same time, straight into the detective's hands. But the prospect was suddenly gone. Twelve years of careful planning. Of closely monitoring the case, with only one other person aware of the great plot. A single confidant who understood the endgame they were playing to. Hunter didn't keep hard copy notes, no secret ledger or safety deposit box diary. He kept everything—every last, atomic detail—in his head. Which was blown to bits.

Anything his brain held, or might have held, was reduced to nothing more than worm food and, later, worm shit.

But who was behind it? The Three Houses, the rulers of London's underworld—affectionately known as the 'London Underground'—couldn't have had the slightest clue what he and Hunter had been up to. Mulligan had been careful, maybe even too careful at times. And he trusted Hunter with his life; he knew the kid wouldn't have flipped on him and gotten himself killed in the process. No way. The hooker could've ratted him out, but that would've meant he'd opened his fat gob up in front of her (which he'd never do) and she went to one (or all) of the Houses with it (which he'd never *let* her do). Sure, she'd been fooling around with him for some time now, but still. Girls like that came and went. They didn't learn anything, they didn't know anything, so they couldn't say anything. This one wouldn't have been any different.

The shooting didn't make sense, either; the scene was both too messy and not messy enough. Mulligan figured it was either done by an amateur or a pro who wanted to look like an amateur. Likely the latter. The bodies were left splayed and sloppy. There was no attempt at corpse disposal or any indication the murders were to be a message for or from someone, a threat of sorts against one House by another. It was a standard shooting, the kind of thing you'd see anywhere in England. Nothing special. And yet... the whole scene was wiped clean. There were no fingerprints or footprints besides Hunter's and the hooker's. No sign of forced entry. The knife was left behind, but the gun was taken. No sign of a robbery, of a dispute, or of a struggle. No sign of anything.

The detective felt his heart dropping to his stomach. He thought about how close he was. How much he had. He could have closed the Three Houses down for good. But he'd wanted more. He'd wanted their affiliates. Their friends. Their families. Their pets. He'd wanted everyone. And now, he had no one. His head started going dizzy again as he realised what he needed to do next. A cold sweat came over him, the shakes returned, and he knew there was a price to be paid for his greed.

It had to be him.

He racked his brain for anyone else, anyone but him.

But there was no one else. He couldn't rely on that prick, Anderson, the department's big 'fuck you' to the detective, and Mulligan had very few friends left. Just one, in fact. The last person he wanted to see. The person he swore never to use again, not for anything, not even for this. But there was no one else.

He picked up his mobile, praying for a last-minute alternative. One didn't come. He swiped the keyboard and sent a text to a number he didn't have saved in his contact list but couldn't have forgotten if his head was bashed in with a hammer.

21 Bshps Av, hmstd. C u in 20mins. M.

His mind told him not to press send. *You will only regret it.*

Detective Mulligan had been on the job for twenty-three years. He'd seen all there was to see. Nothing surprised him any more. Because he'd seen the man attached to the phone number resting in his palm in twisted action. Because he'd seen what that violent fuck did to an entire cartel in the Bolívar case. Because he'd seen how McLafferty met his tortuous end at the hands of the same man. A man who should have been locked up from the sorry day he was born. The man he was now considering bringing out of retirement, out of the darkness, and onto this case.

The detective looked at his phone. Click. *Message Sent.*

He gave in to two basic human flaws in one week; first greed, now anger. Like going back to an ex for one last shag for good time's sake, he regretted it the moment the deed was done.

Somewhere in London, a mobile was about to beep and, from that moment on, the whole of London was going to wish all hell had broken loose because it would've been better than what was coming. What was coming back.

But Mulligan didn't care any more. He'd tried to do his job with grace, charm and professionalism. He'd made an honest attempt at good, old-fashioned police work. But it was no use. For the first time in a very long time, the detective felt the need to brace himself. Already, he could feel something coming that he hadn't felt in a long time. It was a feeling he hated.

The detective, after twelve long years, was about to be surprised again.

Somewhere, right then, Calcain was about to be disturbed. And it was going to be even worse than the detective could've imagined.

*

Compton Street, Soho, London.

Pure darkness, with nothing to see. Just the way I liked it. I couldn't even tell whether my eyelids were open or closed. Peace. Finally. My own world and my own zone. There was nothing to do, nothing to see. All I had to do was exist. Just exist.

I was with Her. I could feel Her. I could smell Her, and I could smell *The Fame*. All I heard was the sound of my breath and the most beautiful music I'd ever listened to, maybe the most beautiful ever made. She sang to me, and I felt special.

Just give in, don't give up baby / Open up your heart and your mind to me / Just—

Suddenly, there was a flash. Lightning without thunder.

Everything was bright, too bright, and I couldn't see anything. My eyes hadn't had time to adjust. *Come on, pupils, do your thing.* The bloody Valium was still dragging me down, making me slow to come to. Or it could've been the heroin. Or it could've been the morphine. No, none of those. It must have been my designer drug, Dark Fire.

Or it could've been all of them at once.

With my sense of sight obliterated for the moment, I waited for a second, sharper sense to kick in. But my peace was already broken. The music had stopped. I could hear my own heart beating again, alive again. Panic set in just as quickly as the pills had pushed it away the night before, and the night before that, and the night before that. It only took a single noise to bring it all back:

Beep beep.

The bloody phone. How much time had passed since I first entered awareness this morning, since I first heard Her? Had it been hours? Or just a few seconds? What the hell was I on these days?

I looked at my phone. I didn't believe it. Mulligan.

21 Bshps Av, hmstd. C u in 20mins. M.

The phone started vibrating, playing a melody too chipper for that time of day. He'd always been an impatient one. But for him to be ringing me, well, something must have had him spooked. He'd never be so eager to hear from me otherwise. And let me assure you, the feeling was mutual. More than mutual.

"Yeah?" My voice was understandably hoarse.

"You coming or what?" His voice was unsurprisingly tense.

"Yeah, gimme a fuckin' minute. I'll be there." I hung up.

My pupils suddenly did their thing, and I could make out the shapes of the room and the things inside it. I reached for my bedside lamp and turned it on. And back into the real world I went. Shitty one-bedroom flat above a gay porn and sex shop. Clothes, drinks, trash everywhere. The roof, the walls, the floors, everything looking about five seconds from collapse. I eyed the bed and the floor. Three hookers. A new record. The lowest by quite a margin since I started competing against myself twelve years ago.

Right. Time to get up. It was eleven p.m. My music was back on, and She was singing to me again.

Eheh eheh / eha eha...

I shut it off. I needed to get ready. Only a few steps to the bathroom, and I turned on the overhead light. It flickered, either from a crappy bulb or shoddy electrical system or both for that matter. I turned the shower on, and the yellow-orange water sputtered then flowed; it was the clearest it had been for months. That was a good omen. The water ran through me and slowly, I woke up enough for my body to recognise and attempt to abort the toxins racing through it. I spun around, stepped down from the shower floor, dropped to my knees, and threw up in the yellow toilet with the orange decay running through its cracks. Looking at it made me sick again. Good. I was getting all the shit out of my system.

Once I'd voided the contents of my stomach, I flushed the foul leftovers and looked at myself in the mirror. The cunt that stared back at me with bloodshot eyes looked tired. He looked baggy-eyed and pale. He hadn't always looked that way, but he'd come to own it. He must have shaved recently. The yellow decay around the mirror frame matched the stuff in the toilet, the stuff in the shower and up the walls. Pills upon pills were settled in piles around the sink, on the lid of the toilet tank, scattered across the grey stained floor. I brushed my teeth, swiped a bit of gel on, and left the toilet. Fresh underwear was essential for a night sure to be of great importance, if for no other reason than to rub Mulligan's face in the fact that, in the end, he'd been the one to call first. *He'd* been the one to need *me*. I threw on a dark suit, leather Ecco loafers, two dabs of aftershave, a grey tie, and the cufflinks I got as a gift from a girl many years before. I glanced around the room. The hookers were still asleep. A fleeting pang of guilt before it was banished. I found my final item of clothing—a red, silk scarf—and wrapped it around my neck. Then I was off. The door to my apartment never shut all the way, but the one downstairs did. I stepped out into wind and rain. It was late September, and we were already on the road to an English winter.

I put one foot down on the sidewalk, and before I could take a second, I heard a campy, high-pitched voice.

"Getting up a little early, babe? Oh em gee, you're all dressed up!"

That was Tanka, Jimmy's boyfriend. They'd been together for six months; the longest Jimmy had been with anyone. Jimmy always had a thing for oriental boys, but it didn't bother me any. He let me have the flat above his shop and everything. He was a good man. A cock-hungry poof, but a good man nonetheless.

"Well, Tanka, you better get used to it. I have a feeling it's all going to be a little bit more civilised from now on."

"Oh, honey," he said in his American accent. "What have you taken this time, and… wait. Are you wearing the hair product I gave you?"

"Oh, yeah. I thought I'd make an effort with this one. And, honestly, I haven't taken anything, not for at least five hours, anyway. But look, I have to go. Say hello to Jimmy for me will ya, pal?"

19

"Will do, honey."

I breathed in the fresh air; a stark contrast to the suffocation of my apartment. I put my headphones on—damn good headphones with proper bass. She sings to me.

I am as vain as I am loud…

I began my journey. Where was I headed again? Oh, right. Bishops Avenue, Hampstead. Northern Line on the tube. I needed the Edgware branch. I'd take it from Tottenham Court Road. My favourite station. Close to Soho, close to the British Museum. Close to the herpes-ridden West End.

I walked through Soho, the land of the freaks of London. It was a great area, really. It smelled of noodles, pizza, and shisha. There was always trash on the ground, and the people there, the buildings there, the gutters there were all as dirty and nasty as it gets. The colours, though. The colours in Soho were amazing. Shops (usually sex shops), bars, clubs, coffee shops, and restaurants all displayed shiny lights, neon lights, shimmering lights with diverse shapes and sizes throughout the night. You'd see all the colours; red, green, blue, orange, and fucking yellow.

I hated yellow.

But not in Soho.

It was everything you'd expect from any city's downtown area anywhere in the world. The streets were vibrant, and the illuminated signs made for a beautiful stroll. Something like moonlight, but better. And the food was quite nice. With Chinatown a stone's throw away, you could get some decent 'chicken' noodles (which were more likely rat). I stopped for a takeaway cappuccino from Bar Italia, the best damn coffee shop in London. I walked past the freaks. The publicly fertile gays. The dressed-up drags. I could make out the City Point skyscraper in the distance. I was close.

I reached into my pocket and checked (a bit late) for the four essential tools a Londoner needs: Oyster card, bank card, ID, and keys. It was all there. You didn't want to be looking for your Oyster card at the barrier before you got onto the platform of the tube. That's a cardinal sin in London. Almost as bad as standing on the left side of the escalator. Your punishment would be a devastating stream of insults from impatient strangers:

"Oh, fucking hell. Get your card, will you? You fucking tosser."

"Fuck off to the right side, you cunt-lipped prick."

All that and much more from your fellow commuters. Too stressed for their jobs, too excited for their dates, too eager to get home, and, my personal favourite, on too much coke. Three seconds makes a lot of difference in London, or so they think, and you don't want to take those three seconds away from people unnecessarily.

Past the barrier, down the escalator, onto the platform, and then I was waiting for the Edgware-bound train. The platform was packed, but I always felt solace there. You knew what you were going to get from the end of the seemingly never-ending tunnel. And when it came, it could take you anywhere you wanted to go. I loved the London underground, and I loved very few things because when you loved something, it was a real shit sandwich to lose it. People say, 'It's better to have loved and lost than never to have loved at all'. I call bullshit.

According to the terminal sign, it was two minutes until the next train came. In tube terms, that could be anything from thirty seconds to five minutes. I waited. I observed. Looking around the platform at night could be very entertaining. The loners sitting on the chair or standing by the platform with their books, Kindles, papers, or phones. The cool (and very loud) gangs of either trendy, all-boy groups or mixed-gender posses. The thirty-something chicks out on a hen do with pink everything head-to-toe and costume store wings. It was Saturday night, eleven forty-five p.m. by then. The clubbers must have been heading to Camden (most likely to the Koko Club). The rest just wanted to get home. I always looked for the single, dressed-up ones who looked a bit teary-eyed. The ones who called it a night too early because they saw their boyfriends talking to other chicks or had unnecessary arguments with girlfriends that could have been resolved within minutes. I'll say this; any other night, such chicks would be getting fucked—and fucked well—in Soho, above a gay porn sex shop. I loved the look of regret on their faces in the morning. It was priceless. But not that night. That night, I had work to do.

The train was coming. It was going to be tough trying to get a seat. I positioned myself as best I could. The train arrived following a warm, comfortable wind. The door opened, and I let the passengers get off, nudged the crying girl, and aimed for the seat closest to the door. Got it. Now to Hampstead. The train was crammed, as anticipated. It was all too close. A guy and girl stood in front of me, and guys always seemed to be wearing such tight trousers these days. The girls, too, tended to wear leggings, if not skin-tight dresses, but I sure as hell didn't mind that. I could either smell the girl's cunt, the guy's balls, or his balls after they'd been in her cunt. Why the fuck would he do that? Why would anyone stick their balls in a girl's cunt? Sick fuck. I looked at him in disgust. He didn't like that but fuck him. Ball-fucking weirdo. I closed my eyes and let Her sing to me.

I do my hair, I gloss my eyes…

*

"The next station is Hampstead. This train terminates at Edgware."

I opened my eyes, and the train was nearly empty. Population depletion on the train was an amazing thing to watch. After Zone Three, it dropped almost instantly. I was off the train, tapping my Oyster on the barrier, out of the station, and into the sweet breeze within moments. The surrounding area smelled of crêpes but was generally fresh. Hampstead was green and the High Street, bohemian. Bookstores, independent clothing shops, and family restaurants were all readily available and all posh, but with a nice touch. It was welcoming. I took a right and had quite a walk to Bishops Avenue. No problem, I had good music with me.

I went past the small pond, walked along the Heath, and finally arrived at the edge of Bishops Avenue, which sat opposite Kenwood House. I crossed the road and stepped onto one of the most—if not the most—expansive roads in London. The houses were far apart from each other, their properties covered in trees. Some left a good driving distance between their front gates and the avenue. They were huge. Not big. *Enormous.* Like miniature castles.

The insides of those houses were amazing, usually boasting sixteen large bedrooms, multiple living rooms, and small forests as gardens. The kitchens were every housewife's dream. I knew houses like that very well. I used to own one.

I walked down the street and found it empty. The problem with Bishops Avenue was that rich Arabs, Uzbekistanis, and other undeservedly, overly rich people bought those houses just to say they owned them. They never used them. Even if they were in London, they'd check into hotels. Luxury ones. But they'd never use their houses. They were nothing more than status symbols.

It was easy to find number twenty-one; it was the one with all the police cars, ambulances, and blue lights beaming around it. Police tape was wrapped around fences, doorways and trees. All you could hear was the static of walkie-talkies and people running from one place to the next but somehow not accomplishing much. When I got close to the front gate, a fat cop, looking like someone from of a Weight Watcher's 'before' picture, stopped me.

"Slow down, sunshine. Can't you read the sign? Authorised personnel only."

I could have had a bit fun there, but I was late. I was always late. I needed to make it quick, articulate, and graceful.

"Fuck off, you fat, sweaty, vagina squirt. I need to see Mulligan. Like your pound-a-go whore of a mother, he's expecting me tonight."

Charming, I know.

"All right, funny man. Unless I see a fucking ID, you're not going anywhere. Like a butterfly…"

He tried to match my wit, but I broke him off. That was enough airtime for him and what he probably thought was a sense of humour.

"I'm going to do what I did to that tart you call 'Mom' and show you something that will pleasantly surprise you."

I took out my badge, the only time and place a guy could see my full name. The only time a guy could find out who employed me.

"Cal… Calcain. Is it… is that real?"

"That's exactly what your mother said. Now, pretty please, with sugar on top… Fuck off. There's a good lad."

He knew the wrong step could have consequences beyond his wildest imaginings. His head was the size of a melon, and the sweat began to bead on his big, fat chin. He let me through. He knew then who he was fucking with. I wondered, *Is he shitting himself because he knows who I work for or because he knows who I am?*

"Calcain…" I heard him say as I walked past.

I hoped I was wrong. I didn't want to be known; fame and my job didn't go hand in hand. At *my* end of the day, fame could kill.

I walked past the gate and onto the long road that led to the enormous doors, which were propped wide open with people coming and going. I walked through the entryway and saw people in white overalls taking notes, measuring this and that, collecting samples. Between them stood a twenty-something, medium-built douchebag with a funky mullet haircut and a late thirties-early forties, relatively tall and well-built man. The latter hunched slightly. As strong as he looked, he was clearly a broken man. Bits of silver hair stuck out here and there, but he wore a nice bespoke suit. He looked tired. His features were still sharp. Slim face, curly hair, strong jaw, and silver eyes that looked up at me. His face was awestruck. He was stunned that I turned up. One of the few men I knew who wasn't intimidated by me, who didn't fear me. He knew me. I couldn't say for sure, but I thought he could be smiling. I doubted it, though. He'd never be happy to see me. He was, without a doubt, the biggest cunt ever. He was the closest thing I'd ever had to a friend.

As I walked towards him, I saw more people gathered around the sofa in front of me. The closer I got, the more blood I saw. I walked forward and suddenly realised where I was; in the middle of a fucking crime scene. Two dead bodies, one crumpled beside the couch, the other on the floor next to it. Male, Black, twenties, gunshot wound to the back of the head. Female, White, twenties, severe head trauma and stab wounds. It was old school. Either an amateur or an act of irony. I didn't understand the scene because I would only be called if this was a serious assassination. Sure, it looked like a murder, but not one with intent. Then again, the sheer butchery of the situation told me it could be a message. But what, and from whom?

I began to sniff around for clues, and after a good look, I was fairly certain about what had happened. I looked at the angle of the bullet wound. I looked at the blood spatter from the stab wounds. I looked at the shape of the bruising about the girl's head. I examined the furniture, the countertops, the windows. From the balcony, I could see a massive construction project underway on the house next door. A group of workers was doing the mundane task of cleaning up a small heap of bricks that appeared to have fallen off the roof and crashed down to the home's driveway. I knew what had happened. Clear as day. But there must have been a bigger story here. I wouldn't have been called if there wasn't one.

I turned around to see the silver fox, with his hands in his pockets, staring at me. He was too close to ignore now. He'd aged, but only slightly.

"Well, it looks like that sand is going to be firmly tucked in your vagina for the next few weeks, Mulligan. Two vics."

"Don't get funny with me, Calcain. I'm in no mood."

"What's the matter? Vet fucked your wife again?"

"Nope. After your mother, the vet simply didn't have much more left in him." He raised his eyebrows. "Don't believe me? Have a look at your mother face. And arsehole, for that matter."

He got me good. First, I needed to employ a tactical retreat.

"Oh, Mulligan, I don't think I'll reduce myself to your level further. I'm far too mature for that." Then for a renewed assault. "Besides, your wife's got my number. Anything that pisses me off about you can land on her face."

Eat that, you cunt.

"I thought you weren't into women any more. All tucked in with cock munchers and chinks."

My allies, he meant.

"Don't you fucking dare use derogatory remarks about the people who've protected me. They've done more for me than you ever did. Or have you forgotten how you left me exposed for all the Houses? Or about how you got me banished? Have you forgotten about Elsie? Because I fucking haven't."

Mulligan's face went red. He looked tongue-tied.

"Why the fuck did you even call me here? To tell you what happened? Fine, here's a story for you. She offed him, then herself."

Mulligan rolled his eyes and spread his arms wide. "That's clearly not what fucking happened here, Calcain. Look at that girl's face."

"Maybe she did it to herself."

Mulligan scoffed, "You're putting me on."

I shrugged. "Bit of an odd way to go about it, I'll admit, but that's the only story I'm giving you."

I crossed my arms. "How about you tell me a story now?"

His shoulders sagged back into the posture he held when I first walked into the room.

He gestured weakly towards the man's body. "That's Terry Hunter."

"So? He likes paying for minge as much as the next person. And she looks high-class, which isn't surprising given he's footballer and all that."

"He was undercover for a while." He breathed hard. "Look, it's fairly high-level stuff."

I held up a hand. "Mulligan, tell me what the fuck I'm doing here."

I could see in Mulligan's face that he didn't want to tell me the truth. He was hiding things. Again. Because that had gone so well the first time around.

Mulligan stepped closer to me and dropped his voice. "Hunter was undercover. He was arranging a deal between Charlie, Russell and Elad. The deal was about the Shard of Glass skyscraper in London Bridge."

Charlie. Elad. Russell. Leaders of the Houses. Rulers of London's underworld.

"Bullshit—"

"Just fucking listen for once, you twat." Mulligan's voice was somewhat hoarse with desperation. "I'm trying to tell you about something a lot bigger than me, you, and all your bloody self-pity. Given the location of the Shard, Charlie, Russell and Elad called a truce, which was restricted only to the Shard and the immediate surrounding area. Each would take an equal piece. No war. No killing. Hunter agreed to arrange the deal because he was the only one all three were linked to."

"How?"

"Charlie was his second cousin, Elad is a major shareholder in Arsenal, and Russell had used Hunter on thousands of occasions to promote his clubs down in the West End. For them, he was the perfect middleman. He brokered the deal of the century. They all trusted him."

I waited for more explanation, but none came.

"That was the worst summary of a story I've ever heard. That told me nothing, I got zero information from that. I might even have less now than I started with. So, please. Tell it again. From the beginning. I need to understand how on earth, except for the family ties, Hunter was so liquid. How he managed to get into such a unique position with all three of them. I mean, he must have only been… oh, poor fuck. When exactly was it you took him under your sick, paedophiliac wings?"

"Ten years ago. I picked him up when he was barely a teenager, right about the time we were dealing with the Cohen and Dillon case near Canary Wharf. Poor family, council estate rejects, dispossessed. He was kicking a can around, but I could see potential in him. Serious potential. Pulled a few strings, got him signed up to a few clubs, and made sure he moved on from there. It wasn't hard; with talent like his, it's easy to get ahead.

"When I found out who he was connected to, I got him an agent who specialised in inter-House deals. Got him involved with all the Houses. That also wasn't hard. He was a social kid. Real good kid. Easily likeable and entirely harmless. Soon, he learned the tricks of the trade. Football became ten percent of what he was about; the rest was all about promotion and sales. Clubbing and women were, of course, footnotes to this. For so many years, I watched him, guided him, and helped him to get everyone to trust him. I told him the truth about his purpose very early on, and he knew he was doing a good thing. Besides, with more money than he'd ever dreamt of, he didn't care. All he knew was that he had to gather data on various activities that could be considered 'uncouth'.

"He was designed to be a key witness. Ten years' worth of work on all sides. My main focus was Russell. He really took Hunter under his wing. Got him involved in the club promotions and everything. Hell, he recently signed over fifty percent of that club, Amika, to Hunter for all his hard work as a gift. With everything Hunter had on him, I was ready to move in on Russell but realised the implications very quickly when Hunter told me what you had told me so long ago."

Mulligan's eyes met mine.

"Leaving West End exposed would open up a massive gang war and power vacuum. With the coalition's budget cuts, we simply didn't have enough resources to defend West End. I don't know whether you know this, but the government is at its weakest point right now; the coalition is failing. I would basically be opening the door to an inter-House orgy with a subtle touch of S&M. Hunter said that, even if we took down two Houses, it would still leave the other gangs and a newly undisputed House ready for war. The mini-gangs could form a franchise and take on the remaining House. Who knows what would come of it? We needed to take all three down at the same time. And so Lady Luck, in the form of the Shard of Glass, appeared and licked my arsehole without wanting anything in return."

He sighed. "But she turned out to be a pipe-hiding, arse-hungry wench and ended up pounding my arse like there was no tomorrow instead of licking it.

"A few developers realised More London's potential just off London Bridge. Basically, Canary Wharf and its skyscrapers are too far for some businesses, but vast empty land across the river from the Square Mile is just right. So, after they built More London, they decided to build—or rather renovate—some old cunted building and push it up, making it the UK's and Europe's largest skyscraper. It just so happens that this building is the old PWC building, just outside London Bridge station."

"Just outside London Bridge Station? Specifically there? What a comfortable coincidence…"

"I know. Maybe the developers got some consultant in—"

"What sort of consultant would know that exact space is the one undeclared area among the Three Houses? I mean, I know those boys at Goldmans and McKinzies play it dirty sometimes, but this? How many people know this? It's just ridiculous!"

"Look, I don't understand it myself. In any event, as soon as the Houses found out, all three rushed in to claim it. To avoid a full-scale war, they called in a mediator. Not someone neutral, as that would ironically be bad for the Houses because that person would be content to side with just one of the parties. They needed someone who stood to profit equally from all the Houses getting a fair deal."

"So they needed Hunter?"

"He was perfect. Intelligent, enthusiastic, articulate, fair—"

"And well trained by an expert?"

He levelled me with a hard stare. "Stick that tongue up your dickhole for a minute. I hate it when you interrupt me. Anyway, Hunter mediated a deal whereby everyone would get an equal share by each providing one of the PPO Services: Promotion, Protection, Operation—"

"I know what PPO is."

"I know you know, just let me fucking talk." He sighed hard. "So Charlie got Protection, Russell naturally got Promotion, and Elad got Operation. This created a very uneasy truce. The gangs would have day-to-day interaction on-site in London Bridge whilst their comrades could be killing each other in Peckham. But they did a great job at it; the deal was well formulated and well documented."

"Well done, Hunter."

"Now, I had all the toss.pots in one single place at one single time doing some serious gangster shit, taking turns burying bodies in the concrete and everything. It was beautiful. Horrifying. But beautiful. I had enough to take them down but thought I'd just get some more dirt, just a little extra. A little cherry on top that could be an essential component if the jury was split."

"But you got greedy?"

"Yes, I did."

Some things never changed.

"I'd worked and I'd worked and I'd worked, and I waited ten years for this. I thought I could wait a little longer. Just a week. One week. There was a meeting at the site today to prepare for the completed work. A high-level meeting. Word had it all three heads were turning up. I knew it was too good to be true, but I asked Hunter to wear a wire. I gave him the equipment at four-thirty, and that was the last time I saw him. At least..." He swept a hand towards the corpses. "Before he lost his head. Next thing I know, I get called in for a bloody murder in Hampstead, and there he is. No coming back from that kind of injury. No getting the case back on its feet, either. Everything lost, everything destroyed, just like Hunter."

Mulligan's capacity for being a prick was incredible. He took a poor kid and put him in the middle of some of the most dangerous people in the world. And what saddens him most isn't the kid dying, it's a bad day at work. It's the mess he caused. It's an inconvenience that I'm certain blocked him from early retirement and a big, fat bonus. He used the kid as bait, simple as that. And when the Houses take bait, they take it, they devour it, and they spit up nothing but bones. I should know.

I was tiring of Mulligan's long-winded story.

"So did they meet in the end, then?"

"Yes, but I doubt they know about Hunter yet. They probably

think he's off chasing girls."

"Right, well, based on what you have—and more important, on what you've lost—this seems to me like a tough case for the prosecution."

"Not tough. Impossible. I gave Hunter explicit instruction not to keep notes, not to give me any specific details. I told him to keep it under wraps so if I got caught out, the case wouldn't be jeopardised. I wouldn't be able to tell anyone anything."

"And you didn't think to consider what would happen if he died?"

"I'd be fucked. I knew that. And here I am. Fucked. I have nothing. He did exactly what I said. He kept everything to himself. Everything hidden somewhere or locked up or stored in a photographic memory, for all I know. I wouldn't even know where to begin looking. But I don't regret it because I had to play it safe. The fewer people with inside information, the better for everyone. I was playing all three Houses in one go, a totally unheard of undertaking, and it was too much. Even for me."

"You bit off more than you could chew, you're saying?" I paused for a while, giving him time to reflect on his fuck-up. "Well, dear friend, I can only express my sincerest condolences and my deepest sympathies at your complete and utter failure today. No doubt you will one day reach this admirable goal— hopefully you won't get anyone else murdered in the process— and you'll look back at today and just laugh and laugh."

I checked my watch. "My gosh, look at the time. I must be getting home now, and it looks like a night bus jobbie to me."

I turned to leave.

"Calcain, I didn't call you here for chit-chat."

I stopped. It was exactly as I'd feared, what my gut had been telling me from the moment my phone beeped that morning.

His kept voice was low, trying to be sensible.

"I…" He took a breath and tried again. "This isn't easy for me to say, by any measure, but I need you to help me finish this. If there was anyone else, I would jump at the opportunity to take them on instead. But you're the only person who can hack this. I want you to come on board, and—"

"Two words—fuck off."

My response was perhaps not so sensible.

"Look," he snapped. "I've had it with this fucking case. Ten years of my life has been about this pile of shit, and now I've lost it. Everything. I did it my way, and I was winning, I truly was, but now it's become a bit like a computer game. You play a hard level over and over again, and every time you're about to seal the victory and beat the final boss, you fail. But you've given it so many shots, you've come so close, you think that after all this time, you really have earned it. And so you find you wouldn't really feel guilty about—"

"Cheating?"

He was almost grinding his teeth as he was speaking. "I tried to avoid bloodshed."

"No. You went into a gunfight with a vagina, and now it's bleeding more than it should, even on a heavy month. So you want your balls back. The only problem is that you had yourself a sex change to get that fancy designer minge, which means you can't get them back."

He snapped again, but this time, he was a lot louder. "I wanted to take down criminals, not make victims. This wasn't just about getting revenge on the Houses. That kind of thing just doesn't do it for me any more. Sure, I could go in with a big gun, kill everyone on my way to the top, and then take out whoever I find there. But the problem isn't killing the boss. I wouldn't mind

34

that bit. It's the soldiers who would die along the way. These junior gangsters have kids. Kids who will grow up and want revenge. And guess what that creates? A vicious cycle of death after death after death. More gangs, more violence in the streets.

"With this case, I could have taken all the Houses down without killing a single fucking person. Not one. I did everything just right. I made one fucking mistake. I waited one millisecond too long to wrap things up, and now that potential is gone. And to be honest, I'm pretty fucked off about the whole thing. So I'm done debating with you. You either take this case, or you can go back to that piss-stained, rat-infested nest you call a home, and you'll remain there for as long as I want you to."

Now *I* was fucked off.

"Woah there, boy. You seem to be coming on a little strong here. Let's not forget who has the vagina and who has the twenty-two-inch cock. You went to fight gangsters thinking all you needed was pen, paper, and good intentions. You had the evidence. But you fucked up. You. No one else. Don't forget that. It was all you. But let's suppose you had succeeded. Let's suppose you had gotten away with your mistake, that getting greedy worked out in your favour for once."

He winced at that, but I pushed on.

"Did you really think they would go down that easy? Allow me to introduce you to the real world. First, they would've hired lawyers, probably from Skadden or some other billionaire-supporting shithole establishment that would probably suck any dick, any time, to win the case. They would've gotten top QCs involved who'd have made any witnesses shit their pants in front of a judge, making them look like retarded, self-serving liars. So that rules out a civil trial. Then they would've killed everyone—and I do mean everyone—starting with your great mate here…"

I pointed to Hunter's body. "And ending with you and anyone else who so much as walked past you on the sidewalk. They would have literally killed off the prosecution. Then they would've entered into a big fuck-off war with each other over who fucked who because they'd all refuse to accept they got played by a shitty, second-rate cop. After months of killing and warring, then the juicy stuff would've started. I'm talking high-level assassinations. Empty seats. Vacuums of power across the city waiting to be filled by who knows what kind of dangerous fuck. And within a year, the River Thames would've been as red as mother nature's overloaded tampon."

Mulligan shut up. He actually shut the fuck up. In the history of our relationship, I couldn't recall that happening. Not once. It was a pleasant surprise, but a surprise nonetheless. I was ready for a protracted argument to come my way. I was already piecing together counterarguments in my head. But if he was going to keep his mouth shut, I had nothing to say, nothing to argue against. I felt a lot of pressure suddenly, like when you go deep underground on the tube and your ears started closing in on you. The silence was killing me. He finally broke it, and the pressure flooded out of my ears almost immediately.

"What are your terms?"

That's when things got interesting.

"My terms for what?"

"For finishing this case."

The case was already dead. We both knew it.

"What do you mean, finishing it? Finishing it how?"

He kept a steady, familiar gaze on me.

"Are you saying you want me to take down all three Houses for you? Is that what you're asking me?"

"I'm asking you to find out who killed Hunter. After that,

yeah. Take down the Houses."

I couldn't believe what I was hearing, what he was asking me to do after all these years apart.

"I believe I just told you to go fuck yourself. Or maybe I told you to fuck off. Either would be appropriate. Maybe go fuck your mother. Or a cat."

"I'm giving you an opportunity here, Calcain. A chance to set out your terms. A way out of your current... mess."

"Are you out of your fucking mind? What makes you think I could even do this? On top of that, what makes you think I won't set my own terms, take what I can get from you, and fuck off to Canada or somewhere?"

"Regarding the latter, I'm confident you won't run off. Because you know if you do, I'll find you. I'll eat you. And I'll bury what remains of you in a shallow fucking grave. Because if you fuck me like that, I'll have nothing to lose, pal."

He paused. I could've given him the look, but I didn't. The look that said, 'I'd fuck your wife in front of you right after chopping your dick and balls off if you even tried to touch me'. I understood where he was coming from. He was angry. He was desperate. And he was right. I could've gotten a good deal out of the arrangement. I wasn't feeling a whole lot at that point as far as human emotion went, and when I did feel something, it was anger. But standing in front of Mulligan, defeated as he was, it's possible I felt a bit of sympathy for him. I'd consider helping with the case. But he and I both knew I had my own reasons for that.

He continued. "And regarding the former. If anyone, *anyone*, in this world could possibly do what I'm asking, it would have to be you. Because apart from having a unique mind, an ability to creatively execute a plan, and a limited but sufficient level of intelligence, you're also well trained. And I reckon no one would want to see them go down as much as you and me. Especially after—"

"Stop. Just stop."

He held up his hands defensively and took a step back.

"What do you say?"

"I say you're a cunt."

"Maybe so," he snapped again.

It seemed he still hadn't gotten that temper under control.

"But right now, I'm the only person in the world who you can make a deal with. So think carefully before losing your one chance at freedom. As much as I hate the Houses, letting you go free could be the worse of two evils, if we're being frank. In an ideal world, they'd go down, and you'd be forgotten. But that's not what would happen. And I'm sorry for that. Before today, I believed I'd happily let the Houses run London with the comfort of knowing a cunt like you couldn't walk free again.

"But after today? Well, let's just say I've had a change of heart. If I was forced to choose between your freedom or theirs, it would be like if someone asked if I'd rather fuck my mom or my dad. Neither option is ideal, but you've got to pick one. And today, by a very slim margin, by just the tip of a needle, I choose your freedom. I'm giving you a chance to just once not be a self-centred, pathetic wretch. I'm giving you a chance to go after your enemies. What do you say?"

It was better than silence. I knew where I stood. I knew what this was all about. He had spent ten years on this, and now he wanted to see it end, no matter how. He wasn't asking for my help. He was cheating.

He was letting me loose.

"I've got terms."

"Expected. Shoot."

"First, I want my so-called self-imposed banishment removed. I want full protection. From you, from the Met, from the junior gangs you guys do business with. I want guaranteed immediate freedom to roam wherever the fuck I like, rather than hiding behind the only people who can protect me, which would otherwise keep me restricted to Soho and to travelling at night. Second, I want money. I want at least two hundred and fifty thousand pounds if I catch the person who killed Hunter and at least a further seven hundred and fifty thousand pounds for taking down each House—"

"Done."

"I'm not finished. I want upfront monies. At least the two hundred and fifty thousand pounds, and regular expenses paid. I will, of course, provide invoices, which you can expect to be engraved with heroin needles on used condoms. Finally, I want you. I want full access to you at all times. I call, you fucking answer. I don't care if your mouth is glued with cunt juice after a night of sucking your mother. I want access to you twenty-four-seven."

"All done."

"Oh, and one more thing. I want my pass. I want to know I can do anything to anyone. I can kill, I can torture, I can stalk, I can maim, I can hack. I can do whatever the fuck I want for as long as I want until this case is resolved. I'll do things the way I feel like, without you getting fucking involved."

"I won't let—"

"Then I'm out. Give me total freedom, without interference, or we're done here."

"I won't let you use some—"

"Yes, you will. You'll let me do things my way, Mulligan. That's the fucking deal, those are my terms, and they're nonnegotiable."

He hesitated. The problem with him was that he was a man of his word. If he agreed, he'd be giving me everything. But the thing was, he had nothing left to lose, so giving me the win wouldn't end up mattering to him one bit. I almost felt sorry for him.

"Fine. But just one thing—Hunter is our first priority. Number one. I want to know you'll do everything you can to catch who did this to him." His voice dropped again, almost to a whisper. "I know I'm on the brink of ruin professionally, and you probably won't believe me, not that I have to explain myself to you in the first place, but Hunter... I'd known him since he was a boy. He was a good kid—"

"Mulligan."

"Yeah?"

"I will get the son of a whore who killed him. What remains of that prick after I'm through will be all yours. Though I can't promise you'll have much to play with."

He looked at me, and I could see tears gathering around his eyes and a small, faint smile. If he'd adopted Hunter, it would've been the second son he'd lost in ten years. He fought the tears back.

"I'll get him," I said again, no longer able to look Mulligan in the face.

He remained silent. I walked away, giving him space. I took a photo of the scene with my phone, then slowly started to leave the scene, observing its details as I passed. I turned and took a final look at the stunning living room full of antiques; a huge, thin TV; silk Persian rugs. And, of course, two new accessories; a dead man and his hooker. As sure as Mulligan was certain that Hunter's death was related to the Houses, I was equally as certain that it wasn't. Still, this was part of something bigger, something that stretched beyond this room and out into the city. Mulligan thought someone knew Hunter was a rat, and maybe someone did. If he needed me to say I was looking for Hunter's killer, fine. I'd say it. I'd look the part. I'd play the game. I'd just take down the Houses while I did it.

Everyone in the room still looked busy, but Mulligan somehow stood out. He always did. He was looking at the window, but I knew I was really the thing in his sights. He always had that kind of awareness. As I left, I heard something from the living room. It made me feel something I hadn't felt for a while. The voice was kind and faint, and I was sure it was Mulligan.

If I didn't know better, I'd say it sounded like, "Thank you."

*

I walked down towards the gate. The fat cunt I had to get past earlier was outside the house now. He took one look at me and jumped up.

"Mr… uh… sir."

"Don't call me that."

"Sir, I was just wondering. Do you need a lift home?"

"Where do you live?"

"Lambeth, sir."

"Don't call me 'sir'."

"Yes, sir."

I needed a good night's sleep. I needed to sleep well. Before taking on a massive project, if you can, it's imperative to have a great night's sleep. My funds were drying up, and I knew I had upcoming expenses, so I couldn't risk not getting paid for the job. I needed to sleep somewhere clean, with a soft bed accompanied by a bathroom not caked in mould. Although my flat was on his way, I didn't ask to be dropped there.

"Do you know any cheap hotels here? Like a Holiday Inn or Travelodge?"

He stammered, as if surprised the person he was talking to talked back. "I, uh, well, I know there's one on Finchley Road? Outside the O2 Centre?"

"Why the fuck does everything you say sound like a question? Is there a hotel there or not?"

He nodded, but it looked more like a tic or a spasm.

"Fine. Take me there."

"Yes, sir."

"Stop fucking calling me that!"

"Sorry, sir."

"Fuck's sake…"

I climbed into the back of his car and put my headphones on. I needed to hear Her voice again. I needed to put my thoughts together. Her music started. It gave me peace. I needed to figure out where to start in an investigation that had no discernible ending or beginning. I heard Her voice.

So happy I could die…

I found my centre and my solace. I didn't realise when we'd stopped, when I'd got to my feet, or when I'd paid for the room, but when I opened my eyes properly, I was standing beside a hotel bed, ready for sleep. How I'd checked in or what I'd said to the fat cunt who drove me there, I just couldn't remember. I got under the sheets with the volume turned to its maximum setting, She gave me my last dose.

Eheh eheh so happy I could die / And it's all right…

As I started to black out, only one thought came to mind—I had work to do.

Chapter 2

Camden Town, Camden

Ask and ye shall receive. I had a great night's sleep. I woke up in a comfortable bed and played fantastic music while I showered with clean water and scented soap. Everything was fresh and clear, and by nine forty-five, I was out of the room and enjoying a huge breakfast with crossings, hash browns, eggs, orange juice, tea. The works. I had it all. And one more spoiling—I caught a cab to Camden Town station.

Outside the station, it was as busy as it got. On a weekend in Camden, they'd close the station doors for those departing because so many people would keep trying to board. And for those left out in the cold, it was a walk to Chalk Farm or Mornington Crescent. I walked past the slow-moving scrum of people in front of me, took a left on Camden High Street, past Inverness Street and towards Camden Lock. Camden, in the absence of a better word, was crazy. It used to be filled with punks; now, it was full of everyone from the alternative scene. You still saw a lot of punks, and the main stores blasting loud electronic music were still there. To me, the storefronts looked like gateways to space; robot models, weird posters, everything neon pink and green and black. It was bizarre. The road towards Camden Lock was filled with shops on either side of the road selling all kinds of market crap, like plastic clothing, T-shirts featuring the face of Che Guevara, cheap electronics, key rings, weed paraphernalia, and so on.

The road went over a small canal, and by that time, you could see a bridge above you with 'Camden Lock' written on top of it. From there on, if at any point you turned left, you'd be hit with a smell that was a mixture of Chinese and Middle Eastern food and scented candles. The smell was unique but by no means repulsive. Just slightly annoying. The Stables Market—the area on the left of the Lock—was filled with statues of horses and stable boys attending to them. The moment you entered it, you were hit by Chinese food stands almost forcing you to purchase a meal. It all got very claustrophobic from there. The rows, with market stands on either side, were just big enough for one and a half people, and everyone somehow looked like they wanted to buy some of the trash being offered, which mostly consisted of bracelets and rings that were worth more before they were put together. General junk like postcards and stock photos of London were also for sale.

At the heart of the Stables Market, there was a shop with two robot models outside it, each of them about ten feet tall. They looked like a mixture of Transformers and Terminators. In the shop, you could hear some of the worst music in the world. It was more like noise than music. Like a bird screeching to a beat. Electro-punk. It hurt my skin. The window displays were stacked with huge boots, clothes made of leather and spandex, and metallic accessories. It was everything you needed to look like a total freak. Nails, skulls, glow-in-the-dark cunt rings. Every base and body part was covered. Like the other punk shops, neon green and pink were the most represented colours, both in terms of product and décor. It was horrible. I mean, if you want to dress like a prick, that's fine. But why would you want to draw attention to it? That said, given the style and aesthetic of my

Guardian Angel, I should've been more tolerable of people like that. At least they had the balls to stand out as freaks on the outside; I was a freak on the inside. Outside, I probably looked like a gentle city worker. If the thing that lived inside of me was to go clothes shopping, I have no idea what he would purchase, though the alien afterbirth of a shop in front of me would probably be a good place to start. With that in mind, I entered B-85 Boutique. London's number one store for punks.

The interior resembled a spaceship more than a shop. The walls and floors were white plastic, accented at irregular intervals with glowing, high-tech lights. It was enough to induce a migraine, but I wasn't there to shop. I was there for information. The man I was looking for was called—get ready for this—Kuken-Ra'ef. Expert hacker. He worked with the CIA for fifteen years. Given that he was only twenty-seven, that should tell you a little bit about what he went through. Smart little kid learns how to hack, hacks into U.S. military for fun, gets caught, and is secretly extradited while his family is well compensated. Turns out, money does buy you love if you're a teenage parent with a partner who is all too ready to run away. He was raped until he loved the CIA, imprisoned, forced to work. After fifteen years, he finally had the CIA by the balls. He single-handedly upgraded their entire security system, blocked it and the people it protected, against any potential invasion, then threatened to take it down unless freed. They freed him but couldn't kill him. If he died, so did national security in the world's most powerful nation. Served them right. He got paid and still gets paid. He set up this shop in honour of the music genre that got him through all the nights of hell he had to endure. It's where he was planning his next move, which would probably be to stay here until he died. Fucked up little kid. Really fucked up. But he was the highest authority on information. He was skinny and tall, with a huge pink mohawk. His looked almost like the robot models out front, often donning tight garments and retro T-shirts. He was covered in tattoos but didn't have any piercings. Poor Ralph Codagan. That was the kid's real name. I bet he was still Kuken Ra'ef on the inside. Somewhere. Maybe.

I went to the counter and immediately, the Japanese manga-looking chick in front me knew I wasn't there for clothes.

"Can I help you?" Her accent was thick, her English almost unintelligible.

I nodded. "I'm looking for Lord Ra'ef."

She was obviously pretending not to know who her boss was. She probably thought I could be a cop. Poor girl. If only she knew how much worse I was. How much harder I could make things for her and Ra'ef.

"Ra'ef? Don't know Ra'ef. Maybe 'nother shop. Thank you, please."

She dipped her head towards me and tried to turn away.

"Hey!" I slammed my hand down on the counter, sending kitschy pens flying and logo stickers drifting to the floor.

Her tiny mouth opened.

"I'm going to say this once. Then I'm going to smash your head on this table, hold you down, and piss in your ear until you're fucking deaf. Then I'll do it to the other ear. Now. Tell *Ralph* that Calcain is here—"

"Calcain." A soft voice cut me short.

It seemed to come from, well, everywhere.

"You always had such a charming way of dealing with women."

It was a neat, clear voice from someone who sounded calm and educated. But where the hell was it coming from? I glanced around the room.

"Thank you, Ralph—"

"It's Lord Kuken Ra'ef!"

"I don't give a fuck if you call yourself Deliciously Chocolate-Coated Coco Pops. We need to have a chat."

"Why me? I can't help you more than Inforno. Go see him."

I. Hated. Inforno.

"Look, Coco Pops. I'll happily burn this highly flammable plastic castle to the ground if you don't show me your ugly face. What were you thinking with all this shit, anyway? The fucking white everywhere… is this an homage to fucking *Star Wars* or some shit? And why the fuck—"

I suddenly felt myself getting shorter. No, not shorter. Sinking. The floor tile underneath me was descending into the ground. I didn't have time to react before I found myself dropping into the heart of a secret underground club, exactly the last place on earth I'd ever want to find myself. The music was unbearably loud and screechy. And there were literally hundreds of people there. Rainbow-coloured lights flashed constantly, and every now and again, water sprayed from the ceiling. It was like an underground warehouse. Everyone looked like technologically advanced vampires and someone was singing live on the stage. Their voice sounded like a car skidding while heavy metal music blared in the background. I got up, and it was nearly impossible to push through the hordes of people. The flashing lights didn't help any. I could make out people kissing, biting, and possibly eating each other, and I'd guess a good ninety-five percent of the club's patrons were on LSD or something similar. They'd probably been partying since the night before. This was where one of my many gifts came into play. Regardless of where I was and how common the other person may have looked, I could find anyone I wanted in any given scene. I was an expert at *Where's Waldo*. It was a pretty useless gift in the grand scheme of things, at least when compared to dodging bullets, flying, being invisible, and having the power to re-virginise a chick. But in situations like that one, it was a pretty neat gift to have.

I spotted Ra'ef (or Ralph, if you wanted to be dick about it, and I often did) in the VIP area. I punched, kicked, shoved, and jumped my way through the scrum to get to him, leaving in my wake a series of yelps and bloody noses. As I got close to Ra'ef's vicinity, I was stopped by what I could only call two giants in boots and thongs. One had a green thong and rocked a gigantic pink mohawk. The other was the opposite. They suited each other. Looking at their knee-high metallic boots and metal gloves, it appeared I needed to show these gents of leisure some respect.

"Right then. I'm here to see Ra'ef."

One spoke with an outrageously thick voice for a guy in a thong, but then again, these fellas were huge—I'm talking jacked—and oozing with power. Who was I to critique their style?

"His name is Lord Ra'ef, mortal. He does not expect you, and so he shall not see you."

Mortal? Was he kidding me with that? Fucking *mortal*? I immediately lost any sense of respect I had for the ogres. Dicks like these fell for their own gear and believed the shit they were told about how their clothes gave them special powers. Punks and goths were the same in that respect, but punks could fuck you up if given half a chance. Goths were reasonable, which made them weak. I thought charming might be the way to go on this one. Well, my kind of charming anyway.

I stepped toe to toe with the one on the left. "I don't know what the hell you are—some sort of fucked up tribute to the Cheeky Girls or Milli Vanilli—and frankly, I don't give a shit. If you don't let me through, I'll stick your mohawk so far up your transsexual mother's dickhole—"

Everything turned black. When I opened my eyes, I could see my reflection. Was I flying belly up over a sea? What I saw looked like a river at night, and I felt like I was floating over the dark water. I felt so light. Wait, no. I was on the floor. The ceiling was made of mirrors. Lots of mirrors. Of fucking course it was. And there I was, on my back, staring up at myself. My heart hurt. Suddenly, the clubbers surrounded my body and started kicking me and tossing me from left to right. I was too weak to fight back. Like a piece of meat among alligators, I was being thrown around and torn apart. I needed to figure out what the fuck had happened. Before I could, I got thrown towards the bar, launched through a tower of pint glasses, and landed behind the bar, under the till. The bar was newly designed and heavily wired. The cables stuck out of all sorts of ports and crevices. I rolled further underneath the bar to shield myself from projectile stilettos and the remnants of margaritas. Right. Time to think. What the fuck happened? I took a few deep breaths. *Okay. So I told that beast in a thong to go fuck himself and then he magics me onto the floor. No, no, no. I tell him to fuck off and then Ra'ef uses some form of electric device to throw me off balance. No, that's not it either. I've moved from fantasy to science fiction. Both are impossible.*

I had to focus on what was probable, and that was this:

I had told Mohawk Mo to fuck his mother, and then he punched me so hard in the chest with his metallic fist that I fell a few metres back and blacked out. I wasn't fighting beasts, monsters, or magicians. They were only human. Strong and

49

freaky-looking, sure, but still just men. That was all. They had the same weaknesses as anyone else. As for the hungry clubbers who attacked me, I needed to do something to make them shit themselves. The giants could, at least for the moment, wait.

I reached for my pockets.

The screen on my phone flashed to life, and I prayed my headphones hadn't gotten busted while I was being beaten. What I was about to do required music. I kept the Lady in my life silent—she shouldn't be tainted by what was about to happen. And nothing got a sick, twisted Londoner like me to do his thing better than a fellow Londoner. I pressed play and heard all I needed to.

I give you everything you'll ever need / And I'll find a way to turn you into a monster / Me and you, we can rule the world 'cuz no one's gonna fuck with me, I'm a monster...

I was a monster. Now, I needed to find a tool. I spotted a piece of wood hanging beneath the bar. I tore it down and found that there were nails sticking out of it. I couldn't have made a better tool in that moment; it was a divine gift.

I'm a monster / I'm a monster / I'm a monster / I'm a monster / I'm a monster, I'll give you everything you'll ever need...

It was time to fuck them where it hurt. I rolled out from beneath the bar, jumped up, and smacked the first punk who came into view. I smacked him hard. Real hard. Like half his face flying in the air and splattering blood on the people around him hard.

I screamed, "Now, which of you motherfuckers wants some of this?"

The problem with moving as fast as I did was not many people realised exactly what had just happened to that poor boy's face or the extent of his injuries, the extent of the damage I was prepared to do there. And some of them were filled with too much adrenaline to care. One of the punks got brave enough to get close to me, and I hit him in the face with the plank, immediately yanking it out and letting the blood spray from his wounds like a sprinkler, misting the crowd. The first punk was still shaking on the ground. The next brave one got it straight in the belly. The way he screamed as the nails penetrated his gut caused the circle of onlookers around me to widen and expand, future challengers second guessing themselves. The music stopped, and the water showering down from overhead ceased.

"Who wants next?" I screamed again, swinging the bloody club above my head.

Slowly, the crowd backed away even further, and just as I was about to feel comfortable and confident in my win, I heard a horrendous groan. It was like scream… but a strange one. Like a battle cry, but by some form of giant house cat. I realised then why the punks had stepped back. It wasn't out of fear; it was to make room for the giants.

As they walked forward, their metallic shoes echoed through the club. I started with a battle cry of my own.

"You pretty sisters finally coming out to play? Not a problem. There's plenty to go around."

They stepped towards me, each step rattling the floor tiles around their feet.

"Fee Fi Fo Fum, I smell a pair of giant cunts." I turned to the group of punks still watching. "You guys smell that? Or is it just me?"

The twins kept coming. I had to remind myself that they were human and therefore mortal. They had weaknesses. They each picked up what could either be a mace or an anal probe with tiny spears at the end, and the fight was on. They didn't play it

Hollywood-style. It wasn't a one-at-a-time kind of deal, with the camera work zooming and panning for maximum drama, all elements working together to ensure the hero's victory. No, there was none of that. They both came for me at once.

Think, Calcain, think. How do you take on two robotic giants? I looked at the bar. Everything there was busted up and reflecting flashing lights, and an opportunity suddenly presented itself to me. I dropped the plank. I didn't need a weapon for what I was about to do. The twins grabbed me and started throwing me around like a ragdoll. I just smiled up at them. They had to be two of the biggest idiots I've met. I took the punches to the face and body happily. I took the kicks with a smile. As bloody as I was getting, I just needed to wait for the inevitable to happen. As soon as I saw it coming, I was grabbed by one of the giants who held me too close for my liking.

"Mortal, you are going to the bottles next. You have disobeyed the law of Ra'ef, and for that you shall die. What fool thinks he can take a Titan like me?" He threw his head back and released a deep, heavy laugh.

I hated chats like that.

I smiled mockingly. "Oh, your worship. I'm going to give you one chance. Just one. If you surrender, suck my dick, and swallow, I'll consider letting you live. Because in the immortal words of the famous sisters from *Shawshank Redemption,* 'You done broke my face, and I reckon you owe me'."

I smiled. He didn't. The next thing I knew, I was flying towards the bar, towards victory. A decent enough landing would do the trick. I fell right next to the loose electric cables, right in the sweet spot, and smiled. The dumb fucks—and their metallic, immortal shoes—were about to be toasted where they stood on the drenched floor. I jumped onto the beautiful, wooden bar top and pulled on the wires. By the time those moronic giants figured out what was about to happen, I'd have enough cable to throw at their feet. I took a gamble and aimed to land the sparking tips as close to them as I could manage, and, as always, when it came down to an act of sheer brutality, I was ridiculously lucky. The cables landed right on their metallic shoes.

Now, how can I describe what happened next? Well, have you seen those huge balloon men used as business promotions, particularly at car dealerships? The ones that catch the wind and wave their hands in the air? Take one of those, give him a little flesh, put him through an oven, toast him good, and that's what I had on my hands; two giants flailing their arms, windmilling them in every which direction, before pieces of their flesh began exploding from their bones. Their skin looked like soup boiling, bubble-gum bubbles swelling before the pus-filled *pop*. Eventually, they stopped trembling on the floor and everything went silent and suddenly dark. I couldn't see a thing.

And I had an epiphany—I'd fucked myself.

I was standing on a wooden table, an island surrounded by an electric sea of death. Silly, silly, silly. I should have planned for that. I wasn't sure if there were any survivors of the original cable drop. What if Ra'ef had died as well? I looked around and the emergency lights flared on. I didn't have a plan, no escape hatch this time around, no backup. I lay on the table and rested a bit. I'd gotten a good kicking earlier. My body hurt, and my head ached.

But I'd been through worse.

I took out my headphones again and let Her speak to me.

D'd'd'd...

I lit up a cigarette and thought about the fact that, if Ra'ef was dead, my only half-decent source of information would be

53

Inforno, and that guy was a cunt through and through. I mean, a *total* cunt. "

Silicone…

Before panic set in, She calmed me.

She looks good but her boyfriend says she's a mess / She's a mess…

I needed to get the hell out of there.

Baby loves to dance in the dark / 'Cuz when he's lookin', she falls apart / Baby loves to dance, loves to dance in the dark…

Without Ra'ef, I was basically fucked.

Suddenly, I heard a faint noise somewhere beyond the music, enough to merit a pause. I took out the headphones.

"The fuse. The fuse, Calcain."

It sounded like Ra'ef. Good.

"What about the fuse?"

"It's above the bar, behind that bottle of dry gin. Be a love and turn it off. There's a good lad."

I looked at the bottles on the shelf behind me, just more than the length of two hands. It was doable if I stepped forward and put my foot on the shelf itself. Using the torch on my phone, I could make out the shape of the fuse box, faint and colourful, a few glowing buttons.

"And if I trip?"

"You'll die, and I'll starve to death. Or I'll fall onto the electric floor and fry like my friends."

"Then I guess you're fucked without me, mate."

"Well, um." His voice sounded strained, like he was struggling to get two words out. "I'd say we're equally fucked, actually."

"Why do you sound so tense? You're usually so calm, Ralph."

"Um, well, first of all, fuck you. It's Ra'ef. Stop being a dick. Secondly, let's just say the fact I'm alive right now is a true testament to my quick thinking and natural survival instinct."

I glanced around the room. "Where the fuck even are you?"

"Please, sunshine. Please. I know you can't afford to have me dead. So, please. Move your ass."

I thought about it for a beat.

"No."

"What? Look, this isn't funny. Get a fucking move on now."

"No. Not until you tell me why Terry Hunter's head is splattered across his house."

"I don't know. I don't give a fuck about dead footballers, but I'm sure you can read all about it, as well as the latest news on Simon Cowell's new controversial show, in *Hello! Magazine*. I've got a copy in the back. Now, please, fuck off and get a move on."

"Ralph, I'm not going anywhere. I know you're in deep shit. It doesn't sound like you can hold whatever position you're in much longer. I also know where the fuse is now, thanks to you. So I'm good. I'm definitely getting out of here. If you die, I can just hit the little switch here and leave. I'll probably even toss off on your head before I go."

"It's fucking Ra'ef, all right? The name's Ra'ef. Stop fucking it up. Secondly, in case you can't tell from the dungeon I live in, I'm pretty fucking depressed. So although I would have wanted a better death—perhaps one where I'd be found choking on my own balls after a night of hardcore masturbation—I'm not afraid of dying. And if I do die here, you're the one who will have to learn to enjoy the company of Inforno, who I am sure you'll get on with like a dick on fire. I'm sure he has everything you need to know, but he'll stick that information so far up your ass not even a proctologist with tentacles for arms could take it out. But, I mean, you know. Choice is yours."

He had a point, but I needed more.

"Do you know what I need to know about Hunter?"

"Calcain. Um. You do know who you're talking to, right?"

Another good point. It was a silly question. It was time to make my move. I put my right foot on the shelf in front of me. It was a stretch, and an uncomfortable one at that. I put all my weight on my right foot, moved the gin aside, and flipped all the switches. The glare from even more emergency lights flooded the room.

I still didn't have the guts to step down off the bar, so I stayed put and looked around for Ra'ef. His voice was fairly close by, but I couldn't see him. What I could see were two enormous corpses on the floor in front of me and around twelve more in the surrounding area. Bloody hell. Mulligan let me go, and within one fucking day, fifteen or so people were already dead. Just like old times. As I looked towards where Ra'ef's bodyguards were first standing, I saw a figure dangling from an old, curved staff— a cane, really—which was hooked onto a metallic tube running along the ceiling. It was Ra'ef. He'd been hanging for dear life from a walking stick. I almost wanted to laugh.

"Ralph. You are a fucking idiot. An absolute moron, oh lord of punks."

He was still holding on, clearly afraid to take the big leap, worried that cutting the fuse hadn't done the trick. I could see him clearly now. Black robe that was almost see-through. Tight leather pants with metallic shins and knee pads. Black and orange-striped vest and tattoo sleeves running from his wrists to his shoulders. A burgundy mohawk, probably as long as his arm. The colour of it had changed since the last time I saw him. Aside from black lipstick, his face was clear. He had sharp, metallic nails and knuckles and horns coming out of his elbows.

"You're such a dick," he said, struggling to get air. "Do you think it's safe to come down now?"

I chuckled. "I honestly don't know. I was hoping you might help me with that, given that you designed this place."

"Theoretically, I'm certain it's safe. But still, you never really know, do you?"

Lord Ra'ef, King of the Camden underworld, was at heart still a geeky twelve-year-old dressed up like a fantasy creature.

"So, a walking stick, 'ey?"

"It's my staff. I carry it with me. Makes me look more authoritative." He adjusted his grip. "And occasionally saves my life, as you can see."

This would've gone on forever if I didn't do anything. I picked up a bottle from the bar, aimed, and threw it at him. I missed.

"What the fuck are you doing?" he screamed as he began to swing from left to right.

"Just giving you a bit of encouragement is all. I thought you said you weren't afraid to die?"

"I'm not! Do you have any idea how expensive that was? That was an 1857—"

I threw another. He'd started to piss me off, valuing his own life less than an object. A beverage, no less. Something that would turn to piss within hours. It was pathetic.

I threw everything I could find at him. Bottles, bottle caps, rolls of receipt paper, a stapler. He was tough bastard, I'd give him that. Torture does that to a guy. I should know. And I did know. He swung from left to right, but he wouldn't drop. My last available projectile was a 1957 Bollinger Magnum.

"Ralph. Either you get down or I throw this at you with all my might. It'll kill you before you drop."

He stopped swinging and looked directly at me.

"It's Ra'ef. And you can hit me as hard as you want. I won't drop. I'll never drop. I am the King of Camden. I am Lord—"

I rolled my eyes and chucked the Magnum at him.

He dropped.

Aside from a minor *splat* when his ass hit the water, nothing else happened.

He, however, passed out instantly.

One thing I can't tolerate is self-aggrandisement. I hate that. And people who refer to themselves in third person. The truth is, Ra'ef was the undisputed Lord of Camden. He owned most of the land and stores and had gained those properties by legitimately pushing people out. His wealth and tolerance of freaks earned him a small army able to withstand any assault in the Camden area. He could've expanded but had no reason or ambition to. The problem with people like him was that sometimes, that kind of power went to their head. They deserved it, they'd worked hard, but they also believed their own legend.

Until they came across me.

Suddenly, a reality shock hit them in the form of a homicidal assault. Then they were quiet. Ra'ef, for example, would never again speak to me in the manner he had for the last half hour. He who controlled Camden controlled the punks. By default, I now had control over the king of punks. The only thing was that he and I went way back, both of us following in Her path. She had tamed us both. His musical taste was different, on the whole, but we shared Her music and Her message, which was still something. She guided us both. For that, we were, in a way, brothers. In fact, we attended one of Her gatherings together. And so I could not betray such an allegiance. I decided not to take advantage of my position.

I slowly jumped off the bar and walked towards him. The room was utterly silent, as though I'd killed the building itself.

He groaned as I lifted him up. He weighed almost nothing.

"You okay, Ralph?" I asked, knowing I should be feeling guilty about how hard I hit him.

"I-it's Ra'ef. I wa-wa-was having my nipples licked and body felt up by four s-stunning b-banshees. You show up. Everyone's d-dead."

"Come on, son. Let's get you out of here."

"No. N-not safe. They're coming. They took many already. Now they want me. B-but they didn't s-send you after me. I'm c-confused."

"Who? Who's after you? What do they want with you?"

He looked like he was losing consciousness, so I jostled him.

"Do they know about Hunter?"

"They want us. The sub-rulers. We once wanted to join... join the Houses. But the Houses didn't want us, so we... we set up a sub-command. Camden, Shoreditch, Soho, China Town and the rest. It created a balance. Relative peace. But some... something terrible has happened. A new breed has arrived. Something worse than anything I—or you—have come across. They don't care about who rules what. They don't care about the current organisation. And worst of all, they don't want to join the Houses. They want to destroy them. T-t-to take down all the Houses. Calcain. They're coming. They're united. One man at the top. They're going to rule London Underground. Undisputed. The Third House. The Third... House."

Just as he passed out again, several punks came rushing in. These seemed to be his emergency team as they had guns. Lots

59

of guns. They were also very well built and were wearing military uniforms, though they still sported mohawks and metallic shin pads and steel boots. They looked at me and realised, if anything, I didn't want to kill Ra'ef. One of them rushed and grabbed him from me, feeling around his neck and shining a light into his eyes. Unlike the other punks, he had very few tattoos. He was probably in his mid-thirties, and he had a blue and white mohawk. I assumed he was a doctor.

"Electric shock?"

"No. I threw a bottle at his head."

He looked up. "Huh. I see."

He turned to the others who had entered with him. "We need to take him to the rest area in Base Twenty-One. I can monitor him better there. He's likely concussed, so it will be a while before he's back on his feet again, but it's nothing major. He just needs rest and medical assistance."

"Who will lead Camden during this time? I need information."

"He has backup systems in place. I wouldn't worry. And besides, he'll only be down for a little while. In the meantime, Calcain, I suggest you leave." He looked around at the carnage. "There may still be some hope for this lot."

"How do you know my—"

"Demon with the Long Coat. Calcain the Monster. I work for the 'King of Information'. If you needed to go to him directly, I assume you needed high-level intel. Unfortunately, without his direct authority, whatever you need to know, you won't find in Camden. I can only suggest Inforno. And before you try and kill your way to some more details, I would remind you that Camden is about to fortify itself, and the people are generally on high alert. Given the events of tonight, whilst I'm sure you can get pretty far, you probably won't make it far enough, though I guess it's up to you to decide how many bullets you want to take. I'd recommend zero."

He pointed at the punks dressed like warriors. "Help me pick him up. As for you…" He turned to me. "Go down the corridor at the back, take a right and then a left. You'll see a small door. That door leads to a lift that will take you inside one of Punky Fish's changing rooms. If you step out of that door, you will be right outside Camden Lock bridge. I'm sure Ra'ef will summon you once he has recovered. In the meanwhile, I bid you farewell."

He was surprisingly polite for a punk, but members of the new generation were often middle class and well educated. They took Ra'ef and left.

I took the route as directed and soon found myself on Camden High Street. The light hit me hard, and I remembered it was only afternoon. Stepping into a nightclub in the morning can really mess with your sense of time.

I walked past the Bridge and headed to Chalk Farm and Primrose Hill for my next meeting.

Whilst walking, I kept on thinking about what Ra'ef had said. Someone wanted to destroy the Houses and rule supreme. Their sole intention was the destruction of the status quo. If the whole of Camden was afraid, then this new group posed a plausible threat. To do that, they must've been sick, twisted, and without mercy. To petrify Camden the way they had, they would've needed to be hungry for destruction.

It seemed I had a competitor.

Chapter 3

Chalk Farm & Primrose Hill, London

I walked past Camden High Street and the last remaining market stalls, reached the Roundhouse Theatre, then finally made it to Chalk Farm station. Further on, I took a left, walked over a small bridge and headed to the village of Chalk Farm. Like most 'villages' in London, it was basically a quiet, posh street with charming boutique clothing shops, restaurants, pubs, organic groceries, and coffee shops. It consisted of a single street and was probably about a few hundred metres in length. At the end of it was a small park with a hill on top from which you could see almost all of central London. It was called Primrose Hill. It once served as a terrible battle ground for me. We were on top of the hill. The enemy at the bottom. Both sides rushing to meet in the middle. Both equally matched in strength. *The Mirror* wrote that the brutality was almost 'medieval'. I disagreed. Medieval killers weren't half as creative as I was. Now, however, the location was back to its previous form; a quiet hill with wonderful scenery.

As lovely as it would've been to keep strolling around Chalk Farm that Sunday afternoon, I was there for a different reason. I'd come to see one Vladimir Tolsky, the owner of Trojia, a coffee shop in the village. They called him Vlad the Impaler because rumour had it he was quite rough in bed and very well endowed. It supposedly felt like being speared. The last time we'd met, he'd wanted to kill me on account of me sleeping with his daughter.

She wasn't even worth the drama it caused, to be honest. Square-jawed, six feet tall, cold, and angry. Shit kisser. Slow in bed. Maybe the reason he'd wanted to kill me wasn't so much that I'd slept with her, but rather that I'd readily provided the above feedback to him afterwards.

The village hasn't changed much since I was there last. Trees on either side of the road covered the almost Parisian shops. Vlad's coffee shop—or, as he called it, the Russian Tea House—was painted red and had colourful stained-glass windows. It was quite welcoming from the outside. The inside, though, was rather dark, with wooden chairs and tables and Russian paintings of past warrior Tsars on the wall. I took a deep breath and stepped inside.

An attractive girl greeted me with a nice, "Hello, welcome, can I get you menu?"

She was surprisingly happy and upbeat for an Eastern European. In an odd way, she resembled Her, and thus I found her charming. Her presence filled me with a mild peace. I needed that after such a morning.

"No, thanks. I'm here to see Vlad. Is he around?"

"No, he is away," she said.

Her eyes were huge and green, and blonde fringe fell above darker eyebrows. She couldn't have been more than five foot four without heels.

"He will be back shortly. Just finishing lunch at Lemonia up the road. Do you want Russian tea while you wait?"

"That would be lovely. What's your name?"

She smiled. "Natalya."

"And where are you from, Natalya?"

"Georgia. It's the most beautiful country. We have wonderful wine."

"I might put that to the test. You work here on weekends?"

In her broken English, she said, "No, I'm just covering my friend. I'm actually corporate lawyer. My friend keeps taking holidays, and Vlad said if she doesn't find replacement, she would get sacked. We used to work here when in law school, so I covered."

She wasn't lying about her career. She'd been there long enough to use terms like 'sacked', and her demeanour was very much like that of other women from the city. I liked her. I wondered if she'd like me after seeing me get what I am about to get from Vlad. Elsie wouldn't have liked it. She was too innocent for this kind of thing. But she was gone now, so it didn't matter.

I sat outside. The weather was surprisingly good for that time of the year. Natalya brought me tea and baklava, both of which I consumed while waiting for Vlad to show up. She came back after a little while to ask if I need anything. I got into general chit-chat with her, and we seemed to have a lot in common. Like the same contempt for people who rated themselves higher than they deserved. She told me about lawyers who often love to talk about work and cases but want to sound cool by not mentioning parties for confidentiality reasons. She said they were morons who thought they were better than they really were, and that having careers in which they actually serve a purpose that benefited humanity wasn't enough for them. Before Vlad came, I took down her number so I could drop a text every now and again.

I waited for about half an hour, and she came out without her apron.

"I am going now. My shift is over. The tea is on the house, so no need for payment. The kitchen is closed, so the chef is minding the shop. Take care, Calcain." She paused and smiled. "Funny name."

"Take care, Natalya. Have a good one."

She left, and as soon as she was out of sight, a shadow came over my body. It wasn't the sun setting. It was the six foot nine, muscle-bound creature who was an interrogator for the Russian army. Not KGB. But a butcher, nonetheless.

"You come, drink my tea, sit in my chair, and you don't even say dobry dien," he said in a deep accent.

"My old mate. So good to see you. Why don't you grab a chair? I've been waiting a while for you."

"I sit. Of course I sit. My shop. But I sit because I like playing with prey before eating."

I believed him. I was sure the concept of cannibalism wouldn't be alien to him. He took the seat next to me and barely fit into the chair. The chef brought him a small glass of what could only be pure, petrol-grade vodka. I got one, too. He appeared surprisingly friendly. I had no idea why, but I thought I'd take advantage of it.

"So, they now let you out during day and outside ass-bashing men area, 'ey Calcain? The Monster. Demon with Long Coat."

"I would have thought, or rather hoped, you'd know why."

"Too many reasons. Hunter dead. New Breed. Increase of Russian oligarchs. You tell me."

"Hunter—"

"No one knows who killed him." Vlad massaged his head, clearly stressed. "That prick, Inforno, wouldn't say nothing, and Ra'ef is keeping things quiet, but secretly he fortifies. The only thing is, he know what he is fortifying against. We don't. We know something coming. But not what. Whatever it is, people are scared. The violence, Calcain. It's severe. Almost to your level. There is one man who leads, but no one know who. I actually thought it was…"

He tilted his head towards me.

"You thought it was me?"

"Well, it would have to be. His style very similar to yours. The Houses ordered you to be monitored, but no one find you. All people know was you don't fly outside Soho during day and don't go past Shoreditch at night. You could not possibly organise what's been happening elsewhere, right? But who knows. It's elusive. Some people don't even know it's happening." He shrugged and drank from his glass. "I don't know."

"How could that be?"

"There have been systematic killings. Couriers and messenger boys. The odd street gangster connected to the Houses. Tactical killings, you know? But not a direct challenge to particular House. It makes dark spots in London, so Houses can't see all corners. By the time it's sorted, a new dark spot pop up. They are like shadow. Very quiet. You don't notice them. Not even Houses took them seriously. But then. Last night. Things kicked off. Hunter dead like that. Woman dead, too. That was, um, how you say, on my face. Or in my face. In *your* face. Dumb fucking language." He sipped more vodka.

"Anyway. It was challenge to all three Houses in one go. But then, it's so bold it could actually be one of Houses. A war is coming. No one knows with who or what or when. The Houses will suspect each another. Who knows if New Breed isn't House in disguise? Everyone is suspicious. That is all I know. It could be gossip." He shrugged again.

Just when I thought things weren't complex enough, I now had three fucked-off Houses ready to go at each other's throats, a full fortification in London's sub-gangs, and a new group intent on taking down the balance so that they may reign, as they think, undisputed. Hunter was the best candidate for a declaration of war. But there was really only one thing that worried me. Vlad was right. That orgy had my dickprints all over it. I mean, ask anyone who knows the upper echelons of London's underworld and they'd tell you. Calcain would be the one to take down the Houses. But I had style and substance not visible to the naked eye. I didn't kill people I considered to be innocent, however twisted that consideration may be. Maybe I'd have killed Hunter. I wasn't sure how innocent he really was in all this. But I wouldn't have killed the hooker. Hookers are about as innocent as they get. From the outside, it certainly looked like a declaration of war. But who was supposed to have been declaring it?

I leaned towards Vlad. "Is my name on the list? Am I a suspect?"

He laughed, sputtered and coughed, and I thought he might have been a little bit tipsy.

"Why do you think I haven't smashed your eye with glass?" He held up the empty vessel in his fist. "Of course you are suspect. But most believe you are not responsible. They say you have more class. Besides, if enough people suspected you, you would be dead by now."

He coughed some more. "I'm not feeling too great, Calcain. My lunch didn't settle. I will say to let bygones be bygones in my territory. Unless you fuck with Russians, you'll be fine. The oligarchs respect my word, and so you're safe to roam. But if you fuck with me, I will tear your balls open, make nice omelette with cheese, bit of garlic, good black pepper, touch of saffron, and feed it to you. Do you understand?"

I nodded. Vlad may have been a lush, but he was a tough old prick. Tough as they came.

"Now, fuck off then."

He left, making all sort of noises as he went. I finished my drink and walked up the street towards Primrose Hill. Just before the hill, though, there was a pub. I walked in, ordered a pint, and got some fish and chips. I didn't usually go down to that pub, but I knew someone who did. I waited for a while, and eventually he turned up with a few friends. It took a few minutes for him to see me, and he played it cool when he did. He had wavy, light brown hair cut just below his ears and a clear face. A colourful scarf was wrapped around his neck, and he wore a navy blazer with blue jeans and brown, pointy shoes. To complement the look, he wore a cream-colored coat. Typical rich kid. Must have been thirty-two by then. He sat with his friends and had a few drinks. I waited. Eventually, he got up, and with one quick shake of the head, he indicated he was ready to see me. He went out, and I followed a good few minutes later.

It probably took about three and a half minutes off my pace to walk to the top of the hill. As I walked, before I reached the peak, I could still make out the words painted on the road leading up before you reached the top. It read: *And the view is so nice.* And it truly was, if you were able to clear your mind of its visions of past carnage.

At the very top, I could see him standing there with the wind tousling his hair and jacket. I stood next to him and suddenly, all of beautiful London appeared before me. From Canary Wharf to the City, West End to the Palace of Westminster and the London Eye. Looking down the hill, typical Victorian English lampposts were pinned along various walking paths, almost as though they were still filled with candles ready to be lit. The sun would set soon. The green in front of me was peaceful, and I was tempted to get out my headphones and turn Her on. The silence and the peace were, however, broken by my old rival, Luke Wellington-Mansell.

"It's been a while, Calcain," he said in a typical, posh, Fulham-style accent. "I was starting to wonder when you'd show up, being that the shit has hit the fan and all that."

"Since when do you swear? You were always almost poetic in how you spoke. And you always thought you could beat me, Mr. Demon with the Long Coat."

"Tried to? If I recall correctly, I beat you three times. Or have you lost your memory during the past few years? And I prefer 'Monster in the Coat'. It's more fitting." He levelled his eyes on me. "You're the monster, after all. Aren't you?"

I stared out over the city. "All three of your victories were heavily disputed, you know that? On account of you cheating and everything. And even if it had been three, which it wasn't, what would that have made it? Three out of forty-seven times? Forty-eight? I can't recall."

Luke smiled and shook his head. "Oh, my dear Calcain. I take it you've not come for a general chit-chat, 'ey? Not here to reminisce about old times?"

"No. I'm not here for that."

Luke paused and thought for a while.

"I take it you already know about the new generation? The so-called New Breed?"

"I have heard. Do you think they're a threat? Or are they just another fad, like Ra'ef in the early days, getting too powerful in Camden before being told where he stands? I mean, every few years people say someone, or some group, is moving in to replace the Houses, but as soon as the threat is identified, one of the three steps up and shows the new twats who's boss. The rest either sponsor the attack or assist, either with intel or immunity in territories. The Houses won't hesitate to unite if it means keeping the status quo."

I shut my mouth. I'd already talked too much. More than I ever did to anyone. He had that effect on me where I felt the need to impress. Not just because he was highly intelligent but because he was as close to an equal as I'd found so far. I needed to stay a step above.

"Calcain, don't be ridiculous," he said, his voice taking on an air of authority I hadn't heard from him before. "Of course there's reason to fear them. But you need to take them for what they are. A threat. And you need to deal with them accordingly."

He paused again. He seemed troubled.

"There is something else you should probably know about, though. I haven't got a lot of details, mind you. I don't fly that close to the sun. But something quite important was supposed to happen last night. The meeting at the Shard. It would've been more than just a peace deal for London Bridge. It was something much more than that, and it had all the Houses excited. I think what you need to do," he said, pointing a finger at me, "is find out what had everyone so jumpy. My uncle wouldn't even tell me what the meeting was about. That's how critical it was. But word of Hunter's death raised suspicions, the leaders got paranoid, and the meeting was called off. The only thing I know for sure is the outcome of that meeting would have changed the game whilst paradoxically keeping the status quo, the golden dream the Houses have for so long intended to keep. It seems they found a solution—a permanent one—that required a change but would benefit everyone in the long run."

He dug his fists into his pockets. "I don't know what the New Breed is, but I haven't seen my uncle this stressed since the start of the recession. Now that doesn't mean we should fear the Breed, exactly. But they did cause the only plan developed in years to be tabled, likely for good. They've ensured war. They've encouraged chaos. So we may not need to be wary of *them* but of what they represent."

His uncle, Russell, was his dad's brother and leader of one of the Houses. By all accounts, Luke was overstepping territories by showing up in Chalk Farm, but no one would touch him. Not least because he was generally a nice guy. His deductive skills were brilliant, and he was ferociously intelligent. Yet all of his intelligence was being wasted at the pub.

"Luke, I have been given a rare opportunity—"

"To take down the Houses. I know. Total freedom to create carnage. Just what you always wanted. Never cared for anything else. Except Elsie, of course." He paused and swallowed hard. "Sorry about that."

I kept my mouth closed. Slowly, the last rays of sunlight faded in the distance. Too few people respected the sunset these days. He wasn't one of those people, and neither was I. The lights in London shimmered from Canary Wharf to the City and now to the towering figure of the Shard. The Victorian lights of the park turned on, and the bright zigzag in front of us complemented the green, dark grass. The lights stretched from the Shard to the BT Tower, to Westminster Palace and to Big Ben. The distant full view of London was like a photo from movies. The shimmering city in the night. My beautiful London. I'd missed that view. The comfortable fresh air hit me, reminding me that the night had arrived. My natural habitat summoned me. It was almost time for me to go. The view, though. It was so nice.

"The city is calling you, Creature of the Night." Luke's voice interrupted the long silence between us.

That had been the name of my band, Creatures of the Night. He remembered. We were intense rivals back then, and it was us who had gone to war on that hill. I needed to respond, but I was too far inside my head.

"Right. Well. I should—"

"You have to change the status quo, Calcain. Replace it with… well, I don't know what. But whatever it is would be better than what the New Breed has to offer. It would also be better than whatever deal the Houses were aiming to make. But before you can do that, you need to stop the inevitable war between the Houses and the Breed. In the past, the Houses would unite against a threat. Stand as one. After Hunter, everyone is at each other's throats. The environment is perfect for an external strike. Especially now that we have such a weak-hearted government. If you want to take down the Houses and the Breed, you need to stop the war, or at least find a way to control it. You need to be in command. If a war happens, so be it, but you need to be the one to decide when it starts and, more importantly, when it ends. You need to create a controlled environment where only the right people die and only exactly when they are meant to. It's the only way to avoid casualties, and the only way to ensure everyone goes down in the end. Otherwise, you'll get caught in the middle, and you will be crushed like a small, dry leaf on a sidewalk."

He turned and looked at me hard. "You need to find out who killed Hunter and started this mess. You also need to find out just who the fuck the New Breed are and why everyone is shitting themselves about their uprising. Specifically, you need to know who's on top. Then you need to find out what the deal was the Houses were planning to settle on. It's going to be up to you to play the game. Pit them against each other. Find out who knows what. Control the narrative. Keep them separate. That's how they'll fall."

I nodded. "Right. I can do that."

"Don't fuck it up. You fuck it up, and you'll end up launching a full-scale war. Just wipe them out, Calcain. Clean the slate. Let London start again."

Whilst the task he put before me was very complicated, I needed to remember I was a hired detective for the Metropolitan Police. My assigned purpose was to find out who killed Hunter. Or I needed to look like that's what I was doing, anyway. Once I convinced Mulligan I'd gotten it sorted out, I could do what I wanted. And carrying out my investigative duties in the name of Terry Hunter would be an easy way to get information. The idea was to somehow create chaos and end it at the same time.

The wind blew, and it was comfortable. It was almost as though London was embracing me, giving me the kind of hug a mother does before her son goes off to war. The London night was beautiful. From that hill, I could see all of its external beauty. The stars in the sky matched the bright, multicoloured sparkles of London's skyscrapers. I would soon be immersing myself in the city's even more stunning—yet equally repulsive—interior.

I took my headphones out and debated my choices; R&B, hip hop, or Her. It was a Saturday night. It would have to be all of them. But first, Her.

I started to put my headphones in. "I have to go."

"Just tell me this."

It was Luke's final attempt at retribution. I thought he was smarter than that.

"I know for you, the destruction of the Houses is inevitable. It was always meant to happen at your hands. I won't argue that. But there are ways to go about this kind of thing without making the streets of London run red. I know the kind of havoc you're planning to unleash, and a lot of innocent people will die as a result. Will that really be worth it? Yes, you'll kill the people you hate, the ones who tried to kill you first, the ones who did truly horrible things to you. But you're going to run into a lot of people who don't deserve the fate you'll hand them just to get to the men at the top. You'll hurt people who were born into this madness, ones who didn't have a choice. People like you. People who didn't ask for where they are or what they became but ended up demons because they were put through hell. You might end up coming against those who may actually care about you. That you may care about. People who love you—"

"I don't have people like that."

"Still. What the Houses did to you, what Mulligan did, it was all beyond excuse. Beyond forgiveness by any measure. It was horrendous. I know that. But Calcain—"

"I promised," I said.

Luke was talking as if he knew what had happened to me, a young cop, all those years ago. But he couldn't possibly know, not really, until it happened to him.

"I swore to their faces that I would get them back. You were there. You heard me. I don't intend to go back on that promise. It's not in my nature. I warned them if they let me live, I would come back. I promised them, and I promised Elsie. And now the monster's coming back."

I put my headphones in and selected 'Paper Gangsta' from the track list.

Remembering me before we began…

"Next time I see you, Luke, the circumstances will be very different. Your uncle is one of them, and if you're still aligned with his House when the time comes, I will kill you. I'll have to."

I turned my back on him and started walking down the hill.

Fakers…don't have no follow through…

I looked back at him, still standing on the hill, unmoving and unaffected by my threat. They were hard but necessary words to say to him. It's like the way people say love and hate are two sides of the same coin. Most nemeses only get that way because the hero and the villain are too much alike.

I paused.

"For what it's worth," I said over my shoulder, "killing you would be one of the hardest things I've had to do."

I don't do funny business / Not interested in fakers / Don't want no paper gangsta...

I played the track over and over. She sang it so well, a story of dreams gained and dreams lost. But She didn't sing of nightmares. For every dream lost was a dream gained. It was only when you let the nightmares come through that problems arose. Because nightmares don't come and go—they stay. She didn't believe in that kind of thing. To her, the monster I was, that I'd become, was still acceptable. She turned me into a dream. She saw me for what I was. Her music saved me from... well... Me.

'Cuz I do not accept any less / Than someone just as real as...

At the bottom of the hill, I could still see Luke staring out over the city. As an enemy, he had honour and pride in his work. As friend, he was unique. He taught me a lot about creating terror for my enemies. And he would be happy to be crushed under my wrath as I took down his uncle. His dreams died a long time ago. He was simply waiting for the inevitable. He was simply existing, wasting his talents at Chalk Farm. If I could feel anything for him, it would be sadness. Especially considering what I was about to do.

I passed Chalk Farm Village, the bridge, the busy road, and enter the Chalk Farm station. Chalk Farm was at the very edge of the city before Camden. From there, at the edge of Zone Two, it was only a few minutes to Zone One, Central London. It's important to note, Central London encompassed the City and West End. Some people called it the City, but that was wrong. And a decent enough Londoner knows why. The City was the financial centre of London—the Square Mile. It was all about international power. The West End had businesses, but it was also a place of leisure. So it was the richest square mile in the world. My favourite metro line, the Northern line, was unique in that it led both to the City and to West End, the territories of Elad and Russell.

I was on my way to West End. I stood on the platform in the station, and it was packed. It was seven-thirty, and London night was about to wake up. But that evening, after a long time, I was free. And London was about to see something it hadn't for a long time.

On the train, the already very tipsy lads hung onto the handles and swung left and right to impress their female companions and other womanly passengers. They played the old London tube games, like standing with your feet close together and balancing yourself in such a way so you don't fall over when the train stops—near impossible on the London tube—thanks to the G-force. As the train passed through each station, it became more and more packed. Only in London will you find commuters who defy all laws of physics and volume in order to fit the most people into the most limited of spaces. For example, at that moment, there could only be room for a small child, or a relatively slim midget, to board the train, but a seven-foot giant standing on the platform at Euston Station believed that if he hunched enough, he could still fit, even if it meant crushing a child, man, woman, or pensioner. He pushed as hard as he could and managed to make enough space for himself. His face showed that he was in pain, and the people around him tried to press themselves away from his girth, which pushed them into the people behind them, who pushed into the people around them, creating a rippling effect of cringing and discomfort throughout the train. Because of this man's insistence on forcing a game of bodily Tetris, every passenger would have to suffer through the awkward closeness, the stench of one another, the shared sweat, and the neck pain. And the man would feel justified, knowing he didn't have to wait another minute for a more comfortable journey.

The Northern line split at Euston, at which point some trains would navigate through the City whilst others would depart towards the West End.

This train terminates at Morden via Charing Cross.

The automatic operator reminded me that I was on the West End service train, exactly where I needed to be.

I heard a noise from the scrum. It was the impatient giant.

"Ah, shite!"

It seemed he, however, was not where he needed to be. His face was priceless.

Those small things made my night. You couldn't make it up. I loved London.

Chapter 4

Goodge Street and Tottenham Court Road, London

No sooner did I get out of Goodge Street Station did I feel my phone buzzing. It was a text from Mulligan.

Solve it yet? Drop by T-Court All Bar One if around.

It hadn't even been twenty-four hours, but All Bar One reminded me that I needed to catch up with a mate of mine I hadn't seen for a while. Ian Chef was a true pal, an Essex lad, a West End lawyer, six-foot-something, and strong. He was as big as he was bright. He'd know a bob or two about just what the fuck was going on, given that he sometimes acted on behalf of Elad—which was ironic, given that he was positioned in the heart of Russell's territory. But I was only a ten-minute walk from All Bar One, so I figured I might as well entertain Mulligan.

I walked down Goodge Street and made my way towards Tottenham Court Road. That area was within my territory and was home to my two major backers; the China Town Oriental Coalition and the Soho Connection. Put simply, the yellows and the gays. I wouldn't normally walk down this road, but the fucking Olympics in London balls-upped the tube, so the Northern line didn't stop at Tottenham Court Road Station. It was all being upgraded, though the athletes and their balls or bikes or whatever-the-fuck had already come and gone. Soon, London would be filled with annoying foreigners who had watched the

Olympics on television and now wanted to visit the city. Fucking foreigners who didn't know London, didn't understand the laws of the tube, and who filled the stores, making it hard for us natives to get what we wanted quickly.

Without them, though, we'd be fucked. Especially now that the Conservative cunts were in power again (by fucking up Liberals and uniting with them—another strange paradox). They cut the shit out of funding, including money for the police force. That meant the police were much weaker, and the Houses had, therefore, been having a great time in the last few months. Anything bad for the public sector was good for the Houses. The internal bickering in the coalition government also made decision-making much less efficient, which gave the Houses ample time to carry out various dark deeds while inquiries were made and options were mulled over. One thing I liked about the Conservatives was their zero tolerance policy on crime, but now that they were busy fighting amongst themselves, stuff like murder wasn't as high on their list of priorities. And God knew by that time, there must've been at least a few members of the government doing more personal dealings with the Houses than they were permitted to.

Soon, I reached the enormous Freddie Mercury statue outside Tottenham Court Road station on the edge of Oxford Street. Freddie was dressed in his Wembley Stadium attire, with his head down and one hand up, holding the mic. I walked past the statue, took a left, and within a minute, I was in All Bar One. I got myself a pint, then looked for Mulligan. I found him upstairs where he was saying goodbye to a few mates. He was sitting in the middle bench in an area half the size of a standard lounge; he wanted to be easily spotted. He looked tipsy. Slightly red skin and slow-moving limbs. One look at me, though, and he was sharp again.

"Any progress?"

I sat down across from him. "No. Just a learning exercise for now."

"Well, we found out who the hooker was." He took a big swig of the beer in front of him.

"Oh yeah?"

"Yep. She wasn't a hooker after all."

"Yeah, I had a feeling."

What I meant was, I already knew that.

"I think it's just seeing a footballer and a beautiful girl in a tight black dress like that makes everyone think hooker. Poor girl. Her name was Leyli Scarlett."

"Persian?"

"Yep."

"Name change?"

"Also yes. It was originally Saghirlatt."

"Persian word for 'scarlet'. Well, actually 'scarlet' is the English word for 'saghirlatt'."

"Huh. Well, apart from simply wanting to go to bed with a rich, popular figure, I wonder what she was doing there."

I decided to take advantage of Mulligan's intoxication. "It's a great mystery, isn't it? Like just who the fuck your dad is. I mean, there is such a great variety of options, so many men it could be. Your mother wasn't terribly picky, was she, mate? So it's just a *huge* and very diverse pool of candidates."

He smiled. He may have outgrown me and my playful ribbing. It all depended on what he said next.

"Well, getting back to the real issue at hand…"

He'd outgrown me.

"I wasn't giving you a friendly update. I was instructing you as your superior. You, not we, need to find out who she was. I am not wondering about her identity; I'm ordering you to find it out and report back to me. I want to know her background, what she did for a living, any strange activities or odd occurrences that may have cropped up over the past few months." He slid me a slip of paper across the table. "Here's her address and her next of kin."

She lived in Shoreditch, though her next of kin lived in Kensington, which was partially rich Persian territory. Naturally, Russell was the patron leader, but the day-to-day operations were run by a Persian collective of businessmen, professionals, and private member clubs.

I folded the paper and put it in my pocket. "I'll have a look, but I can't say her kin is terribly important for my purposes."

"Well, it's important for mine. She's been killed. Hunter's been killed. Someone must be to blame, Calcain. It's not like they were victims of fucking spontaneous human combustion. There was a shooter, there was a stabber, maybe one and the same, maybe not. I haven't got a lot of answers right now. In fact, I've got no answers, only questions. Maybe her kin and history will answer some of those questions. And if not? Well, fuck, just pick a House, any House, and narrow it down for me, will you?"

I nodded. "I'll go back and re-examine the scene at some point. Maybe I missed something. Doubt it. But maybe. And I'll have a chat with her next of kin tonight."

I stood. "Do you want me to figure out who your father is whilst I'm at it?"

He gave me his usual smirk, as quick as a twitch of the lips.

"No, no, I know who my father is. My problem was easy. I just needed to find the right man. Your problem, however," he said, shaking his head, "is much, much different. Grave circumstances indeed. What you need to do first is identify which species your father is from, and then, once you've ascertained that, try to deduce what instrument and by what miraculous act your mother managed to breed with such an animal."

He drained the remaining contents of his pint glass. "If I were you, I'd start with lizards and work your way up."

He stuck a thumb in the air.

I smiled. He hadn't outgrown me after all.

"You know, if you hadn't banished me, at least in the way you did, you wouldn't be in this mess right now."

I felt the mood change.

"You were out of control, Calcain. Killing everything in sight. I begged you to stop, but you wouldn't listen. I needed to put an end to it. I did what needed doing, and I'd do it all again, though perhaps a bit differently."

I leaned down and put my palms flat on the table. "I had them, Mulligan. I had all of them, and you betrayed me. You can say you did it because I was getting out of hand You can say it was because of the carnage, but the fact remains, friend—you tried to turn me over to the Houses to win their favour, to get them to cooperate, nothing more. I saw it coming, though. I knew what you were thinking. I was already making moves. I was smarter than you. But I wasn't faster than them. And speed beat brains that day, didn't it?"

Mulligan's face was going red. "Calcain, listen—"

"Elsie was just a girl. A little girl. No parents, no siblings, no nothing. She came to my door hungry, and I fed her. Twelve years old. She still had a shot, she still had potential, she could've been something."

It was all true. Darling Elsie. Orphaned, like I'd been. Alone, like I'd been. I saw myself in her but also something better.

82

Something worthier.

"All I had to do was keep her safe from them. From you." I put my face close to his. "All I needed was a day. One day. And they'd have been gone, and I'd have taken her somewhere far, far away from here. Sure, you'd have had to clean up the mess, but we'd have sent you a real nice postcard. You gave me up, though."

"You were obsessed with taking them down. The morgue was filling up with bodies. What did you want me to do?"

"You knew they wouldn't find me at the house that day. Say it. Say you knew."

"I didn't know she'd be there, I swear."

I slammed a fist into the table. "Say it!"

I could hear his breathing getting heavy. I wasn't sure if it was from fear or anger, but I knew what was coming, could feel it bubbling up from inside my chest. I could hear Elsie's tinkling laughter in my mind and tried to push the Monster down.

"You let them take her, Mulligan. You could've stepped in, but you left her at their mercy. A little girl. My little girl. And they left her in the street for me to find. Raped and tortured and dead. I was sitting beside her body when they grabbed me and dragged me off for my own punishment. Do you know what they did with her body, Mulligan?"

He kept his jaw clenched and shook his head.

"Neither do I. But I think of it a fuck of a lot, let me tell you." I dropped my voice and got close to him to make sure he heard each word I had to say. "If it hadn't been for you, the Houses would be gone, and Elsie would be in college studying marine biology or literature or whatever the fuck she wanted to study. She would've been a lot smarter than either you or I, I can tell you that much. Instead, by the sheer force of luck, I was saved by the Soho and China Town gangs. I'd be dead right now if it weren't for them. And it would've been your doing, pal."

"You were uncontrollable. You were leading everyone in the department to their deaths—"

"Careful now," I snapped. "You wouldn't want me to lead you to yours."

I finished my drink and turned my back on him. He lifted a lazy hand to flag down a waitress and asked for another pint. I put my headphones on as I left the bar, and She started singing for me.

Don't want no paper gangsta...

I was off to Kensington. The land of the rich.

*

South Kensington Station and Sloane Avenue, Chelsea

Outside the station, I spotted a couple of toffs outside waiting for a cab. The problem with those areas was they reminded you of the scale, the huge gap, between the middle and working classes in London. The people around there wore expensive clothes and had the latest of everything, from gadgets to cars. The only interaction they had with the working class was on a professional basis only, with the working class being hired by those in the middle. Often filled with an undeserved sense of self-satisfaction, middle-classers had a surprisingly good sense of humour. And they all looked like Luke; light jeans, brown or dark blue coat, shitty shirt (often floral in nature—what the fuck), longish hair, and red trousers. They all looked alike, regardless of race.

I took a left and walked down towards Sloane Avenue. The people there all fall under the same brand, even the girls. Mini dresses—brand names, of course—high heels with red soles. They were all likely on their way to a club called Güù or Skãnk or some shit like that. To them, a wild night out in an exclusive private members club was as close as it got to living a dangerous, exciting life. God forbid if Harvey Nichols, Harrods, or Selfridges closed. They'd start up a riot. They did smell great, and their makeup looked amazing. The brunettes almost all looked like Kate Middleton, with their hair smooth and shiny. Money has that effect on women; Kate Middleton looked diseased before joining the royal ranks.

In my ear, She was still singing "Paper Gangsta." In the song, She had high hopes and was given so many great promises. Promises she believed. Then they dropped her so cruelly and brutally and coldly. A young woman's ambition thrown in the wild to be savagely destroyed. But she turned the tables. Whatever was thrown at Her in the wild was the thing destroyed. That young ambition had a lot of fire behind it. She'd fallen so far down but got up and conquered the world. *That's my girl.*

The house at seventy-nine Sloane Avenue was large but not a mansion. Presumably, the family was paying to live in the area, not so much for the house itself. I turned off the music, took my headphones out, and shoved them in my pocket.

I rang the bell.

Fuck, what the hell was her name? Shit.

I only had seconds to think.

Before I could remember her name, the door opened, and the person I saw was—to say the least—stunning. But young. Probably sixteen. She had long, black hair hanging close to her elbow, like a dark waterfall. Big, beautiful eyes stood out even more with the carefully drawn eyeliner, a sensible amount of foundation, and a lipstick the same colour as her lips. Light olive-coloured skin was complemented by the tight, tan T-shirt and blue jeans.

If only she was older.

Despite her looks, she also had a proud feel about her. This was a girl you learned to respect before she'd consider a date. She wouldn't allow herself to be viewed otherwise.

"Hello, can I help you?" She smiled when she spoke, but that did not contradict her pride.

The accent was Queen's English, despite the fact she was Persian. She must have been born here or at least raised here from a very young age.

"I work with Scotland Yard. I'm here to investigate the death of—"

"With?"

She picked up on the caveat. Smart girl.

"Are you employed by them or are you just nosing around for them?"

I needed to break her. "I'm a consultant. I'm here to find out who killed…"

Then I remembered. "Leyli."

I went in blunt; hearing the name of a recently dead sibling isn't easy, no matter how proud the person is.

Her still face was betrayed only by the small movement of her nose and a slight watering of the eyes.

"Journalists like you have been on our case since…" She sighed. "Look, we don't want to know who killed her."

"I'm not a journalist. I just need to ask a few questions." I toned it down. "Your sister's death is a horrible pain to bear. Trust me, I know how it feels to lose someone you love, especially in a manner like that. I'm here to try and bring some closure to a terrible tragedy. And I need to act quickly. The man who hired me, Detective Mulligan, should have called or sent word in advance of my arrival."

She paused a moment to think. "I'll give you fifteen minutes. But if you turn out to be a journalist, I promise you this—I'll make you the goriest headline to ever hit London within an hour."

I nodded. "Thank you."

She held the door open wider. "Come in."

As I step inside, the sheer scale of the house hit me. High ceilings—my favourite. The kitchen was in the distance, and the reception area was complemented by two human-sized vases, Persian carpets on the floor, and other general accessories. As I stepped forward, she led me to the living room on my left with massive sofas, a chimney, and tea tables accompanied again by vases, antiques, and another large Persian carpet. There were small carpets with miniature designs framed and hung on the wall. There are also quotes from the Qur'an and Shia Islam written in gold and hanging between them. They were done beautifully in fine Persian calligraphy.

"Sit down here, and I will get the rest of the family. Can I get you tea or coffee?"

Persians were kind-hearted and always hospitable, even to their enemies.

"Tea would be fine. No milk or sugar."

"You drink tea like a Persian."

"I just like the taste."

She smiled for the first time and left.

A few minutes later, she returned with three other women. Apart from one who was considerably older, by at least nineteen years, the others looked roughly the same age; early to mid-twenties, a maximum of six years apart between the oldest and the youngest. The oldest was probably ten years older than the girl who had greeted me, or slightly less. Apart from weird-looking noses, they all appeared fairly similar and fairly stunning. Pretty much all the young ones were dressed the same, with their makeup nicely done. The more mature woman wore a long but somewhat slim-fitting dress with golden designs on it. She was a touch chubby but carried herself extremely well. She had an aura of class about her. Her maturity was complemented by her kind smile and features

"Good evening, sir."

I stood as the women entered.

"My name is Belgheese Saghirlatt, but you can call me Bell for short. I prefer it to Geese, which is only slightly less complimentary." She smiled as she tried to break the ice. "You have already met my daughter, Jade, who, in the midst of protecting the family, not only rudely did not introduce herself but also did not get your name."

I was almost stunned by the level of her politeness. She was soft-spoken, but a Persian accent was hidden behind her words. Persians spoke slowly, and when it came to pronouncing words starting with 's', they made a point of pronouncing 'es' before the word. For example, they would say 'es-tar' instead of 'star' or 'es-peak' instead of 'speak'.

"Madam, I am Detective Calcain. As I have explained to young Jade, I work with Scotland Yard. I am here to investigate the passing of your daughter, Leyli."

She paused, taking a deep breath as she collected herself. She would not cry in front of strangers.

"Tragedy follows her name. You know the story of Leyli, Leyli and—"

"Majnun," I nodded. "Layla and Majnun, the Persian tragedy similar to that of *Romeo and Juliet*."

"It predates Romeo & Juliet, but I am impressed you know the story. Or at least the title."

"I have read extensively on ancient history and particularly on Persian history. Part of my work involves international affairs, and you can't really understand modern Iran without first understanding its history."

"Reading is not the same as visiting. You should. I can see you may have some ancestry in you, though I cannot tell how strong or weak."

"Well—"

"You drink tea like a Persian. You maintain politeness, even when speaking to a sixteen-year-old. You smile at the name of Persian culture. You are Persian enough. Speaking of tea, Jade, please, tea for us and the guest. Some dates, fruit, and zoolbia bamieh."

"Maman!" Jade said, sounding slightly offended not to be taken as seriously as an adult.

"Baby, please."

With this soft request, Jade left.

The family sat on the sofas arranged in a rectangular formation around the room with a table in the middle. I sat on the south sofa, with one of the girls on the east and the other two on the west. Bell sat in front of me, north of the table. Two of the girls had high heels on, and one to my left had boots on. The sofa was nice enough, but even with the chimney burning and keeping the air warm, I always found it impossible to feel comfortable on a stranger's sofa, certainly not with so many stunning girls around me. I sat on the edge of the seat and wondered why on earth are they were wearing shoes indoors.

The momentary silence was broken by Bell. "My daughters, Mahsa, Roya, and Kimia."

As she pointed, Mahsa was to the west with Roya. Kimia was alone to the east. In the group, Kimia was the oldest and most closely resembled Jade, especially in the way her demeanour demanded respect. All looked tired. The makeup barely hid the redness and the puffiness around their eyes. They'd clearly been crying.

"Madam." I didn't have time for chit-chat.

As professional as this exchanged needed to be kept—I was representing the police force after all—I needed to get to the point fast. Ideally, there would've been time for an ice breaker, but I got straight to the matter at hand.

"I need to know a little about Leyli in order to draw a picture of what happened." I knew what happened. "I need to know who she was and how she knew Hunter."

"She should have killed that dog herself," Mahsa said, raw emotion and anger underlying her voice.

Her curly hair bounced as she spoke. "He treated her like garbage. That's why people shouldn't mix with dogs. But still, she still loved him. She thought he could change. He got far less than he deserved. Now everyone is saying my sister was some kind of killer." She scoffed. "Ridiculous. She was killed because of *him.*"

"Now, Mahsa." Bell raised her hand calmly. "We are here to help find out what happened. You must appreciate, Detective, that my daughters are not in the best possible shape, so you must excuse the emotions and anger that will no doubt emerge."

"I do understand. It is a terrible time for any family." Nice and professional.

Roya demonstrated the same emotion as Mahsa when she spoke. She had very straight, long hair and was holding Mahsa's hand.

"How do we even know you're not a journalist. We've been hounded without a single second to think and haven't even had a chance to grieve for our sister."

"You have only my word. I can show you a badge, but I expect you've seen enough fake police badges from journalists recently, so that wouldn't give you much faith. I could tell you exactly who I am, every detail about my work and history, but it could all be lies. It won't help to build trust between us. You have only your instincts for that. I will say the circumstances surrounding Hunter's and Leyli's deaths are controversial, and as such, I have been hired by Scotland Yard to closely examine the events before, during, and after the crime. I see things. I understand things." I met the eyes of each woman, hoping to instil in them a sense of security. "I'm an expert at what I do."

"My apologies, Detective." Kimia spoke for the first time.

She had a small smile on her face and inquisitive eyes. But the smile was a front. She was not happy.

"Why is the death of a footballer so important? I mean, forget the media. There have been a lot of shifty, supposedly official people knocking on our door. People who look a lot like you."

She said what they'd all been thinking, and I was sure she was telling the truth. I would be amazed if people like that—fake officials, fake experts, gang members and House leaders in disguise—hadn't been around. Kimia knew there was something more complicated going on. Looking around the room, it became clear they all did.

A relatively honest response would do.

"That's not surprising." I had to choose my words carefully. "Hunter held a very special position with us, the details of which would no doubt put you in danger, so I won't be sharing them with you today. So, yes, you are correct. My involvement in this case was necessitated by the fact that this goes beyond the death of a footballer. I'm here because Hunter was more than that."

"Well, then that must mean you are here to investigate not Leyli's death, but rather Hunter's. And my sister is, at best, one of your clues." Kimia kept her chin straight and head high.

"I assure you, the police will be looking into the circumstances of both deaths—"

"But you are only looking into one."

She was testing my very limited patience.

"It will serve all parties to find out what happened. I'm not here to promise anything. I've been asked to find a killer. It would follow that finding out who killed Hunter would also shed light on who killed Leyli. Unless you think there's some reason to believe two people were killed in the same place at the same time by different killers harbouring entirely different motives, which, I must say, is extremely unlikely. Statistically improbable. Maybe even impossible. I will find out the truth, and when I do, justice will be dispensed."

I ground my teeth together, feeling a familiar tension spreading through my muscles. I was getting annoyed.

"I'll share this with you, and only this—right now, the working police theory is that your sister was hired by a House of the London Underground to assassinate Hunter. I won't share why that's the position or how we're coming across such information, but that's where the police are at on it."

Kimia's voice got soft. "Is that really what they think?"

I nodded. "Yes. But I disagree."

Granted, my disagreement was in actuality my knowledge of the facts of the case, my understanding of what happened in that room. However, this family might have information for me. And

92

if not, I could at least tell Mulligan I did my due diligence.

"But you were her family. Maybe you know things, things the police don't. Things that might be helpful for me."

Bell leaned back in her seat. The other girls sighed, bar Kimia who crossed her arms. She still didn't trust me. And who could blame her?

Kimia stood her ground. Suddenly, Jade came through the door with tea, sweets, and fruit. The silence didn't break even as she moved around the room.

She left a few dates on a plate for me, along with honey golden sweets; a puff pastry ball and something resembling a thick, orange spider's web. They looked soft and sweet, and I picked one up to have with my tea.

"That's zoolbia bamieh," Jade said with a small measure of excitement.

It tasted sweet, milder than honey and soft in my mouth.

"Do you like it?"

"Yes, it's quite nice. Complements the tea really well."

"Detective Calcain," Bell said after having remained silent for some time. "You take to sweets and tea quite well. Zoolbia's primary ingredients are flour and honey. They restore much of the body's exhausted minerals and glucose and are therefore a favourite among opium and morphine addicts. Those needing a fix also tend to have increased anxiety and discomfort that is often calmed by tea and zoolbia."

I didn't respond and continued eating. She had a point. It was fantastic and got me thinking about the excitement of being finally, totally free to go back to living my life the way I chose. Doped up, whored up and drunk. I looked at the time, and it was nine forty-five. I realised that day had been the longest I'd gone with nothing more than a beer in my system. No drugs. No pills. I might as well go cold turkey, really clean myself up. It was a nice thought, though. Unlikely to happen. But nice to think about.

"That's very interesting about addicts and zoolbia. I wasn't aware."

"Would you like to discuss it further, Detective Calcain?"

"Indeed, but it'll have to be at a different time, madam. Meanwhile, I have the pressing business of dealing with your daughter's murder."

"You speak like a lawyer. 'Meanwhile.' A forceful change of conversation, don't you think?" She paused as she sipped some tea. "Tell me what you need to know."

It seemed as though she wanted to pit her deductive reasoning against mine, to tell me that she, too, was on ball. I cared very little for that.

"Tell me about Leyli and Hunter's relationship. How they met, how long they went out for, what they were like together, things like that."

Mahsa spoke up. "They met at Amika, an upmarket club in Kensington. She had no idea who he was. Sure, he's famous, but he's no David Beckham, you know? Anyway, she'd just broken up with this guy she'd been dating for seven years, and he was the super jealous type, and it was getting a little bit crazy. But Hunter was quite the gentleman at first. He didn't try anything. I think he could tell she wasn't interested in anything serious yet. They started out as friends, and that was all. She even went out with this other guy a few weeks after meeting Hunter, and Hunter wasn't fussed. They just kept hanging out, and they got close. Hunter was always charming and respectful, very quick to apologise. He treated her like a goddess. She eventually gave him a chance, and they went out."

"That was one and a half years ago," Jade interjected.

"Yes," Mahsa said, nodding. "That's when they started dating, and he was great. He had a Persian grandmother on one side and a Persian grandfather on the other. Obviously, he was mixed race, but not so distant from his roots that the Persian elders would disagree."

"Some did, though," said Jade abruptly.

Mahsa sighed. "Yes, some did. It wasn't really a racist thing, you understand? We were born here, but our blood is Persian. Comparatively to other ethnicities, there are just so few of us remaining, so we need to ensure our children don't forget their real homeland, that they maintain our customs and traditions. So yes, some elders voiced their concerns. Our family has a special status among Persian people. We have links to groups both inside and outside Iran and across all political circles." Her face darkened. "All except those blood-thirsty extremists, the Mujahideen. Our father was killed by one of them during a terrorist attack in London."

"The Mujahideen say they are reformed, but they are a cult," Jade again interjected. "They kill Persians and even joined forces with Saddam to attack Iran. They've murdered innocent families. Don't believe the news. They are backed by the Saudi royal family to ensure Iranians are divided, though—"

"That's enough, Jade," Mahsa said. "Anyway, after the death of our father, our uncle was the next highest elder, but he was so afraid we would ask him for money after Dad's passing, as if we're a family of beggars, that he ignored us. Not a single phone call. Totally un-Persian. My dad paid for his education and for his house, but the soulless moron didn't even call us once after Dad died. As if we needed his money. Anyway, without the support of the elders, Leyli was effectively shunned by most of the community. But Hunter was partially Persian and respected the culture. He wanted his kids to go to a Persian school, for example. And for that, the remainder of the community was quite happy with him. And since Persians don't rely on community as much as other cultures—we tend to be more integrated with wider social circles—the shunning really didn't impact us. Mostly just my mother."

She paused to take a breath and sip her tea. I kept quiet and let her continue.

"Things between them were going really well, but that changed very quickly after about six months of them dating. Leyli started to come home late or not at all. That might not seem like a big deal for a girl her age, but after our father's death, Leyli was working two jobs to support the family. She was the oldest, and Kimia came after her, and those two worked hard for us. But Leyli became dejected after a while. Hunter was buying her expensive gifts she couldn't maintain. Huge, shocking gifts, like a Bentley. She needed to spend a week's wages just to keep the car running. Eventually, he persuaded her to quit her job and let him support her. She couldn't keep up anyway, so why suffer? Mom wouldn't accept any money from him, but he—"

"He persuaded LeilyLeyli otherwise," Jade interrupted, angry. "In doing so, he managed to do something no one else before him had ever managed to do. He managed to take away her independence."

Mahsa continued, "Our father died young. And living here isn't cheap. Our mother can't lose face in the community, both the local community and the Persian one. So we kept the house. What Dad left us covers the bills and the food, maybe a little extra. The rest is locked away in Iran. We support our own lifestyles. Leyli left uni halfway through to provide for us. She took two jobs, one as a personal assistant and one as a bar girl. Her salary covered our school and leisure fees, which meant we could continue receiving private education. She gave me time to comfortably finish school, graduate, and get a job at Goldman Sachs, and Kimia was also able to complete her classes and get certified as a lawyer. She works for Linklaters now. With my and Kimia's salary coming into the household, Leyli became a little obsolete, but she still gave her money to the family. She…" Mahsa stuttered as she slowly became overcome by grief. "Sh-she said her mission was incomplete until Jade got where she wanted to be, too. That's how she sacrificed herself for us. So you can see," she said, anger filling her voice, "how we didn't give a fuck what the community said about her going out with that sonafabitch. She was so much sweeter and so very much more kind-hearted than most Persian women. She was our gem. Our saviour. Without her, none of this would be here."

She gestured around the room furnished with upper class furniture and décor.

Jade went to Mahsa and hugged her, both of them crying. Then there were tears all around the room, though none from me or Bell. The world I lived in was so much crueller than a story of an older sister making a sacrifice. I wanted to ask what Bell was doing all this time, if the wife of a wealthy man had been reduced to cleaning houses. More likely, that's the fate she would have had, had it not been for Leyli's work and persistence, and perhaps it was that edge of Leyli's sacrifice that got to me more. She'd rather work herself to death than see her mother lose face.

It felt inappropriate at that moment, what with all the waterworks, but I needed to close the gap between the sacrificing sister and the murder.

"The extent of her sacrifice is truly amazing. It is not easy to be a good child to one's parents or to be a good sibling. As much as I hate what I have to do now, I'm afraid it's urgent I ask for a bit more from you all." I paused to take a sip of my tea and let the girls collect themselves before continuing. "How did Leyli turn from this model daughter to quitting her jobs, to playing into Hunter's hand, to being so dejected?"

Kimia's voice was cold. "Well, she realised the money she was bringing in was nothing compared to what we were bringing in. I mean, she still did wonderful things for us, like paint the house and fix things up—she was very practical for an attractive girl. In any event, soon, if Mahsa and I booked a holiday, paid for flights and a hotel, she'd hardly manage to afford dinner. She used to take us to Brighton and Cornwall. Mahsa and I started taking the family to Singapore and Florida. She went from the financial power source to third in line, but she still insisted on paying for things around the house. And she worked with Jade closely on her schoolwork. But between the money we had coming in and trying to keep up with Hunter, she gave up the bar job. The money wasn't worth what it used to be any more, and without that job, she'd have more time with him and..." Kimia's voice shook, "more importantly to her, more time with us."

She wiped away coming tears before continuing.

"It didn't take long for her to give up her day job, too. Early on, Hunter was busy training during the days and had his businesses to look after, so Leyli was free to work during the days. I thought it was strange. They went away on holiday every now and again, but sometimes she wouldn't see him during the day for weeks at a time.

"Given that we're in a deep recession, Leyli did a fantastic job keeping her career as a PA intact. I mean, she was amazing at her job. Always ahead of everyone, wanted by all the senior partners at Ernst & Young. Then, about three months ago, she began to spend more time with Hunter. She would often stay at his house, and we began to see her less and less. We didn't mind too much—we knew she needed to live her own life—but when we did see her, she'd often seem very troubled. At first, she just wasn't her usual, bubbly self. She blamed it on work pressure—there were layoffs, which put a lot of the burden on her—but eventually, it became clear there was something more to it. She didn't look showered and neat, like she usually would. She was losing weight. She had these marks on her wrists, like burns or cuts. She always had an excuse for them. 'Oh, I was doing such-and-such with a candle', or 'oh, I tripped on the stairs and took a tumble'. Worst of all, she'd started staring off into space for minutes on end, not saying anything or doing anything. Six months ago, she said Hunter wanted to get married, but in order to do so, he wanted her to dedicate more time to him. She wasn't exactly excited about that caveat. She said Hunter was becoming less receptive to Persian culture, going back on his plans for their future children to be raised with our traditions. She also said he would say things to her. Awful, cruel things. She showed no emotion when she told us that, though, like her spirit had been wrenched from her body. We asked her if she wanted to leave him, and she refused.

"About five weeks ago, she finally quit her job to become his full-time girlfriend. Ironically, she ended up having even less time for us."

I could tell Jade wanted to say something, but she stopped before she did, her mouth opening and snapping shut.

"Every time we saw her from that point onwards, things seemed to have become worse," Kimia said. "She was going out a lot more in the evenings. She looked exhausted, and she started saying strange things, like Hunter was threatening her and had people watching her. Stuff like that. Then she had a huge row with Mom about three weeks ago, and she never came home again."

Jade's face changed at that point. I thought at first she was about to cry, but she quickly changed expression. It was, to say the least, suspicious.

"Did you see her at all after that?" I asked, moving my eyes away from Jade.

"Oh, yes," Kimia said. "And we emailed a lot. Her best friend, Hannah, is going out with my friend, Mark, so I always saw them when I went out. Sometimes she seemed completely fine, like her old self. Other times, she spoke in riddles, saying something terrible was coming. Maybe it was related to what you said before? About some gang house?" She looked at me with earnest eyes.

I shrugged. "It could be, sure."

She looked at her hands. "Anyway, I didn't know what was going on, but I begged her to leave him. I swear, I begged her." Her eyes met mine. "Something wasn't right."

She began to sob.

"Can any of you think of anyone else who might have been around Hunter or Leyli around this time who might have had closer access or more insight to offer?"

Kimia wiped her nose on one of the napkins Jade had brought in with the tea. "Her friend, Jessica, was around them a lot. She was Hunter's dealer and ran in the same circles, so maybe she would know more than us."

I sat forward on my seat. "I would like to speak with Jessica."

She nodded. "She lives in Lambeth North. I've got the

address on my phone. I can email it to you or text it."

"I'm a bit old-fashioned. Can you write it down for me?"

"Certainly." She pulled a pen and pad of paper from beneath the table and wrote the address, passing it to me.

It was near Fitzroy Lodge, my old boxing gym.

"Do you have any other questions, Detective Calcain?" Bell asked calmly.

I was admittedly rather surprised by her self-control. She seemed calm and relaxed, considering what had happened to her eldest daughter. She didn't cry. And with this question, it felt as though she was trying to hurry me out of the house, which, of course, made me wonder—was there something she didn't want me to know about? Might the family have more information than they were sharing? Was all the reminiscing just a distraction?

"I do have some more questions, yes. How was her state of mind when you last spoke with her?"

"She met us for breakfast yesterday morning," Jade said. "She seemed like the old Leyli again. She was kind, sweet, and loving. She even called Mom from the coffee shop. But I was the last one to speak with her. She called me at about nine last night. She told me she loved me, and that I was everything to her. She also said everything was going to be better from now on. She was crying, but she was mostly saying positive things."

"Mostly?"

"No, well…" Jade looked panicked, and Bell and Kimia both turned to her.

Jade swallowed. "She did sound positive. But I thought she sounded maybe a little sad because she was thinking of leaving Hunter."

"Did she tell you that? Or are you guessing?"

Jade shrugged. "Just a guess."

"Anything else? Did she say anything to any of the rest of you?" I looked directly at Bell, but she merely shook her head.

Before I could go ahead with further questions, the door suddenly rang. Jade went to answer it, and as she opened it up, all I could hear were the screams of women and the deep voices of men.

Bell looked at me immediately, and I thought her expression was almost relieved.

"Excuse us. Family and friends are beginning to arrive, and it is time for us to grieve. I fear you must leave, but this house will be open to you in forty days' time when our grieving ritual comes to an end."

She turned to her now-eldest daughter. "Kimia, give the detective your number." She looked at me. "Kimia will represent us going forward. If you have any questions, just direct them at her." She ushered me past the throngs of friends and family members. "Farewell, Detective Calcain."

I had a strange feeling as I was walking through the crowd, like someone was looking at me as though they somehow recognised me.

I left the house and entered the fresh air of a late October night in London. I had many more questions about Leyli's final days, and something told me that Jade and Bell may have had the answers, but there was nothing else I could do. Not for forty days. The front door shut behind me, but as I turned to leave, it reopened and Kimia slipped out. Admittedly, she caught me off guard.

"Hi," she said, crossing her arms in the cold.

I was about to take my long coat and scarf off, but she stopped me.

"Don't worry. I won't be here long. Look, I'm usually out in

Sketch, so if you have a question, you can find me there. I just wanted to tell you two things, but you have to promise to be careful with this information; I don't want anyone knowing where it came from."

I held a hand up, as though I was swearing an oath in court.

"Okay." Kimia's eyes shifted up and down the street. "First, Leyli told Jade her argument with Mom before she stopped coming home wasn't about Hunter. I asked Mom about it, and she said it was something about her and Dad getting divorced before Dad died and Dad taking that trip to get away from her, which resulted in his death. I just find that story a little…" She hesitated over the right word. "Incomplete. And an argument about that out of nowhere seems a bit sudden and odd."

"I have to agree."

She rubbed her hands together to warm them up in the cold air. "Also, the last thing she said to Jade on the phone was that Hunter was coming home soon, and she had to get ready for a magical night. Then she promised she'd be Jade's fairy godmother again. That's what Jade used to call her when she read her stories as kid." Kimia began to break again.

"I appreciate you—"

"Oh, I guess there's a third thing, actually," she continued. "From what I understand, the leader of the United Persian Collective has sworn revenge. It has an elusive masked leader feared by many. A Persian supremacist. Some call him 'Moghan'. It's an Arabic name but refers to a masked Persian warrior. Maybe that's part of it? I just…" She stopped, looked back at her front door and turned to me again. "I just don't know, you know?"

Sketch was a crazy bar near Kensington and bloody expensive. Jade suddenly came out, asking Kimia to come in.

Kimia started to follow, but turned back to me and said

quietly, "I know there was more to Leyli's fight with our mother. Don't get me wrong. I'm certain Mom didn't kill Leyli, but…" She shrugged. "Maybe there's something there." She straightened her hair before going back inside. "I look forward to seeing you soon."

She left with a smile and a quick stroke of my arm, which I would've been flattered by if I hadn't seen the role she was playing for Jade or any other potential rubberneckers. She needed it to look like she was chatting me up and nothing more. I couldn't help but feel a little disappointed.

I walked the streets until about eleven so I could get my head in order, strolling along Kensington High Street via Knightsbridge. You could get some seriously pretty-coloured lights along the way.

I needed to know if Kimia's suspicions about her mother were correct. Bell wasn't involved in the murders, I already knew that, but maybe she had other pertinent information. House information. In addition to that, I wondered what Jessica's role was in everything, if she had one. What might she know? What might she have told other people?

My main mission was to take down the Houses, but it was hard not to be distracted by the intricacies of Leyli's family life. There was too much to consider, more than I had hoped.

I got to Kensington High Street station with Her still singing "Paper Gangsta" in my ears. I took the Circle line to South Kensington, then the Piccadilly line to Leicester Square and continued my walk. I needed a drink. I needed a fix. I needed to think. Fuck me, it was worse than I thought. Much worse. I was dealing with a new breed of an organised criminal group that posed a legitimate threat to the Houses. I was dealing with the murder of someone with a lot of powerful friends with as many powerful enemies. I was dealing with a vengeful mother, who may or may not have had more knowledge than she was willing to share. And at the heart of the thing, I was dealing with two victims whose deaths weren't at all what people were believing them to be.

It was all too fucking complicated.

I needed to simplify it.

I needed a fix.

I needed a drink.

I needed a hooker.

*

The Shochu Lounge, Charlotte Street, London, eleven forty-five p.m.

It had been a shit day. A really shitty day. I started with a great breakfast that soon turned into a massacre in Camden, and at that point, the day, as statistically impossible as it was, got progressively worse. The only other time that could have happened would have been during World War II. Still, it could be worse. Couldn't it?

I got off at Leicester Square to the manic, busy crowd. I fought my way past them and walked straight up to Tottenham Court Road. On my way, I jumped into Foyles and picked up a graphic novel. The train journeys were beginning to take their toll, and I needed entertainment. I went straight past Tottenham, and a few turns later, I was on Charlotte Street.

Now, Soho was one of the most happening places in London, but regulars like me sometimes needed a break from the busyness. The tourists had wised up to the area and, as tourists always do, fucked it up for the locals. I had to admit it was good for business, though. As time passed, we regulars were gifted with a few restaurants and bars just outside Soho, far enough to lose the tourists, close enough to be able to crawl back drunk. On that road was a tiny door that went downstairs to the Shochu Lounge, which was connected to a Japanese restaurant upstairs called Roka, and was by no means cheap. But the cocktails hit you right, and right when you needed them to. Especially when you felt like I did then.

The surrounding walls were covered in modern Japanese art. There were sofas around the bar, which was centred in the room and had a huge block of ice in the middle that the barmen chip away at every now and again for drink orders. The lights were dim, and red and black were the prominent colours of the décor. The wall to the south of the bar had a shelf holding large, egg-shaped jars with wooden tops. There are a few more of those jars around the bar, as well as a few super-sized ones. They contained Shochu, an ancient Japanese vodka and the prime ingredient in the lounge's cocktail mixes. It was also my favourite drink.

As I walked in, a woman greeted me and asked if I had a reservation. My answer was, of course, no. But my good Lithuanian pal and barman signalled me in. That always made me smile because everyone knows a primary trait of an alcoholic is feeling at home in a bar and considering a barman a good mate.

"Good to see you again, Calcain," he said with a smile as I sat on a stool beside a table closest to the bar.

"Get me something strong. I need to wake up."

Lithuanians may not be very famous for their Japanese Shochu cocktails—in fact, they're not known for it at all because why on earth would they be?—but this man knew how to make a bloody cocktail. I liked his name; Darius. He was an expert. All you needed to tell him was the kind of mood you were in, and he'd match you with the perfect cocktail. If you were sad, he might cheer you up with Sunshine Blue. If you were ready to celebrate, maybe it will be a champagne-rich Nightingale. He always knew what I needed, and at that moment, what I needed was a moment of clarity before I crashed. He mixes me up a dark Manhattan with Shochu as its base.

"My friend, you look like you actually have joy running through your tired face. Happiest I have seen you for a long time."

"Considering I was nearly killed several times this morning, I reckon I've done pretty well. Glad this face ain't lost its figure. As long as I've got that, I should still be able to keep my luck with the ladies, pal. If not, I always have my wit."

"Your wit? Maybe it's better to just keep working on the face. Here, this will cheer you up." He held out a hand. "Give me your phone. I will put on the music you like."

He took my iPhone, and first She sang 'Paparazzi' for us all, and when that ended, She started in on 'Scheibe'. It was a sterling effort on Darius' part. My cocktail matched both my mood and my music, and I found myself drinking alone in a dark, modern lounge whilst my favourite girl sang for me. Yes, things could definitely have been worse.

Before I finished my drink, another appeared on the bar before me, and Darius and I made small talk. As the third drink arrived, I noticed a small sofa open up near the bar, and I navigated my way to the dark corner.

I closed my eyes and saw things better than I had all day. She kept singing.

I don't speak German, but I can if you like…

The beat hit hard and fast, my pulse increasing with every bass note. She started singing in German and suddenly, the day's events came into focus. The music got louder. My heartbeat throbbed.

When I'm on a mission / I rebuke my condition…

In my mind, I saw the hotel and then Ra'ef and the punks, and then someone else, someone in the club, but he wasn't dressed as a punk. Who the fuck was that? Did I know him? The mental images continued and I saw Vlad, and then Mulligan saying goodbye to friends, one of whom looked very familiar. Then I remembered Bell's house, the look on her face, the hard stare of her eyes. I was reminded of the secrets she was probably keeping. I wondered what she knew and what she'd tell and what she'd done or would do. A vengeful mother with a feather could do more damage than a psychotic murderer with a chainsaw. I was certain she'd played a role in this saga, but I wasn't sure what that role might be. At the centre of everything was Hunter. And at the centre of him were the Houses.

Then a stark image came before me. When I was fighting my way past the guests outside Leyli's family home, the first person I saw outside kept turned away when he saw me. Was he the same person I saw with Mulligan? The same person at the club with Ra'ef? Mulligan's people might have been following me, and I found that very fucking annoying. But I didn't have time to focus on that.

I opened my eyes, and the bar was empty. Darius was cleaning up and drying a few glasses. He looked at me and smiled.

"Calcain, I worry you may have lost your touch on drinking. You are lightweight now, no?"

"Darius, believe me. This is the most awake I've been in a long time."

"Yes. You do look a lot more focused. Happy for another?"

"No, thanks. I need to get home. Listen, thank you for the drinks. They really are magic."

I walked over and put a fifty on the bar for him. "Here, keep the change."

"Calcain pay? Ha! Since when?" He grinned at me.

"I've been employed, my friend."

"When? Yesterday?"

"Yes, yesterday."

"To do what?"

I paused, smiled and made my way towards the stairs and answered him over my shoulder. "To do what I do best, pal. To do what I do best."

I walked up the stairs, and as I reached the top, I felt like I was king of the world, a feeling interrupted by Darius rushing up behind me to give me the phone I'd left behind. That Darius. The Shochu Lounge. They always made me feel great.

As I stepped out of the stairwell, I relished the feeling and walked down Charlotte Street, putting my headphones in and selecting the next track for Her to sing to me. Her voice, my buzz, it was all wonderful. But it was the kind of wonderful that only lasted about forty-five seconds.

*

The floor in a road off Charlotte Street and Soho, London, one thirty-five a.m.

Just as I was about to let Her sing 'Electric Chapel', everything went suddenly dark. I couldn't breathe. I felt myself lifted up and thrown to one side. Before I could move, I was dragged to what I assumed was an alleyway, and all I felt were punches to my stomach and kicks all across my body as I lay immobile. I felt the pressure you get at the back of your throat right before you throw up. I was dizzy. I couldn't move. All I could do was lay down, take it like a bitch, wait for my new friends to exhaust themselves. But they just wouldn't tire out.

Suddenly, an energy I can't describe ran through me. I only got that sometimes when I was in serious shit. I could see an orange light running from my head down my torso and through my limbs. It was probably a stress-induced hallucination, but it woke me up enough to get my eyes open and see a gift, a gem of brick within reaching distance. I launched my body towards it, grabbed it in my fist, and with all my speed, I smashed it against the first thing that came flying my way. It turned out to be a bloody industrial rubbish bin, and hitting it felt something like smashing your fist against a steel wall. Pain shot through my arm, and I crumpled, brick still in hand. *You had one shot. You ruined it.*

The loud bang and sheer force of my action worked, though. The hits stopped coming, and my attackers put some distance between us.

"It seems our little lady has still got some force in her, Donnie," said one.

I could only make out bodies, not faces. There were three of them. East End accents.

"Well, blimey, Davie," said another. "Bloke wants another 'ard one up his cunt. If I was 'im, I'd sit right on my twat and keep me mouth shut."

"Shut up, you morons," said another voice with a clearer London accent. "Well, Calcain. Seems they were right about you. You can take kicks and punches like a donkey, and you sure look like one, too. I'll be short, which I hope won't offend you. My governor couldn't let you back on the scene without a proper welcome, now could he?"

The other two giggled.

"Now, I'll say this once. Just once. Are you listening?"

He waited. I nodded, head spinning.

"Mind your fucking business. You want to find out who killed Hunter and that little whore? Be our guest. But once you're done with that, you need to fuck right off. Simple. You try any shit above your fucking duty, and I'll be visiting you again. And believe me, next time I won't be so generous. Got that, sweetheart?"

One of the other two spoke again. "What he's saying is, mind your twat. You take the wrong turn, and we'll fuck it. And I sure would enjoy fucking a tasty cunt like you."

"Excuse my friend here; he's a horny little chap. Likes beautiful little girls like you. I'll take that as a confirmation you've heard and will obey what I've said here today. Enjoy the rest of your evening."

The trio began to walk away, and I finally found my voice, shattered and raspy.

"Hey," I said. "The three stooges."

I got up and leapt forward with the last bit of energy I had, and they jumped back from me, startled. I smiled and took a deep breath.

"Tell your master that I've no desire to find out who he is at the moment. Because *I'm* the one feeling generous tonight. He doesn't concern me for many reasons, the main one being that you lot showing up here with whatever the fuck this little routine was supposed to be is simply an indication of how my arrival on the scene has already made him shit his pants. But please be sure to relay to him that I will eventually find him, and when I do, I'll fuck him. Just not now. And I won't hold this little display of

111

yours against him; his fear of me is understandable. But next time I bump into any of you three, I'll chop your balls off, shove them right up his ass, wait for him to shit them out, and then feed them to him. I will repeat that process until I'm satisfied he thoroughly understands the etiquette and intricacies of eating shit. Now, please. Fuck off."

I borrowed a part of that speech from my friend Vlad. If you ever want a good, long insult, always consult a Russian.

The men slowly walked away, checking over their shoulders every few steps to make sure I wasn't following. Once they were gone, I headed back towards Charlotte Street, keeping the brick in my hand just in case those pricks decided they wanted to go for round two.

Seconds after I turned out of the alley, a woman walking past me was accosted by three people in hoodies. They ran towards her, smacked her in the head with some kind of object, and took her bag. She screamed and fell to the ground. They ran too fast for me to do anything, and the woman was starting to groan. People emerged from their homes, bars and restaurants at the sound of her scream and stared at me with hateful eyes.

I didn't understand why they were looking at me. I took a time-out to objectively view the scene. A small, helpless blonde woman on the ground. A recently beaten man, still bloody, still armed, standing beside her.

Of course it fucking looked bad.

I needed to get the fuck out of there and fast. I heard sirens in the distance. I hated the sound.

I ran along the side roads towards Soho, my brain working overtime. Crime on Charlotte is rare, but with cuts and tax rises by that prick prime minister, people were resorting to anything. The prime minister was a Conservative and, using Thatcher as a role model, was all about cuts. The deputy was a socialist and therefore all about tax hikes. Together, they made up the huge, thick, girthy, hungry cock going deep into London's arse right now. No lubrication. Just ruthless anal carnage. That said, I didn't sympathise with the thieves. Fucking pricks needed to find jobs.

I kept running. I'd grown attached to the brick and didn't want to drop it. I eventually found myself in front of Foyles and on the edge of Soho, took a quick turn here and there, and finally, I was back in my protected territory. The various Gaylords—gay gang lords—nodded at the sight of me, and I showed my respect by nodding back. They were the people who had saved my life. I turned onto Compton Street and could make out Jimmy's sex shop. Jimmy was a Gay-Overlord and was the first to take me in on account of knowing me since I was kid. He was a good man. I thought I could've been that for Elsie.

Tanka stood outside the shop, his jaw dropping at the sight of me.

"Oh em gee, oh my God, Calcain. What happened to you? Where have you been? Is that a brick in your hand?"

"Tanka, I'm not in any mood for this. I just need my bed. Be a pal, and let me be."

I immediately felt bad for brushing him off. His looked shattered. He was probably the only person at that moment who gave a shit about me.

I stopped alongside him. "Look, I've just been through a bit today. I'll explain tomorrow."

"Do you want me to clean up those cuts, baby?"

I realised I'd probably have scars all across my face after the beating I took. I touched my face, and it was slick with blood.

"Not right now, Tanka, but tomorrow would be good."

"Jimmy was looking for you. Said he'll come by tomorrow

morning."

"Oh? Did he say why?"

"No. Just that he needed to talk to you and wanted you to be at the flat tomorrow."

"Okay, thanks. Goodnight."

"Goodnight, baby," he said with a look of concern in his eyes.

I opened the door and walked upstairs. My flat was empty, and the overhead light was weak, occasionally flickering. The ladies had gone, but the sound of water dripping in the toilet tank was ever-present. I looked at the huge poster of Her on the wall opposite the bed and breathed deep, letting her calm me. I took my clothes off, donned an old T-shirt, and went to the toilet. I looked at my bloody mess of a face in the yellow-stained mirror. I washed the blood off and put some iodine on the wounds, though certain scrapes were still seeping. I turned the tap on the sink, and it dripped enough water for me to have a relatively dry teeth brushing and a small drink. The moisture tore my already raw throat apart. I limped back to bed, my body aching.

The flat was warm, despite the cold wind disturbing the windows every now and again. I plugged my phone into the charger, restarted 'Scheibe', and got under the covers. What a shit day. What a shit fucking day. So much information. Too much. So much ass kicking—mostly my own. So much drinking and fuck all food. It's no wonder why I'm fucked. There are only three things on my mind. Jessica, Kimia, and the fucker I was fairly certain was following me.

I took a few migraine tablets and eventually found myself at peace for a brief time. She stopped singing, I dozed off, and that shit day finally came to an end.

Part II

Chapter 5

The Thames Side Inn Pub, London Bridge, London

Detective Mulligan was drinking by himself again.

It was late night on Saturday, but he couldn't tell you the exact hour.

He'd been drinking most of the day due to upcoming 'meetings'. But even if the meetings weren't going to happen, he'd still be drinking. It had been a shit twenty-four hours. He got himself another pint and sat outside, looking at the River Thames. To his right was Tower Bridge (East End), to his left was the Millennium Bridge (West End), and before him, just across the river, was the Square Mile (the City). All roads lead to the homes of the Three Houses. East was Charlie's territory, West was Russell's, and the City was Elad's to the front. He'd had them all firmly by the balls. Now, he had nothing.

He took a deep sip of the pint in his left hand and an even deeper drag on the cigarette in his right hand.

Well, he had something, he supposed: a creature whose lust for blood and death would eventually tear the Houses apart. Calcain was his strongest card to play, and Mulligan had bet big. Unleashing a caged lion into the wild makes no guarantee it will still be a good hunter; it just means a hungry predator is on the loose. If it paid off, it would all be worth it. If it didn't, there wasn't much left to be taken from him besides his dignity.

The detective felt confident that he had absolute control over the situation. He'd given Calcain his assignment. Now all Mulligan had to do was sit back and watch the show. Calcain had been so promising, maybe the greatest detective in London. He was so talented, but that talent was overshadowed by an unquenchable thirst for blood. And after what the Houses did to his city, to Elsie, to him, his pursuit of revenge became all-consuming. Mulligan remembered the days before Calcain turned, days when he was energetic and enthusiastic about the work they did together. But that was just a memory now. He'd become a shadow of what he used to be. The detective thought he could still be saved; he just didn't want to be.

"All right?" the barman asked, stepping outside to speak to Mulligan. "Ringin' the bell for last drinks in a bit. You want another one?"

"No, thanks," Mulligan said after taking a puff of his cigarette. "I'll finish this and be on my way. Cheers."

He raised his glass to the barman.

The last few droplets of beer ran through the once-great detective's throat, refreshing it from the dust and the smoke.

He began his walk by the South Bank. He'd meander along the River Thames from London Bridge to Waterloo Station and take a taxi from there.

He walked past the Millennium Bridge and the Tate Modern, which stared directly at St. Paul's Cathedral. He lit up a smoke and took in the view. Maybe the Houses and Calcain deserved each other. Maybe they were each other's Yin and fucking Yang. Maybe this would all end in mutually assured destruction. Or maybe Calcain was the only fucker who loved London enough to fight for her. To die for her.

Something was brewing, though, that might be beyond Calcain and the Houses. The key to the survival of the Houses has been acting like holding companies for subsidiaries, i.e. the sub-gangs. They gave the smaller organisations what they needed, namely guns and drugs, and those groups were then on their way to achieving great things with a franchise and an easily recognisable brand that said, 'You fuck with me, and you're fucking with Russell, Elad, or Charlie'. But the sub-gangs were getting too powerful. And sometimes the patronages collided.

For example, Harlesden was once a powerful yardie territory. Charlie, being Jamaican, naturally gave them his backing. Then the favelas started cropping up as a result of Elad's investments in emerging markets that created an influx of Brazilians in London. They happened to move into Harlesden, which resulted in a war. But, shockingly, they called a truce. A truce not backed by either Charlie or Elad, who wanted the sub-gangs divided and weak. But they called a truce anyway, and became quite powerful, and Harlesden could rival Brixton in terms of gang power. When it came to Brixton and South London, it was practically gang anarchy. With technically no patronage, they could run free and do what they liked. That said, if they were called upon, they would answer because they knew the Houses had the financial and military resources to destroy them. The Houses wouldn't hesitate to unite to keep the status quo. The Houses could destroy Harlesden overnight if they wanted to. But they only called a truce when the danger was imminent and real.

And that was at the heart of the problem.

And key to the detective's greed.

The detective wanted to know why the Houses called a truce when no sub-gangs called a challenge. That meeting wasn't about

117

the Shard. It couldn't be. That sort of stuff could be done over the phone. They were scared of something, and whatever it was cost him his game. His case. And Hunter. Calcain didn't have to look far to find out who killed Hunter—it was Mulligan. Or rather, it was his gross negligence. Hunter was good kid. A very good kid. He had such a great life with the gangs; he could easily have switched sides with nothing to worry about. But he risked his life, and lost it, all in the name of justice. And the detective's incompetence.

The detective continued to walk, admiring the moon shining over the silver River Thames. He went past the OXO Tower, and further down, he could see the London Eye. He lit another smoke.

He reached Waterloo Bridge and took a long look at the graffiti on the skate ramp close to the bridge, surely painted by middle class kids trying to be street. That was a weird thing about London. Class had no relevance to crime. Everyone, of all backgrounds, could easily affiliate themselves with a gang. That's what made the detective's life so difficult. Just when you caught a prominent gang member, it turned out his daddy is a hedge fund manager who could afford the best damn lawyers, and, on a rare occasion, could even afford a prosecutor.

At Waterloo station, the detective hailed a black cab and sat down comfortably. So spacey. So roomy. He thought about the panicked Houses, the sub-gangs likely wanting to use that fear to seize control. The Punks could do it, if Camden, Shoreditch, and Soho united. The Black gangs, pissed off by a commercialised Charlie, could want a coup d'état. Harlesden could unite with Brixton. Or all of it could happen, leaving the Houses vulnerable and ready to fight at all corners of London. And now Calcain was right in the middle of the escalating pandemonium. What was he planning to do? He was everything Hunter wasn't. Cold. Cool.

Calculating. Manipulative. A self-proclaimed monster. He was out in the world again, released onto the masses.

Too many thoughts were running through the detective's mind. Intra-gang war, inter-gang war, outside influence, and, finally, Calcain. Fucking Calcain.

He suddenly noticed the taxi taking a wrong turn onto a motorway.

"Ah, mate," the detective said to the cab driver. "I think you took a—"

Suddenly, the doors locked. The driver smiled and a blind rose up between the front and back seats. The windows looked bulletproof—he wouldn't be able to break them. He probably should have been more frightened, but he knew all he could do was sit and wait for whatever—or whoever—was coming. He opened his bag and took out a bottle of single malt whiskey as the car sped up, heading towards the North Circular. Deep breath. A few more swigs of whiskey. He was glad he'd gotten the single malt. It was his favourite drink, and he wouldn't mind it being his last. Though, considering the circumstances, the last liquid in his throat would probably be his own blood.

It had been a shit twenty-four hours. And it was about to get a lot worse.

Chapter 6

Compton Street, Soho, Lambeth North, and Regents Street, London

My eyes.

I couldn't open them.

It felt as though my eyelids were glued together, blocking out bright light and drawing a red curtain in front of my vision. I took a deep breath. My chest hurt. I couldn't move my arms and legs. Or I could, but if I did, a sharp pain shot through them. And my head hurt. I forced my eyes open, and through the blur, I could only see intense light. I reached up to shade my eyes, and my arms ached.

"Good morning, Calcain," a voice said from somewhere in the room. It's Jimmy." His voice was charming, soft, and clear.

"Where-where the…" My throat was as dry as the Sahara Desert, and it hurt like someone had raped it with a cactus.

"You're at your flat. It's eleven in the morning. You gave me quite a scare. Here, open your mouth and drink this. I fear it won't be pleasant, but bear with it."

I opened my mouth, and he poured what could possibly be the sweetest and most horrendous drink down my throat. My body immediately rejected it, and I reeled my body over the side of the bed to throw up. My head spun, and I collapsed.

It was dark again.

"Calcain" His voice sounded very far away. "How much did

you have to drink yesterday? And when was the last time you had your fix?"

I came to again, still dizzy. "I-I'm not. I don't…"

"You're hung over. On the edge of going cold turkey. Which might work for the heroin and cocaine in your body, but not the Dark Fire. How long has it been? Thirty-six hours or so? And how much did you take before that? Must have been a massive, almost suicidal, dose from the look of you."

I'd been on a steady diet of Dark Fire for years. It kept me fucked and sent me into fits of amnesia. I'd forgotten so much of my past already, but under the influence, I'd also forget things as they were happening. I could take a dose and come to a few hours later with absolutely no memory of what had happened during that time. I started taking it when I was still on the force, before missions, especially when I knew I was about to do something I'd rather not remember. I'd started developing a tolerance to the amnesia side effect recently, so I wasn't forgetting as much as I'd have liked to. And you can't quit it in one go. If you do, the withdrawals could kill you. You have to ween yourself off it slowly. I hadn't taken it since the night before I got Mulligan's text, and I sure as hell didn't intend to quit.

"My arm…"

"I had you hooked up to an IV drip, trying to hydrate you. You ripped the needle out just now. Good work on that."

"I need to get up. I…"

My head was far too heavy, and words were near impossible to come by. My throat felt like it was filled with sand, and each word had to be dragged through it. I thought about Dark Fire. How could I have been so stupid? On top of missing my fix, I'd had bugger all to eat since I last left the flat and lots to drink. I was exhausted.

Jimmy spoke again in the darkness. "Calcain, you need to drink this and hold it down. You'll be here for days otherwise. Open up."

I did as he said and opened my mouth for another dose of crap. So sweet. It crawled down my throat and almost turned into a frog on its way to my stomach, jumping up and down. My insides were twisting, and so was I. I controlled myself, though, squeezing my hands together as hard as I could. Jimmy put his hands on top of mine until they started unclenching. Soon, I felt the drink settling my stomach. Suddenly, like drinking water after suffering from thirst, my head cooled down, and my body rested. It was the feeling you get when you come out of the sauna after a tough gym session and get under the cold shower. Everything suddenly became clear. My senses were back, especially smell. My flat stunk. With my mind back in order, I was able to recognise what I'd been fed. Sovereign. It's the equivalent of taking methadone when you're a heroin addict; it's supposed to cut back on withdrawal symptoms and help you quit the hard stuff.

"Feeling better?"

"Yes. Thanks, Jimmy." I felt cold and wet. "Did you pour water on me?"

"No. That's your sweat. Cold sweat. A side effect of the Sovereign. You've gotta sweat the toxins out."

I touched my face, and my fingers slipped across my skin. I heard knocking on the door, and suddenly, Tanka's voice was there. He mumbled and gave something to Jimmy before leaving.

"You should be able to open your eyes now, Calcain. You shouldn't feel too dizzy."

I heard Jimmy stand and move around the room.

My vision was still blurry, but that was from the sweat. I

rubbed my eyes, and soon everything was clear. I sat up on the bed with my back resting against the wall. I was cold. Jimmy came back from behind the kitchen worktop with a mug he'd tried his best to clean. The mug was sitting on a tray with food, and it all smelled divine. He placed the tray across my lap, and I could see hash browns, croissants, conserves, two fried eggs, and venison sausages. Coffee in the mug and orange juice in the glass next to it. The perfect treat for a hangover.

He had long hair and two fingers-worth of beard. He was in his late forties, and his brown hair and beard had streaks of grey in them, but he looked good for his age. In spite of the silver and gold he wore, he tended to dress conservatively, looking more like the owner of an old-school record store rather than a sex shop. He was often spotted in a suit and brilliantly coloured scarves. Paired with his shiny blue eyes, his sharp look screamed ruthless intelligence.

Jimmy's heritage in Soho went far back, his granddad having been one of the people who made Soho what it was today. Jimmy owned quite a few shops and strip clubs across London, but most of the money he made came back to Soho, Camden, and Shoreditch—the three sisters—to rejuvenate the area as much as possible.

His equality campaign was strange to me. He spoke passionately against homosexual men appearing on TV because, when they do, they are presented as flamboyant, needy, and precious. They were portrayed as weak, more like little girls on their periods than men who happen to prefer other men. I met him first on a case where I was dealing with a serial killer targeting the LGBTQ community. Jimmy proved to be a huge asset, but he also had very little sympathy for those killed—a few of them happened to be on TV. Our teamwork proved successful, and we'd remained friends since. I saved his ass the few times he had run-ins with the law, so when I was banished, he and a few others provided me a safe refuge, in spite of vocal objections and open threats of gang war.

Thanks to him, Chinatown and Soho kept me safe from the men who wanted me dead. He gave me a flat in the middle of Soho, where protection could be easily and quickly provided. Being raised in Soho made him realise the importance of drugs in the underworld, so he went to uni to study not only chemistry but also medicine. A qualified doctor and a drug expert made him an invaluable gang lord. Though his team was relatively small, their quality is amongst the best—he controls the Paladins, former SAS and Delta Force members who settled in the UK in large part for their gay-friendly atmosphere. Under Jimmy's wing, they'd been given more than they asked for and would go to hell with him if he asked. Jimmy didn't use fear to obtain respect and loyalty, but rather kindness, patience, and generosity. He commanded respect without having to ask for it.

"Are you planning to quit Dark Fire?"

"Eventually… maybe," I said, making my way through the food he'd given me. "What happened here was I quite literally forgot to take a fix. That's all. I wasn't trying to go cold turkey. I had a little thing come up."

"So I've heard."

"Oh, yeah?" I swallowed down some orange juice. "What have you heard?"

"Enough to know you probably won't be doing odd jobs for your fix or food any more. It seems you've taken on a lucrative project, Calcain."

"Well, I'm no longer banished, if that's what you're referring to. Police protection is back on."

Jimmy stared out the window of the flat, looking over the street below. "It seems Mulligan got you involved in something big. I knew I was lying to myself when I thought I could stop you from this game or get you off your path to self-destruction. But I need to know. What are you getting yourself involved in this time? And, more importantly, will this involve your previous ambitions?"

I laughed. "Previous?"

"To take down the—"

"I know what you're referring to, Jimmy. But what made you think those ambitions were behind me? They were just..." I stabbed my fork into a piece of sausage. "Put on hold."

He turned to me. "It's madness to try to wage your war right now. I've protected you from more than your enemies; I've also protected you from information I knew would get you reinvested in all this mess. Dangerous things beyond you and beyond the Houses are just waiting for you to unleash chaos."

"I know. You mean the so-called New Breed. Once I find out who they are, I'm sure my suspicions about their lack of relevance to anyone or anything in this city will prove true." I shovelled hash browns into my mouth. "If you must know, I've been hired to investigate the death of Terry Hunter and the girl he was with."

He watched me for a long minute. "I don't think you're telling me everything. So let me remind you that on a daily basis, I have to reassure the Houses that I don't have a ticking time bomb—you—about to blast out of Soho. If you take any steps against the Houses, you will bring them to our doorstep. Russell already called me in yesterday and warned me about you overreaching. We're not strong, Calcain, and with the punk king in an uncertain state, we have no back up from Camden.

Shoreditch and us cannot stop the Houses on our own, not least because Russell's base is right around the corner from here. He's literally one road away at all times. And it's his patronage and proximity to Soho that keeps the other Houses at bay. If you piss him off, it won't just be you but all of us who go down in the fire." Jimmy was breathing hard, and I realised how angry he was with me. "Investigate what you will, but as long as you're part of Soho, I won't let you bring death here."

"Jimmy," I said, my voice hoarse. "Of all the leaders and gang lords, I respect you the most. You see things for what they are. How else could Soho have survived independently when it's actually part of the West End? You have Russell so confused. He thinks he asserts absolute control when, in reality, he has none over you."

I paused, thinking as I drank some coffee, which warmed me through and put me in a good mood. "My task is to investigate two deaths. The Houses have a massive vested interest in finding out how one of the deaths occurred. For that reason, they won't touch me, at least not until my work is done. My ambitions beyond that are just that—mine. Soho won't be touched. And as for Russell, he probably thinks asking you to keep a leash on me will keep me in line. He can, of course, fuck off."

"Calcain." Jimmy paused and watched me. "Just do me this favour—stick to your investigation. Just that."

"Jimmy." I smiled. "My newfound freedom, my police protection, it's all limited to this investigation. As soon as I find the killer, I've served my purpose, and I'll be, as they used to say, recycled. Almost instantly."

"Recycled? Don't you mean disposed of?"

"No, I mean recycled. They'll find me, torture me, take my organs and sell them, then throw the rest in a recycling machine.

They did that. They really did. Charlie's recycling plant contains ten percent human flesh."

Jimmy laughed, then took a hash brown from the plate. He was relaxing, his appetite returning. There was a small measure of truth in what I'd been telling him. Yes, my priority was Hunter's death. But I'd solved that. So no, the Houses—my ambition—were not on the back burner. They were front and centre. But Leyli had been on my mind. I was beginning to appreciate just how irrelevant she was to the work I was doing and how relevant she was to her family. The longer I stalled, the longer they went without answers.

"Soho has been good to you, Calcain. It's your home." He paused and looked around the room. He sighed. "Just when I thought this dump couldn't get worse." He pointed at Her poster. "That's pretty big."

"It's from when she went to India."

"Looks a bit like Audrey Hepburn, the way she's drinking tea with those glasses."

"Yes. To me, Her beauty is in her simplicity. Although Her music is amazing, She looks so very ordinary underneath the mask. Misunderstood. Only Her core followers see Her for what She is."

"And what is she?"

"A symbol. Not just for the outcast or the outwardly freaky, but for those with too much madness, sadness, and monstrosity inside."

"Sounds like someone I know." He drank some of the coffee. "Look after yourself. I've left some tonics and a few other bits to help you cope in the bathroom. And some Dark Fire. Don't need you having another episode like you did last night." He stood beside my bed. "Take care, and call if you need anything. Be safe, son."

I smiled up at him, and he left. He'd shown infinite kindness to an infinitely undeserving individual.

*

It was about twelve-fifteen by the time I got my gear together and was ready to go. I was feeling a lot better, and the weather was fairly warm, so I decided to walk to Leicester Square and catch the Northern line from there. Being that it was a Monday afternoon in October, it wasn't as busy, and by the time I reached Waterloo for the interchange, there was hardly anyone there. It took less than a minute on the Bakerloo Line to Lambeth North, an underestimated area of London that's shockingly close to the river and a perfect strategic point as far as the police and gangs are concerned, given its proximity to Waterloo and the river Thames.

Lambeth North was also home to Fitzroy Lodge, one of the oldest boxing gyms in London. It's humble in appearance, but the training is beyond comparison. Jessica lived not far from the lodge in a new development apartment.

I walked up to the apartment block, and it was clearly luxury, with a killer view of the London Eye and the river. The area surrounding it wasn't amazing. The neighbouring blocks comprised of lines of council houses, corner shops, and a church. If you were dropped in the middle of it, you wouldn't think Waterloo or, indeed, the river would be too close by. But the people in the new high-rises were rich professionals—lawyers, bankers, accountants, and so on. Jessica, I was sure, was neither. She probably supplied most of them with drugs and lived here to be close to her clientele.

I walked to the reception area, and the security guard, a Nigerian guy and no doubt a 'student' as far as the immigration service was concerned, greeted me.

"Are you here to visit someone, sah?"

So polite. He was slim, and when I walked in, it looked like he was playing a game on the computer. People with an unclear immigration status lived a very hard life and often had to resort to various forms of low paying jobs to support themselves. Some worked hard. Some didn't. My friend here seemed like one who didn't. I decided I liked him.

"I'm here to see Jessica. She's at number forty-two."

"Is she expecting you, sah?"

"Perhaps. She may have received a call in advance, I'm not sure. I'm happy to meet her in reception."

"Okay, sah. Let me call her and check."

"Thank you."

He dialled her number and a few minutes later, he put down the phone and pointed to the lift. "Level four, sah, to your left. Thank you for your patience."

The lift was one of those fancy high-tech ones that played music and video for the ten seconds a passenger was on board. People always needed to be fucking entertained.

I walked down the corridor, and before I got to the apartment, I noted the door was partially open with two eyes peeking out from the other side.

"Are you Carl Cain?" a woman's voice came from behind the door.

"Calcain," I corrected her. "I take it you've spoken to Kimia?"

"Yeah."

"May I come in? Or would you rather we grabbed a quick

cuppa?"

"No, no. Come in."

She opened the door and granted me entrance. She was probably in her late twenties. Ginger hair. Pale skin. She was wearing tight jeans with high heels. A plain pink T-shirt. Her apartment was dirty, but not one-tenth as dirty as mine. It was a stoner's apartment. Posters filled every inch of space on the walls. The floor was covered with cigarette packs, ashtrays, used pizza boxes, empty plastic milk containers, bits of cereal, and cereal boxes. The surfaces of the room were occupied by crisp packets, DVD cases, and so on. A MacBook sat on the table in the living room, complemented by a surround sound system and a massive widescreen TV. The living room was large, as was the kitchen. Considering the state of the apartment thus far, I didn't even want to consider what the bedroom looked like.

If I was going to describe the smell of the place, I'd ask you to imagine a dead skunk that's been rotting for a while being burnt slowly. It was an almost oily smell, like snail discharge. If I didn't know better, I'd have said a decomposing body couldn't be that far away. I kept it professional and breathed through my mouth.

"I'm sorry to disturb you. I assume you were just leaving?"

"How d'jou figure tha'?"

"Well, you've got your heels on. Not something I'd just be wearing around the house."

"I should hope not, da'lin. Heels wouldn't suit ya." She laughed, and I smiled. "And in a tip like this, I wouldn't walk around barefoot eiver. Maybe I can't find my shoes, d'jou think of tha'? Wearing high heels doesn't automatically mean I'm going out."

She was playing detective. I decided to play, too.

"Not automatically, no, but the jeans and makeup are pretty good contributing indicators, as is your handbag on the table by the front door."

She smiled and shrugged. "Well, I guess that's why you're a detective."

"Well, I'm not a detective, per se. I'm just assisting the police in their investigation into Leyli's passing."

"Oh, yes," she said, her eyes going a bit sad. She shuffled bits of rubbish to one side of the couch and found a soft spot to sit. "I haven't even had time to cry for her. You make yourself comfortable. Do you want tea or somfin'?"

The last thing I wanted was something out of this place entering my body. "No, thanks. I just ate."

"Well," she said. "Aren't you going to get out your notepad or somfin' like them detectives on TV do?"

I never used a notepad unless I needed to jot down complex addresses or names. I tried to give the impression I was just aiming to have a normal conversation with whoever I was speaking to. I liked to look them in the eye and make things less formal and more friendly.

"I don't think that'll be necessary."

"Oh," she said, her shoulders relaxing. "That'd be all right. What do you need to know?"

"Firstly, I should warn you, you will likely get a visit from the police in the next few days. I'm working on their behalf, but consider me an independent contractor. Whilst you may think admitting to certain things—especially in relation to the use or distribution of drugs—may incriminate you today, it won't. Everything you say to me is off the record. Bullshit all you like with the police, but keep it honest with me, understand? Especially because you may have information that could get you hurt, and I might be able to prevent that."

She started looking nervous, but she held my stare, wanting to exude confidence.

"Well, firstly, I get wha' you mean with the police and them. They can't talk to me unless we do an interview under caution and that. But no one's gonna hurt me 'cuz I'm gang protected."

"Are you?" I said, incredulous.

She stuck her chin out. "Yeah. SE4 Crew."

"SE4 Crew?"

They must have been a mini-gang of youths from Bermondsey. Charlie's territory. I wondered if they'd even had patronage from him. Most of the time, being gang protected means if someone fucks with you, they take a couple to the back of the head. Gang protection comes easy to family members, old friends, former gang lords, CEO's, accountants, lawyers, and anyone else with significant ties to the Houses. If you kill a gang protected person, you risk open war and torture when you're found, so most guys figured it just wasn't worth it. And I highly doubted Jessica—a socialite drug dealer who'd been to a couple of raves with a few bad boys—was likely to be gang protected.

"Can I see your wrist?" I asked.

"Why?"

"If you're gang protected, you'll have a tattoo on your wrist."

She crossed her arms. "Oh, I don't got one."

The only ones who were gang protected and didn't have the tattoo to show for it were Muslims; it was against their religion, so they just wore green and red bands around their wrists.

"The reason you don't have it is because you're not gang protected, and the fact that you think you are when you're not leaves you especially susceptible to danger."

"No, 'cuz Mark said I can—"

"I suspect Mark is a small-time dealer, so I can assure you... he can't protect you from what's coming. Now, Jessica, I don't want to sit here and talk gang etiquette. I don't have the time, and worse, I don't have the patience. Fact number one..." I held up an index finger. "Hunter and Leyli are dead. Fact number two..." I held up a middle finger. "You have information some, including me, might find valuable. Fact number three..." I held up a ring finger. "The Houses will kill you for that information, especially if they see the police here. They'll torture you until they know what you gave up, then leave your dead body for the birds. Fact number four..." I held up a pinkie finger and met her stare. "If you tell me what you know, I can better assess whether you're in danger and how much danger you're in. I might even be able to help keep you safe." I paused and let that information sit with her. "Are you ready to speak now?"

She looked stunned but came around. "Okay, I'll tell you all I know. But I ain't gonna say 'nuffink to the police."

"I couldn't care less what you tell the police, as long as you tell me everything."

"Okay, well, I've known Leyli and them for a while. We went to school toge'va. They were hard-working girls, but I always got myself in trouble. But for all my faults, I was still best mates with the smartest kid in class. Leyli was just like a natural genius. She would come out, she'd party, she'd do sports and everythin', but somehow her schoolwork was always spot on. When I basically gave up on school, Leyli begged me to continue, but with her family and that, she had bigger things to worry about.

"My family makes a bit of money, so I could afford dropping out. I spent most my times partying in places like China-white and that. Inevitably, when you go out like I do, you meet people—celebri'ees, rich people, dealers. I met Hunter through Mark Odeli. He runs a gang and supplies high-end party people. Hunter has better suppliers than Mark, but I guess they were just mates. Hunter was a proper gent. Nothing like the people around him. He spoke so well. He was respectful to women. Probably one of the top catches in London. I introduced them, you know. And he chased her for months until she gave him a chance." She got lost in reminiscence.

"Jessica, I need to know everything you know about Hunter. Mark, too."

She shook her head. "Look, Mark'll—"

"Trust me. There are much more dangerous creatures waiting for you than Mark."

She hesitated again and swallowed hard. "Mark told me Hunter, apart from being a football player, was an important figure in the London scene, even though he was very young. But towards the end, Mark was saying Hunter was playing a dangerous game. Dealing with gangs—big gangs—beyond our reach. The super-gangs and bosses."

She was referring to the Houses.

"Mark said Hunter was planning something big, but a new gang freaked him out."

"A new gang?"

"Yeah. Something about a new super-gang like the big guys who run everythin'. I suppose there can't be many of them, so a new one is big news. They didn't have a name, but I heard they were called a new species or some shit like that."

"A New Breed?"

"Oh, that's the one. Definitely. The New Breed. But Mark said that didn't matter as far as we were concerned. We'd just align ourselves with whoever won. As long as we had our customers, who cared who was running things? But Hunter told him this new thing—this New Breed—was different. Mark didn't tell me why or how. Just different. He said if he told me, I'd be in danger."

Nonsense. He clearly fed her the MI6 chat to make himself sound special. In truth, he hasn't the slightest fucking clue what was going on. It sounded like Hunter was putting a bit too much trust in this Mark guy, which I didn't quite understand. Hunter was a pro and wouldn't have readily opened his mouth to anyone, especially not to a bullshitting drug dealer and especially not when his balls were on the line.

I turned to Jessica and realised she was already looking panicked. Good. She'd tell me everything now.

"When was the last time you saw Hunter and Leyli?"

"Hunter, gosh, that must be two or three weeks ago now. Leyli, though, that was two days ago. She had an argument with her mom. She told me her mom had started to scare her. Apparently, her mother knew a masked Persian warrior or something who wanted to avenge a betrayal, but I swear I know nothing else. All I know is Leyli didn't want that, but her mother warned her to deal with something to avoid it. She made a joke of it afterward, so I didn't take her seriously. I mean, a masked warrior?" She laughed, then reached for her phone. "Look." She dragged her fingertip across the touchscreen phone. "This is the last text I got from her."

I looked at the phone.

14:27 – *Jessica had texted you out tonight babe? x*

14:39 – *Leyli's response was, sorry babe got a date with Hunter, I'll call you later xxx*

"Did she call you?" I asked.

135

"No. I called her at nine, but there was no response. My baby…" She began to sob.

The remainder of my conversation added very little, but it wasn't a total waste of time. It turned out Mark had a base on Old Street in Shoreditch—Camden and Soho's sister territory. It was just outside Browns, the strip club I ended up in every now and again with Ian.

I got all the other details I needed from Jessica and made for the door, paying all possible attention not to touch anything. Just before I left, I posed an old detective question—the sort of shit investigators save as a small footnote in the back of their brains that could later come in handy. The answer I got, however, brought with it a motherfucker of a revelation.

I paused in the doorway. "Does anything else at all come to mind from over the last few weeks that struck you as odd or interesting? Anything that stood out for some reason, even if you're not sure of the reason, and stuck with you? Don't worry about how important you think it is; often, it's the small details that can make or break a case."

She paused, thinking. "There is one thing, I guess."

"Go on."

"Everyone's talking about this new thing. This new gang or whatever taking over. But I remember one night we were all getting pretty fucked up, and Leyli kept saying, 'It's not one, Jess. It's two coming together'."

"Two groups uniting?"

She nodded. "Yeah. She said, 'They're not new, and they're not taking over. They're old. And they're taking it back'."

Shivers ran not down my spine but right below my belly.

Jessica shrugged. "But she was fucked up, so who knows what the fuck she was going on about."

I felt almost sick, but not quite. Excited more like. This would be a challenge. Two groups, not one. Two groups coming back, not starting over.

The game had changed.

*

Old Compton Street and Regent Street, London

There was no one at Mark's address on Old Street, but it looked lived in. A quick look around, and it was clear it was a weekend flat. They were quite common, flats rented under different names for people to store their stuff and to bring guests back to on the weekends, while their actual homes were somewhere far away. When weekend flats were stormed by police, they'd find nothing; there would be no evidence to tie the dealer to the flat.

The presence of this location meant two things; Mark was doing better than I thought he was, and I'd have to wait until Friday to speak with him. With no major leads, I just needed to wait and consider the information for a while.

I was getting peckish around four-thirty, so I stopped by M&S on the way home and picked up a turkey sandwich and some juice. When I turned onto Old Compton Street, I spotted a brunette in a tight, shiny blue mini dress and high heels. She was shivering in the cold October weather and trying to smile at anyone who walked by her. I had my headphones on, and Phil Collins was singing 'In the Air Tonight'. The wind gently caressed the brunette's hair, and my world slowed. She was beautiful, lightly made up, each smile able to warm any cold heart on this very cold day.

She was what we called a 'newbie'. A newbie in Soho was

137

basically a person who heard our neighbourhood was where the whores hung out and decided to go there to sell her or his body. Of course, some whores did hang out there, but the West End was about the escorts, hotel lounges, and high-class bars. Soho really didn't do street prostitution any more. To me, she appeared to be a victim of the economic disaster that had been plaguing London.

It was just past five and getting dark. Now, I was a whoremonger of the highest order. A monster. Probably the worst person she could've come across. And yet, I couldn't help but at least want to know her story. Not to help. But to see if she deserved to be where she was. That way, I may just be able to protect her from what's waiting for her at the hands of someone else, someone who would degrade her rather than use her. Those were different things. You needed to love whores to understand that.

As I stepped towards her, the wind whipped my coat and scarf, and I tried to keep my composure. She looked at me. In the blistering cold, I froze, not because of the weather but because of her charm. Lost in the oceans of her eyes. A deep, deep blue. Enough to see my reflection.

I stopped in front of her, and she smiled, the sides of her lips trembling.

"Nice night," I said, smiling back.

"I think it's still afternoon." She had an obvious New York accent.

"In London, regardless of what the time is, the evening starts when the sun sets. The sun has now pretty much set."

"Then maybe you should have said nice evening." She paused, looking self-conscious. "Sorry, I talk too much."

Something about her seemed broken.

"I'm happy with 'nice night' or 'nice evening'. Whichever

you prefer. What brings you to Soho this beautiful Monday n...
evening?"

She smiled. "Well, to meet you, silly."

Poor effort. Really poor effort. How did she end up here?

I tightened my coat around my chest. "I didn't know I had
friends."

"Well, now you do." She stepped towards me.

"Anything else?"

She shrugged. "That's up to you."

Her lines were rehearsed. She sounded educated. I wanted to
toy with her.

"How much?"

Her smile faltered.

"How much for a quickie?"

Her smile faded entirely. She didn't expect it to be so blunt.
I almost feel bad for doing it.

"I-I don't... I mean, I just—"

"My beautiful lady. I take it that this is the first time you've
done this?"

She nodded. "Y-yes."

"And yet you chose Soho of all the places."

She dropped her eyes to her feet. "I-I heard..."

"On a Monday. Of all the days. A Monday in Soho." I
smiled, waiting for her to recognise the joke, to realise I had, in
short, been fucking with her.

When she did, she laughed, and it was lovely.

"Look," I said. "Why don't we get a coffee, and you can tell
me your story. The going rate for street business is fifty pounds.
I'll pay you seventy-five pounds and pay for that coffee, but
you'll need to come to my place, which is just a few minutes
away."

"Would I have to…"

"No. Not even if you wanted to. I've had a lot of sex and for the next few hours at least, I don't feel like any of what *The Sun* and *Daily Mail* would call 'lewd sex acts'."

She laughed. "Okay. But I'm a bit turned off you read that trash. I'm more of a *Guardian* girl myself."

"A liberal? Well, you'll find me both liberal and conservative, depending on my mood, as well as by whom and which part of town I've most recently been screwed over in."

"Charming." She smiled.

I took her to Bar Italia, and it turned out she wasn't just cold but also thirsty and hungry. We then headed up to my flat, and the sheer shock on her face was brilliant. The good news was, as she embarked on this new, exciting, illustrious career in the hospitality industry—providing intimate vaginal services to the horny gentleman—she'd never see a humbler abode than mine. It was effectively and decisively dirtier than a train station toilet, with an aroma achievable only by the industrial and chemical enhancement of a genetically enhanced pre-historic skunk. It reeked of a filthy cocktail of whore juice with a touch of tarragon for flavour.

But in spite of that, the place was relatively tidy, bar the needles, bottles of alcohol, and similar paraphernalia on the floor. The two sofas were clean enough for someone to sit, and that's exactly what she did. I sat on the sofa opposite her, next to my bed. She was sitting beside Her poster. I put my iPhone on and had Her sing 'Fashion!' on loop.

I am, I'm too fabulous / I'm so…

"Well." I broke the silence. "What do you think?"

"Well," she said. "You sure have a favourite musician."

She gestured to the enormous poster of Her, as well as to the few smaller ones hung around the room.

"She sustains me."

"How does she do that?"

"I'm a… I'm sort of a monster. I don't get people, and for the most part, they don't get me. She, though—her music—somehow speaks to me, contains me, and stops me from doing crazy things by doing it herself. How she dresses, how she acts, how she speaks; it's me on the inside. If I have her to keep me contained then, on the outside, I can look normal. Or close to it, anyway."

She looked slightly uncomfortable but also like she was trying to contain her laughter.

"You better get used to this," I said, smiling. "You'll find your clientele to be at the very least awkward and at the very worst painful, and I use that term loosely. Take my friend, Ian, for example. A prostitute once refunded his money because she couldn't take it any more."

She continued to smile, but she looked tense suddenly. She didn't find my comment funny. I asked her what drink she would like, and considering the vast and impressive collection she saw around the room, she seemed unable to choose.

Messy as my flat was, it held many things I considered precious. Next to her feet on the floor, beside some used tissues, a ninety-seven-year-old vintage Georgian wine stood proudly. Next to my sofa was a bottle of Dom Perignon 1902 Magnum champagne.

Regardless of what she saw, she showed restraint and reservation only class or fine parenting can offer. She asked for an orange juice. I had a brand I would describe as being inspired by oranges rather than pressed from them, and I readily provided it to her. She hated it. It had been in my fridge for as long as I could remember.

She still turned down my offer of fine alcohol. Maybe she was already full of life's luxuries. Maybe she'd had enough of the bittersweet taste of the finer things. Or maybe she was just raised to never show hunger or admiration when shallow luxury is thrown at her. Or maybe, just maybe, she doesn't fancy a heavy drink on a Monday afternoon.

I leaned back in my seat on the couch. "So what invited you to this fine and time-honoured profession?"

"Is this the *why are you selling yourself* talk?" she asked bluntly.

"Again, get used to it. Every one of your johns will ask the same thing."

She hesitated before opening up. "I'm a PhD student. I came here from New York. I dropped out last year for more reasons than I care to articulate. Then when I decided I wanted to get back on track, I found out the tuition fees had gone up. I was going to ask my family for money, but before I could, they called to tell me my dad had died. Heart attack. We lost our house in the Upper East Side, and my mom and brothers moved to Harlem. They live in this tiny apartment, but they refuse to leave Manhattan. My family has been there for generations. Anyway, I don't have money to get back, and I can't ask my mom for money, so I'm stuck. Two weeks from now, I'll be homeless, so I need cash for rent, food, and for getting back to my studies. The quickest way a girl can make money anywhere is by doing what I'm doing here. Well, this and stripping, but I can't really dance."

"A very comprehensive answer. What are you studying for your PhD? And how much will it cost to get you back into school?"

She sighed. "I'm a sociology major. My dissertation is on

the interactions between different social and economic classes in places like the Square Mile or Manhattan, both of which are considered *the* City rather than any old city."

"I'm a City boy myself, so please do throw in some detail." I smiled. "Maybe I can help with your research."

"Well, one of the basic philosophies I'm working with is that the only place people of different classes have genuine and culturally unique interactions on a regular basis is in the City. It's the only place where you can see people of lower classes ordering around and making demands of people of upper classes. For example, a trainee son of a millionaire working for a partner as part of a firm of accountants who had humble beginnings. It is only in a professional environment, specifically in the City, where you see a genuine interaction of people as equals."

"So you've been doing this research for two years? Since you came here from New York?"

"Well, yeah—"

"You know much about gangs?"

Please, I thought, *please ask if I'm talking about the Houses.*

"Are you talking about…"

Come on, you got it.

"Like, thugs?"

Shit. Considering the City was under Elad's control, she had a massive gap in her thesis. But it sounded interesting enough.

"Your career path will expose you to all sort of classes, sure, but you'll run into some scum eventually."

"I guessed as much. But it would help with my research."

"So, in answer to my other questions?"

"Oh, seventeen thousand pounds."

"And why did you choose to do this particular research, then?"

She thought for a beat. "I come from a family that used to have a bit of money, and when we didn't any more, we still kept our values. My dad's death landed us very low on the social totem pole, but that still doesn't change our values and beliefs, which are fundamentally upper class."

"So in addition to this idea about the City being a kind of level playing field for all social classes, you also want to know if wealth was taken from the wealthy, would those with class still stand out?"

She nodded. "That's putting it simply, but yeah."

I leaned forward. "How does snobbery fit in? There are plenty of middle and upper class snobs who don't know the first thing about discipline and charity, both of which I would consider upper class values. Some of the poorest people I know donate more—often more than they can afford—to others. I think it's how a person is raised that's important, not their class. You were just raised right. That's all there is to it." I sat back. "But then again, you're the PhD student."

I was about to change the topic when I felt the ground shake and a heard a bang so shockingly loud I thought my roof fell. There was silence immediately after, but I knew what was coming. I jumped on the American just before a second loud bang shook the house, my cups, lamps and bed light all falling from their secured locations. The shock was so intense the flat shook in its entirety. I felt the American holding me tight.

"It's okay. Don't worry. Regardless of the impact, the explosion is actually far from here. There won't be any more. Relax."

She was breathing heavily and only mustered enough energy to utter, "Okay."

I tried to reassure her.

144

"What's your name, anyway?"

The question went against my convention of not asking prostitutes their names, but she wasn't a whore for my purposes, which was the biggest compliment I could give her.

Her voice quivered slightly, but she answered me. "Shelly. And you?"

"Well, Shelly, my name is Calcain. Feel free to crash here and so on, but I need to go see who's fucking up my city. They're making a war zone out of my baby."

I knew she wouldn't steal anything. She seemed kind, and that should be rewarded. I considered getting her a job with Jimmy that would pay for re-enrolment in her PhD program rather than have another whore killed on my street.

I got off her, and she sat up.

"Calcain? Where's that from?"

I paused to answer before I rushed out the door.

"London."

*

I made my way through small alleys and passageways towards the direction of the screams and sirens. The noise led me straight to south of Regent Street, just off Oxford Street, not too far from Oxford Circus.

Just as I'd expected. Two burning cars.

The first one had the bomb underneath it, the second one happened to be nearby. If I had to guess, and I hoped I was wrong, the first one contained a House member. The second one, if I was lucky, was empty. If I was lucky. The police have the cars surrounded, and firefighters were getting organised.

One thing—don't fuck with English firefighters. Ever. It was only a few seconds from the moment they were in place to when the fire disappeared. Seconds.

From my distant vantage point, I could make out several carcasses inside the vehicles. The first car—containing the bomb—was an Aston Martin DB9. The second was some kind of Ford 4x4, maybe a special edition. By the look of things, I'd say that one held a mother and her kids, which wasn't as good as if the car had been empty, but not as bad as some of the alternatives.

I had twenty seconds at best. I ran towards the cars and spent about ten seconds examining the DB9 before someone started towards me, at which point, I ran towards the 4x4. I had time for a brief look before I was grabbed and thrown outside the police protection zone. That was okay; I'd gotten what I needed.

There were two bodies in the DB9. The driver had an amorphous star shape embossed on a ring on his finger, which was stuck to the roof of the car. That symbol and the number plate indicated he was a close associate or full-fledged member of Russell's house. The person next to him was probably a floozy.

As I suspected, the second car had held a woman and a few children. That part was good. Not for the family, of course, but I couldn't deal with more than one House casualty at a time. The stakes were too high.

The attack didn't seem like the work of another House or even a sub-gang. Whoever carried it out wasn't even playing the same sport as my usual suspects. We didn't do car bombs in London. Fallujah, maybe. But not London.

The explosion didn't take the shape of your average car bomb. Those were usually placed below the passenger and driver seats. This one was placed by the bonnet. It was a bomb stuck in a hurry, maybe even tossed from a motorcyclist. The explosion must have happened while the vehicle was moving. The blast occurred in front of the Apple store in a no parking zone with double red lines, so it's likely he was moving when the thing went off. Your typical car bomb would explode with the switch of the ignition.

It was a fucking mess, and right by Oxford Circus of all the places. The bomb appeared to be a deliberate act of recklessness, and therefore not an amateur. Though it could have also been a vigilante, pissed off about who knows what and looking for revenge. Whoever or whatever the culprit, someone was clearly trying to fuck things up, and they were being unashamedly obvious about it. I was starting to get annoyed. I intended to teach them shame.

I was suddenly dragged backwards, hard and by the neck. There were at least two people. I was losing consciousness but still aware of my surroundings. I smelled the dirty water of back alleys. I heard the back doors of a building open and close. I passed out briefly, and woke to being dragged up a flight of stairs. Just as I was about to pass out again, I was pushed through two wooden doors and finally dropped on the floor of a warm, comfortable room.

I spent a generous amount of time coughing and holding back vomit. Slowly, the squeezing feeling in my neck began to fade, and I realised whose room I was in.

I was fucked.

I guessed I was in an old Victorian building by the look of the décor. Persian carpets lay across the floor, Chinese vases sat on oak wood end tables, and old paintings and antique furniture rounded out the scene. It looked like what you might find in a typical posh hotel, but it was an office. There was a big fuck-off star at the front of the desk to tell anyone unfortunate enough to

147

look upon it that, if they thought they were fucked before, they were about to learn the true meaning of the word. They were about to be prison fucked. By Lord Russell, nephew to Lord Wellington, and nightmare of the West End.

I was royally fucked.

I needed to manage things perfectly. I only had one chance.

"Why is it," I heard the voice behind the desk say "that wherever there is a serious fuck up, like a squirt of period stain on brand new bed linen, Calcain isn't that far away?" The voice was posh, deep, and sophisticated. More importantly, it wasn't Russell's.

"I-I guess…" The words tore at my throat. "I guess trouble follows me everywhere. Like this rash I caught ages ago. Never goes away."

"That's the best you can come up with?"

"Considering the throatal rape I just suffered, yes. Speaking of, are you on your period? I could do with that giant tampon."

"That can be arranged."

He used a soft 'g', like a Frenchman, and I suddenly realised who I was talking to. A cunt.

"H-hold on. Are you—is that Smitty?"

"Julian Hemsworth-Smith."

"Hm." I paused. "Cunt."

"Watch your tongue, scum."

"No, no, no, you watch *your* tongue."

I slowly got to my feet. His hair looked like overgrown pubic hair. He was very pale, with freckles. White shirt, brown coat. A thin silver chain decorated his skinny prick of a neck.

"Or what, Calcain?"

"Or I'll cut it off, and you won't be able to lick your mother's minge any more."

"Johnny." He pointed at one of the big guys behind me. "Discipline, please."

I knew what was coming, but I didn't have the energy to avoid it. So I just tensed up and prepared my body as best I could. Damage control. Then I got a huge, mighty powerful kick to the stomach. I felt like I got hit by a car. I fell down, coughing. I almost blacked out again, but I focused on my breathing. I started to taste blood as I was dragged to my feet by one of the brutes.

"The problem with you, Calcain," Smitty said, not looking at me but writing on a paper in front him with the desk lamp shining on his face; the sound of his pen on paper almost louder than his voice, "is that you seem to think your actions, including your rudeness, make people fear you. You couldn't be further from the truth. The more you gab away, the more I understand you. You're not some genius detective. In fact, you're pretty incompetent. You bark when you're scared and, as we know, a dog that barks never bites."

"There you go again," I said, shuffling away from the guy holding me. "You chat shit you heard from movies without actually experiencing anything yourself. You're just Russell's bitch. You have no power. You've adopted a gang boss persona from *The Godfather* or some fucking place. You're nothing, but you think you're something. That's why people call you a c—"

"Do you want me to discipline you again?"

"Fuck you, cunt. You talk about barking dogs but trust me, if you piss off a Doberman, it'll bark the whole time it's biting your balls off. Now what the fuck do you want with me? I'm as busy as your mom on Friday nights."

He paused and realised I wouldn't be entertaining him.

"What were you doing—"

"At the scene of an explosion? I'm a fucking detective,

149

Smitty. What do you think I was doing?" I shook my head. "It was a big fucking mistake bringing me here. I'd bet anything the bomber would have circled back around to the scene to make sure he hit his target. I could've ID'd him then and there, but here we all are," I said and smiled around at Smitty and his cronies, "with our thumbs up our asses while the bad guy runs away."

Smitty clenched his jaw.

"You know, this whole thing could have very well been an invasion deep into Russell's territory, a big fucking threat against your boss. How are you going to explain that to him, then?"

I knew my words would be like poison to him because deep down, Smitty had no fucking idea what he was doing, and he'd believe anything I said. He was Russell's useless cousin—utterly incapable of anything—so his parents asked Russell to look after him. Russell was very fond of Smitty's parents; they looked after him a lot when he was first starting out and was disowned by his father who, to teach Russell a lesson, bankrupted his son's business. Russell then carried out a successful hostile takeover of one of his dad's major property companies. His successes kept coming after that, and Russell was happy to look after Smitty, putting him in charge of marketing and PR and assigning a few top guards to look out for him.

Russell loved Smitty so much he couldn't be touched, not without repercussion. But that didn't mean he couldn't be fucked with.

Smitty sat up straight. "Firstly, I do not appreciate being called a—"

"Cunt?"

"Yes. Secondly, seeing you roaming around so freely during the day is, of course, a cause for concern for us. Especially when bombs start going off. I asked my men to collect you in case you had information regarding the bomb because, as you said yourself, a criminal very often returns to the crime scene."

"Oh, you're such a fucking moron. When have you ever heard me accused of being a fucking car bomber?" I paused for breath, controlling my anger.

He opened his mouth to reply but was interrupted by a phone call. He lifted the handset from its base. "JHS," he said. He paused. "Um, Julian. Julian Hemsworth-Smith?"

He glanced at me, then away.

"Don't use that term with me. I said don't call me that. Just tell me what it is, and I will pass it on to Russell. Okay. Okay. Yep. Yes. What? *What*? And... Okay, understood. B-b-but you're sure about this? It was only a few... I need to see the CCTV footage. Yes. Thank you. Goodbye."

The room was silent. He looked at me again, this time will less suspicion but with a new degree of reservation. He was being very careful now.

"Everyone except for Calcain leave the room."

"But, sir..." one of the guards said.

"*But fucking what*?" Julian snapped. "Just fuck off right now."

As soon as they closed the door, Julian looked at me and spoke clearly and slowly.

"Well, you're free to go. One thing I can be sure of is no one with even the slightest understanding of the Houses would be crazy enough or stupid enough to pull this off. Not even someone with an army behind them would do this. Not even you, the Demon in the Long Coat."

"Who were you just talking to? What did you find out?"

"We're all fucked, is what I found out."

"We? How so?"

151

He paused and rubbed his eyes. "It was Justin in the car."

"Justin? You mean—"

"Yes. *That* Justin. Russell's brother."

He was right. We were fucked.

Chapter 7

Abbey Road, St John's Wood, London

The news sent shockwaves through me. I knew Justin. He was a good kid. Bright. Talented. Didn't give a shit about gang warfare. As a further testament to his benevolent personality, the man had started a trust in the West End, helping poor school kids find apprenticeships in the city. He got on brilliantly with his brother but didn't have fuck all to do with gangs. Julian was right. No one in the world would have had a grudge against Justin, so if he was dead, it was because of his relation to Russell. It was a message.

In theory, there were only two people with balls big enough to do something like this: Charlie and Elad. That's what Russell would think, anyway. He'd see Justin's death as a clear declaration of war.

Julian rubbed his temples. He knew as well as I did what would be coming. He was petrified, but he was also blessed because at least he knew. Anyone riding the streets didn't, though they'd find out soon enough. But I felt for Julian because right then, he had the worst job of anyone in the impending London war. He had to tell Russell his younger brother was dead. Killed.

"This is bad," he said, looking up at me. "This is no game, Calcain. We're in the shit. All of us. Russell is going to kill everyone." His eyes were wide and terrified. "Everyone."

He opened a cupboard next to the desk and picked up a bottle of single malt whiskey and two glasses. He poured both cups, then drank each. "Sorry," he said, filling both glasses again. He passed one to me. We drink in silence for a few moments.

He sighed. "So," he said. "What do you think? Charlie? Or Elad?"

"To be honest," I said, thinking as I sipped, "I can't think of a motive for either of them."

"It's over that fucking kid, isn't it? What's his name? Hunter? Fucking prick. I knew he was trouble from the first moment I saw him. I was glad when they told me he was fucking killed, and about time, too. Trying to be everyone's best friend."

I saw an opening, so I took it. He couldn't tell me anything I didn't already know about Hunter's death. But maybe he could tell me something else.

"What do you know about Hunter?"

He shrugged, defeated. "Everything. What do you want to know?"

"I want to know why you think he was killed and by whom."

Julian would have been party to some pretty high-level discussions at Russell's side.

"You call me a cunt, but if you'd met Hunter, you'd know what a real cunt really is. He sucked up to all the three leaders but to Russell especially because Russell made him a fucking West End prince."

I sensed a hint of jealousy in Julian's voice.

"Apart from upper management, everyone fucking hated him. You'd think his proximity to the big guys would have made him—"

"Untouchable."

"Right. The problem was, he didn't align himself with any specific House. He was in a league of his own. I mean, if you

154

killed me, you know Russell would respond. Same as if someone killed Wayne, you know Elad would step in. But with Hunter, being beloved by all but affiliated with none, no one really knew what the threat was or if there was one at all. Either all three would react or none of them would. It was a fifty-fifty shot, and I guess someone rolled the dice."

I admired his honesty.

"Some might say today's bombing was retaliation by someone who thought Russell had killed Hunter. But who? And why would Russell have killed Hunter in the first place? What could Hunter possibly have done to make Russell so angry? And why leave the scene instead of simply making him... you know. Disappear? I'd hazard to say it didn't have anything to do with Russell at all and might instead have something to do with this New Breed I keep hearing so much about."

Julian rolled his eyes. "Oh, please. Don't tell me you believe the NB bullshit. It's bollocks. A ghost story for junior gangs. If Russell was concerned with them, they'd be dead by now. The Houses would have taken care of them." He leaned forward, conspiratorial. "Between you and me, I think the Houses actually like having the New Breed around. They keep the London gangs in check, too scared to operate outside their territories, too nervous to cause problems. Sooner or later, the Houses will elect one of themselves to take down the NB, pick some nothing group of thugs and say 'these are the guys' and make a big show about it. That way, the gangs will remember the big daddy will always be one of the Houses."

He refilled his drink and continued.

"If I was going to point a finger at someone for Justin's death, I'd say Charlie. Hunter was Charlie's cousin. If he thinks Russell killed Hunter for some reason or another, it would make sense for him to go after Justin."

I sipped from my glass and thought aloud. "So two people have died who had no official affiliation with either House but were close enough to big players for there to be suspicion of revenge. And Elad seems to be the odd man out. Nothing's happened to his loved ones, so could it be possible he's behind both deaths? Trying to fuel misgivings between Russell and Charlie?"

Julian shrugged and sighed. "That's very possible, as well." He paused then looked at me seriously in the eyes. "Calcain, if you were hired by Scotland Yard to investigate Hunter's death, then I don't propose to interfere with you going forward because you can bet your bottom dollar Justin's and Hunter's deaths are connected. West End is yours to roam free. In fact, you have our protection and temporary patronage. I need you to find out exactly who killed Justin and quickly. On the off-chance Justin's death wasn't perpetrated by Charlie, I need to know before Russell does something he can't take back. I'll buy you as much time as I can, but you have to hurry. If Russell goes after Charlie, London will burn. Give me your number and I'll feed you information as I get it."

I wrote my number on piece of paper and handed it to him. I stood to leave, and I saw Julian's lips moving, as if preparing how to break the morbid news to Russell. He looked broken and afraid.

"Oh, Calcain," he said before I could reach the door. "I'm going to text you details about a guy called Sutton. He used to be one of Thatcher's young cronies and now heads a government policing committee, or something like that. He trumps the mayor when it comes to gang-related activity. He regularly deals with the three Houses. Super old-school. More on side than any other government employee we've dealt with. He'll lead you in the right direction."

"Thanks."

A thousand ideas started coming to mind, plans and motives and suspicions, but I had to get Julian's thoughts on something.

"What about this for a theory: What if all this has nothing to do with the Houses? What if the person who killed Hunter is the same person who killed Justin for reasons unrelated to the big bosses? Or maybe two different killers with two different motives having nothing to do with the gangs? What if it's all just a big misunderstanding?"

He almost rolled his eyes. "The odds of that are astronomical, to say the least."

However it came about, whatever the reason or intention, open war was upon us. Someone, some beautiful saint, was doing what I'd planned for so long, pitting the Houses against each other, playing into their paranoias, ensuring mutual destruction of all three. Whoever was behind it, their execution was raw. Admirable. But raw. And it was sure to cause problems for me one way or another.

I would've done it better.

*

I skipped the madness outside and walked until I got to Edgware Road. From there, I caught a taxi to Chalk Farm. I needed to get out of West End before I became a suspect. I called Mulligan a few times along the way but received no response. I'd made it clear to him in the beginning that I wanted him on board and responsive at all times. He was currently in breach of contract. Funny. He was always punctual.

157

As soon as I reached Chalk Farm, I ducked into a local cafe, got a dark coffee, some fried eggs, and hash browns, then planned my next move.

I needed to get in touch with Sutton first, then revisit the scene at Hunter's to see what the police no doubt missed. I then needed to hit the gym, keep a low profile over the next few days, and head back to Old Street on Friday to talk to Mark. I also needed Mulligan to get back to me. It wasn't that I was worried— Mulligan could take care of himself—but very deep inside, I had an odd sense something wasn't quite right.

I called up Sutton, and his PA told me he was at home in St John's Wood on a street off Abbey Road. Perfect. After that, I'd pay a visit to a friend in Camden and then hit Bishops Avenue in the evening.

A ten-minute taxi ride later, and I was outside Sutton's place. It was a large, luxurious townhouse. At least eight bedrooms. I knocked on the door. A man I assumed was his butler opened the door and granted me entrance. Inside, there were a lot of old vases and handmade carpets. I wasn't sure what it was about wealth and large vases, but they seemed to go hand in hand. I didn't get it. I waited in the living room on a sofa until I was summoned to Sutton's home office, a few doors past the living room. There, in a white, pristine room equipped with plenty of high-tech gear and four large monitors showing the news and financial markets, sat a man behind a glass desk. He was looking at the screen of the iMac in front of him.

He looked in good shape for his age, which was probably pushing sixty. He was on the phone and reviewing a file at the same time.

"Yes. Yes. Yes, b-but... I know, David, but it is simply just not as easy as that," he said in a very posh, educated London accent.

Tenth generation upper class, Sutton studied at Oxford. His type was almost a rarity in aristocracy. Most heirs opted to live off Dad's money until it ran out rather than putting that fancy degree to use or contributing in any way to our society.

He continued, having stopped shuffling through the papers. "If you want to deal with it that way, do it, but don't then ask why the policy has failed and crime is on the up because you simply won't take advice. What has…? One second." He looked at me, one hand covering the speaker on the phone. "Calcain, is it?"

I nodded.

"My apologies. This call just came in a few seconds ago. Do you fancy tea or a sandwich?"

"I'll just have some dark coffee. Maybe with some cookies or biscuits?"

"Of course." He looked at the butler. "Darwin, do the honours, will you?"

"Very good, sir," Darwin said.

"Just one moment," he said to me as he pointed at a nearby sofa.

I sat down, and he turned his attention back to the phone.

"Right. Where were we? Oh, yes. Look, what has happened isn't a random act. It's a… let me finish. No, let me finish. It's some form of a revenge attack, but I assure you no one in the public knows what's happening, and in no way can they connect it to the kid's death. Tragedy happens all the time. Easiest thing to do is to say it's a faulty car and that we're getting an inquiry together to investigate the car maker, and by the time we're done with all that, it will be old news. Or… no, no, absolutely not. A Russian assassination of a Russian spy or business associate, you mean? Like a war between Oligarchs? That's what you want to tell people? Amid the growing Russian influence on the streets? They'd never cop to that, even to raise reputations; they're still too fearful of Putin. And when they do find out the truth, they'll expose it as a police cover up, and then there would be real trouble. You want to move it as far away from the streets as possible. Just do what I'm telling you. Fine, let me think."

I watched Sutton, knowing full well what—and who—that conversation was about. He caught my eye, and I gave him the best coverup I could think of on the spot.

"Tell the people it was an attack by the Real IRA against an old republican guard, only they got the wrong car." I shrugged. "Mistaken identity."

"Exactly." He beamed with excitement and repeated what I said into the phone. "IRA is old news. It's like talking about an old episode of *Doctor Who*. It may have interested you at the time, but not much any more. Exactly. I'll dictate a press release within the hour, and all you need to do is read it to the cameras. Then, after that, we need to sit down with Teresa and properly talk about the implications. No, we need to talk about it tonight, David. I'll come by at twenty-two hundred hours. Very good. Cheerio."

He put down the phone, typed a few things on his keyboard, then turned his chair to look directly at me from behind his desk. He'd clearly been in the army. He looked the type. And sounded it.

"My apologies, Calcain. I'm sure you know what has happened and indeed who has been killed. Terrible times and indeed, worse times are ahead."

I needed to play him a bit. "I'm not sure I know much."

"Come off it, man," he snapped with a smile. "Let's go ahead and clear this up now. I know you. I know who you are and what

160

you're about, so let us speak as equals, shall we?"

I nodded. "Fair enough."

"Good." He settled more comfortably in his chair. "So what's your view?"

I figured direct was best. "Well, I don't think a House was involved at all. It's either a coincidence or someone is trying very hard to make a mess of things, though I'm not sure why yet."

"Aha! Very good," he said, jubilant and excited. "But you see, heads of Houses don't get to be heads if they're idiots, now do they? Of course not. They're quite intelligent, which is what makes them difficult. Now if they were old mobsters, they would be stupid, strong, and forceful. But these three are sophisticated and highly calculating chaps. An idiot would say Charlie killed Russell's brother out of revenge for Hunter. A reasonably intelligent person like yourself, however, would argue that killing someone as important as Russell's brother is a declaration of open war, which would not be wise right now in large part because of the various sporting events coming up that will be held in Charlie's territory. He wouldn't want a war, not when he's about to make the money he is. Now Russell is more an executive than an underworld leader. Why would he want Hunter dead? He wouldn't. Charlie knows this, just like how Russell knows Charlie would never order his brother's death. There's no reason. And there's too much at stake. But still, we're speaking about someone who has lost a beloved sibling, so we must ask ourselves: how clearly will Russell be thinking after the initial news breaks? How will he act? That, old chap, is what we need to figure out."

I thought for a while. Sutton's reasoning was sound. I needed to match his rhetoric and put us on the same playing field. He could prove useful to me.

"It seems to me that we are at the brink of an event horizon, and Russell is the one who will either pull us back or push us through. If I was to make a guess, I'd say his love for his brother would make him strike at Charlie, but it's how hard the strike will be and what Charlie will do in response that's important. Emotion often beats reason. Even the most reasonable man can think without reason if his emotions are thrown into disarray. Russell has the ability to strike very hard. And I think he will. I also think the person who plotted this thought likewise."

Sutton's response was interesting. "But what if it was Charlie all along, and he used extraordinary cunning to do something so terrible and out of character no one would think him guilty? Or indeed, what if it was Charlie, not Russell, who was overcome with emotion? What if Hunter's death was too much and Charlie took revenge, thinking Russell was involved. And what of Elad? He will have much to gain if two Houses are weak, leaving him an open field for a coup."

He was being almost deliberately confusing. It was a strategy he likely used on the prime minister to sound like the smartest person in the room and gain absolute control over a situation. But it wouldn't work on me. I knew this game too well.

I smiled and said with some small level of jest, "What if it was this New Breed?"

He gave me a quick smile back. "Is that meant to be a test?"

"A test for what?"

"You know what I mean." He chuckled lightly. "You want to see if I believe the rumours about the New Breed."

"Well? Do you?"

He sighed. "If such a thing even exists, I do not think it's related to these two murders. If any so-called New Breed was involved, they would have been destroyed immediately upon

Hunter's death. I'm not even going to entertain it. The simplest answer is often the correct one, and the simplest answer is that one of the Houses was involved. I'm not sure how, and I won't make an official conclusion until I have considered all relevant factors. So far, though, there is nothing wrong with saying Hunter's death—however and by whomever it was perpetrated—resulted in Charlie acting out of emotion and striking at Russell. All things considered, Hunter was almost as innocent as Justin."

"Do you know why Hunter was so important to the Houses? What it was that earned him so much influence and beneficence?"

"I assume you already know enough about him, don't you?"

"I know about his connections to this faction and that, but it's his rise to such a privileged status I'm unclear about. Other people are connected to all three Houses, for one reason or another. So what made Hunter more special than any of them?"

He paused a while, then said, almost deep in thought, "Fame."

"Fame?"

"Yes. Fame. He had it. Other people connected to all three Houses as intimately as he was didn't have it."

Sutton opened his bottom drawer, took out a bottle of vintage dark rum and two glasses, then put ice in them from the mini freezer behind him. He poured the glasses half full and gave me one. He then leaned back in his seat, sipped his rum, and continued.

"When we speak of gangs, most people think of troubled, poor children in council houses making a living. Running around in tracksuits. Dealing cannabis. That's certainly what I thought for a while until I learnt of the Houses. The day-to-day gangs are known to people. Indeed, they are the subjects of some fascinating low-budget films. They are visible to everyone in shopping centres and high streets. The Houses, though, are invisible. They are the titans of London's crime scene. The dealer in a council house gets his cannabis from his supplier, who in turns gets it from another person, and so on, until you reach the source, the thing that makes it happen, the creator and originator of the crime. The Houses pay border patrol, the police, and the home office, not always in cash but certainly in kind. They stay out of public view, yet they know everything and control everything in the underworld. For example, Elad's influence in the City is beyond comprehension. No development is made without his blessing, and no major merger occurs without his involvement. Their collective empire took years to build. But they have an Achilles heel. Their success is in their invisibility. They are the unseen. They are the unheard of. No one knows who they are. But in the new age, they needed to enter more legitimate markets, and so they needed a face, and that face had to be likeable and popular."

He smiled and took a few more sips of his drink. "Do you see where I'm going with this?"

I nodded. "Yeah, I think I do."

He continued. "To expand their operations in the way they wanted, they needed fame. To be able to advertise their ventures openly. To get in front of new international businesses. To market their services. To that end, their strength of being invisible was now their weakness. Not for too long, however, for in Hunter they found that fame. The face that was happy to market very specific businesses—usually unconnected to crime—and attract just the right attention. Hunter was on side. He did this work for them, and he did it brilliantly. Like a work of art. I know he was a poor kid at one point and not much is known about his early rise but at a certain point, his rise became meteoric. He somehow managed to remain loyal to all three Houses. His art was masterful. I admired him most, though I also despised him for how much more powerful he made the Houses. You see, my dear boy, Hunter could walk to an area and cameras would follow him. So if a drug deal was to occur without the Houses sanctioning it, he could simply walk there and the paparazzi would walk with him, ruining the whole transaction."

He refilled his drink, and I reached forward for him to refill mine. He then took out a thin cigar and offered me one. I obliged. He turned on the air-con and lit up the cigars.

He puffed a few times. "Now in regard to his death, the way I see it, he would only have two types of enemies: those motivated by jealousy and those motivated by the desire to destroy the Houses, someone like yourself."

It was clear from Sutton's eyes that he carried a kind of darkness in himself as well. I guessed he'd need to for the kind of work he did.

I smiled. "Well, I can assure you I had nothing to do with it. I only got up from hibernation, if you will, after his death."

He smiled and chuckled. "Of course you didn't. That would be an act too insane even for you."

Maybe he didn't know me as well as I thought he might.

"So what's your next move?" I asked him, my curiosity getting the better of me.

"As you know, I work in the government and have done so for a while as their liaison minister in charge of crime control. The way it works is we agree a certain amount of crime with Houses, and they stick to it. They make the money they need to keep their operations afloat, and I keep the streets cleaner than they'd be otherwise. If anyone goes rogue, the Houses deal with it themselves, leaving my team and I to concentrate on bigger, more important things. As for my next move, I'll be speaking with the prime minister to see what assistance we can offer the Houses to keep them from going at each other's throats. Needless to say, Scotland Yard's not holding back; they're using all available resources to find the people behind these attacks. I will also recommend to the prime minister that the army should be on alert in case things kick off, granting me temporary authority to order the military to intervene if need be. I am happy to keep you posted. My understanding from Julian is that you were already hired by the legendry Detective Mulligan to get on with investigating this matter. Julian and I have agreed he will personally provide extra finance to you to speed up your investigation, as you're more likely than Scotland Yard to crack this case. I have agreed with him to provide you with what I know and give you any guidance you need going forward. Is there anything I can assist with currently?"

I thought a while. If Sutton thought Charlie could be behind Justin's death and this was all some conspiracy—and there was no such thing as the New Breed—we were running two different routes. I was going to keep on the New Breed investigation and make my conclusion once I'd spoken to Mark on Old Street. I wouldn't discount Charlie being involved, but I'd let Sutton confirm that for me.

"For the time being, I just need a contact to update me on various changes that have happened since I've been dormant. If I could have your email and number for quick questions, that would be very helpful."

"No problem at all. Here are all the details you need."

He handed me a thick, luxury business card, and I put the details in my phone. The best course for me was to head to

Camden to check on Ra'ef. Sutton was great at the history of the Houses, but he didn't have the current intel Ra'ef would. Sutton's information wouldn't be as extensive, either. He seemed very good, but he could only look at things from an outsider's perspective. I needed Ra'ef, and if he was still unwell, I'd be stuck with Inforno. Fuck Inforno.

The rest of my conversation with Sutton demonstrated his sheer knowledge and intelligence, which was amazing and far-reaching. He knew the streets and the functions of the Houses very well, and in an almost statesman-like manner. He knew how to separate his professional function from his personal feelings about the influence of the Houses.

Before leaving, he gave me a few files for reference, which would possibly alleviate the need for me to go back to Bishops Avenue. He also gave me the credentials I needed to hack into Scotland Yard's records online, if necessary.

"It was a clean execution," he said. "Absolutely no trace of other people being involved. They simply can't be related."

"I'll make my own deductions."

"I thought you would have made them by now. Was it not you who could crack a case faster than a first impression?"

"Yes. But on a good day. I'm a little rusty." I stood at the door. "One last question. Do they still agree to specific crime rates? I mean, do they still declare how much killing, rape, murder, extortion, and general mayhem they intend to carry out?"

Sutton looked at me, sharing my dismay at my question and looking genuinely frustrated. "My dear boy. Yes, they do. And they breach it all the time. And the government does nothing. Just a slap on the wrist. You and I both appreciate the problem here. In some ways, we're the same." He let that comparison hang in the air between us. "What's your next line of inquiry?"

"I'll be going to a small-time gangster's house on Old Street on Friday for a few questions. In the meanwhile, I'm going to keep a low profile. I'll also review CCTV images to see what I can gather on Justin's death, though I doubt anything will come from it. Have you heard much from Mulligan at all?"

He hesitated a second. "Nothing. Though I have received news he hasn't turned up at work. It should be nothing to worry about; he probably called in sick. I haven't checked. Forget about Mulligan for the time being. I've already reviewed the CCTV images and found nothing, but I'll send them to you all the same. Keep me posted, and do let me know if you need anything. Darwin has a cheque for you outside. That will be from Julian. Cheerio."

"Thank you. No doubt I will be in touch." I smiled and turned to set off but was abruptly stopped by Sutton.

"One more thing, Calcian, if you don't mind."

"No, please, go ahead."

"You don't believe in the New Breed, do you?"

"No," I lied. "You were right. I was just testing you."

If he didn't know Mulligan was behind Hunter, then Mulligan played his cards close to his chest for a reason. That said, I liked Sutton. He'd be useful.

Not just for this investigation.

But for my wider project.

*

With all the shit on my mind, I needed clarity, so I decided to head back to Camden and check on Ra-ef. I needed him alive and well. I needed some direction on this case.

Getting a taxi was a bitch, which was unusual for a Monday

night. Frustrated, I walked from Sutton's house in Blenheim Place off Abbey Road and followed it until I reached Abbey Road studios. Moronic tourists were always trying to recreate the Beatles' famous album cover on the zebra crossing. How fucking original. Like no one before them ever thought of it. Fucking tourists.

As I continued walking, a taxi stopped for me. Finally, my luck was changing. I looked inside and saw Natalya, the Georgian lawyer.

"Need a lift?" She smiled.

I smiled back. "Yes. Thank you."

"Where are you going?"

"Camden."

"I am going to see my friend again, so it's on the way," she said with excitement.

I got in the car, and the traffic gave me the opportunity to get to know her a little bit more. She was charming and sweet but wouldn't talk about Tbilisi, the Capital of Georgia, where she was from. She talked of Georgians' ability to maintain their unique identity, even after so many years of invasion by foreigners. After a while, I decided to change the subject.

"So, are you seeing anyone here?"

"No, I am not." She chuckled. "But that is private and so naughty of you to ask."

I smiled back. "Madam, please, if I was a gentleman, I wouldn't be where I am right now, both literally and metaphorically."

"So naughty." She hit me gently.

I laughed off the flirtatious swat. "Anyway. Tell me, where do you go out?"

"I go out mostly in Chelsea, Es Dable Yu Siri area. Like Jak's and sometimes Eclipse or something? Also, Home House and Mayfair area. Like last night, I went out in Home House. I was so drunk, I was like dead. I found out I spent nine hundred pounds on cocktails with my friends." She blushed.

"Home House? The douchey private members club? That joint? Only middle-aged dicks and Indian businessmen go there. Ridiculous. That said, I commend you for partying on a Sunday. Very noble. I take it you went to work today?"

"Yes. But I was in bed until like nine-thirty."

I liked her accent. 'Daaed' instead of 'Dead', 'Drank' instead of 'Drunk', and 'siri' instead of three. It was cute.

The rest of the conversation followed suit, and when we parted ways, I got her email. She headed to Chalk Farm, and I went back to Ra'ef's cyber store, which was closed for maintenance. I went back to the market to find a contact.

At that time, Camden was busy. Really busy. But it was busy with bohemians and punks, which give it colour. The smell of oriental food there wasn't foul like it was in Chinatown. It smelled more like Soho, with hemp and scents filling the scene like you're standing in a stoner's room. But a sensible stoner. You just feel calm. And hungry. The madness of Camden Market is complimented by the fact that at times, you feel like you're in an old Middle Eastern bazaar.

I walked through the madness, and at the centre of the market, through the various clothes, homemade soaps, one-of-a-kind paintings, and vintage CD stands, I saw a Rasta behind a small stand blasting electronic music. His base was at the intersection between tight walkways, so he couldn't be missed. He sold the CDs, but the music was so loud, you could hardly hear when he told you the price. He sat at a desk behind the stand, occasionally rising to dance to a beat. LaShawn was a colourful opener to the stables market. He was a hardcore Rasta, preached love and solidarity, and slept with any tourist he could talk to for more than ten minutes. He always had killer weed on him, and his accent was fresh off Kingston, Jamaica. As I approached, I could hear him at his most charming.

"Listen. Dem men just preach 'ate. What I say is dat love can exist between people 'cuz we all yuman. All got two eyes, ears, and a mout. Two ears to listen, one mout to speak. We must listen twice more dan we speak. Dis ting I learnt from me books, so come down to the crib tonight, and I'll show you. I got killa weed. Den we talk about me civil rights books, and dedications to Bob Marley. I like you Spaniards 'cuz you got passion. You feel d'love, you feel d'emotion. See you den. One love. Take care."

Lovely. Utter nonsense. But lovely. Two Spanish girls. Not bad. He had some charm on him.

When LaShawn saw me, he turned off his music. He knew I didn't like to shout. If I had to shout, I may have decided to call him by his real name—Mustapha. I may also not have understood his Jamaican accent and ask him to speak in a more English Harrow College-educated, half-Somali, half-Ghanian accent— which would have been closer to his mother tongue. What would that do to his reputation?

LaShawn and I knew each other too well. Too well for his liking. Too well for my liking.

His shocked face entertained me.

"Let's not be too surprised. You of all people should know I have returned from banishment."

"M-m-manz, ah heard—"

"Let us put the Jamaican accent away, shall we?"

He froze, swallowed, and continued. "I heard you were back. I just didn't think you'd be in Camden so quickly, at least not after Ra'ef." He spoke in a clear English accent that rivalled a royal, quiet enough, though, not to be overheard.

"I know, I know, I fucked him up, but it was Ra'ef being Ra'ef; he deserved it. And frankly, I couldn't give two shits about punks putting a price on me."

"N-n-not that, Calcain."

"Then what?"

"You mean you haven't heard?"

"Heard what?"

"Ra'ef is in a bad shape. He's not at all good. They're afraid he may have bleeding on his brain."

I shook my head. "Can't be. I was there when it happened. He was just concussed a little."

"You saw him fall, but you did see the impact all that metal shit in his hair, clothes and face did to him?"

"What are you talking about?"

Then it clicked. It wasn't the fall that did him in; he'd probably been impaled by a spike from a three-dimensional tattoo or the pointed end of a hair piece. If he did die, it would be a pretty shit way to go. I tried to think about how I'd feel if he died. I thought and thought, and I didn't feel anything. I couldn't have cared less if I tried.

"If Ra'ef dies, who'll take over?"

"No candidates have stepped up yet. Ra'ef was so young and organised. He had a strong subcommittee but not necessarily a successor; he didn't think he'd need a second one in line. But anyone taking over will have their work cut out for them."

"And why is that?" I could already guess the idiotic answer I was about receive.

"The New—"

"Breed. Right?"

LaShawn nodded. "They're getting stronger and need more territories. Ra'ef was about to host a very important meeting between Camden, Shoreditch, and the Lords of Soho. He wanted to create a united coalition to provide defence if things kicked off and the New Breed attacked all the gangs."

I learned two important things just there. First, Ra'ef had a peculiar way of releasing rumours of an event after said event has occurred, not before. So I had no doubt the meeting had already happened and likely happened some weeks ago. Now, I accepted Ra'ef believed in the New Breed, but I doubted the meeting was about them. It was more likely about what to do when the Houses decided to destroy the New Breed; he was freaked about the potential for carnage. I needed to know what he knew, and I couldn't do that without Ra'ef himself.

"Where is he being treated?"

"UCLH."

"All right."

"One more thing. If you want to get info about his condition, the guy at the comic book store on Inverness Street knows the last-minute stuff and passes on the details. He's the one to go to on Ra'ef-related business, apparently. Doesn't know shit, though."

"You mean Mega City?"

"Yeah, that's the one."

Perfect. I got what I needed. If I knew Ra'ef, he would've left me a message. He'd probably even guessed the exact date and time I'd turn up for it.

"Thanks, pal. Have a good one."

"Calcain?" he said quite nervously.

"What is it?"

"Is there going to be a war? I mean… like the one before?

When Camden and Soho nearly went at it?"

"No."

He relaxed slightly and sighed in relief.

"This will be much worse."

He looked at me in shock. What did he expect? Battles between small gangs were nothing. They were a small upgrade from council house kids stabbing each other. This thing that was coming now would be true warfare. And whoever went down would take most of London with them.

*

I went down Camden High Street and down one of the side roads. To the right was Inverness Street, which was home to a very small band of colourful coffee shops, restaurants and bars. There were small stands and tents selling T-shirts and other wares, and in the middle of it all sat Mega City Comics. It had been there for as long as I could remember, and even though it was comparatively small, it had all the comics you could imagine crammed into a tiny shop. It was every comic and graphic novel reader's paradise. The owner was pretty cool and didn't give a shit about laws and copyrights. He'd happily buy stuff from the U.S. and sell the material prior to their official release in London.

He knew his customers well, but he served a second purpose. He was a messenger. If you had a document you needed picked up by a contact, you went to him, and, for a small fee, he'd hold it until your contact collected it. But there was a catch. Both you and your contact had to be members of the Courier Club, one of London's most secretive and heavily vetted organisations. The Courier Club's main purpose was to pass on messages by any means necessary.

Many newspaper illustrators, for example, were members, and their method of transmitting information by way of the comics page was nothing less than genius. Consider if you had a guy in trouble with either the underworld or the police. You'd tell your contact to lie low until a particular cartoonist drew a monkey in her daily comic in the *Metro*. Your contact waits and checks the paper every day for the appearance of the monkey. When he sees the monkey in one of the artist's panels, it means he's good to go. The same process is behind strange advertisements in the classifieds section, like 'Vacuum cleaner cleaning services: We'll clean your vacuum cleaner for a small fee' or 'Want to contribute more tax to the economy? Call Steinburg Tax Consultants, the new tax consultancy for the socially conscious since December 2012'. Together, these two advertisements might be a directive indicating the recipient is clear to assassinate Steinberg at 20:12 p.m. that evening.

This highly complex system was the brainchild of Ra'ef and his former associate, Inforno.

I walked into the store, and the clerk smiled. There was a girl in front of me, who was quite attractive with an exceptionally nice ass tucked neatly inside a pair of leggings.

"I'm here to pick up a series I've pre-ordered for my boyfriend," she said. "My membership name is Lana."

I leaned on the counter next to her and opened my mouth to greet her—to charm her, as it were—but a meaty hand landed on my shoulder and yanked me away. It was the owner. He had a long, grey beard and matching hair. Purple glasses. Probably early fifties.

"Don't harass my customers."

I pretended to be shocked. "Daniel, I'm hurt. I'd never harass anyone, especially not a girl as—"

"Stop." He put up a hand. He handed Lana her receipt. "Have a nice day."

She smiled at the both of us. I'd charmed her without even trying.

"Take care."

I gave her my cheesiest smile. "You too."

Daniel wasn't amused, that much was clear, but I didn't care. "Can I get my comic, mate?"

He handed it to me and waved me out the door.

In order to decipher the message Ra'ef had left me, I decided to go to the Spanish tapas bar two doors down and order a coffee with banana cake. I reviewed the comic page by page. Ra'ef's messages tended to be particularly well hidden, but I'd like to think I'd received enough of them by now that it would stand out to me.

It was an early issue of the *Preacher* series about a disillusioned preacher with the power to command people to do his bidding, an ability referred to as 'the Word of God'. His companions were a blonde chick and an Irish vampire. I read through the issue and couldn't identify anything Ra'ef may have considered a message for me. I examined the front and back covers. I read through the text again, looking for anomalies in the language or images, and still, there was nothing. Maybe that was the message. Maybe he knew nothing. But that would have been a very fucking convoluted way of conveying that information. Frustrated, I closed my eyes and thought about Ra'ef and the ways he'd described me in the past. Savage. Monster. And then it clicked. I flipped back through the pages until I came across a cowboy standing in the background of a panel. He was supposed to be the Angel of Death's replacement. In his hands, he appeared to be holding a Bible, but a closer inspection revealed it wasn't a

Bible at all. It was a book by Dante. His most famous poem. My worst nightmare.

Inferno.

Dante's *Inferno.*

I knew what Ra'ef wanted me to do.

But why?

In the comic, the cowboy appeared to be making strange gestures with his hands, which continued from page to page. It was sign language. It was the message.

The others are coming. The end of the Houses. One of the three has begun its campaign prematurely. Not ready. Desire for an old power. An absolute power returns. Danger for all. Danger. Danger. Danger

I took the message to mean Russell was about to strike when he wasn't ready and that Ra'ef believed in the New Breed. The comic was imported from New Jersey, so I took it that was where he had chosen to ride the tide out. Leaving me in the middle of things. Honourable man, that cunt.

It was clear what I needed to do. I just had to accept it. I wanted to revisit the crime scene first, but not before heading to the toilet for some Dark Fire. I couldn't risk another bout of withdrawals taking me out for a day or more. I'd quit one day. But not cold turkey. Fuck that.

*

I spent the next few hours high, drunk and generally fucked up in the tapas bar; I wasn't sure how many hours. I ate, I drank, I persuaded some keen chick to give me head in the corner of an alley outside. She was still going at it like a pro, holding me with both hands and playing vacuum cleaner, her wedding ring the only thing shining in our immediate space. She seemed too young to be married, no older than mid to late twenties. Her husband had taught her well, though. I was totally spaced out. I couldn't remember what I was supposed to be doing. I had some shitty ass comic in my hand about some gay cowboy preacher. Why was I holding that?

The girl sucked away. I was waking up. I still couldn't remember the specifics. But I needed to see Inforno. And I needed to go to Bishops Avenue. I put on my headphones, and She started singing to me, 'Cherry Cherry Boom Boom'.

Eh (eh-eh), eh (eh-eh) / There's nothing else I can say...

Her voice soothed me, got me focused. The chick finished her job, and I threw some money at her out of habit. She seemed offended. I apologised and asked for it back. She seemed even more offended.

I went back to the bar and picked up another banana cake. She continued to sing.

I met somebody cute and funny...

I had the track on repeat. It was a great pick-me-up song. I left the bar, and it was pitch black outside. I stumbled to the tube, but it was closed. I'd clearly been out of my head for a while. I walked down towards Mornington Crescent, looking for a cabbie. I spotted a guy holding another by the hand with his six-seater car's door open. The guy being held was on the phone and at the same time shouting at a few friends nearby. As I walked past the car, I saw a strange-looking GPS inside it, and I realised what had happened. The man being held was a passenger in a cab. He and his friends had tried to run away without paying, but the driver caught one. He was begging his pals to come back. I looked at the cabbie and slipped a few notes in his pocket.

He looked at me in surprise. "Do you know these idiots?"

"No, and I'm not covering their fare."

"Then why?"

"You're probably losing out on a lot of business right now by waiting here and making sure this kid is held responsible for his actions. Don't want you to go home too light."

The guy being held spoke Spanish to his friends. I gave him a look that made him shit himself.

"If I catch you doing this again, I'll kill you."

The driver smiled, and I continued on my way, hailing a black cab with its orange light on. I climbed in.

"Bishops Avenue. Fast."

"You got it."

I opened both rear windows and let the breeze roll in. I was still fucked up, and before I knew it, I was on Bishops Avenue. I directed the guy to the house and gave him a generous tip.

The front of the house was still guarded, so I went around back and hacked into the security alarm. Fuck knows how. Somehow, I found myself back in the living room. The murder scene. The bodies were gone, replaced with white chalk. Pretty. Blood and brains were still there, albeit dry.

Now for some detective work.

I wasn't there to figure out what happened; I already knew that. I was looking for notes or photos or some other form of evidence Hunter may have gathered on the Houses. Things only Hunter would have been able to see, access and report back about. Things I would be interested in. Things the New Breed, to the extent that it's real, would be interested in.

Using my phone and the details Sutton gave me, I accessed the notes on the case. The security pin was mistyped three times prior to deactivation. There were remote signs of struggle in the living room. Other than that, the police had nothing.

I walked upstairs and looked through each room and drawer, behind every painting and inside each safe. The notes indicated that the police believed nothing was stolen and therefore the killer was someone hired to carry out the execution. Jewels and cash aside, there may have been other more important, more precious items hidden away. Evidence. I looked through the usual areas where a safe of such importance could be, like in the ceiling tiles above the shower or awkward spots behind removable drywall. There was nothing. Hunter was clearly very careful. I went outside, and the bricks that had fallen down were still near the house. I scanned the garden. Still nothing. I scoured the house inside and out. There was absolutely no information hidden anywhere. Which meant he probably did one of two things: hid the information externally or, as Mulligan believed, kept it all in his head to avoid detection.

Fuck me.

I sat on the couch beside a large bloodstain and listened to Her. I lit up a small cigar. After a while, I called Mulligan again. Still no answer. I was getting worried and made a mental note to contact Scotland Yard in the morning.

I finished my cigar and left. On the way out, I noticed something: footprints. Fresh ones. I follow their path back to a tree in the garden, where I discovered a matchbox in the tree. The prints led to the house and back out, but there was no indication of anyone having been inside since the crime scene was closed. At least no one official. The yard was muddy, and the left footprint was deeper and more emphasised than the right. The only explanation was that person with a limp slid out of his shoes—trainers by the look of it, not police force issue—and walked barefoot through the home. Whoever it was must have been looking for the same thing I was. Information. He saw his opportunity and seized it, but he was in a rush, hence the dropped matchbox. It was a generic box you could pick up at any bar, but the logo advertised Browns strip bar on Old Street in Shoreditch. Only two of the ten matches had been ripped out, so this person was likely there recently. And it wasn't lost on me that Mark's base was on Old Street. He could've been connected. I was starting to enjoy this.

I walked up Bishops Avenue towards Hampstead station, caught a taxi, and powered towards Soho. I needed a good night's sleep and to keep a low profile until the Justin situation blew over. I didn't need to be associated with that.

In the cab, I was accompanied by the most beautiful woman in the world. She was singing to me so beautifully.

I think about the unknown person behind the whole mess. I wish I could send him a bouquet with a note attached: 'I'll find you, you fucking fuck'. And when I did, I'd make him tell me everything, down to the very last footnote. And then I'd fucking kill him.

Dark Fire was still burning inside me, and with great music and the promise of milk and chocolate digestives, I dozed off. Until I got to Soho. My home.

*

By the time I reached Old Compton Street, it was two forty-five a.m. True to form, Tanka was outside smoking and looked shocked to see me. I must have looked like shit.

"Listen, Tanka, I've had a rough couple of days. Give me a rest, will ya?"

He crossed his arms angrily. "Sweetie, if I don't do it, no one will. You look terrible. Tomorrow at nine, I'm coming upstairs with a healthy breakfast that's going to fix you right up. Some minerals, some vitamins, maybe some potassium. Coconut juice, even."

Poor guy. He really was a nice person living in the scummiest part of London.

I smiled. "Thanks, Tanka. You're a true pal."

"Well, evidently I'm not your only paaal…"

"What do you mean?"

"The American lady you brought in has been in and out of your place with shopping bags and stuff. It no longer stinks in the corridor."

"Fuck. Has she thrown anything away?"

"Oh yeah. Lots of stuff."

"Fuckin' hell, Tanka. Why didn't you fucking call me? She could have raided me dry."

"Listen, anything that makes your crappy place a little less crappy is a good thing in my book. Even if it means you going bankrupt. Anyway, I spoke with her, and she seemed really nice. She told me—"

Before he could finish, I rushed upstairs. My door was locked. I rummaged through my key ring for the key for the flat door, remembering that apart from alcohol and drugs, there wasn't much to raid. Except my notes. All my work on the gangs and the Houses compiled into a handy journal. What if she was working for them? I opened the door to absolute darkness interrupted only by two candles on a table next to my bed. As I walked towards them, I noticed all the rubbish on the floor was no longer there. The floor—including my rug—was clean. The window was cracked, bringing in fresh, cool air, and the smell of food, in particular cake, made the flat feel like a home. As great as it all was, I couldn't bring whores there. It was too… nice.

On the table, the two candles sat on either side of a plate with a chicken breast, mashed potatoes, gravy, and mixed vegetables. A small glass of red wine was also beside the plate, as well as a set of silverware. The table had a white table cover and red tablecloth on top. Shelly was asleep in my bed on what appeared to be new sheets.

I sat down and ate the meal before me. It tasted wonderful. I washed the dishes in the sink, blew out the candles, and lay next to her. She was holding a teddy bear.

She shifted in bed, half-awake, and put her head on my shoulder. I put an arm around her somewhat reluctantly.

"I got the money from your drawer," she said in a hoarse, sleepy voice.

"I didn't ask you—"

"You didn't need to."

She dozed off again. I reminded myself of my golden rule. Don't ever fall for a whore.

But Shelly wasn't one. Was she?

On the opposite wall, she'd framed Her poster. It all somehow felt... right.

Chapter 8

Old Street, Shoreditch, London

It was finally Friday. Sutton called several times to feed me information. He continued proving himself to be highly intelligent, and we enjoyed good banter. It felt almost like we were working together, which wasn't something I'd normally entertain. Sutton was different somehow. And the tidings he was giving me were terrible.

Russell was grief-stricken and had demanded that Charlie explain himself. Charlie, on the other hand, couldn't understand why Russell considered him the culprit. He reasoned that Russell must have thought Charlie guilty of retaliation. But in order for retaliation, an initial sin had to be committed, which led Charlie to the only logical conclusion: Russell must have killed Hunter, a fact that now had him, too, in a frenzied state. They were within weeks of open war, if that. There had been a few volleys, some low-level killings, but nothing yet that could be described as a declaration of war. Elad had declared alliance to both parties and neither at the same time, stating openly that if Russell and Charlie went to war, he'd be there to take down the winning House, which was sure to be weaker by the end of the initial battle. Historically, the checks and balances of the three Houses that made up their mutual dominance helped their respective business interests, but open war would change everything, and the threat of such an event meant the government would intervene at some point, probably at the last minute. I wondered if they'd be strong enough to handle it.

Sutton asked to meet so I could share some information from my side, but I'd cropped up on too many gang radars, which had mostly limited my investigating to the City and East End. So I didn't really have fuck all to give him, but I needed to prove myself useful so I could continue dredging him for information. I didn't want to talk about my findings; it ran the risk of him thinking me an idiot or untrustworthy, and I needed to avoid both perspectives.

And on top of all that, Mulligan was still missing. He'd been gone a few days, and Scotland Yard was starting to panic, though not as bad as I was. He had the answer to every question I had about his ten-year investigation into the Houses. Without him, I was at square one. I had no immediate reason to suspect his disappearance was linked to the crimes; it would've been very shabby work by the person behind this chaos, as it would not only expose them to the wrath of the Houses but also the full force of Scotland Yard and the Metropolitan Police. The powers that be may not have liked Mulligan, but he was popular enough for all in mid-management to authorise a wide-scale search. Which is exactly what had started happening, with nothing to show for it. I knew he wasn't dead. I could feel it. But whether or not he'd be dead soon was a different story.

But for now, it was a beautiful Friday night in London.

I was eviler on the weekends. More of a monster.

More patient.

More scheming.

Shelly was out studying and catching up with friends for a drink afterwards, which was a good thing. I needed to be alone. Alone in my living room. Sitting on the single sofa with the room lit by a handful of candles. A glass of Pampero dark rum on ice. The drinks were going down smoothly. I had showered and changed into in a black, long-sleeve T-shirt, black G-Star jeans, a brown belt, brown loafers, and a brown coat. I needed those clothes. They were easy to change out of, appropriate enough to grant entrance into any restaurant or club, comfortable to run in. I sat in deep thought. Totally relaxed.

In that absolute tranquillity, the only noise being the delicate sound of a candle burning, I reached the mental level I needed to in order to search. To find. To question. To hurt. To kill. It was time to let Her in and time for Dark Fire. I turned on the 'Scheibe' remix, and it exploded into the room. I took my drug of choice and blew out the candles. I entered the zone.

There was darkness first. Then a small red and white dot that burst into a smoky shadow in front of me from which She appeared. She smiled.

"You seem worried."

"I fear I'm running around with no real purpose. I'm stressed. Mulligan is missing. Sutton is my only other lead, apart from Inforno. But my biggest fear is I am looking for a mad person with no real purpose other than to destroy. The same traits as a psychopath. The same desire for carnage. Chaos. Insanity. Same hatred for the Houses. Same level of indifference for life. I fear I know his next move, which will be premature—and without proper planning, it will result in pandemonium."

She smiled.

"Doesn't that remind you of someone? And if it does, would you do what this person is doing? Or do you think you'd have other plans?"

"What other plans? My plan has always been to destroy the Houses for what they did to me. What they did to Elsie. What they did to London."

"Then why not stand aside and let it all happen?"

She had me there.

She continued. "I think there is a method to your madness, as there must be a method to the madness of the person you are seeking. Find that method, and you will find the madman. People misquote you every now and again. People hear you say 'Find the hate, and you will find the monster'. But what you mean is find the—"

"Hurt…"

"And you will find the Monster. Can I get an Amen?"

"Amen."

"Don't give up. Marry the night."

With that last word, a powerful light shined in my eyes, then everything so far was laid bare in front of me:

What happened to the man following me early on? Was he still around? He wouldn't have stopped. Has he paused? Or can I just not see him?

I need to speak with Jessica again.

I need to speak with Kimia. She was hiding something.

Another death is near that will move us closer to war.

Mulligan needs me.

Wait.

The light was brilliant. It felt like it was tearing through me.

I should have looked for Mark rather than waiting for him to show up at his weekend flat. He's probably in danger. He knows too much for a two-bit gangster. He knows way too much. I've been waiting for him to come home. But so has the killer. And that's why the man stopped following me. He's been at Mark's. Waiting.

In a shock, I opened my eyes. I needed to get to Old Street.

Immediately.

*

I grabbed my tools and rushed out of my flat, jumping down the stairs. The fastest way to Old Street would test my patience; it meant waiting. I loved the tube. I hated to wait for it. But patience was a strength of mine. I hoped.

I ran to Tottenham Court Road and jumped on the Central line to Liverpool Street. Things were starting to make sense. The killer knew me. He was following me to see what line of inquiry I'd investigate first, then he made his plan from there.

How could I let him escape me? Everyone I'd been in contact with was in danger. Jessica, Kimia, Sutton, Shelly—even fucking LaShawn. That was why Ra'ef was keeping away. I wasn't dealing with a New Breed, per se—I was dealing with their assassin.

If I got to Mark early enough, I could save him. But not without a fight. Because the assassin was already there.

I caught the first taxi I could as soon as I get off at Liverpool Street station. The City boys and girls were out for Friday night drinks, and they were in my fucking way. I had to crush a few couples on my way to the taxi.

"Where to?" the driver asked.

"Old Street. The faster you go, the more money you'll get."

My man drove well, powering through bus lanes. A minute or two later, I was within running distance of Mark's house, but the traffic logjammed. In the distance, I saw a Black guy—about six feet tall with loose clothes and braided hair—walking towards Mark's house. It must've been him. I threw a twenty at the taxi driver and ran towards Mark, screaming.

"*Mark, get the fuck down!*"

As I ran faster and got closer, I thought he saw me, that he could hear me. Just one intersection before—

Everything went dark. I opened my eyes. My head was spinning. It was all hazy.

"Mate, you all right?"

Slowly, the blurriness went away, and I saw a bunch of artsy people and a few suits gathering around, looking at me in surprise.

"Mate, I think you're in shock. You got hit pretty bad."

"Wha… what happened?"

"You ran across the street and got hit by a car. I got his number plate, if you need a witness."

I got to my feet, but my legs were weak and I fell to the ground. I was too dizzy to move. They gave me water and tried to call an ambulance before I stopped them. I didn't have time for all that. I thanked everyone and told them that someone would be meeting me. They dispersed, and I slowly made my way to Mark's apartment building. But before I reached it, I was grabbed by my arms, which were in absolute agony, and pulled into an alley. My fucking thighs hurt.

"Who the fuck are you?" a voice said.

I looked at my perpetrator. It was Mark.

"Oh, thank fucking God." I sighed in relief. "I've been looking for you. You're in danger. We need to talk."

"Why am I in danger?"

"Well, for starters, there's an assassin waiting for you inside your house."

"What? Why?"

"Well, because… wait. Is your name Mark?"

"No."

Oh fuck. Fuck. Shit. Fuck. Big mistake.

"Get the fuck off me," I snapped.

He let me go, his expression turning curious. "Hold on. Is Mark in danger?"

"You know him?"

"Yeah, I was just going to visit him now."

"Then for fuck's sake, get the fuck out of my way!"

He stepped aside, and I was running, my fucking back killing me. I finally found myself in front of the flat. The door was secured, but I'd brought enough tools to break in and then destroy a small army. I picked the lock and entered the small flat, gun drawn. A rush of energy filled me immediately, and it took me just seconds to clear the entryway before I ran towards the small living room on my left.

There. Right in front of the TV, which was blaring. On a lounge chair, with a bowl of cereal by his feet, Mark sat with his back towards me. He didn't react to my entrance. Next to the sofa was an old antique table covered with newspapers, bottles, and weed.

As I approached him, I noticed a smear of blood on the floor. I didn't need to see his face to know. Mark was dead. I picked up the remote by my feet behind the sofa and turned off the TV.

I lowered my gun. I was overcome with anger. I'd lost my lead. I should have waited here until he came back, but my real mistake came a lot earlier—I didn't take being followed seriously.

Followed.

I was followed.

Suddenly, the anger inside me turned into a chill. My heart was beating so fast it made me nauseous. It felt like it had dropped right down to my stomach. Fuck butterflies; I was feeling pigeons battling in an epic war.

I was too late to save Mark. He was probably killed hours ago, so the assassin hadn't been waiting for him.

He'd been waiting for me.

The car that hit me wasn't an accident.

Jason distracting me wasn't a coincidence.

And now he was behind me.

He was about to assassinate me on someone else's behalf.

I heard a click.

"Don't look back." The voice was muffled and definitely not Jason's.

A third person in the room.

Keep calm, Calcain. Use fear to your advantage. Breathe.

"I wondered when I'd meet you," I asked with a calm voice but with a heart beating as fast as a rabbit. "Surely you'll let me see your face before finishing me off?"

I heard a small chuckle.

"The infamous Calcain. The unknown Calcain. The man hellbent on destroying the Houses. The apprentice of the once-great Detective Mulligan. It's strange, isn't it, how we almost seem to take the exact same path towards completely different destinations. I have to say, you're so much more injudicious than the adversary I thought you'd be. Such drastic levels of imprudence resting on such feckless pillars of dexterity, yet with a solid level of ingenuity."

What a clever sentence. I offered a clever response.

"Your mom."

"Funny." He didn't sound like he thought it was funny.

"Not as funny as how your whore of a mother looks when we play babies. You should see her in a nappy. Sucks dick like a toddler would his mom's tit and swallows all the milky goodness

191

that comes out. But you'd know all about that, wouldn't you, you cunt, considering what you've been doing to my city."

"Speak in any way you want, but do not dare disrespect my art—"

"Oh, fuck right off right there."

Self-praising cunt.

"Don't tell me I've been chasing after one of them twats who considers chaos 'art'. You know fuck-all about that, so please don't give me the art chat, okay? Please. Kill me, if you want. But save me the art chat. You fucking drip of a vaginally inserted paint brush."

"Calcain, please don't get snippy with me. I watched all your moves, and now I have you cornered. Your one lead is, as you can see, spent. Now what do you have? Where will you go? I am within inches of you, and you have no idea who I am. I've followed you like your own shadow on many occasions. And yet, you've managed to do nothing, you've found nothing. Nothing."

I laughed. "Hold on. I do know you. I knew I recognised your voice. Aren't you that tart I analled last week? The one with the rash? I've been itching ever since."

He was certain enough of my impending death to share a small bit of information, but not certain enough to show me his face. There was a reason he hadn't killed me yet. He wanted to see if I knew anything or had told anyone else what I'd learnt. That curiosity is what was keeping me alive. I still had a chance to find a way out.

"Make fun as you like, Calcain," he continued. "But you have nothing that can threaten me. I knew your every move to get here, which is why I have you cornered, and you have… well, nothing. Your very existence is irrelevant to my work. I am a much higher authority than you in the art of tracing, detection, and deduction. Now, the question is, do I kill you and enjoy feasting on the remains of my so-called adversary? Or do I let you live and continue your role as a suspect, knowing you'll remain oblivious to my movements around you?"

I couldn't give him any information.

"Well, as further food for thought, don't forget this—if you kill me, who'll fuck your mom? You certainly don't do a good enough job from what she tells me."

"So very funny. I think I'd much rather kill you, actually. As a token of vanity. I will be the man who killed the great Calcain—or rather, the great Mulligan's apprentice."

I was onto him. He won't kill me now, not even with a silencer. He'd rather play it safe. He'd waited inside this horrid, dirty, stinky flat for the past days. He lacked creativity. He was probably some form of accountant. Cared a lot about details. Wouldn't be pragmatic about it. Everything had to follow suit. If I made it through this encounter, I'd enjoy killing him. If I didn't, I only cared about one thing.

"Is Mulligan alive?"

"So serious all of a sudden," he said, surprised. "I feel charitable, so I'll answer your question. He is alive. For now. But he plays a very limited role in the scene I'm creating, so he'll be dead soon. Maybe if I kill you first, he'll start talking. I think he thinks you're the only one who can rescue him. So if you die, he'll have no hope. He's more use to me than you, considering how long you've been away. Yes. That's what we'll do. Kill him, Jason. And do bring me his heart."

I smiled. He was leaving his puppy to do his dirty work. I couldn't let that happen. I needed him to make a mistake. I needed a hint. I needed to scare him.

"I'll promise you this," I said. "Whoever you are, I will find you. I swear I will. And when I do, you will beg for a ruthless death. But what you'll get will be slow, and it will be terrible. And it will only be a sign. For the Houses. To let them know I'm coming."

"Calcain," he responded. "You don't even know if I work for the Houses or if I'm working against them. But know this—The Houses as you know them will be gone. There will be a new order in London. I'm after more Houses than you can comprehend, and even you won't be able to stop me in time."

More Houses? What the fuck was he on about?

I heard slow footsteps going towards the rear of the flat. A window opening and then closing. Good. Now, I needed a plan. I still had my gun, but if I tried to shoot Jason, he'd shoot back, and he had the better angle. My body still ached from being struck by the car, but I was strong enough for one swift, sudden movement.

"Jason, I know what you're thinking. But the thing is…"

One.

Swift.

Sudden.

Movement.

I tilted to my side, lifting my gun hand to where my head had been positioned previously, pointing it at Jason. I pulled the trigger as I flipped sideways. I felt Jason's bullets whizzing past me, but with so much adrenaline pumping through my veins, I couldn't tell if I'd been hit. I heard him falling. I jumped behind the sofa to take cover. I peeked around the cushions and could see Jason was bleeding. But he had his gun pointed towards me. He was about to shoot. It was now or never. I shot up from behind the couch, pulled the trigger, and put a bullet in his throat.

He dropped. He stopped moving.

I took a few breaths. I needed my nerves to cool. My heart was beating fast, and the rush of blood made everything seem like it was happening in slow motion. I got up and slowly walked towards Jason. I put my hand around his throat, his blood seeping out from between my fingers.

"Jason." I leaned my face towards his. "Tell me who your friend was."

He couldn't speak. It was understandable, considering the damage to his vocal cords. I hadn't considered that when I took the shot. But there was a rattling on my left. Jason was knocking his knuckles against the floor of the flat. He turned the underside of his arm up to reveal a tattoo. A square with a cross in the middle. I already knew Jason was a hitman. But now I knew he was a very specific kind of killer. His insignia indicated that he was someone who took one job, just one, so his family would be taken care of. There were dozens of men—and a few women—running around with the city with those markings. The Houses used them regularly. They were recruited at random, but they took poison a few hours before the hit, and they'd die shortly after the deed was done. It was a perfect system. No prison time for the doer. No way to trace the assassination to the Houses. And a family grief-stricken but cared for.

Jason's head lolled to the left. He was dead. Better by me than by poison.

I searched the flat for clues, anything that might indicate what Mark knew or what someone would think he knew. His body was clean, his pockets empty. But all small-time gangsters were the same, so I knew where I could find at least one clue. I opened his mouth and took a good look at the treasure chest that shined back at me. Then I took pliers to his molars and pried his gold teeth out one by one. As I expected... one of them was hollow. Inside, I found a tiny, rolled piece of paper. *Richard Oliver.* I thought for a while. If the information was sensitive enough to be hidden away so painfully, it could only be one thing: a password. I picked up his laptop off the floor, turned it on, and when it asked for the password, I typed *RichardOliver*. I got in. I opened the web browser, and the page automatically redirected to a Hotmail account with his username already populated. I tried *RichardOliver* again, and I accessed his inbox. There was just one email. From Kimia.

Thanks for that, Mark. I've looked into it myself. I keep coming to something or someone wanting to take it back. Take back what I don't know, but it must have something to do with either Richard or Oliver. Whatever it is, it's about an ancient power. Let's chat when you're back. You know where to find me. I've got something I want to show you—can't figure out what it means, but I'm sure you can.

Small-time gangsters. All fucking idiots. I needed to have a little chat with Kimia myself now. But before I did, I had to head to Browns; I needed a description of the killer.

I looked at Jason.

I felt a bit sorry for what I was about to do to him. But it was essential. I needed to send a message.

I put on Her track, 'The Queen'.

I can be / The queen you need me to be…

My tools.

A saw.

Some pliers.

A drill.

I had everything I needed to get to work.

All drug dealers have explosives in their houses to ensure that, if the shit hits the fan, they can destroy all evidence;

fingerprints, fibres, DNA, everything. Within a few minutes, they're set to go off when I want them to; tomorrow's headline would be interesting.

I cleaned my wounds, washed the blood off me, and fixed myself up with whatever I found in the bathroom. To alleviate the pain, I took some Dark Fire. I waited for the shakes and the calm that followed. I blacked out for about twenty-five minutes, then I was back on my feet and leaving through the back window.

I headed straight to Browns. Some drink and ass would sort me out.

I felt like shit.

*

Browns had a massive sign out front and two huge security guards. They were nice enough and would grant you entrance if you followed three simple rules:

One. No touching.

Two. No cameras.

And three. Put a pound in any pint glass placed before you by a stripper.

The interior was about the size of a pub. It had a small stage with a pole and a DJ next to it to your right as you entered. To the left was the bar. At the far end, in the front, sat the private booths. The bar was frequented by the kind of men who couldn't afford a decent gentleman's club and instead fed on Browns' good-quality women; of course, the term 'women' was loosely implied. Before a dancer went on stage, she'd walk around the audience with a pint glass, and anyone she passed had to drop a pound in. She'd go up on the stage and take her kit off during the dance, and it was your job to memorise what you saw and wank off later.

You could also get a private dance for fifteen quid.

I knew the owner, so I stood by the bar, ordered a pint of Foster's and a packet of salt and vinegar crisps, and waited for him to come down. The people there were truly the scum of the earth, but the drinks were cheap, and some of the chicks weren't too bad. Not great. But not bad.

I took a sip of my pint and was approached by a stripper propositioning me for a private dance.

"Fuck off, love. I'm not in the fucking mood."

I'd hoped my attitude would put off the other strippers, but before word got around, a petite brunette with a great toned ass approached asking for a pound in her pint glass. She was doing her round before going on stage. I obliged. I never fucked with that rule; it was the most important of the three.

She got up on the stage and did her thing while I stood and watched, drinking my pint and eating my crisps. I was still aching a little from being hit by the car. I'd definitely feel it in the morning. I examined the matchboxes available on the bar. They didn't look like the pack I took from Hunter's garden.

As I neared the end of my pint, and certainly the very end of my crisps, Michael O'Leary, a forty-something Northern Irish fella with a tight pink shirt and light blue skinny jeans, approached me. He had a beer belly the size of a camel's hump and made his money in construction. Now he owned a few pubs and bars, including the illustrious Browns.

"All right, Calcain? Long time no see. Keeping out of trouble?" He shook my hand.

"You know me. The way I keep out of trouble is to be right in the middle of it. How are you, Mickey?"

"I'm good. Just had another argument with the wife. Since I married this English lass and she took my surname, she's had trouble being mocked and that. Now she wants to go back to her original surname. She's realised that, once you marry an O'Leary, there ain't no gold at the end of the rainbow. Just a penis. So, as I said, she wants her old surname back."

I laughed. "You know, I haven't heard of racism directed at the Irish for some time."

"Yeah, well. It happens. But I'm sure you didn't come to play catch up for old times' sake. And you know Melody went to become a doctor. So why are you really here?"

He didn't know anything about Houses. His patronage came from Inforno who, though officially connected to Elad, was pretty neutral.

I needed to be careful with Mickey. He didn't need to be privy to the specifics of why I was there. He knew that, as far as the game was concerned, the less he knew, the better.

"I need to find someone who's been here. White. English. Not sure about the age. Pretty sure it's a male, though I could be wrong on that. Never know. Most notably, the person I'm looking for had a limp. Maybe permanent, but maybe not. Could be he was injured briefly, so if you can think of any regulars who suffered a leg injury, that might be a good start. Also," I said and handed him the matchbox I picked up outside the house in Hampstead, "I found these."

Mickey picked up the box. "These matches are from the VIP area."

"VIP? Here? Damn, Mickey. This place is becoming quite the establishment."

"Fuck off, kid." He chuckled. "We have back rooms for VIPs now, but your man could be one of a hundred. I'll check with the girls. When did he take this?"

"Let's say three weeks ago. Look for someone with a special

199

request to stay private."

I'd guess at someone tall or heavy based on the depth of the footprints at the house. Likely the former.

"Tall. Above six foot. They may have been asking about local gang traffic. I'd guess he's also quite wealthy. I can't speak to how fine his attire was, but he likely carried a lot of cash."

"Sure, leave it to me, pal. I'll see what I can find out."

I stood to leave. "Oh, one thing. I need an answer by tonight. Three in the morning at the latest."

"Fuck, Calcain. There are at least fifty girls working here on a rotation of ten a night, six days a week. It will take me at least a week to get something to you."

"No. It would take you a week to get an answer for anyone else. It will take you a few hours to get an answer for me. Because I asked you nicely." I looked him straight in the eye. "Because we're friends."

He held my stare for a long moment before looking away. "Fine. I'll get you what you need."

"Good. I need you to articulate the serious need for this information. Then I need you to get a burner from somewhere as far away from here as possible and send me a text or an email with a full description and any other details you scrounge up. Start your text with the word 'sovereign', so I know it's you."

"Fine. I'll get that to you. But what if I get a few different descriptions? Like a short man with a limp and a tall fat man with a limp?"

"How much will it cost?"

"Nothin' for you, Calcain. Not after all we've been through."

"Thank you. One last question, an easy one. Where does Inforno work these days? I need to speak with him."

Mickey laughed. "Surely, you know where he lives. I

mean—"

"I know exactly where he lives. I'm asking you where he works."

"I thought you hated each other."

"I despise him more than an elephant hates fighting a fucking poacher in the ocean."

"That's a bit dramatic."

"Not dramatic enough, believe me."

He laughed again. "Well, you know Old Street is Tech City now. So guess where he is."

I thought about the vicinity of Old Street and the close roads and big IT companies near it.

"Very close to Old Street?"

"Yes."

"Near Moorgate?"

"Indeed."

"Finsbury Circus—no. Square. Finsbury Square?"

"Yep."

"Fuck me. Seriously? How did he pull that one off?"

"Figure it out."

"Fucking Bloomberg. The largest financial information company in the world. I love the mayor of New York. But fuckin' hell, he needs to sort his security."

"The funny thing is, he still works as a lawyer in that law firm at Finsbury Circus. He's on a secondment to assist Bloomberg on some overhaul or something."

"What a cunt. That means he's probably already hacked the shit out of the place."

"The sort of cash he's been making is just fucking laughable. And that's for his work on the secondment. You don't want to know how much he's thieved."

"I might just turn up and have a little meeting with him, then."

"When you do, be nice to him. You guys should get on better. You make a good team when you try."

"He defines everything I hate about everything. I hate him more than—"

"An elephant somethin' somethin'. I got that."

I smiled.

"You want to stay for another pint? On the house?"

"No thanks, mate. By the time I'm finished with it, I'll probably have paid triple its worth on your pound-a-pint scam."

He laughed. "You're a class act, Calcain."

I smiled again. "I look forward your text later. Take care, bud."

"I better get on with that, actually. Take care, sunshine."

I slipped past the enthusiastic guests coming in and stepped outside to a wonderful greeting from a fifty-something Black guy in a track suit and a big, fluffy jacket. He wore a cap and had enough gold teeth to pay a millionaire's ransom.

He nodded at me.

"You want some China kid or some minge, you let me know," he said in a strong East End accent.

"Will do, sir. Have a good night."

"Goodnight, kid."

The fact was, I knew where Inforno lived, but I had my reasons— far too many of them—for wanting to deal with him outside of the home.

I put my headphones in. I selected 'Americano'.

I met a girl in East L.A....

I started thinking to the rhythm of the music.

If you love me, we can marry on the West Coast / On a

202

Wednesday...

Jessica. I needed to find Jessica.

Ah ah ah ah ah America, Americano / Ah ah ah ah ah America, Americano...

Lambeth North. That was my next move. Northern Line to Elephant and Castle-Bakerloo Line to Lambeth North.

*

I got past the porter with a similarly worrying ease and found myself in front of Jessica's door. Several harsh knocks later, it still didn't open. No signs of forced entry. If she'd been murdered in her apartment, the killer would have been known to her. The locks were designer luxury, recently installed, and unpickable; she would have had to let the killer in.

I ran downstairs and explained to the porter I hadn't heard from Jessica in a while and was worried about her safety.

"Don't be worried, sah. She can take care of herself. She is safe. However, I can't violate tenant privacy, so her whereabouts are confidential until..."

I smacked a fifty down on the front desk.

"I can't..."

Another fifty.

"Look..."

Another fifty.

"Listen..."

One more fifty.

"This is all I'm putting down."

He hesitated. "Put down another, and I'll see what I can do."

Fuck it. I threw down another and smiled as he pocketed the cash.

"She left about twenty minutes ago. She was dressed like she was going out."

"Out where?"

"I don't know, sah."

"Was she on her mobile before she left?"

"Yes."

"Do you know who she was speaking with?"

"She said a few names, but I cannot remembah."

"How about Kimia? Did you hear that name?"

"Oh yeah, definitely."

"Did she order a cab?"

He nodded. "Yes."

"Where to?"

"Can't remembah. On Fridays, I order a lot of cabs."

I smiled. "You sure you can't remember?"

"Definitely sure," he said, giggling and taking a bite out of a hot chicken meal stinking up the reception area.

As soon as he took another bite, I grabbed him by the neck and pulled him towards me. The food was caught in his throat. He couldn't scream. I dropped him to the floor and kept squeezing.

"Listen, you chicken-gulping goof of a giggling ogre. I don't ask fucking twice for something I've paid good money for. Your head is entirely useless bar that temporary bit of information it's holding. Other than that, it's too hollow even for a fucking paperweight, you disgusting, repulsive, repugnant piece of thirty-day old vaginal discharge. Now I'm going to ask you one fucking question. You're going to answer. You're going to answer or else I will squeeze your throat so hard you'll be sucking dick out of a straw for the rest of your life. You hear me? Nod if you hear me."

He nodded, and I loosened my grip on his neck.

"Where did she catch a taxi to, then?"

"Cun—"

"I hope you're not trying to call me something that will make me very angry."

"Cu-cun—"

I squeezed his neck harder.

"I dare you to finish the word. I dare you…"

"Sah…" He struggled for air. I loosened my grip "Sah, I-I am n-n-not calling you nothing. It was Cun-Con-Conduit Street. Numbah nine, s-s-sah."

Oh. My mistake. I let go and helped him up.

"You sure it was number nine?"

"Yes, sah. I'm sure." He walked behind his desk, his suit now covered in dust and dirt. He pulled a book from a low shelf and opened it to reveal detailed cab orders.

"See? Numbah nine Conduit Street."

That was the address for Sketch.

"Are you sure the taxi is legit?"

"Super security, sah."

"Here's another fifty." I set it on the desk between us. "I'm sorry about earlier. I work for the police. I need to make sure she's safe."

"I understand, sah. But please control your tempah."

"I'll work on it. If she gets back in the next hour, call me on this number."

I gave him a blank card with only my number on it and walked out. I felt a bit bad for the guy.

Jessica had gone to see Kimia, to where Mark would've been heading if he hadn't been killed. Sketch. I figured Jessica had gone looking for information she should've stayed far away from. Kimia, too. They should've all kept the fuck away, but they clearly weren't scared of what was waiting for them. After they found out what happened to Mark and Jason, they would be.

I got on the Bakerloo line. Straight to Oxford Circus. I changed the song on my iPhone, and She sang 'Brown Eyes'.

My gear wasn't too torn up, and since I had freshened up at Mark's place, I was probably looking clean enough to enter any bar in London. By the time I got there, it would be closer to eleven. The perfect time to enter a club.

*

As soon as I got out of Oxford Circus, I started texting a few contacts, and by the time I got to Sketch, I was on the VIP guest list with a fucking table of drinks waiting for me. That's what I loved about being a Londoner—if you're connected enough, you can get in anywhere. I approached the scantily dressed blonde chick manning the door outside the club with her two burly bouncers watching the queue.

"Hello, love. I'm on Rachel's guest list. Name's Rutherford."

She looked through the pages on her clipboard.

"Can't find you here, hun. Rachel's guest list is full. Goodnight," she said dismissively.

You had to be super polite to people like her because she was the one with the power to let you in or not.

"Sorry, hun," I said with a smile. "I may not be on the list you have there because I'm a VIP. I probably don't look it, but I am."

One of the bouncers handed her a second clipboard.

"What's your name, again?"

"Dan Rutherford."

Sometimes club promoters would pass out information about guest list no-shows, and for a small fortune, some lucky partier could use such information to gain access to an elite venue. This was one such occasion. No Dan Rutherford? Enter Calcain.

"No, hun. I have Dan as ticked. He's gone in. Do you have any ID?"

Fuck a duck.

"No, love…"

"Then you're not getting in."

What followed was an annoying and lengthy process. I called my contact and got him to contact her manager. By the time the manager was dragged to the phone and touched base with the girl at the door, it was still another fifteen minutes before she granted me entrance, just to fuck with me. In the meantime, I waited in the fucking cold, the bouncer telling me more than once to shove off. I asked the girl twice if she'd heard anything from my contact, and both times she denied it. She folded the third time.

"It will cost twenty-five pounds to get in. It's a special night. Sean Paul is performing."

I entered past the girl, paid with my card, got my hand stamped, and collected my voucher.

There were three bars and clubs, one on each floor. I scanned each level until I found Kimia and her crew in the club on the ground floor. It was a big space with a bar in the middle. There were probably nine in her group. She looked safe. The dance floor was packed, and to the far left, Sean Paul would be taking the stage. That's when I'd make my move.

I went to the bar upstairs and, to my pleasant surprise, I bumped into Natalya and her Russian, Italian, and French friends.

I ordered a few shots of Patron XO Café, then a vodka cranberry, followed by a dark rum and coke. A mojito, too. Every now and again, I pretended to go to the toilet and check on Kimia.

"Did you see the toilets?" Natalya asked.

"Yeah, they're clean."

"No. I mean how cool they are."

I hadn't actually gone in the bathrooms. "Yeah, they're really high-tech."

"No. Maybe you haven't seen the toilets. The main ones."

She took me to where the toilets actually were, and they looked like gigantic eggs. They were in a large hall up the stairs, and there were about twelve of them. Twelve giant eggs men and women could enter. Big enough to fit an obese man. It was pretty cool.

As we went downstairs, I squeezed Natalya's hand. She turned and kissed me. I held her face with my hands and gently caressed her hair with my fingers. She looked at me and smiled.

"You are very naughty."

I felt a thunder surge through me when I kissed her, but I didn't know why.

I smiled back. "What I can I say? I apologise."

"I have to go now. But call me."

I was a bit tipsy by then, and things were going faster than my mind could comprehend. I heard a few screams from the ground floor club. The headliner would be on soon. It was time.

I ran towards the stairs as he began. I saw Kimia a few metres away from the stage, dancing with her girls. She seemed distressed; her dancing was erratic, her moves harsh. She kept begging her friends to dance with her. Notably missing from her circle was Jessica, who I spotted at the table drinking and staring at her phone. As I made my way through the crowd and downstairs, the music became louder and the bass stronger. I hated Sean Paul. I hated his style. In the distance, I could see Kimia having some kind of argument with her friends. She wanted to dance, but they seemed tired and wanted to sit. They left. She danced. It was time. The chorus of the song was good.

I, I'll do anything I could for ya / Boy you're my only / I, I'm gonna flip these beats on ya / You don't even know me...

The lights were dim, and it was as though I was walking into the abyss. Utter darkness, but the music was loud. Kimia was by herself and all over the place. I approached with my head down and danced in front of her. I moved close enough to dominate the erratic energy around her moves and submit them into a simple rhythm that overpowered her style. She was no longer dancing to the music or the beat. She was dancing to me. To my moves. My motives. To my beats. I could see that she was tipsy, wearing a tight, short, black mini-dress with high heels. Now that she was moving slowly, moving her hips as necessary, her charm began to overtake me. Her head was down, her hair covering her face, and she still hadn't seen me clearly. And when I thought I'd tamed her wildness, she counterattacked, putting her hand on my shoulder and beginning to gently snake. Her ultra-sexuality dismissed me as a worthy candidate and put me in my place as a desperate, hopeful, and now ambitious applicant with a limited chance of success entering zones well above my league. She slowly moved her hand up my neck, her hips gyrating slowly but with precession and delicacy. To me, it was a dance. To her, it was art. I was not the tamer. I was a prop. I would soon overstay my usefulness and will no doubt be disposed of accordingly.

I, I'll do anything...

As we got closer, she started to lift her face to kiss me. I had to play hard to get; she couldn't see me yet. I slid behind her, and in a sudden move—perhaps impressed by my bold act—she pressed herself against me. Now the snake was closer, much more erotic, the moves much more exaggerated. Still, she kept her grace.

I'm gonna flip these beats on ya...

I slowly kissed her neck. She liked the feeling. The song reached the last chorus, the volume of the music and the beat increasing. Alexis Jordan was on the stage.

Got to love you / Got to love you / Got to love you / Got to love you...

The beat and music reach their peaks.

I, I do anything I could for ya...

Kimia was still at work, mesmerising me with her sexuality, but I snapped out of it when I suddenly saw my reflection in someone's glass of Blue Lagoon. I remembered I had work to do. I played with her, gently caressing her body. I needed to feel her reaction to what I was about to do. I closed down on Kimia's neck and moved up to her ear and whispered to her.

"Richard Oliver."

Her body froze in my hands, putting a quick end to the sensuous movements she'd been making half a second previously. It wasn't the first time she'd heard the name.

*

"So I take it he's dead, then?" Kimia said, sipping her gin and tonic, gently breathing to catch her breath.

"Yes. He is."

"Shit." She continued to drink, her hand shaking as she lifted the cup. "That means Jessica's..."

"In very serious danger, yes."

"Shit."

"Now. I'm going to be as nice as I possibly can. So tell me everything you know, and I will protect you, your family, and Jessica. Leave anything out, and I'll let the bad men tear you all into as many pieces as they like."

"Don't get too excited, detective. I'm protected by both the Persians and the Russians. I'm untouchable. It's Jessica I'm worried about. Those who give me protection won't give it to her."

Another chick protected by sub-gangs who knows fuck all. I wasn't going to argue this time.

I sighed. "Fair enough. Who are Richard and Oliver?"

"Okay. What I'm telling you I'm not sure about. It's just speculation. But you need to understand, I'm in a terrible spot here because—"

"You think your mom could be a murderer. I know. What you tell me will be confidential, and don't worry, I've no reason to arrest or otherwise detain your mom. I don't think she falls too deep within the remit of my investigation. Just tell me what you know, or at least what you think you know, and you have my word that if your mom is involved in anything she shouldn't be, I won't assist with or get involved in taking her down. Not without your blessing, anyway."

She nursed her drink. "My family is looked after by the upper-class Persian community in London. And they sometimes... well, they do things to people who may hurt the community. Nothing scary, usually just putting pressure on businesses, but sometimes—very rarely—they engage in violence."

"Murder?"

"I'm not sure. Maybe. Anyway, when I heard about Leyli, I

211

approached Jessica and Mark who told me they'd do their own investigations but that I should use my contacts in the community to find what I could. I know a few people, and when I spoke to them, they went completely mute. After a few days, one of them finally opened up and said I should look closer to home. Which made me think, because I've always known there was something special about my mom. My sisters and I all have childhood memories of her sort of disappearing for a few days at a time or leaving late at night and coming back early in the morning. When I grew up, I thought maybe she…" Kimia smiled.

"Was a prostitute?"

She giggled. "Well, yeah."

"But you don't suspect that any more, do you?"

"No. Not at all. What little understanding I have of my mom's youth points to her being trained both in the Iranian and Israeli Defence Force. This is from discussions I overheard, random pictures in her personal albums, and the odd letter here and there. What she did afterwards, though, I don't know. She obviously settled down and became a housewife, but I don't think her activities stopped altogether. There was something strange about her. Don't get me wrong, she was a kind and caring mother—the best—but she was always so calm in terrible situations. And still—as of a few days ago—she went out in the middle of the night. I used to think it was some form of exercise or that she couldn't sleep. But things changed when Leyli hooked up with Hunter and he, at her request, asked around about my mom. Leyli didn't like the answer, so her relationship with Mom deteriorated. But neither would tell me why. So I sent Jessica and Mark on a new errand—to find out who my mom really is."

Maybe Mark wasn't killed because he had information on the Houses. Maybe it was because he had information on Bell.

"And they came up with?"

"Nothing. They asked as much as they could, but fundamentally, they found nothing."

"Are you certain?"

She nodded and shrugged. "Nothing of substance, anyway. All they found out was that there was talk about a new group and something to do with Richard Oliver."

"What was the new group called?"

She looked up and rubbed her left temple.

"New something. New kids? New children? New-borns? Oh, wait. New... New Breed. Definitely New Breed. And a Third House."

This was the second time I heard about the Third House. It may have meant Elad was behind it all. With two Houses at war, the third House gains. But it didn't smell like Elad's work. Besides, Ra'ef also referred to a Third House when he could have easily just said Elad by name.

"You need to tell me everything you know. Don't miss a single detail. Your life is in serious danger as of this moment."

She looked shaken. I was pushing too hard. I needed to calm her down.

"Look, don't worry too much. I can help you if you tell me everything."

She nodded. "Well, Mark and Jessica met this guy. I don't know who he was or anything, but he said a change in the status quo was coming. Something about the new group—New Breed—taking over. And that was why Hunter was killed. But he wouldn't say anything more unless we paid him. Before we could arrange payment, he died in a car crash on his way from Brighton. Police said it was drunk driving, and they weren't treating it as suspicious. Anyway, he said he had uncovered a name behind this New Breed, and that was Richard Oliver. He said this Richard Oliver is the contact for the New Breed, and that if we found him, we'd find the answer to everything. Mark said he was due to meet another contact—he didn't say who—who was going to tell him more about Richard Oliver. We were due to meet tonight, but... you know."

Her eyes looked fearful.

"I spoke to a few of the Persian elders here about gang warfare and how we were protected. They told me something had spread about a change of alliance but that they were negotiating with a contact to make the transition smooth. They said it wasn't something I should speak about with my mom. They said the community was divided over the change and my mom was one of the most senior members against it. They said the key to the change was my mom's agreement. I never thought it was that serious. But my mom's movements have become a little erratic. She has already sent my sisters to Iran to protect them until we get to the bottom of the killing; they just think Mom's worried about Leyli's death being deliberate and revenge coming our way. I stayed; she couldn't persuade me otherwise. And that's basically it, so..."

"No, it's not. There's something you're not telling me. I can tell from the tone of your voice that something is missing."

Her voice shook. "There's just one thing. My mom didn't approve of Hunter, I think in part because she didn't agree with a change of alliance. One of the elders said my mom could well be linked to this Richard Oliver guy and that she was playing politics so she'd get a more senior position in the community by being somehow 'persuaded' to join the new alliance. That latest information is what I wanted to tell Mark tonight, and I swear that's all I know."

It meant nothing to me. There could be thousands of Richard Olivers and, for all I knew, it could've been nickname. Then again, that could be useful—if it was a name known on the streets, it could lead me somewhere. And I knew one person who could give me some direction on that. Sutton. This would be a good excuse to catch up, and I'd have something to share with him, which should help me gain a bit more of his trust. I needed as many allies as I could get.

There used to be a time when House business was so secret people literally didn't know they existed. Now people knew about patronages and even about the New Breed. I couldn't wrap my head around how the word was spreading so easily.

I looked at Kimia. She was watching me nervously.

"Look," I said. "It's going to be okay. I said I'd protect you, and I will. But you need to listen to me carefully."

She nodded.

"First, you'll be escorted to your house where you'll pick up your passport, a few changes of clothes, and nothing else. You and Jessica are going to Paris tonight. You'll be staying in the Vendome area for the next couple of weeks; it's controlled by Russell's French cousin. I've arranged a special ferry for you. You are not to leave the Vendome vicinity without prior approval and must be escorted by the agents I assign you. You're not to tell your mom about our conversation. You have my number, and any new information that comes to you comes immediately and directly to me. I do not recommend you seek out any additional information on your own; if you do, you will be doing so without my protection. Are we clear?"

She hesitated. "If I listen to you word for word, will I live?"

"Yes," I lied.

There were no absolutes.

"Okay."

My phone rang. It was Mickey.

"You got a name and description?"

"I couldn't bloody believe it, mate, but with the information you gave me, I managed to narrow it down to literally three people out of hundreds."

"And they are?"

"A chap called Joseph Nicholas Silverstein. Wanted a dildo slapped on his face."

"Not him. Next."

"A Mr. Ahmed Odeh. Girls said he particularly enjoyed the filthiest salad—"

"Next."

"Um."

I heard him shuffling some papers on the other end. If the next name wasn't who I thought it was, I'd be straight back to where I started.

"Right, the last name is Richard Oliver."

My heart pounded. "What did he look like?"

"He was a weirdo. Had his face partially covered all the time with a thick scarf and hat. It's not uncommon for people of status to cover their faces here, and we don't normally question it. But he was into freaky stuff, like being spat at and watching the girl strip whilst cutting himself. Not straight cuts, though; looked like some kind of design. He did have a limp a few days ago. He talked about how much he loved London, that it's the greatest city in the world, things like that. He wore a black suit and black leather gloves. That's all my girl remembers. Hasn't come back since last Tuesday."

"That's fine, mate. Text me any more details she comes up with. I just need to check something. Can you stay on the line please?"

"Sure."

Fuck. So I was dealing with an utter lunatic. The supposed kingpin of the New Breed. Richard Oliver.

I took a sigh of relief. This motherfucker wasn't as careful as I thought he'd be. The game was about to change, and I was far behind him. I'd catch up, though.

I reached for my pocket and took out a small device with a single red button on it. Pressing it would activate one of two mobiles. The first mobile was in my dear friend Jason's hand; it shouldn't be too far from the rest of him. On activation, it would make a phone call to another mobile not too far away and connected to a whole heap of bombs and explosives. They'd tear the whole fucking flat apart.

I pressed the button and heard a loud explosion on the other end of the line.

"Fuck!" my Irish friend said.

"Cheers, pal. Have a good one. As I said, let me know of you hear anything else."

I hung up. Time to move.

I called Julian and arranged protection for Kimia and Jessica. He was happy to oblige, though clearly under stress from the situation with Russell's brother.

He told me, "Russell is preparing for carnage, but within reason."

Whatever that means.

A short time later, two bulletproof Lexus pulled up to the club, and the drivers asked for me at the door. I handed the girls to their chauffeurs: a Chinese guy call Xi and a Black man called Dwayne, each with a shaved head.

It was pouring outside. I put Kimia in the car, and she looked

217

at me worryingly.

"Don't worry," I tried to reassure her. "You'll be fine."

She kept her eyes steady on me. "Something terrible is about to happen, isn't it?"

I didn't want to lie again. I'd get caught in one eventually.

"Keep to Paris. Don't look back." I turned to the driver. "Xi, it's all you, mate. Get them out of here. Check in with me when you arrive."

The car disappeared into the distance.

There was no more avoiding it. I needed to have a chat. With fucking Inforno.

*

By the time I was back on Compton Street, it was nearly two-thirty in the morning. Tanka was standing right outside the shop having a fag.

"Calcain…"

"Not right now. It's been a shit few hours."

"I can tell. Your face is smashed up."

"I know pal, but I'm just not—"

"Jimmy left you a note." He took a drag from his cigarette. "It's on your front desk. Your girlfriend is probably asleep. I think she cooked you dinner, though."

"Fuck. I was hoping to nip down to Bar Italia for a toastie, to be honest."

"Her food is much nicer. Homemade. I feel like I'm being cuddled when I eat her food."

"You seem to be really chummy with her."

"If you're not careful, I might switch my gay button to *off* and steal her away. I've no trouble switching teams for a catch

218

like her."

"She's all yours, pal."

"You really wouldn't care? At all?"

"Nope. In my line of work, it's hard to give a shit. And I have a code. I don't fall for hookers."

"But she isn't one."

"You know how I met her?"

"Yes, I do. It was the first time ever she had tried it."

They must have been talking quite a bit in my absence.

"Right. Well, it's late, so I'm going to crash. You up for longer?"

"Nope. I'm closing at three, so there are just a handful of perverts left to cash out."

He smiled, and I saw genuine happiness; he really did enjoy serving the London perverts. Or maybe he enjoys being in the company of Jimmy and me, knowing full well not many people got the treatment he does; respect.

"Well, if anyone makes trouble, just wake me up," I said, trying to be nice.

"Thanks, Calcain. But I should be able to take care of myself. Now get some rest in the arms of a real gem. A true stunner who actually cares. A rarity in this part of town."

"Cheers, mate."

I went upstairs, and again, the table was full of food. Chicken with some form of potato and tomato side. A glass of Chardonnay next to the plate, and a can of Coke in a bucket of melting ice. She knew what I liked. Fucking Tanka. Or maybe I was the one who told her. I couldn't remember.

Before I could sit down, the roof started shaking. Someone was up there. Not to worry, I knew who it was.

I climbed out the window and onto the roof. There, standing

219

next to a burning trash can and holding a six-pack of beer, was Ian Chef in a three-piece suit. He was over six feet tall and heavily built.

"All right, mate?" he said in a slight Essex accent.

"Yeah, I'm good. Feel free to, you know, make yourself at home."

"Well, I heard you were roaming around a little, so I thought it'd be rude not to come by."

"Indeed."

"So what's the new gig, then?"

"Do you really want to know?"

"I don't think I give a shit. I'm a lawyer. Need to know basics. Fuck everything else."

"Agreed." I stood beside him at the fire. "You still with that chick?"

He handed me a beer and bottle opener, and we took long pulls from our drinks after saying a quick 'cheers'.

"Nah, she left me. Said she wanted someone a little bit more down to earth."

"Fuck it. Plenty more fish in the sea. She was a whale, anyway. You don't need all that."

"But I did everything I could to impress her. She said she didn't want to go out with boys any more and wanted a man. So I decided to act it out. I took her out a lot. We saw *Shrek* at the theatre. I enjoyed that. Then I took her to the Shochu lounge and spoilt her. Then she said she wanted a more down to earth character."

"Did you take her to Wagamama?"

"A borderline fast food restaurant for date? What sort of cunt would do that?"

"I would."

"And you're dating who these days?"

"Your mom."

"Good luck with that; she isn't easy to please."

We drank a bit more and moved on to matters more serious. Ian didn't know shit, but he told me the Creatures of the Night— my staff—were aware something was happening and were waiting for my word. A good detective always had a team on the street to gather information and jump into the fray when the time came. It was the Creatures I had with me during my run-in with Luke on Primrose Hill. We were outnumbered, but you can guess who won. Amongst the Creatures was also Vas who, with a Jamaican mother and an ambassador African father, was connected amongst both British and African communities. When I was banished, the Creatures separated, as they no longer had police protection. But now, it seemed, they were back.

"I don't know what exactly is going on, Ian, so tell them to stay vigilant. Tell them to tool up and prepare to leave London in an emergency. If I don't avert this disaster, they'd want to be as far away from here as possible."

"You think they'd leave you here in the middle of things on your own? Fuck that."

He was right. They wouldn't leave without me. So be it.

After a few more drinks, Ian left, and I went back to my flat.

I warmed up the food, then put on a cartoon sitcom on my phone to watch as I ate. I followed my meal with some milk and cookies, then cleaned the dishes and got ready for bed. I looked at Her poster in front of me and prayed I'd dream of her. I took a few headache tablets and lay down on my side of bed, with Shelly sleeping on the other.

"You're never home," she said in a broken voice.

"I have a job to do."

"I know. Do you need help?"

"No. Are you okay? Do you need anything?"

"No, I don't need anything."

I tried to nod off, but she turned and hugged me. She was wearing a soft teddy.

"I'm glad you're home safe," she said.

"Yeah, me too," I whispered, holding her.

Careful, Calcain.

Part III

Chapter 9

Somewhere, London

Years ago, Detective Mulligan was assigned a case he didn't want. It was his first 'fuck you' from Scotland Yard after they refused to prosecute a gangster called Charlie who was in charge of one of the major mob Houses in London. He was told to drop it. He refused. It left things a bit sour between Mulligan and his bosses.

Blood was splattered everywhere. Bits of body parts were strewn across the room. Maybe the needles were the worst part; Detective Mulligan hadn't dealt with that before. Or maybe the worst part was the fact that the victims were all children. They couldn't have been older than four or five.

The large basement in Hackney, East London, was a messy place. An old TV was still running. Milk cartons and used fags littered the floor. As did disassembled dead bodies with needles protruding from every eye in sight.

The second 'fuck you' from Scotland Yard was when he was put in charge of training juniors, which meant he had to sift through new officers at the bottom of the barrel to see if he could find someone useful. When he did, they were usually reassigned. The rest stayed by his side until they eventually left the force, which sometimes took fucking days, months, or even years. The

Great Detective, as he'd once aptly been nicknamed, was losing his patience.

"So, er, basically we're dealing with a paedo, aren't we, sir?" That was Chapman. He had an average figure and short, blond hair. He wore a tailored suit. Like a mini-Donald Trump. He'd been around for a while—clearly long enough to make such idiotic deductions.

The detective snapped, "For fuck's sake, Chapman, how fucking stupid—"

"Of all the stupid things I've heard." A distant voice drew nearer. "That has got to be one of the most retarded things I've heard you say, Chapman."

Chapman didn't take kindly to insults. "Well, we're not dealing with midgets here, pal. They're kids. Children and that."

The voice responded, sharp and authoritative, but young. "Chapman. Tell me. What does 'paedophilia' mean?"

"It's when you like little kiddies' bums. You get a kick out of it."

"Incorrect. It means 'lover of children'. There are paedophiles who live their whole lives without being inappropriate with a child."

Chapman rolled his eyes.

"It's true. That said, our line of work addresses the more fucked up side of things, most often by way of child rape, sexual assault, or molestation. Now tell me..."

The owner of the voice stepped out of the shadows and into the light. He was a young man. Around six feet tall, sharply dressed in a black suit and pink shirt, a black handkerchief around his neck. A long coat draped over the tailored suit.

"Do you see a lot of love in this room, Chapman?"

Chapman's eyes scanned the scene. The twit looked utterly

224

confused.

"Where is the evidence that these children were raped or sexually assaulted or molested?"

"I…"

"It would do you well to communicate with the forensic examiners on your cases moving forward, officer." The man's voice was low, almost threatening.

He continued walking towards Chapman. "Bruising on the bodies—what's left of them—seems to indicate only that the children were being held down. So far, there's no indication of anal or vaginal penetration. No evidence at this time that there was anything at all sexual about what happened in this room. No love here. Just malice."

He stopped in front of Chapman, clasping his hands in front of him. "So, please explain how you came up with paedophilia as being a suitable explanation for this crime. I'm just dying to know."

There was an air of charisma about the man. The way he looked. The way he acted. His every movement was calculated. He wasn't afraid or disgusted by what he saw in the room. He seemed to be soaking it in, shivering at times as he consumed the visual before him.

"Well…" Chapman struggled for an explanation. "If you think about it…"

He came up empty.

The young man started pacing the room in demonstration. "I'll tell you what happened here. Nothing. There's no equipment, no tools, no blood spatter, no smears, nothing. This isn't the crime scene. It's the body dump. Look over here." He pointed at a torso propped in the corner of the room. "The blood has gotten dark and congealed, more than the others, so it's likely one of the earlier kills. Note the clear knife wounds to the chest. But if we look around, we don't see that pattern throughout all the kills. It looks like he moved onto a scalpel at some point, maybe some form of a bread knife, then the cutting pattern disappears entirely."

Mulligan was curious. "Why is that?"

The young man looked at Mulligan sharply. Now eye to eye, the detective noticed the young man's eyes were much darker than he'd anticipated, and behind them burned an intense focus and inherent fury that made Mulligan consider taking a step back.

"Boredom," the man responded.

"Boredom?"

"Yes. Boredom. Even psychopaths get bored of doing the same thing over and over; it's human nature. But it's safe to say there's one thing this guy's not bored of."

Chapman piped up, "The eye thing?"

The young man hit him with a sarcastic grimace. "Yes, Chapman. *The eye thing.* Sticking the eyes with pins is very gruesome and very specific to this one individual." The young man closed his eyes and shivered slightly and quickly before opening them again. "I think we are dealing with a performance here. Something the killer did to appease a crowd. Not a cult; I've yet to see any indication that these were ritualistic killings. I think this man is a literal performance artist, and to show the crowd he means business, that his art is real, he starts with the needles-in-the-eyes thing. He disposed of the kids here because this place fucking reeks like embalming fluid year-round due to the attached funeral parlour upstairs."

The young man began to lose his patience, and his voice gradually got angrier. "He's just a pretentious fucking cunt who probably wears some special robe and bows to some form of fucked up applause that increases in volume as he reveals a child. Like a fucking magician." The young man's anger reached a boiling point. "He then takes two pins, shows them to the crowd with a flourish, then holds the child down and inserts the needles. Twisted fuck. The kids are probably homeless or from unstable homes, possibly immigrants or minorities. Kids he doesn't think will be missed. Kids who mean nothing to him."

His eyes were crazed, tracing invisible patterns on the floor. His voice was low.

"I'll get him for this. I'll track down every participant. I'll tear each of them apart one by one," he seethed, breathing heavy before shaking his head, as if coming to.

He composed himself and looked at Mulligan. "Well, I think I've learned everything I need to here. I'm going to do some field work and make a few queries."

Without permission or a request to be excused, the young man left. With his departure, detective Mulligan felt charisma and intellect leave the room. But there was also something dark and uncontrollable about that young man. He was angry. Maybe even psychopathic. He demonstrated a certain level of patience only an obsessed killer would have at his disposal. He stayed on the scene until he consumed all the information, made a plan, then moved on to the next phase.

The detective was impressed.

"Tell me, Chapman. Who is that young man?"

"Calcain, sir. Detective Calcain. He's new."

As the detective was about to make a few notes, his notepad suddenly melted in his hands. In a panic, he looked at Chapman and saw his eyes falling slowly down his face.

"You all right, sir?" Chapman gurgled as his face dissolved.

The room began to spin and fall apart. Detective Mulligan

tried to step forward, but his shoe was firmly stuck to the floor. His lips were stitched together. He couldn't scream.

Then everything got dark. Very dark. And then it was pitch black. And then it was silent.

Detective Mulligan suddenly came to. He was sweating, but he couldn't wipe his face; his hands were tied above his head. His feet were chained to the floor.

He could tell he was inside, but he didn't know where. It was damp.

He was blindfolded, and his entire body was in pain. Maybe he'd been tortured.

"Ah," a nearby voice said. "So you awoke after all. Well done. We've been worried about you. I'm glad you're okay. We didn't want you dead, now did we?"

Mulligan's ears felt full, and he couldn't hear properly. Footsteps approached the detective, and in a sudden, sharp movement, his blindfold was removed.

It was blurry at first, but his vision slowly cleared to reveal a smile. A dangerous smile. From a familiar face.

He thought first of Calcain. *What have you done? What have you done to deserve this?*

"I guess your first reaction is surprise. But even an idiot like you should be able to put all the pieces together now," the person said. "The reason you're here is to tell me, well, everything you know. You've been here quite some time. Heavily drugged, of course. Now, I'm a patient man, but my supervisor over here isn't."

The person pointed to another very familiar face.

Mulligan was gobsmacked. Caught off guard. Betrayed.

His feelings evolved quickly. Fury to anger. Anger to outrage. Outrage to sadness. Sadness to fear. Fear to panic. And now, finally, panic to calm.

Calcain was in danger. That much was clear. The detective couldn't do anything about it, but of all the people in the world he'd ever met, Calcain could handle himself best. He'd probably have fun doing it.

The detective smiled. He broke his silence with a hoarse voice.

"Do your worst, you fucking cowards. I'm not saying shit."

Detective Mulligan had seen some pretty horrendous cases over the course of his career. He'd dealt with turf war murders, retaliations and, worst of all, gangland punishments.

But no one punished like Calcain did. He didn't bring hate. He brought horror.

After all, McLafferty, the child killer with the needles, was tortured for a month before he was found, skinned alive, barely clinging to life to answer to his charges.

The people before Mulligan now would likely try to kill him, but in spite of the pain that awaited him and despite his myriad disagreements with Calcain—despite Elsie and despite his banishment—Calcain would come for him. And unspeakable horrors would await his captors.

Then a third person walked in. Someone who would have been kind to Calcain.

The detective would do his best to get word to Calcain, to send messages or signs or signals. He hoped Calcain would be able to read them.

Mulligan started plotting, but before he could form a coherent thought, the world went dark again.

Chapter 10

Moorgate, Westminster and Chiswick, London

It was time to make my move on Inforno, but first, I was meeting Sutton in Moorgate at Thirty Finsbury Circus. Finsbury Circus was a very strange place. Four nine-floor buildings enclosed the Circus, and they each looked like Victorian mansions. Inside the Circus, however, things were extraordinarily high tech. Close to Old Street, Bank, and Liverpool Street, Moorgate was a great place to work and have an active social life. Really, anywhere in the City was good for those things. But Moorgate was the best.

There was a wonderful little park in the middle of the Circus with huge trees. It was a good place to wait for people in the summer, but not so great in the winter when wet snow was pissing down.

I walked up the small steps, which led to the main door at number thirty. The doors were old on the outside, but inside, I was greeted by two sets of automatic doors before reaching a shiny, high tech reception desk. Behind it sat a young brunette.

"I'm here to see Mr. Sutton"

"Your name, please?"

"Calcain. He's expecting me."

"Of course, just bear with me one moment, please."

She picked up her phone and told the person on the other end of the line I'd arrived, then asked me to have a seat on one of the sofas until Sutton came down.

The usual 'Can I take your coat?' and 'Would you like a coffee?' was offered, but I refused.

A short while later, I heard footsteps approaching before Sutton appeared wearing a three-piece, striped suit. He was carrying two lever arch folders.

"Calcain, old boy. How are you?" He sounded cheery, like he was trying to break the ice, though it had already been broken.

"Not too bad. Thank you for seeing me on such short notice."

"My pleasure. Shall we go to a meeting room or would you rather go for coffee?"

I contemplated the venue options and didn't see much of a difference. "How's the in-house coffee?"

"The best you can possibly get in any City office."

"High praise. If there's a secure meeting room here, I would be agreeable to stay."

"Right you are. Nicola, is the Southwark meeting room free?"

The receptionist typed on her keyboard. "Yes, sir. Should I book it in for an hour?"

"Yes, please."

We walked across the corridor to the left and entered a twelve-seat meeting room surrounded by glass and windows which overlooked the Circus.

As I sat down, Sutton poured me some coffee, and I took a few chocolate chip cookies from the table. The coffee was great, as promised. So were the cookies.

"So, what brings you down here on such a lovely Saturday?" Sutton said, sitting down and opening his files.

"I was attacked. On Friday."

His expression changed. "Oh, dear. Are you all right?"

"I'm fine. Thank you. It comes with the job."

"I can get my personal doctors to look at you, if you want."

"No, I'm absolutely fine. I'm used to such treatment. But some things aren't quite fitting together for me. I've been thinking over the evidence, and I'm not finding an immediate pattern or connection. I'm beginning to think I've missed something."

"Well, why don't we try and put out heads together and make some sense of it all. What do you have so far?"

Perfect. I needed information.

"Well, my strongest clue is a name. Richard Oliver."

Sutton rubbed his chin. "A rather daft name, don't you think? Could be a first and second name, but with no surname perhaps? Or could it be an inversed name, with the real name being Oliver Richard? Could go either way."

"I think it's more likely a code, but I can't deduce what that code might be. Regardless, someone has claimed the name as their own, but I'm sure they're not called that. It would be far too risky to use your real name."

"I'll look into it, but in all my knowledge of the Houses and gangs, I've never come across this name before. Ever. This could be connected to that, uh, oh, what's it called?"

"New Breed?"

"Yes, the New Breed. I agree it would be highly unlikely that someone who has attacked the Houses, or so we think, would use their real name. But then again," Sutton said and moved closer to the edge of his chair smiling, reeking of intelligent thought, "think of it this way, young Calcain: What if this person is in fact using their real name, and it's just that they are not well known yet? Everything—and I do mean everything—this person has done thus far has been blatant. So, why not use their real name?"

232

"Indeed."

I thought for a while. Sutton's mind was highly intellectual and could be put to good use.

"What do you know about the New Breed?"

"Well." He leaned back in his seat. "It's hard to filter through all the nonsense. I hear all sorts of stuff, but most I can't take seriously. What I *am* confident about is that there is some form of organised resistance to the Houses. But whether they would be capable of an attack of this scale is hard to say. I doubt it. The odd thing about this whole scenario is how long it's taking the Houses to find the killer. They have immeasurable resources and contacts, and still nothing? Then again, you could be considered their lead detective, so maybe they're relying on you to figure things out."

It told me nothing, and that was the problem with the New Breed. There was virtually no information on them.

"Look," he continued. "If there is one person who could help, it would be—"

"Oh, dear."

"Inforno."

Shit. Even bloody Sutton was telling me to speak with him.

"Why do you have a problem with Inforno?"

"He's an annoying, pretentious, self-satisfied moron. I despise him. To speak with him is to ask help from a rival at work or in love. Our relationship is complex, though one thing we can both agree on is our mutual hatred of one another."

"Indeed, it is mutual. As I've been told, he says similar things about you. I've never spoken to him since Ra'ef is my point of contact, but he may be worth a try."

"He just makes good guesses. He has no information. He's a Ra'ef wannabe. I don't even know why people consider him one

233

of the leading authorities on information in London."

"Surely he has earned his reputation by now?"

"As I said, he just makes very good guesses."

"Well, perhaps a good guess is all we need right now."

He had a point. Being directed, in whatever direction, is useful.

"Speak to Inforno, Calcain, and then let me know what you find out. It may be that what he knows can be added to some of the junk I have at my end and a pattern can start to form."

"Certainly." I stood from the table. "Thank you for your time."

"Any time. You're okay otherwise, yes? Any ill health? Financial problems? Please do tell me; I would be happy to help however I can."

He was a very nice guy at the end of the day.

"No, sir. I don't work for free, so I've got it covered. But thank you."

"Not at all. But working free is no bad thing."

"I suppose skills gained are sometimes worth more than any immediate financial reward might be."

"Right you are. You do look a little discoloured, though. I can send you my personal doctor—"

"Thanks very much, but that won't be necessary."

He showed me to the door, and we parted ways.

I had exhausted all my options. There was only one way forward.

*

Old Compton Street, Soho, London

I walked straight back to my flat, chatted with Shelly, and

had a little something to eat. I was feeling more natural with her. We were each doing our own thing, but I was starting to get used to the idea of having decent food at home when I got back and to the place being generally clean. I warned myself, again, not to get too comfortable.

I braced myself. Time to see Inforno. I had a few clues, and he just needed to give me a good enough guess. That was all I needed from him. I'd take it from there.

I said goodbye to Shelly, went downstairs, and took a left.

I rang the very first bell to the left of Tanka's shop, Electrical AZ Hardware, an electrical goods/sex book shop. The flat next to mine.

A clear-cut North London accent responded through the metal box beside the front door.

"Oh, hello?"

"Paul, it's Calcain."

He hung up.

I rang again.

"Oh, hello?"

"Paul, it's—"

He hung up.

I rang yet again.

"Oh, hello?"

"For fuck's sake, Paul, it—"

He hung up. Again.

I knew what he was up to. I had to entertain him. So fucking be it.

I rang again.

"Oh, hello?"

"Er, Inforno. It's Calcain."

"Oh, yes. Calcain. The fuckhead druggie wannabe dick-

235

tective. I suppose it's true that once you've had enough private dicks up your bum hole, you'll become one yourself. How can I assist you?"

"Listen, cunt—"

He hung up.

I was getting agitated.

I rang again.

"Oh, hello?"

"Inforno."

"That's my name, don't wear it out."

"Why did you hang up this time?"

"You know I don't like the 'c' word, my lovely. Now, what is it I can assist with?"

"I need some information."

"My name is Inforno. My job is information. You come to me for information. Everyone does. So I ask again—what is it I can assist with?"

"I'd rather say in person."

"No. Sorry."

He hung up.

I rang again.

"Oh, hello?"

"Inforno, we need to talk in person. If you don't let me in, I will break in then beat what I want out of you."

"Oh, really? And what makes you think I'm actually in? If I recall correctly, last time this happened, you broke in only to realise the bell outside this door was linked to another property halfway across London, where I was talking to you from a phone connected to this speaker. Which gave me enough time to call the police. Before that Mulligan bailed you out."

There was a fire alarm going off in the sex shop across the

street. It was echoing in his speaker, so the motherfucker was either in or very close by.

"Listen, Inforno. I just want a chat. I'm backed by the police and Russell. If you want to answer to them—"

He hung up.

I rang again.

"Oh, hello?"

"Listen, you motherfucking dick. I need to have a chat whether you like it or not. You hang up again, and I will break this door on your fucking head."

"I don't like threats."

"Fuck you, you cunt—"

He hung up.

I smashed the door.

I ran upstairs at top speed; all he needed was a few seconds to disappear. I arrived at a flat fundamentally the same as mine, except with a thousand more computers, screens, and wires installed.

Inforno was a relatively well-built guy for a computer geek, just short of six feet tall with dark hair and blue eyes. He wore a tight black T-shirt complemented by dark jeans. He was in his early thirties, and his biggest sense of pride came from being ranked the third best *Warcraft* player in the world. And being the second source of information after Ra'ef. And being a cunt.

I rushed towards him, and when I was within an inch of getting my hands on him, he pulled a level and suddenly, I was flying.

Actually flying.

Downwards.

Falling.

To the shop below.

Trap fucking door.

I crashed through the counter table and blacked out.

Moments later, I woke up surrounded by dildos of all shapes, sizes, and colours. All of me hurt. My back hurt a little more than the rest. I think the vagina sofa nearby broke my fall, but I must have bounced off it and straight onto the anal beads.

I got up and brushed the glass from my shirt. I looked up and was surprised to see Inforno looking down at me from the hole in his floor.

He looked pleased with himself.

In the blink of an eye, he reached for something on a nearby table, then he poured a black liquid all over me.

It was hot. Not boiling. But hot.

I tried to move out of the splash zone, but I tripped over my own feet. Whatever the liquid was, it was slippery. I could hear the son of a whore running down the stairs and out the door. I wanted to follow him, but the room was spinning.

I collapsed again.

Get the fuck up, Calcain.

I got to my feet and stumbled out the door, past visitors with shocked faces and a totally relaxed shopkeeper; he was probably used to the trap door trick by now.

Every time I breathed, I felt sick.

I made it to a convenience store near the shop and took few bottles of water. I didn't bother paying for them. I ran outside and poured the water all over me, and it froze the black liquid instantly. Within a few seconds, I was stiff as a statue, totally unable to move. Tourists walking past threw coins on the ground in front of me, confusing me for a street performer.

Inforno had made a twat out of me.

I fucking hated him.

As luck would have it, Tanka came running my way, though it was more of a fast hopping; even his running was camp.

"Calcain, what happened to you?"

"Oh, nothing. Nothing at all. Just decided to make my cash performing for the masses in the streets, you know. What the *fuck do you think happened?*"

I screamed the last bit. I was pissed. Every second that passed, Inforno got farther away from me, and I wanted to demolish him right then and there.

"Okay, honey. What do I do?"

"I don't know. Whatever this shit is, water makes it seize up."

Tanka touched stuff on my body. He thought a while.

"Tanka?"

"I'm thinking, babe."

"What the fuck are you thinking about? I need you to break this off me right now."

"No. You don't want that, honey."

"I'm pretty sure I fucking do."

"No. You don't, because this is an oriental industrial glue. Whoever poured it on you probably got it from Chinatown. You try to break it off, it will take your flesh with it."

"So how the fuck do I get it off?"

"I'll be right back."

He returned a few minutes later with a kettle.

"Tanka, what the hell?"

"It's the only way, Calcain. We need to make the liquid, well, liquid again. Now get ready."

"Tanka, no. If you fucking—"

"Honey, it's not boiling; that would burn you. It's just really, really hot, and it will really, really hurt."

"Tanka, you fucking Jappo—"

Before I could finish, he poured it on me. It felt like a hundred needles penetrating my skin and injecting acid underneath it.

It.

Fucking.

Hurt.

But I slowly got my movement back. The black liquid began to drain off me. Not all of it. But enough for me to move.

"Now, soldier," Tanka said, looking at me more seriously than I'd ever seen him. "Let's go get the fucker who did this to you."

I didn't understand why, but his order had some charisma to it. I wanted to hurt him for the hot water but couldn't. Maybe because it was the first time I'd seen Tanka on the offensive.

I wanted him to join me in hunting down Inforno, but he was the boyfriend of Soho's most powerful lord; I don't really want or need him to get hurt.

"I'll go," I said. "I don't want you to risk—"

"Shut up, and let's go."

As I walked, I could feel my movements becoming more fluid until I could eventually break into a run. The only question was where the fuck Inforno ran to.

Tanka spoke Japanese with the owner of the shop beneath Inforno's office. The owner, fearing Tanka's status, didn't hesitate to tell us that he saw Inforno run towards Euston.

I shook my head. "I need to go upstairs, Tanka. This fucker is chatting shit. He has no idea where Inforno is. He just wants to please you."

If you're in this job long enough, you pick up on these things. People can be so afraid of you, of being tortured for information they don't have, they'll give up false facts just to be left alone.

I ran upstairs, but as soon as I reached his flat, I slowed down. I wasn't planning on falling down any more shit today. It hurt falling down. It fucking hurt.

I looked around the flat and saw something equivalent to a server room. There were literally hundreds of different computers, servers, cables, monitors, keyboards, handheld devices, and general IT stuff scattered all across the flat. Some screens were just flashing different colours or static whilst others were showing cartoons, interactive maps of London, Bloomberg News, BBC News, foreign news outlets, and a couple of films.

I navigated my way to what had to be his main computer desk and could see that he'd hacked into the Scotland Yard intranet. The in-house server.

I look at the name Inforno had typed into the search field of the Scotland Yard database: 'Richard Oliver'.

There were eleven thousand five hundred and sixty-two results. I clicked on the one result listed under 'possible associations', and only a small paragraph showed up:

'Richard Oliver' is either a person, a nickname, or a name of a newly formed criminal organisation that has been operating in London for around two and a half years. They are engaged in anti-mob vigilante actions, though they are mostly peaceful. Suspected vandalism at their hands ranges from defacing cars to breaking windows. They are not a threat. It is unknown whether their leader is or goes by the name of 'Richard Oliver'. The group has shown a worrying level of sophistication and organisation. No members have been caught or identified. The name 'Richard Oliver' was brought to our attention strictly through word of mouth.

Caution urged when suspecting or approaching this person/group. This matter is linked to HOUSES project.

And the most fucked up part:

If you have obtained any information on the above or need further clarification, please contact DCI Mulligan ex.1865.

Mulligan had lied to me. He knew more. Un-fucking-believable.

I turned Inforno's server room upside down, rummaged through every drawer and every file, and found nothing of substance. In spite of all the hardware, most of his stuff was saved to some form of secure online Cloud system, making it impossible for me to access anything he knew. I was incredibly fucking annoyed. First Mulligan. Now this. Only two people knew about Richard Oliver; one of them was missing, and the other had just escaped my clutches.

I needed to figure out my next move, but my mind was racing too fast for me to come up with a plan. I was drawing a complete blank. I needed to calm the fuck down. And I only knew one way to make that happen.

Enter Dark Fire.

*

I came to.

It was deep into the night, and I didn't know any more then than I did that morning. I was still in Inforno's room, sitting alone with a bottle of dark rum. I couldn't remember anything from the last few hours.

Not a thing.

I blinked, and when I opened my eyes, it was close to two thirty a.m. I couldn't remember shit. I was nowhere near solving

242

Justin's murder, to identifying Richard Oliver, to sniffing out the New Breed, to figuring out how Hunter fit into the puzzle of the Houses. In the heat of annoyance and anger, I put my hands on my face. I felt defeated. I'd never been so slow in getting a case moving. Never.

It was three forty-five a.m. In the darkness and the peak of my depression, I woke up to Her singing 'Bloody Mary' in my ear.

I didn't recall putting it on.

Dum dum da da da / I won't cry for you / I won't crucify the things you do…

I punched the ground and watched the dust fly, and from the dust, She appeared before me, like a genie out of a lamp.

"What's wrong, champ?" She said, Her voice alluring and majestic.

"I'm lost again. After everything and all the time I've spent, I've only got two words. A name. It could mean everything. But I'm lost."

"Since when has it been about the conclusion? It's always been about the chase with you. The journey. The conclusion is just a short, pleasant, proud time before the next challenge. Enjoy the chase while it lasts because, let's face it, it's only a matter of time before you crack this thing."

I smiled.

"You came up with a simple and brilliant plan to catch him. From this point onwards, things are going to change. Just believe in yourself."

"What plan?"

She smiled. "Now that would be telling."

A plan. I had a plan. And suddenly, as though I was struck by lightning, I remembered. I'd spoken with a few people

243

throughout the night. That prick Inforno was coming back. He had something at his place that meant fuck all to me but everything to him. His grandmother's necklace. So cliché. I was waiting for him to come back. Tanka had hacked into his CCTV system and shut it down. He didn't know I was there.

I looked down at my lap. I was wearing my SKINS running trousers and shorts on top of them. I was wearing trainers. I was in my gym kit. I'd already planned for his arrival; I was going to chase him. To race him. I couldn't remember what was supposed to happen after that.

I knew him well enough to know that he was waiting. He'd probably been waiting a while, long enough to make sure no one was there. I bet he was planning on a quick snatch and grab, in and out, just like that. But that wasn't what was going to happen.

I heard him slowly coming up the stairs. The necklace was in my hands. I don't remember finding it, but it must have been Grandma's. He was about to make a stupid mistake to get it back. And I was about to make sure he paid for it.

He was close. I could hear each deliberate step he took. He opened the door, and I was waiting right behind it. We were in total darkness. He turned on a powerful torch and swung it around the room.

"Shit," he said. "Where the fuck is it?"

I crouched behind him.

"Fuck," he said. "It's going to take me hours to put this all back together."

He bent down to pick up a box, and I saw my opportunity.

I jumped with all my force and in a split second, he turned around and caught me in mid-air with a device that resembled a mobile phone.

Except it wasn't a phone.

It was a fucking Taser.

It knocked me on my ass.

"*You motherfucking moron!*" he screamed. "You think I wasn't expecting you or one of your cunts waiting here? I thought we had a fucking deal. You don't touch me, and I don't investigate shit about you, and yet... wait. Calcain?"

He turned the Taser off.

As I came to, I kicked the Taser out of his hand.

He tried to make a run for it, but I grabbed his leg. He tripped, and I punched him as hard and as quickly as my body— running on Dark Fire and Taser shocks—could allow, which wasn't much.

Eventually, he pushed me aside, but I had too much mental resolve to let him get away this time.

He ran out of the room, and I chased after him. At the base of the stairs, he was met by a roundhouse kick from Tanka and fell straight down. I jumped on him again, but I was still weak, and Tanka was small. Inforno managed to pry himself free and take off again, but we were right behind him.

I'd heard before that Inforno, like me, was a runner. And maybe that was true, but I could outlast him. I just needed to make sure I didn't lose sight of him. I needed motivation. I put my headphones on, and She started singing 'Boys Boys Boys'. And then 'Paper Gangsta'. God, I loved that song.

I ran after Inforno with everything I had, Tanka not far behind.

London at around four a.m. on a Sunday was a strange place. The survivors of the night were still out. Couples crying or arguing, as they'd likely been doing for hours. A few people were looking for cabs. Others were lingering and chatting. But in any event, the streets were empty, so we had free reign to run in the road. He and I both knew every single pothole, sharp corner, and trash can in this neighbourhood. So, it brought us to this—a race.

And it was literally anyone's game.

He had an advantage in that he could choose the track; he could jump, take sudden turns, and adapt to things right in front of him that I would have limited time to react to. So I had to remain focused. I followed him and listened to Her sing 'Retro, Dance, Freak'.

We ran out of Soho and then hit Leicester Square. He couldn't raise many alarms, as he was already wanted by the police. I took a quick look back to make sure Tanka was close by. He was.

I chased Inforno towards Trafalgar Square and almost ran around it before going through Whitehall towards the river.

My focus was clear.

My target was locked.

I would outlast him.

I would outrun him.

The race continued until we reached the borders of the Westminster station and Westminster Bridge. By that time, he'd ran several miles at fairly high speed and couldn't have much left in him. I knew that because I felt the same. He had two options. He could run in front of the Parliament and wait in front of the cops, which wouldn't be ideal in his circumstance. Or he could run across the bridge, then jump off it. With the level of energy we both had, swimming was out of the question. He could even drown. I could drown.

He chose the bridge.

The Thames moved as fast as lightning and roared like thunder. London's river was angry that night.

He jumped across the barrier and waited on the edge as I

approached him.

"Take one more step, and I will jump! You hear me? I will jump!"

"Now, now," I said, smiling and keeping my distance. "Let's not be silly. We were having such a lovely race. Why quit?"

He was panting. "What I want is in your hands. But what you want is in my head. If I die, you lose everything."

"The thing is, you don't know shit about shit. That's your style. You take rumours, and you make really good guesses. That's it."

"Then why did you come to me? If I don't know anything, why did you come to me?"

Because I needed a good guess.

He continued, "See, you think you know everything, don't you? Well, guess what, dickhead. You don't know any fucking more than anyone else. The answer is right in fucking front of you." He looked at me, wide-eyed, like he was waiting for me to understand. "Don't you get it? The Third House?"

I didn't know what he was getting at. I kept silent and let him ramble on.

"You still don't see it?" he said in a state of shock. He laughed. "Think about it for second, mate. Think about what you know, and look at what's in front of you. Look at it."

Was he being literal? I searched his body for tattoos or markings or some other visual cue and saw nothing.

"Look, give me my grandmother's necklace. Keep your distance, and I'll tell you what you need to know."

I reached for the necklace in my right pocket, but it wasn't there. I must have lost it at some point during the race. I pretended to hold it in my hand.

"Tell me what you know."

"Show me the necklace."

"Fuck you. Tell me what you know, or I'll throw it in the river."

He shook his head. "You're so fucking blind." He thought a while. "It's true there's a power shift happening. You're right on that bit. But it's not about the Houses or the gangs or any of it. Think, Calcain. Who stands to gain the most from the furore? The so-called 'New Breed'? If they were another gang coming up, they'd have been dealt with by now. So why is it that they haven't been, huh? Look at what's been happening. Elite House targets are being taken out. A war is on the brink of eruption."

"Okay, and?"

He levelled me with a stare. "And there's an architect."

"An architect. Who?"

"Where's my grandmother's necklace?"

"Not until—"

"No." He raised his voice. "Where is my grandmother's necklace?"

"I lost it. I thought it was it my pocket, but it wasn't, and I'm sorry for that. But I can protect you if you just tell me what you know."

He shook his head, tears welling. "I've already told you so much. I'm fucked. You may not get it now. But you will later."

"You know more. I know you do."

"I'm not the architect, Calcain."

"Then who is?"

He sniffed. "It's Luke. Your old nemesis. Gayest fucking rivalry ever. You're so up each other's asses with praise and love. Ask him what he hasn't told you. Because if I say anything else, they may kill my grandma. You need to figure the rest out yourself. But I can't face her without her necklace. She gave that to me and said that, if I ever sold it, I would have reached the lowest of the low. I would only let her down if I sold it. I have done some fucked up things, terrible things, but I didn't ever sell it. Every time I see her, she checks to make sure I still have it. She'll never believe a fucker like you stole it. You ruined everything."

"Look, Paul, I promise I can help you find your grandma's necklace and protect you—"

He screamed, "*You don't call me Paul! Only my grandma calls me Paul! My name is Inforno!*"

And then he jumped.

And I followed.

At that stage, I didn't care if I died. I just wanted whatever was in Inforno's head.

So I fell down deep into London's angry mother and felt her cold, shivering heart. And then there was darkness.

*

The Thames was cold. It was very fucking cold.

But I made it to shore. Everything was a bit blurry, and I must have been fucking far from where I first jumped in.

I'd had Inforno in sight for a while. I tried to reach him, but the tide took him away. He was lost. The Thames, though, spared me. It wasn't the first time it had happened. Hopefully, it wouldn't be the last.

I slowly got up, and my entire body hurt. I had a terrible headache.

I saw a few teens staring at me, and I asked them the essentials.

"What time is it?"

A curly-headed boy responded, "Two in the afternoon, sir."

"What day is it?"

"Sunday, sir."

"Right. Where the hell am I?"

"Chiswick, sir."

"Thanks. Hey, stay in school and don't do drugs. Drink milk."

"What, so we could end up like you?"

"No. So you don't end up like me."

"Okay. Will do, sir."

I needed to get home. Fast. I got in a black cab and headed straight back to Soho. I called up Sutton along the way and told him everything. He was amused by it all and said I needed to think more about what Inforno meant when he said the answer was 'right in front of me'.

Sutton paused. "What does he know that you can't see?"

Chapter 11

The Tate Modern and the Lime House, London

The papers were running wild with stories about an explosion on Old Street. It wasn't so much the explosion that drew their attention but the fact that the remains found appeared to have already been separated prior to the explosion. Separated and arranged into alphabetical order. And nailed to the walls.

I called it a work of art.

They called it the work of a psychopath.

In any event, the person who wanted to kill me in that room in Old Street had no doubt gotten the message.

Don't fuck with me.

A lesson I had sincerely hoped my dear friend and one-time nemesis, Luke Wellington-Mansell, would have known about.

It had been almost a week since I'd learned of his betrayal of the Houses. I'd been looking for him ever since, only to learn he was abroad and coming back that day at three in the afternoon. There was an exhibition in the Tate Modern he'd be attending at six in the afternoon.

I'd be waiting for him there.

During the week, I helped Sutton as he was struggling to persuade the government to take decisive action in relation to the open war due to explode shortly. The government didn't care. They would rather see the gangs tear each other apart. They said they had bigger things to worry about.

The streets were getting more dangerous, and a lot more people were dying than deaths being reported. Missing persons reports were on the rise.

Word had spread.

Charlie and Russell were about to go to war.

I spent almost every day at Sutton's office, working with him to persuade the government to at least protect some areas, but they were staying firm in their position. They wanted to see the criminal underworld bring itself to an end; they didn't see the damage they'd have to deal with in the long run.

Since working with Sutton, I learned that what kept the Houses at peace for so long was the Shard of Glass. A simple deal of peace around the skyscraper. The crucial deal that Hunter had been caught in the middle of. The reason people thought he'd been killed.

For that reason alone, Luke had a lot to answer for. That his name was mentioned, even as a guess by a desperate Inforno, was enough for me to take action.

Luke could be very dangerous if he wanted to be. But why would he betray his uncle? I waited outside in the cold London weather, beneath the Tate, to find out.

I watched Luke arrive, browse and eventually catch my eye.

He could tell.

I knew.

He approached me and kept his voice low. "The old liquor bottling plant. Lime House. See you there in four hours."

I smiled. "Sure thing, mate."

I left him to his exhibition.

*

I waited for Luke to arrive. I was prepared. I brought all my tools. I trusted he'd bring his.

I was standing in a typical abandoned factory, with lots of open space, a high ceiling, and random liquids splashing down from cracks in the roof, echoing around me. I put on my music. I closed my eyes.

In my ear, She sang for me.

Rub that glitter and grease around / Rub that glitter grease around / Rub that glitter and grease around / Grease around…

I was in my own private concert. I watched her dance. She walked around a watermelon-coloured car on stage, with a piano where the engine should be.

Then I sensed him.

I breathed in his Tom Ford cologne, which he only wore on special occasions.

To a normal ear, each step he took would be almost inaudible. To my ear, they rocked the factory's very foundation.

I nodded my head to the beat. I kept my eyes closed. She sang on.

So I rub that glitter grease around…

I took a deep breath. I could feel him in front of me—about ten yards away.

Slowly, I opened my eyes.

Long, dark coat. A scarf around his neck, which reached down to his wrists. Black shirt. Skinny trousers. Low-heeled boots. Standing there with legs shoulder-width apart. Fists closed.

He was ready for war.

The music ended, and I paused on the next track.

"Well, here we are," Luke said gently.

"Indeed." I took deep breath and continued. "Why, Luke? Just tell me why."

"If you haven't figured it out already, then perhaps try and…" He paused. "Deduce it."

"I can't. If I could, I wouldn't have needed Inforno to help me."

"Inforno figured it out, and you didn't?"

"Just tell me why, Luke."

"Well, for starters, I enjoyed a very privileged position as the guy who would be the least likely suspect due to my general indifference to the criminal underworld and, of course, my relation to my uncle. But did you stop to think that maybe I just hated how things were run? How terrible the streets of London have become? That House approval is needed for all major events? The thing that annoyed me the most is that the public is totally oblivious to the Houses and their influence. And the people who knew how things were being controlled—people like you, people who hate the Houses—have done nothing. You stand around and talk about it, but you're too scared of the Houses to put into action any plans you come up with. You're petrified. If Mulligan didn't stop you, believe me, you would have stopped yourself. At the end of the day, those who claim to love London don't do anything to save her. So I had to step in. The government chosen by the people should run the streets, Calcain, not some House leader who is a glorified thug."

"I would have ended—"

"Really? You? You would have ended them? Okay, how about this; you were banished, yes, but you weren't mutilated, were you? You still had your hands, your arms, your legs. Didn't you? Your mind worked just fine, didn't it? So why is it that, instead, you decided to be a freelance killer in your banishment?

Why not continue your mission? You act like you have a solution to everything. But you don't, do you? No. Instead of working towards an end for the Houses, you became an addict." He spat the word out. "I'll be honest, when Mulligan banished you, I was over the moon. I thought you were no longer restricted. Caged. You were a monster unleashed."

He looked deep into my eyes and with anger in his voice, he continued.

"For so many years I waited..." He hesitated. "For you, Calcain. To do something. Anything. But you did nothing. You didn't even call me, and Lord knows that if I had stepped a foot into Soho, Russell would have killed me.

"When Mulligan released you, I was hopeful. Excited that Calcain, the bane of Scotland Yard's existence, was unleashed yet again. The cunning. The monstrous streak. The madness. Even to date, I thought you killed Hunter to secure your release and therefore unleash your plans. But more and more, I think you had nothing to do with it at all."

It didn't matter that I knew Luke hadn't killed Hunter. He was the architect. He had information. So I had to play it cool.

"Are you saying you didn't do Hunter in?"

"Oh, do fuck off, Calcain, please."

"Then who did?"

He was getting irritated. "As I said, I thought you did it."

I paused. "Did you try to kill me, Luke?"

"You were beginning to get in the way, and I couldn't have that. Seems you managed to slip away."

"And the rest? The car bombing?"

"I wasn't responsible. You don't think I run this operation alone, did you? All I did was keep out of the way."

"Then?"

"Oh, please. What difference would it make for you to know all the details about the big, bad scheme? Surely you're aware I can't risk you remaining alive after this."

"And surely you realise that would mean killing me. Here. And now."

"Yes. And—"

"Wait."

His mouth twitched into a snarl, but he remained patient.

"Where's Mulligan?"

"Don't you worry about Mulligan."

"Where the fuck is he?"

"After everything he did—"

"I'm not going to ask again, you—"

"He's safe. Happy? You're not. But he is. And now you can die knowing that fact."

He had so much information, and I had almost none of it.

"You sure you don't want to tell me anything?"

"I'm sure. And you can't charm it out of me, Calcain. I only volunteered to come here to make sure you were... dealt with."

I shook my head. "You're a fucking puppet. You know that, don't you? An irrelevant pawn for someone bigger and far, far more important than you have ever been or apparently ever will be. I had high hopes for you, too, you know. You've let me down."

There was a long, uncomfortable pause. Luke broke it.

"Well, for better or for worse, we are where we are. Just like old times. So, Calcain—the Demon in the Long Coat—are you ready?"

"Just one minute."

I needed to take Dark Fire. I didn't want to have any recollection of what was about to happen. I'd write down what I learned in the moment and save the notes for future examination, but how I extracted that information from Luke and what happened afterwards would all be forgotten. I didn't want to remember any of it. I swallowed the drug down.

"Ready?" he asked.

"Yes. I'm ready."

I put my headphones on and played the track I had reserved specifically for this situation, a momentous encounter with someone I loved and hated in equal measure.

She screamed as 'Bad Romance' started to play.

Luke and I—both trained boxers—ran towards each other at the same time, and the fight began.

I threw the first punch straight to his gut, and he followed up with a ruthless hit straight to my hip. I ducked his next left, but he connected with the right, landing a fist in my stomach. The action left his face open to a clear right hook, which I gave him with all my power. I had a clear upper hand.

He made the tactical decision to try for a kick, taking our battle from a fistfight to something more barbaric. I obliged.

All the while, she was singing to me.

I want your love and all your lover's revenge / You and me could write a bad romance / oh-oh-oh-oh-oh-oh-oh-oh-oh-oh-oh-oh / Caught in a bad romance...

I hit him with a strong uppercut, then he did the same, and we both fell to the ground, spitting blood. With our backs against the concrete, we were separated by a longer distance than I thought. At least a few metres.

I heard Luke speaking to me through a bloody throat.

"I sometimes forget if I'm fighting the man or the monster."

"I sometimes forget, too."

"Ready for round two?"

"Hell fucking yes."

We both got up, but I was dizzier than I'd expected, like I was coming to from a concussion. Luke was stumbling around, too, and I figured he felt the same way.

"It doesn't need to end like this, Luke." I wanted to kill time trying to reason with him until I got my feet back." Just tell me where Mulligan is, and I'll let you go. Until next time, anyway."

"You'll kill me as soon as you find out."

"How do you know?"

"It's the kind of thing that makes you the monster you are. Frankly, I fucking love it, though I will say it's a bit less endearing when you're on the receiving end of things."

I smiled, and we both turned to each other to reengage. But suddenly, about eight people started running towards us holding baseball bats and knives. I'd been about to accuse Luke of an ambush, but his expression was just as surprised as mine. Maybe the Houses had found out about what he'd done. Maybe these men had been sent to kill him. But the Houses would've supplied its army with guns, so whoever these men belonged to didn't want to draw attention, regardless of how remote our location was.

I took a deep breath and stood shoulder to shoulder with Luke, both of us facing down the incoming assault. I managed to kick the first one I engaged in the face and take his bat. Using that, I stabilised a few others before being speared to the ground by a fifth person.

Then the ground underneath me began to shake, and I and three of the others crashed down to a lower floor. It was a good fifteen-foot fall, and I landed flat on my back. For a minute, no one moved. But I was fucking angry.

I took a carbo-gel I always kept in my pocket in case of

exhaustion, and I started to feel its effect almost immediately. I pushed myself as far as I possibly could and got to my feet. The newcomers were doing the same. They must have been paid well for my head.

Hits and kicks turned into pushes and shoves. I was feeling exhausted from my fight with Luke, but I needed to pick up the pace if I was going to survive . In fact, I needed to get fatal.

Three guys were coming back to consciousness on the floor. I grabbed the first one I could, put him in a headlock, and snapped his neck. The *crack* was louder than usual. I smiled.

"Right, boys," I said. "We can do this the easy way or the hard way. The easy way is death. Quick and simple. The hard way, though, is a bit more... how do I put this? It's a bit more exciting." I looked between the last two standing. "What do you say?"

The slightly larger of the two ran towards me, and I grabbed him by the neck. I squeezed and pulled as hard as I could. I felt something rip. I heard the gurgling sound I'd never tire of. He fell to the ground, and his friend looked at me, confused.

I smiled at him. Then I held up what remained of his friend's throat.

Petrified, he decided to make a run for it. That wouldn't do.

I ran and tackled him to the ground. I kneeled on his back, grabbed his face, and yanked it back from behind.

"Who sent you, sunshine?"

"Someone far more fucking dangerous than you. You might as well end it now."

I knew his type. He wouldn't tell me anything. No use fucking about.

Another loud crack.

I could hear the sound of struggle upstairs, but I couldn't tell who was winning. A loud, echoing gunshot sent shivers through me. Luke wasn't packing a gun, as far as I could tell, and neither was the gang who attacked us. But someone must have had one. I decided to let that distraction, whether Luke was killed or not, be my means of escape.

I looked around and located a wet tunnel at a far corner of the basement. Amongst all the filth, I could still smell fresh air wafting in from it. I entered the utter darkness, and after a few minutes of swimming in liquid filth, I made it out to the edge of the river.

I spotted three Land Rovers in front of the factory and Luke's Bugatti Veyron. The cars were empty, which seemed strange because you'd think a getaway driver would be necessary for a plan such as theirs. But they obviously hadn't come prepared.

I climbed into Luke's Bugatti and hacked his car's system with my phone. I was ready to drive off into the sunset. But there was a problem.

I'd left Luke behind. It was eating at me. If he was alive, he'd need me. And if not, they'd desecrate his corpse. I remembered Elsie's small, battered frame in the street. I'd set out to kill Luke, sure. But I couldn't bear the thought of what they'd do to his body. I could still help him. I could protect him from the Houses if he told me who was behind it all. I just needed answers, then I could keep him safe.

I put my headphones on again. She was still singing 'Bad Romance'.

I crept back into the factory, and She took it from the top.

Oh-oh-oh-oh-oh-oh-oh-oh-oh-oh-oh-oh / Caught in a bad romance…

The volume was so low, I could hear full well what was being said in front of me. Then a sight filled me with nothing but raw rage.

Luke was on his knees, bleeding from his lower left abdomen. His face was torn apart. He'd been savagely beaten and shot. But he was alive. His hands were being held up and out by a person on either side, whilst a third stood in front of him. They were all fairly big guys, dressed all in black, with leather coats. And they were all focused on Luke.

There were others on the floor, presumably dead. Quite a few. Luke still had it.

"Well, I've just looked down the little hole your mate just made," the one in front of him said, looking at Luke. "Unless me torch or me eyes have got it wrong, I'd say your little chum just done all me mates in. Now, that's not acceptable. Not at all. We can't have any of that."

"I care very little what you think or want. I know who sent you. Just end it," Luke said, confident and proud even as he looked death straight in the face.

"You know as well as I do that we can't really end this until you tell us what you told your little pal. You sure have screwed a lot of people over, and I can admire that. I can. But it seems you've finally double-crossed the wrong person."

"I'll make this clear—I didn't double-cross anyone. I never betrayed your employer. In fact, I have been fully supporting him this entire time. I helped him get to where he is. Why would I then ruin it?"

"Well, he fancies you a bit of a poofter. Says you may have a soft spot for our friend Calcain. Maybe you let something slip when you were sucking his willy."

"Fuck you."

The burly guy in front of him immediately smacked Luke in the face with the back of his gun. It infuriated me.

"Now listen here, you fucking cock-munching poof. What the fuck did you tell Calcain? What does he know? If he does anything to ruin my employer's plan, everyone you know and love will be done in. You hear that? I will personally tear them limb from limb. Understand?"

Luke spat up blood and probably a tooth or two.

"As I said, I didn't tell him anything. I can't. I swore on something you'd know nothing about."

I thought he might have been speaking to me on the sly.

"Tell your master that I met him here to settle an old score."

"Well, you won't be able to any more, I promise you that," the burly guy said, smiling. "But I guess we're going to have to find another way to get the truth out of you."

"You're wasting your time. Calcain knows all of this goes back to the government's resistance to act on pandemonium. He'd ask himself why it is that in spite of working so hard, the government won't heed advice."

He was definitely speaking to me.

"Why would the government let this war of the Houses happen? At some point, the prime minister would surely want to intervene, but why hasn't he? These are not hard questions. He knows this all goes back to Whitehall. He also knows it goes back to a more ancient war of the Houses."

"Well, don't you worry about that, sunshine. I'm not wasting my time. I'm going to enjoy what's about to happen."

It was time. I slowly got down and secured my shoelaces again. I'd need to sprint. If I made a single mistake, I'd die. If I was going to die, I'd die by Luke's side. If I was going die by Luke's side, I'd die listening to Her scream.

I put both headphones in and move to restart 'Bad Romance', but I heard Luke speak before I did.

"Don't."

"Then what did you tell him?" the burly guy asked.

"It's not worth it," Luke said, and the shake in his voice told me that, too, was for me.

You're wrong, Luke. To me, it's everything.

I blasted the song in my headphones.

I sprinted as fast as I could, and the two on either side of Luke clocked me instantly, letting him go.

The burly guy pointed his gun at me and shot. He missed, and I was close enough to tackle him and grab his weapon. The two remaining guys kept kicking me, unaware that I had the gun in my hand. I shot one of the thugs in the eye, and the other one made a run for it before I shot him in the back of the neck.

I got up at the same time as the burly guy. He was feeling the pain. I shot him in the gut. It wasn't enough to kill him, but it was enough to hurt him. I spotted a knife on the ground near me. I dropped the gun and picked it up.

I sat on top of him, pressing against the stomach wound whilst looking at him eye to eye. I needed to see his eyes clearly for what I was about to do to him.

"Who sent you?"

"Fuck you. He's—"

"I know, I know, he's far scarier than me. I get that. But once they find you—and what remains of them—he'll think twice about telling people he's scarier than me."

I looked at Luke on the ground. He was gulping and coughing, something between vomiting, crying and moaning in pain. He was bleeding heavily. His face was a mess. We were friends once. Nemeses now. But friends once.

I should've helped him, but I was seeing blood. I looked at the fuckface responsible.

"Do what you want, you fucking poofter. I'm not scared," he said.

I put my mouth close to his ear. "You should be scared. Because I'm about to sever your head from your body."

His eyes showed nothing less than terror. I never got tired of that look from people who deserved it.

It occurred to me that this was the same fucker who attacked me on Charlotte Street. Fucking fantastic. A reunion for the ages.

I had 'Bad Romance' on loop. I took out my headphones, and it was so loud I could still hear the song.

Walk, walk, fashion, baby / Work it, I'm a free bitch, baby...

I couldn't hear anything any more. I put my knife on his throat, and everything went dark. When I came to next, it was done.

I ran to Luke. I should have gone to him earlier, but my body was engulfed in fury.

"Calcain. My dear Calcain. You came back."

"Rest, Luke. I can save you. Just hold still. I'm calling an ambulance."

"The deed is done. I'm done."

"Stop being dramatic. You're not done yet. We still have a fight to finish."

"No, we don't. This is it. You fought well. I was so proud of you. You know, I've felt horrendous about my betrayal. But I did it because I wanted a change for the better. I love London as much as you. I couldn't stand what it was becoming. To that end, I've failed. I've turned it into something much worse. It will be in the hands of a guardian far more terrible than the leaders of the Houses. I wish so much that I'd had faith in you, that I'd aligned with you. Because I know deep down inside—very deep—you're a good man. I would kill the monster, Calcain. But not the man inside."

"Luke—"

"No, listen. Today you proved it. You did. The monster would have run away today. But the man... the man would have come back for me. And you did. Now, please. Save her. Save London." He coughed, and blood sprayed from his lips. "I'm so sorry."

"Luke, please. I've never begged anyone, but I'm begging now. Please..."

Then, in my arms, his head suddenly became heavier. The shimmer in his eyes began to fade. The once proud expression, even behind the blood on his face, dropped. There, in an abandoned factory in Limehouse, my dear friend and one-time nemesis, Luke Wellington-Mansell, died.

Holding him tightly in my arms, I whispered into his ear.

"I will punish them for you."

And then I wept. And I cried. And I screamed.

Luke was the only person who truly knew me, who truly understood me. He was my most intelligent enemy. With him dead, I was broken.

She still sang.

I want your love, and I want your revenge / You and me could write a bad romance / Oh-oh-oh-oh-oh-oh-oh-oh-oh-oh-oh-oh / Caught in a bad romance...

Deep in my sorrow, everything turned dark and black.

I was bad romance.

*

I came to. My face was on the ground. My eyes hurt. My back hurt. My entire body ached. I couldn't even move my neck. I

265

lifted my head slowly and looked around to find nine decapitated heads in the shape of a heart in front of me.

It was the same factory I was due to meet Luke in. I was obviously looking at some sort of aftermath. I couldn't recall anything that had happened, but I'd clearly won. Luke had lost. I could see his broken, bloodied body, but he was laid down like a prince. He could've been sleeping.

Please, please tell me I'm not responsible for this.

Slowly, things started coming back to me. Then my phone vibrated. 'Bad Romance' was still playing on my phone, and I'd written a lengthy note:

Luke was killed. Not by you. The beheaded thugs did it. He said nothing of substance aside from the word 'whitehall'. Another victim of Richard Oliver. Avenge him. Avenge London.

The note went on, but I'd read the rest later. I needed to hand Luke to Russell's family.

Whoever organised the ambush would eventually come to check the factory. They'd see what I left them.

The houses were already at war. Now I was at war with Richard Oliver. He couldn't take me out. He'd have to fight me.

A few members of Russell's House picked up Luke's body. They were sympathetic to me; they'd been briefed on our history, and they were genuinely sad. Luke was very well loved for his kindness.

"This war is taking so many casualties, 'tragic' is no longer a serious word here, is it, sir?" one of the House members said to me.

"No. This is Hell. The Hell we should try and avoid."

He nodded. "Do you need a lift?"

"No. I'll find a way home."

"We'll leave the rest in there. Seems like you're trying to

make a point."

"You're correct. Good night."

They drove off with Luke's remains, and I walked a long way to the nearest Boris Bike and cycled home.

*

By the time I got home, it was about three in the morning. Tanka stitched me up, and I showered off the remaining blood. Absolutely exhausted, I heated up the dinner Shelly had left out for me and ate it as I watched cartoon sitcoms. When I finished eating, I brushed my teeth, took some headache pills in readiness for what would come in the morning, and got in bed.

"You're late again, babe," Shelly mumbled.

"I know. I had to… I was delayed."

She pretended I was her husband. I pretended she was my wife. I slept deep and in comfort alongside her.

Chapter 12

Westminster and The Old Vic Tunnels, London

I woke up in absolute agony. My whole body hurt. My head hurt. My eyes hurt. My back really fucking hurt. I also felt shockingly hung over. I remembered drinking half a bottle of brandy with my dinner the night before. That must have done it.

I reached in my drawer and take some headache pills. The water went through me like acid, burning my mouth, my throat, my stomach. Everything. I felt sick having drunk it.

"Why oh why is it I find myself looking at you in the same manner pretty much every time I come to see you here?"

That voice. Jimmy. Fuck.

"Well," I said through the cactus in my throat, my voice going through it like raw meat in a grinder. "It's because I'm a night person. And you're catching me at… what time is it?"

"It's ten-fifteen."

"Right. I'm a night person, and you're catching me at ten-fifteen. What are you expecting, exactly?"

"Doesn't matter. It's time to get up. It's Saturday. The people are out and about. And you could really do with some fresh, cold London air." He grinned at me from across the room.

"Why are you so fucking cheery?"

"Why shouldn't I be?"

"You're usually such a miserable old cunt."

He laughed. "It's probably the fresh air that does it for me. Early November. It's really a lovely time. November is so rarely rated for its contribution to the seasons. Or maybe…" He paused. This is the real answer coming now. "Maybe it's because Russell has ordered everyone to assemble and prepare for war with Charlie. Maybe that's why I'm feeling good. Because to be frank, this will likely be my last full day."

Like falling into a pool of water riddled with loose, live electrical cables, the last twenty-four hours rushed through me and woke me up. I remembered everything. I was so fucking close to getting the answers I needed. I'd lost too much for it all to disappear now.

"No. You have to stop. I'm so close to—"

I tried to get up but blacked out and fell straight back in bed.

Jimmy looked at Shelly. "Give him some food, would you? He's feeling exhausted."

"I don't want any food," I said. "I'm full. I just want some time. Even just a few days."

"It's too late. He gave the order. Charlie has as well. We're going out tonight. Russell wants full control of Whitechapel by two in the morning. We'll probably get started at midnight."

"Jimmy, please. Speak to the lords of Soho, tell them—"

"Calcain. It's over. Word has it Charlie made a point of the war last night in Limehouse. I'm not sure how to break this to you, and Lord knows I felt like hell finding out, but…Luke's dead."

Violent image from the previous night rush over me.

"I know he's dead. I was there. And Charlie didn't do it."

"I'm sure that's what you think you saw and what Dark Fire has you convinced you saw, but it was Charlie's men who killed Luke. They then decapitated what appeared to be his entourage and placed their heads together in the shape of a heart for whatever fucked up reason."

"No, that…" I paused.

There was nothing else I could tell him. The people who attacked us only told me who they weren't; they didn't tell me who they were.

"Russell has lost faith in you, Calcain. He's heard reports of you running around, drinking, taking drugs, and getting into fights. You're nowhere closer to resolving this than you were at the beginning. With Luke dead, that's two innocent members of Russell's family."

"But—"

"The war is on. I just came to warn you. You should leave London. We won't be able to protect you any more. You're alone in all this now. Entirely. The Met has given up on Mulligan. They think he's probably dead, either because he knew too much or he was under so much pressure he decided to off himself."

"He wouldn't do that."

"Are you certain? *Really* certain?"

He didn't wait for a response and instead got up and went to the door. He seemed seriously disturbed.

"Fuck this!" I screamed. "Take my word, I will fucking stop this. And I'm not leaving London. Not until this shit is done."

He smiled. "I knew you'd say that. God bless you."

He closed the door and left.

Shelly looked stunned, and her voice was quiet. "Look—"

"Whatever you're about to say, I suggest you don't. This is far bigger than you think. And you don't know anything about it."

"I do, Calcain," she snapped. "I know all about stuff like this. I've lost people to this shit your kind seems obsessed with." She shook her head. "You're all just children with guns."

"*Look at me!*" I screamed. "You have no idea what I have been through in the last twenty-four hours, let alone the last few weeks. My body is broken. I've lost a very good friend and escaped death by the skin of my fucking teeth far too many times than you can guess. But seeing blood in my city would be worse than death to me."

"Oh, really? Calcain the Hero to the rescue? I've worked hard, too, to make sure you're okay. I've cooked for you and cleaned your dump of an apartment. And then you take that awful drug and can't even remember what I do for you. All these nights you've been shaking and sweating in your sleep, crying for help. Who do you think has been the one holding you? Who do you think tells you it's going to be okay? Who do you think has cried seeing you tear yourself apart in your dreams? Your mind may not be working when you're in that state, but your heart is, and the way you hold me at night tells me how much you love me. I know you do. I don't want you to remember the hell you go through when you're coming down off that shit. But I do want you to remember how much I love you."

That shut me up. In the past, I'd woken up from those dreams with the bed broken or with whores around me holding knives and looking petrified. But since Shelly came, I hadn't had that. I'd been told I was a monster in my I sleep. So why hasn't she run away? What must she have endured?

She continued, "I know this may sound insane to you, and you may never consider it. But come with me, Calcain. Come to the US. We can both start fresh."

Her face was eager and earnest. She meant it.

"I don't know what you've been through. But it must have been hell. That said, I can't leave London. You don't understand what happens when the Houses go to war. They destroy everything. Everything. Including innocent people. As long as I believe I can stop this, I can't leave. I have to try."

"Calcain, please—"

"Shelly…"

She ran towards me and held me in her arms, weeping.

"So, what then?" she asked. "You're just going to leave me? To go die? After everything? I've cried with you. I've cooked for you. I've cleaned for you. And after all this, I'm still here. Right now. Begging you. Don't go out there. There will always be something bad, something dark, something to fight. When the Houses fall, something else will take its place. There will always be crime. You can't change that, Calcain…"

She was crying hard, almost screaming. It tore what remained of my heart apart.

"Please. Just stop."

"No."

Shelly kept speaking, but my mind went blank. I thought that, with a little more time, I could crack it, but they might kill me before I do. I needed a week. I only had a few hours. And I had no protection from the Met, China Town, or Soho; I was basically open game. Anyone who'd ever wanted me dead would have their chance. If I left my flat, it was likely I wouldn't be coming back. But I had to try. Which meant I needed to get violent. I'd already sent my message in the shape of heart. He would be afraid, but I still needed to live long enough to find him.

Shelly's tears subsided. "Come on, Calcain. Let's leave. Please, baby, let's go."

She called me 'baby'. It felt good. But I couldn't go with her.

"No, Shelly. I'm sorry."

"Why?"

"Because I'm ready to die doing what I love."

"Which is what?"

"Killing motherfuckers who fuck with my city."

My iPhone was playing on the dock. She was singing 'The Edge of Glory'. The piano version.

I'm on the edge of glory / And I'm hangin' on a moment with you...

I wished Shelly could be with me forever. She was the first person to really love me in a long time. But I had work to do. If I went with her, too many people would die. I couldn't let that happen. I needed to stop the war. And until I saw his fucking corpse in front of me, I needed to save Mulligan.

"Fine," she said, slowly leaving the bed. "Then you're doing this by yourself. I'm not going to stand here and watch you die."

She picked up her bag and left the flat. The room was suddenly so empty.

I showered and prepared myself.

It's hot to feel the rush, to brush the dangerous / I'm going to run right to, to the edge with you...

I skipped the bulletproof vest and opted instead for a navy three-piece suit. It was fitted and tailored to my specifications to allow for the storage of several different types of knives. I attached my gun to the waistcoat and wore the suit jacket over it. Then I pulled on my long, dark green coat—also equipped with tools—over the suit. The tie didn't have a function; I just wore it to look good.

I looked around at my flat. I probably wouldn't see it again. And in spite of how it looked, I loved it. I look at Her poster on the wall one last time as She screamed.

I'm on the edge with you (with you, with you, with you, with you, with you)...

I put my headphones on. It was time for war.

*

I knew a guy called Michael Lavender who worked at Whitehall. I'd be meeting him later to see why the government wasn't intervening in the House war. I was also set to meet Sutton for coffee by Westminster station for one last ditch attempt to get our heads together for a solution. I agreed to meet him at two exactly, so I needed to move quickly. Sutton, though he may not have known it, was my only hope to put all the pieces into place. He had information, resources, and access that I didn't, especially now.

There was a letter on the ground outside my door. I picked it up. It was from Ra'ef. And it was dated that day.

He'd written it in a code specific to Soho: space invaders. The messages always showed the same basic image of a crowd of space invaders, and depending on which aliens were missing, you could make out a series of between one and fifty-five words.

The message, once deciphered, read:

An ancient war between the Houses. When all is destroyed, who gains the most? In that, you will find your answer. Who is Richard Oliver? I have been made an offer which I will accept at one-fifty-nine in the morning. Finish before then or run. Far.

Ancient war of the Houses. The oldest war they had was getting rid of the old guard back in the late eighties, early nineties. But if we were talking ancient, that would be the war between the Richardsons and the Krays, though at that time, they weren't Houses, per se. And if any of their descendants were remotely involved, I was fucked.

*

By the time I got to Whitehall, I could already tell London was different. It was as though she'd caught a cold. The streets felt creepier. I felt like I was being followed.

I stepped into Michael Lavender's office and asked for him. Of all the fucking times of the year, the man was on annual leave. But his PA said he had left a message for me.

I stood outside and read it.

Our hands are tied.

Fucking great.

I was sick and fucking tired of hitting brick walls with every single fucking step I took. I fell down, holding my face. I wasn't crying. But I was screaming in my head. I didn't care who saw me on the street. I just didn't.

There was a time I would've given myself thirty-six hours maximum to crack a case. But it was November, and I was stuck. I'd lost all forward momentum. I was far from the answers I needed. There were only a few other people who may have known something that could help, but when I called, they didn't answer. I've got coded messages from Ra'ef, Jimmy joining the fight, Sutton doing the little he can from his governmental position, and Mulligan still fucking missing.

I was failing them all. Plus Luke. Shelly. London. Everyone.

I was not Calcain the Great. I was his shadow. A high failure. A spectacular one. But one thing I could do was at least sink with my ship. If ever I was to be remembered, at least they'd say I didn't run away. Assuming they found my body.

I still needed to meet with Sutton. Maybe he had found something I could help with. I wanted to contribute. If I couldn't, I'd go back to my flat and wait for the end. Or maybe I'd join

Jimmy—he'd helped me so much, the least I could do was die with him.

I looked at the time. One-thirty.

I needed something to get me through my meeting with Sutton. Not Dark Fire. I'd had enough of that. I turned to the one person who, apart from God, I could always turn to. The one person who had picked me up without fail over the last four years. The person who helped me avoid depression. The person who saved my life.

Her.

I put my headphones on, and She started singing 'Alejandro'.

Don't call my name / Don't call my name, Alejandro…

I stepped into the Starbucks near Westminster station—where I was due to meet Sutton in half an hour—and took a seat next to the window overlooking Big Ben. It was magnificent. I ordered my drink and returned to my seat. Immediately in front of me, a mother and her child sat down. The mother was a standard, upper-middle class, blonde white woman, having probably just visited her husband for lunch and now likely heading to West End to shop. The daughter was a very, very cute big-eyed toddler who seemed eager to impress her mom with her encyclopaedic knowledge of things.

"Caap," the child said.

"No, babe, that's a *cup*," the mother said in a posh Fulham accent, pointing at the cup.

The kid smiled with delight. "Maffee… ma… maffee."

"Hun, that's a *muffin*."

The kid grinned. Watching their interaction cheered me up. The mother saw me smile and smiled back.

"Shoog… shooga."

"That's *sugar*, hun. With an 'r'."

"Me!" the kid said, laughing.

"That is you!" the mother said.

The kid clapped.

"Nooth." She pointed at her mother's face. "Nooooth"

I smiled. The mother looked at me, then at the little girl. "That's my *nose*."

The kid laughed again and clapped some more before turning silent for a bit as she observed the world around her.

I rewound 'Alejandro', but I kept it quiet so I could still listen to the mother and daughter speak.

The kid pointed out the window, towards Big Ben.

"Heeuf. Heeufs. *Heeeeufs*!" she screamed.

"No, darling." The mother smiled.

'Alejandro' dropped its first beat.

"No, we don't live…" The mother craned her neck to see the direction her daughter was pointing. "Oh, yes, you're right. That's where Daddy works."

"Heeeufs."

"No, darling. *Houses*."

'Alejandro' dropped the second beat.

My heart started racing, as though it was about to explode out of my chest. Almost like having a loose electrical cable shoved straight in my spine.

The mother continued, "*Houses*."

I stood up, dropping my cup as the mother cracked the case wide open for me.

"It's the *Houses*, darling. The Houses of Parliament."

I ran outside and across the road. To the Houses of Parliament.

I reached deep in my pocket, hoping I had my ID with me.

How could I have been so stupid?

She was screaming 'Alejandro' in my ear.

The 'New Breed' was anything but new. All the allusions made to me about an old power coming back weren't in reference to some shitty gang making a run for the top. They were talking about the fucking Parliament.

I walked around the parliament building, my body shaking before two statues.

Who is Richard Oliver?

Richard the Lionheart.

Oliver Cromwell.

One represents a king's divine and ultimate power. The other represents the power of the people over the king. No man is divine. No man is above the rule of law.

An ancient war between the Houses.

The House of Commons. The House of Lords.

How could I not have known?

Russell and Charlie at war meant carnage. The Houses would decimate each other. It would make the coalition look incompetent. The government would fold. And who stood to gain the most from the collapse of not only the Houses, but also of the government itself?

The answer was inside Parliament.

I showed my ID to the guard at the front door, and he let me pass with a lingering stare. I kept rewinding 'Alejandro' and thought hard as I paced the room.

Who would take over if everything in the City fell? Elad's interests in the City meant he was heavily invested in the government. He'd gain nothing from the destruction of both sides. So who, then?

"Who takes over if the government fails?" I said to myself,

thinking out loud.

"The Lord Chancellor," a voice responded.

An old statesman in a three-piece suit. Incredibly posh accent.

"The Lord Chancellor?"

"Yes."

"Could I trouble you to ask—"

"No. Find out yourself. Go down the corridor, take a left, and then a left again. The name and portrait are outside the office."

"Thank you, sir."

One person could hold this office. The one leader of the Houses connected directly to the queen. A distant relative. Russell. Would Russell kill his own brother? His own nephew? What would he gain from the carnage? Political power? Is that it?

Or maybe it was his father, Lord Wellington.

I ran past a marble staircase. The gothic building was riddled with old portraits of great statesmen and politicians, including the guy who'd just helped me—the Lord High Steward and Lord Speaker.

I followed his instructions, past the various corridors, until I reached a sign that read *The Office of Lord Chancellor* to the left. I turned and stood outside the office.

'Alejandro' was coming to a close again.

So was every last bit of hope I had inside me.

I felt like a ton of bricks had fallen on my head. I felt broken. Lost. Gobsmacked.

The Lord Chancellor looked down at me from his portrait, appearing regal and majestic in old, black legal robes with a golden pattern throughout over a three-piece suit. And a wig on top.

I closed my fists so tight, I thought my fingers might break. His name was written in gold underneath the portrait:

Ebenezer Albert Charles Jonathan Sutton, Baron Sutton, PC – Lord High Chancellor.

Lord fucking Sutton.

The first man I'd trusted in years.

Slowly, it dawned me. Who knew more about the Houses than anyone? Who gained more from the collapse of both the criminal and the executive powers? Who advised the government on it? Did he ever advise them to stop the war or did he just lie to me?

But something didn't make sense. If the prime minister died, the queen would make a formal decision on a replacement. There was the deputy prime minister as well. And in party politics, if one man died, he could be replaced with a new party head. Not someone from the House of Lords. I didn't understand.

My fury took over.

I would beat him to death. I didn't even want an explanation.

I opened the office door, expecting to see him in there. It was empty. His desk was covered in benign legal papers. I hacked into the computer on his desk and found nothing. I rummaged through his drawers and filing cabinets. Everything I came across was irrelevant.

Then I did what detectives do best. I looked through his trash can.

And found a photo of me.

It was taken years ago, before I was banished, and it was tossed out alongside an invoice from a company called Confidential Shred-All Limited. It stated that of the ninety-seven boxes they'd received, all but one had been shredded, and that last one hadn't been processed simply because they don't destroy electronic data. I called them immediately and asked an old contact to pick up the box and send it to my address in Switzerland.

In the meantime, I ran out of the office. In the main corridor, the Lord Speaker was still standing there.

"I beg your pardon, my Lord Speaker," I said to him, keeping my respect to a maximum.

"Ah, so you've educated yourself, I see."

"Yes, sir. Though I do have a question." I showed him my badge.

He stared a moment, then collected himself and smiled. "Please proceed."

"My Lord, forgive my ignorance, but why is it the Lord Chancellor would become the high executive should the government fail? According to convention—"

"Convention in this scenario, young man, is nonsense. As you are clearly aware, the United Kingdom has no constitution. It is instead guided by an unwritten convention, which governs behaviour. That means that, if a minister does really badly, he will resign according to convention. He'll know when to resign, though he will be reminded if he forgets. In party politics, if the prime minister dies, replacing him should be an easy domestic transition. That's how we have dealt with it in the UK. Except…"

He hesitated. I tried to look as relaxed as I could to make him think he was dealing more with an eager apprentice than a detective.

"Except, since the coalition, we have dealt with constant bickering and disagreements. You see, to stay in power, the conservatives and liberals have made ridiculous concessions. It follows that the rumour is the coalition agreement has an addendum. A secret agreement. Put simply, to keep the left-leaning Labour party out of power, the prime minister agreed with his coalition partner that in the event the government resigns, a neutral person would take power—with mutual votes between the parties already agreed upon—who will lead the government until the next election. Which means, for the first time in UK politics, a definite inheritor of power was chosen, someone guaranteed to become leader should the government fail. A man by the name of Lord Sutton. For this reason, the balance of power between the Lords and Commons has been a bit shaky. The two Houses often don't see eye to eye, especially as the commons hold more power. But with the Lord Chancellor's recent powers, and the government failing to get a grip on things, that power seems to have balanced, at times, even in our favour."

He leaned towards me. "The government has failed already, you understand. There are riots, explosions on Regent Street, mass decapitations. Nothing is safe anywhere. Nothing is sacred. And the only reason I'm sharing this information with you is that I resigned today."

"Why leave now?"

"Because Lord Sutton has bigger plans. Plans that threaten that which I swore to defend so many years ago."

"Which are what?"

"Democracy. I am powerless to stop him. So I shall take my leave." He straightened his jacket.

"Thank you, my Lord."

I respected his departure. He'd told me enough. But before he left, he turned and whispered something to me.

"Whatever it is you're investigating, I wish you the best of luck. But know this… you are dealing with a very dangerous and powerful man. But even the wisest fall to vanity before an imminent win, which is what he thinks he has. If you are going to strike, now is the hour."

And then he was gone.

And I was due to see Sutton in a few minutes.

It seemed the Houses had been nothing more than pawns in Sutton's plan to seize real power. Absolute power. Parliament. The Houses comprised only a small part of his plan. A finishing touch. With Russell and Charlie targeting one another, I suspected Sutton planned on making a deal with Elad to rule the underworld or face utter destruction. So he was fucked. All the Houses were. Not to mention the government. Not to mention me.

Sutton was probably quite happy with himself, but he wouldn't be for long. I had the box saved from the shredder. Maybe something in it could ruin him. But by the time I could get to Switzerland and pass all the data I'd acquired to the French press—who would love nothing more than to take down the United Kingdom, those ungrateful pigs—Sutton would have already enjoyed absolute power for a few hours. Yes, he'd be destroyed, but not before everyone was dead.

It would be a pyrrhic victory. And it wouldn't be good enough. I needed to win it right away. By killing Sutton in broad daylight.

I realised it was about one o'clock and ran outside the Parliament towards Starbucks. I couldn't be late. I didn't want to risk Sutton turning up, seeing I wasn't there, and disappearing.

As soon I stepped into the road to cross to the coffee shop, I flew backwards. Far. Almost ten feet.

Everything turned dark again, but I wouldn't give in to my sudden, stunning fatigue. I refused to pass out. I needed Sutton. I couldn't let him get away.

My ears were ringing and eyes blurry when I got to my feet. My hands were shaking. There was glass everywhere.

Before me, Starbucks was in flames. There had been an explosion inside.

An explosion meant for me.

I was the last part of Sutton's plan. The last small hurdle to get out of way. How better to get me out of the way than with a big explosion to precede the biggest gang war London had ever seen? How better to prove the government's incompetency than with an explosion right near the Parliament, showing its inability to protect itself, let alone its people.

My left hand, bloody and torn from the explosion, suddenly felt soft, cool and comfortable. I looked down and saw my fingers being held by a small, chubby hand. The kid from Starbucks. She must have survived the blast by the skin of her milky teeth.

"Ith okay," she said.

I looked at her and smiled. "It's absolutely going to be okay, hun."

Her mom looked at me, in shock from the explosion but still happy to have survived it. I reached into my pocket and gave them both a stick of gum.

I suddenly had all the resolve I needed to find Sutton. For this little girl. For her mom. For Elsie. For London.

Enough feeling sorry for myself. I had work to do.

I put on my headphones and listened to the song that had saved my life, the one that stopped me from jumping off a bridge at my lowest point so many years ago. The song that told me, regardless of everything I was going through, *It's going to be okay*.

I remembered preparing to off myself back then. I was standing on Millennium Bridge in Southwark overlooking Saint

Paul's cathedral and Tate Modern museum. I was ready to jump. Then I heard an angel tell me it was going to be okay. Her voice stopped me. I looked around for the angel but couldn't find her. Then I realised the voice was coming from a boat party below me. It was one of Her songs.

Standing outside Starbucks, I hit play and I soon felt alive. I didn't have time for Dark Fire. I didn't have time for anything. Just to do what I did best. To be a Monster. Once I beat him, I would eat him.

I texted Sutton using an app I invented for the agency that gave me my badge; it would give me the recipient's geolocation.

Bang! You missed. Have another go.

I received GPS coordinates within seconds of the text being sent. He was standing in front of Westminster Cathedral.

I walked towards it and saw him from afar. He was across the road, in a long coat, watching me.

What's going on the floor? ...Just dance / Gonna be ok...Just dance...

He sent me a text.

What are you talking about? I've just arrived.

I texted back.

I have a little thing I need to show you.

He responded.

Come over. Let's get a drink.

I shook my head. The audacity.

So you can run me over again? No, thanks. Let's get a drink on my side. We have lots to talk about. See attached.

I sent him a photo of the Shred-All invoice, with the note about the electronic material circled.

That means nothing to me.

I smiled up at him as I sent my next text.

Then you have nothing to worry about, mate.

His next text took a while to arrive.

What do you want?

I responded.

To eat you. Slowly. Painfully. With a glass of red wine.

His next message was quick.

I can give you anything. Why don't we make a deal?

I almost laughed out loud.

You don't have anything I want.

But then he sent a photo of his own.

It was Mulligan. He was chained and bloodied. I couldn't tell where.

A text followed.

Tick-tock.

I didn't want to waste time, not now and not where this was concerned.

Make me an offer.

He'd been prepared for this, all of it.

Old Vic Tunnels. Six.

Too late.

Who knew what kind of chaos he could rain down on London by then?

This is my only offer. Old Vic Tunnels. Six. Or he dies. If something happens to me here, now, I'm taking you with me. Kaboom.

He sent a photo of himself wearing a vest of bombs. The same vest he was wearing at that moment.

He texted again.

One on one. You have my word.

I turned his own words on him.

That means nothing to me.

He was walking.

I'll be there at six. You can play hide and seek until then.

A red bus pulled in front of me, temporarily blocking my line of sight. When it left, Sutton was gone.

I sent another text, but the mapping tracker still showed him to be standing where I last saw him. I ran across the road and found his phone abandoned on the sidewalk. Before I could pick it up, it began to smoke, and with a minor spark, it set itself on fire.

Great. Self-destruct.

If he was planning to blow up the tunnels, he'd be taking one of London's biggest stations with him—Waterloo. It was near the Shell station and would probably take some the building with it. There were active garages in the area, too, including one in the tunnels. The place dripped petrol. An explosion there would be devastating. So I had no other option. I had to meet him, if for no other reason than to stop him.

Luckily, he needed me alive. If I died, he'd have his carnage, but only for a short while; the contents of that box would destroy him. He'd try to torture its location out of me. In fact, he'd probably show up with a whole posse to do just that. But I could build a posse of my own.

I call up Tanka, Ian Chef, Basya Stephens, and a few others, as well as former members of Creatures of the Night. Then I checked into a hotel, had a shower, freshened up, and ate a full meal. My group would be meeting at five-fifty outside the Old Vic Tunnels.

It was now or never.

*

The Old Vic Tunnels were exactly what they sounded like—tunnels owned by the Old Vic theatre company, behind Waterloo station.

When you entered the tunnels, it was pitch black. They were the same size as the ones you'd expect to find in any metro or underground platform, but their design was strange. They seemed more like several rooms connected to each other by small corridors. The maze of tunnels was mostly used for gigs and art exhibitions, and it was grimy, damp and riddled with graffiti. Rats were not uncommon.

I understood why Sutton chose this place. There were plenty of hiding spaces and only one clear exit route. It was deep underground, so no one could hear you scream. It was dark. A perfect place to play a deadly game of hide and rape.

I waited outside the small entrance door, which had an open padlock on it. As my group reacquainted themselves, I gave basic instructions.

"If there's more of them than you can handle, run. If the situation is looking grim, run. If you are scared at any point, run. If you think can make it alive, run. When in doubt, run."

All in all, there were seven of us. It would be enough. I'd killed plenty of Sutton's men already, and as small as my team was, we were highly effective. Ian Chef towered over his opponents at six-foot-four, and he was strong. Tanka may have been a borderline midget, but he was quick and accurate. And Basya Stephens was an amateur boxer well connected in the Caribbean and African communities.

I opened the door and lit the hallway with my iPhone before Ian pulled out a gigantic torch that lit up the room with the power of three suns.

"Ian, what the fuck?"

"What?" he asked in a subtle Essex accent.

"Are you here to fight or blind these people?"

"It's better than darkness, isn't it?"

"If they didn't know we were coming before, they sure as hell do now."

"Uh, ladies?" Tanka said, frustrated. "Can you please kill each other later?"

"Fuck it," I said, walking forward into the absolute clarity offered by the light, before it flickered, and we fell into total darkness again.

"Ian?"

"Fuck, mate," he said. "The fucking battery's ran out."

"Are you serious?"

He was. So I turned my phone light back on, and we kept walking into the tunnels. The ceilings were a lot taller than I remembered. They were pitched and gothic-looking, scary in the darkness.

As I walked forward, I nearly tripped. I pointed my light at the thing that had snagged my pant leg and discovered the corpse underneath me.

It was fresh.

"Shit," Ian said, pointing his own phone light around the tunnel.

There were more.

The corpse closest to me was no more than a few hours old. The cause of death looked like a sword to the neck.

Fuck.

"What do you think, Ian?"

Ian examined the corpses, walking around to cover as many as he could, reporting back as he moved from one corpse to another.

"There's nine. Sword or knife wounds all around. Ridiculously sharp. The killer is left-handed. And professional; it only took one person to do all these lads in. All killed recently, so the killer beat us by a few hours at most. But one problem…"

"What?"

"They're all enemies. Our enemies. If I were to guess, I'd say it looked like they were waiting for us. We'd have been walking into an ambush. Which leads me to believe these are Sutton's men. Someone beat us to the battle."

I didn't doubt him. Ian used to work with the SAS. He knew his shit.

"Any ideas?"

Ian rubbed his chin as he thought. "Incredible strength and expert swordsmanship. Could be using a samurai sword, like a katana but better. Sharper. Lighter."

"Could it have been Sutton himself?"

"I doubt it. The killer snuck in behind them, and this was all about stealth. This is an expert assassin—"

"Or hashashin." The voice came from somewhere farther down the tunnel.

I ran towards a point of concentrated light before us and found a person sitting against the tunnel wall dressed head to toe in black fabric, holding their gut with their right hand and a sword in their left, the tip pressed against the ground. I stepped forward, and the sword shot up.

"Stop. That's enough. Keep your distance," the person said, their voice muffled.

"Who are you?"

"Someone who came for revenge. But now, after so many agonising weeks, I'm convinced I came to the wrong place."

Their gear was designed for special military personnel. They belonged to a very specific force. My deduction was instant, but I remained silent.

The sword lowered back to the ground.

"There's a few with him still. I'd say you have enough men to take him on. Now. But certainly not before. You were walking into an execution."

I knew why the assassin was there, and it was for the wrong reason. I offered what comfort I could.

"How badly are you hurt?"

"Bullet. In the gut. I would've died if I hadn't seen you. And I hate myself for that. To be rescued by you."

I ignored it. The assassin had every right to hate me; I took too long with this investigation. I could've given answers right away.

I knelt down. "You fought bravely. It's been a while, hasn't it?"

"Too long. But there is no limit to what desperation will do."

"Did you find what you were looking for?"

"Yes and no. And you know why. You always knew, didn't you?"

I thought for a while, then responded honestly. For once.

"Yes. I've always known what happened to Hunter. It took me all of about five seconds to deduce. I was more interested in what would follow. It was entirely selfish. If my investigation was limited to Hunter, then it would have been resolved by the time I left the scene, and I would have been escorted back to my flat and back to my banishment. And there was more I needed to know and understand, more I needed to do as far as the Houses were concerned. And then everything got complicated. Either way, you had no business here. You should have spoken to me before doing this."

291

The assassin was quiet for a long time.

"If that's true, that you prioritised your own freedom over the truth, then you're no different than the creature you seek."

I saw the argument. But still.

"I am nothing like him."

I stood and instructed one of my group members, Geoff Death, to look after the assassin.

"Careful, Geoff. You're dealing with a middle-aged woman. Handle her gently, assassin or not."

Bell met my eyes. "My argument with my daughter. That's still on your mind, isn't it? She asked me to protect her. That's what our argument was about. I said the only way to protect her would be if she told me what was happening. She refused on the basis that it was for my own good. I didn't take the danger seriously, and I refused to help until she told me what I was protecting her against. I failed her. I was her mother. But I killed her. Not at my own hand. But by not being there." She put a hand on mine. "If you are a monster, then Lord only knows what I am."

"You are a mother, and you did all you could. Nothing you could have done would have changed your daughter's fate. Farewell. Send my regards to Kimia."

Geoff ushered her back out of the tunnel towards safety.

With what limited light we had, we pressed forward to the next tunnel, taking care to be quiet and rarely using our lights. As we explored, I noticed movement in a distant puddle of water. I pointed my phone at the ceiling above the puddle. No drip. It must have been a rat. Or one of Sutton's men.

I signalled for my team to take cover and hid myself behind a concrete column.

It was time to call out the beast.

"Here, kitty, kitty."

292

Silence.

"Come on now, Sutton. Let's do this man to man."

Silence.

I snapped. "Oh, fuck off, you old cunt. It's going to happen either way."

Behind a column in the distance, about fifteen metres away, I saw a small, red light. Moments later, a shot rang out.

I shrank against the wall. He had missed me.

"Ian," I whispered, hoping he was nearby.

I couldn't fucking see him.

"What?"

"Can you hear me properly?"

"Yes. Hence, *what?*"

"They've got fucking night vision goggles. They can see us. Why didn't we think of that?"

"Because we're fucking plonkers."

I heard some shuffling to my left.

"We need to even the playing field."

"And how the actual fuck do you think we can go about that?"

A long silence.

"Ian?"

"Let me fucking think."

Another long silence.

"I swear to fucking—"

"What if no one could see anyone?"

"What the fuck does that mean?"

"I've got a smoke bomb." He didn't say anything else.

"That's it? That's the fucking plan? A smoke bomb?"

"Well—"

"That's the fucking dumbest idea I've heard from you, and

you're the fucking cunt-in-chief of stupid ideas."

"Fine, then let's hear your brilliant fucking solution."

He got me there. I had nothing.

"Come on, then. Share with the class."

"All right, fuck. We'll do the smoke bomb. Just toss it."

"No warning?"

"No warning."

Ian threw the smoke bomb, and within seconds, I heard screams in the distance.

"They've got fucking bombs!"

"Shit. This tunnel is coming down."

"I can't see anything!"

"Everyone, wait."

Finally. Sutton.

I screamed to my team, "Push ahead now, lads!"

Gunshots followed. Dozens of them. Maybe hundreds. Until they come to an abrupt end. I heard clicking. They'd emptied their clips. Mumbled voices ahead of us asked one another for extra ammo, but the conclusion was this—they were out.

We crept forward, and I could make out some of what they said.

"Are they dead? I think I got at least two. I can't see shit, though."

"Yeah, I got a few myself."

"Go check the bodies."

Sutton again.

"Be careful. Some of them may still be alive."

Slowly, the men approached.

I'd given strict orders. Absolutely no one from my team was to attack unless they heard the word 'go'. So everyone stood perfectly still in their hiding places, waiting for my signal and ready to strike.

The fighters edged closer, and soon, they were in reach.

"Go!"

We all rushed forward, catching them entirely off guard. I grabbed one by the throat as he ran past me, and with a rather annoying and awkward *crack*, I put the poor guy to rest. I heard screaming and shouting, but none of it belonged to my men. With that confidence in mind, I retreated from the immediate battle and searched for Sutton.

I turned on my iPhone's light, but with the smoke, it was almost impossible to see. All I could do was make my way in the direction Sutton's men came from. Once I successfully put the battle behind me without being noticed, I ran straight through the next tunnel, beaming my light from left to right.

Nothing.

The noise of the fight behind me became distant. Almost inaudible. But a horrible smell started over taking me the deeper I got into the tunnels. It was the sort of smell you'd encounter at the oldest, dodgiest garages, and I remembered there was a garage beside the final tunnel, where people upgraded their cars to make them arty.

I slowed my pace and still caught nothing in the light of my phone. Everything was silent, aside from the sound of water dripping every now and again.

I took a sharp right, and Sutton's face was suddenly within an inch of mine.

A painful strike to my head. Then darkness.

I didn't have time to give in to another concussion, so I got up. I was dizzy.

Before I could see in front of me, I felt a sharp pain in my stomach and fell down again, this time on all fours. Then there was an even sharper pain in my back, and I dropped to the floor, belly first.

I was in agony. I felt like I wanted to vomit.

"See," Sutton said somewhere above me. "I just don't understand why people insist on knives and bats when a golf club does the same job but much more inconspicuously."

His footsteps moved around me.

"It's lovely to see you again, my boy. You are quite the adversary, though to be honest, I never thought we'd make it to this point. I meant to do away with you long ago, but it's true what they say—you just can't find good help these days."

His footsteps stopped near me.

"Tell me where the box is, and I'll let you go. Simple as that. No questions asked."

Acid pooled and gurgled up from my throat.

"No? Nothing? Not a peep? Well, suit yourself I suppose."

A sharp pain ricocheted through my right thigh. I felt the bone fracture. It burned.

"I'm promising you, Calcain, I'm a good man. I really am. I'm doing this all for the greater good. You of all people should be able to understand that, to see what I am trying to create here. You've done more than your fair share of evil in the name of a righteous ideology. Isn't that true? So why is it you so adamantly refuse to give me the same opportunity?"

I forced myself to speak. "Tell me, my Lord. Might I make a different bargain with you?"

"I'm listening."

"Your mother was an unfortunate, wasn't she? In the Victorian sense of the word, I mean. A whore. So how about I exhume your rotten, dead whore of a mum, fuck her brains out—what's left of them, anyway—then re-bury her in a shallow grave.

I can be your post-mortem stepdaddy."

I used all of my remaining strength to get to my feet and push him back. He stumbled through a puddle in front of me, and the sharp pain in my back dropped me again.

Quick steps moved towards me, followed by three sharp strikes to the back as he shouted, "I will not listen to such vulgarity!"

He paused, and I heard his jacket rustle. Straightening it, I imagined.

His voice was calm again. "You remind me of Luke. A man of pure principle. He, too, dreamed of a London without gangs, without an underworld. He told me that he'd do anything to make that dream a reality. But compromise proved impossible for me and him. I practically begged him to kill you. He had no hesitation when it came to seeing his own uncle dethroned. But when it came to you? He simply wouldn't hear of it. Which demonstrated to me that he had outlasted his use. We had... philosophical differences."

It sounded like he was trying to wipe himself dry from the spill in the puddle.

"The idea of the New Breed is that to get rid of all gangs, you need to replace them with a single gang controlled fully by the government."

I rolled onto my side, aching as I did. "Luke wanted to put an end to all the killings."

"Yes, and so do I." His voice got dark with passion. "But to end the killings, Calcain, you first need to kill all the killers. That's the only way. The *only* way."

"You didn't have to kill him."

"I know. It was short-sighted of me. I doubted your resolve was so strong that you'd actually decapitate a small army just to make a point. I should have just stayed in that boy's flat that night and killed you myself. But. Well. Hindsight."

I crawled to a wall and put my back against it with my legs outstretched. Sutton watched me, smiling as he leaned on his golf club. He had the clear advantage, and he knew it. I needed to buy some time.

"So. A New Breed, huh?"

"Yes. A New Breed. You see, you can't just destroy the three Houses and then create a brand-new criminal organisation from scratch. It would need a foothold in the underground. It just wouldn't work. So I had to choose one to function as a shell, for lack of a better term, for my new project. I've selected Elad because his organisation would best suit the city, and he's easier to deal with. I'll make him an offer he can't refuse: full government protection to absorb the other Houses, which would, of course, make him entirely dependent on me. Then all I had to do was put the pieces in play for Russell and Charlie to destroy each other." He paced and swung the golf club absently at his side. "I'm designing an entirely new breed of power from the corpses of London's leaders. I'm making something better and bigger. A Third House of Parliament. A Third Chamber of Power. It needed a Lord Protector to put it all together. But I have no desire to rule forever."

"When did you make Elad the offer?"

"I haven't yet. But the time is near."

"And what makes you think he'd join you?"

"Because he would have no other option. It's that or death."

"But if he dies, you wouldn't have that shell to work with. So you need him to join you."

"Which he will."

"And if he doesn't?"

298

Sutton silenced me with a sinister look that stood in contrast to his normal cheerful demeanour. "He will."

He stared at me for a long moment before smiling, his body relaxing again. "Let's get back to the matter at hand. My box. Now—"

"Do you have a cigarette?"

"A cigarette?"

"Yes."

Sutton thought about it. "I might."

"Can I have one?"

Sutton hesitated but obliged. He dug a pack from his pocket, put a cigarette in my mouth, and lit it for me. I took a few puffs.

"Thanks."

"Of course. We are friends after all, wouldn't you say?"

"Sure we are." I exhaled. "So let's make a deal. But first, I need to know about Mulligan."

Sutton laughed. "He's alive, he's alive. Not too far away, in fact. Just downstairs. He's been very helpful. Not at the beginning. But he's been persuaded."

I took a few more puffs.

Sutton paced the room, playing hopscotch in the puddles. He paused and looked at me.

"I thought about getting you on board in the beginning, you know. We both have the same passion for London and hatred towards arrogant fools with too much power."

"So why didn't you give me a call?"

He shook his head. "We're just too different. You're too head on, you understand? I'm more…" He searched for the word. "Insidious. More like Mulligan. Patient. And careful. The plan I was devising was very delicate."

"Mulligan had a plan himself. But that got fucked up, too.

299

And it fucked you in the process."

"I need to ask this. Did you—"

"No, I didn't kill Hunter. I know who did, though."

"And her?"

"Her, too." He sighed. "Bad business all of that. After I'd heard, I knew it would only be a matter of time before the Houses kicked off, and war would be inevitable. I just sped things up a little. I needed to act quickly to make sure I didn't lose control. As did Mulligan. In fact, in many ways, this race in its entirety has been about two people. Me. And Mulligan. It had nothing to do with anyone else. The question was who could turn this to their advantage quicker. I opted for selective assassinations and fuelled the concept of a coalition government by spreading damaging rumours." He smiled, looking at me eye to eye. "Mulligan, though, opted to unleash you: the creative detective, the bane of Scotland Yard. The once young and passionate Detective Calcian. A man of principle. Principle misplaced, but principle nonetheless."

I took a few more puffs of the cigarette.

"Shutting Mulligan down was my first use of the Third House. Without him, I was free to execute my plan in a hurry. I could have stretched this whole affair out longer, but I must say, I did fear your deductive skills. So I decided to deal with you, but there was one problem. You just wouldn't die. You, like Hunter, were connected to all the Houses, on every radar, but aligned with none. If both you and he were dead, it would surely signal an outside force coming down on London's underground. I followed you many times, which is how Bell caught my scent. She spotted me outside her house. She must be dead now, but she was good. I wish I could have recruited her."

His ego was astounding.

I said, "She wouldn't have joined you."

"Maybe not. You wouldn't have either. And here you are again, still refusing to die."

I rolled my eyes. "You really are fucking long-winded, aren't you? How about you tell me where Mulligan is, and I'll tell you where to find your fucking box, and we can both be on our way."

He pondered a while. The fact was, to him, the battle was won. Mulligan or not, he had me. Mulligan's weapon. The monster he had unleashed as a means to checkmate Sutton. I'd been captured. What now?

"Okay," Sutton said after a while. "There's a garage next door. On the floor is a small door which leads to a bomb bunker. That's where Mulligan is. He was bleeding quite a bit when I last saw him, but if you hurry, he may survive. If you give me the box, I'll lead you to him, kill you, let him go. That's the best I can offer."

I laughed. That wouldn't do. I had a deal of my own to make, and I'd bought myself enough time to execute it.

"You're right. We're nothing alike. I'm much more of an artist when it comes to destroying the Houses. More creative. I want it to be theatre. Drama. And your methods are just so fucking boring. You act like it's a corporate takeover."

"In a way, it is."

"It's not." I shook my head. "There's something you should know. The House leaders would never listen to me. Not now and not back then. They've never given me the fucking time of day unless I was causing trouble. But they would listen to Mulligan. And you've just told me where he is. I could just kill you and go get him myself, and he'd talk them all out of this war. He'd make them understand."

"Why would you want that? You hate them as much as

anyone. More, even."

"I don't want that. But I don't want whatever the fuck this is, either. The Houses will be destroyed, I promise you that. But I will be the one to destroy them. After what they did to London. What they did to my friends. What they did to me. It will be *me* who takes them down and no one else."

He looked a little surprised. Good.

"You were always too academic, Sutton. And you took things far took personally. The thing about making plans is that only about one percent of any plan goes exactly as expected. One percent. The rest you need to rock." I took a long drag on my cigarette. "Think about my plan tonight, and think about yours. Both of us upended by a fucking ninja. An actual ninja. In London. Without her, the lads and I would've been effectively toast. But fate favours the brave, or so they say." I smiled up at him. "You gotta roll the dice, Sutton, that's the only way to survive in this world. That's the one rule. That's why I asked you for this cigarette."

He eyed me as I took another puff.

"I had to take a chance, and it paid off. You handed one over." I kept my gaze deadest on his. "And now I'll have one shot to light you up."

I flicked the cigarette at him. It landed right behind his shoe.

Sutton laughed. "You missed."

"No, I didn't."

Sutton's expression changed slowly as his back began to burn. It was petrol I'd knocked him down into before, not water. But how could he have known that? The tunnels fucking reek of it. He began to spin around, patting at the flames on his back, and I mustered the last bit of energy I had to kick out and knock him towards the petrol, each of the bones in my leg feeling like they were being broken all over.

He stumbled when I made contact and fell into the puddle, turning into fire. It wasn't a gradual burn. It was more like an explosion. I could barely make out the shape of his body inside the flames.

He disappeared as darkness overcame me again. I fell, not through the floor but towards a comfortable, soft, warm abyss. A cold breeze blew across my face. I felt light. I saw Her flying towards me.

I looked at her. "Did I do well?"

She smiled. "Yes. But you're not done yet."

"I can't take any more. I've done enough. I've done good. That's it."

"I'll be waiting for you when you're finished. Here, on the edge of glory."

"I don't have anything left. It's over."

"You need to fight a little more. Buck up. It's going to be okay."

With those words, I felt energy surge back through me and fly at supersonic speeds back into myself.

Every part of me ached. It was freezing. Agonising.

I opened my eyes, and Ian's face was hovering above mine.

Breathing hard and with my heart racing, I slowly came to and found myself still in the tunnel, surrounded by my team. I was lying on the ground with my head in Tanka's lap. It hurt too much to speak yet.

"Pour some more water on him," Tanka said.

"I'm not pouring more water on him. Jesus, you're as much of an idiot as you are a bum basher, ain't ya?" Ian said. "Calcain. Mate. You all right?"

It felt like my mouth was glued together.

"He's fucked," Ian said. "I don't think this cunt's gonna make it. We need to keep him awake."

"So," Tanka said. "Pour some more—"

"I mean by speaking to him. Maybe giving him the odd slap or somethin'."

"We should get him out of here."

"I don't think we should move him. Not yet."

A cold splash of water made me miss a heartbeat.

"Wha..." The sound tore at my throat as I made it. "Wha...What the f-fuck is wrong w-with you? Didn't you hear what this cunt just said? No. More. Water."

"Oh, thank fuck," I heard Ian say. "I fucking told you, Tanka. I said no more water."

"Well, he's talking, ain't he?"

I pushed myself into sitting with a crippling headache. Everything was spinning around me. My body ached. Ian and Tanka tried to stop me from standing but to no avail. If I was going to find Mulligan, I needed the pain to go away. I couldn't take it. I reached into my coat pocket and swallowed some headache tablets and followed them up with a hit of Dark Fire. Within moments, the pain started to fade.

I was back.

"How the fuck are you even moving?" Ian asked.

"I have work to do. What time is it?"

"It's about nine."

"Nine? How the hell—"

"It took us ages to find you, and when we tried to get you out of here, you kept saying no. You said you had to stay here. Then you stopped breathing."

I scanned the room but didn't see a corpse. "Did you see Sutton?"

"No, we figured he beat you then went off to do his thing."

"Not giving me much credit then, are you?"

304

"What happened to him?"

"Last I saw, he was burning into a neat crisp. Might've gotten away on foot. Not far. Gotta be dead by now, but his body can wait. I need to find Mulligan."

"Well, for what it's worth, there's a pretty big, deep ditch just to the left of you. Can't see shit down there. We thought maybe you'd fallen in, but maybe Sutton did. As for Mulligan, we haven't seen—"

"He's here. There's a garage next door with a hidden door in the floor. That's where he is."

"How do you know that?"

My head was aching. I snapped. "Because I'm a fucking detective."

"Still a dick, too, I see."

"Everyone except for Ian and Tanka got out. You need to send word to Scotland Yard, Camden, and Shoreditch. Tell them Calcain concluded his investigation. They need to hold off the battle for as long as they can until I find a way to convince the Houses to stop."

"Calcain, the war will have started already up there. The call to arms was at nine," Tanka said with a broken voice.

"What? Jimmy told me—"

"The war for Whitechapel will start at midnight, but there's already talk of gun shots. Things are escalating early."

I took a deep breath. "We've still got until midnight before the worst of it gets under way. There's still time to get the word out. But finding Mulligan is key. He's the only one who can stop the whole thing."

I imagined what it must look like outside. Everyone assembled. Everyone ready for the carnage. They wouldn't be easy to slow down. They weren't like soldiers. When they started, they wouldn't stop.

Part IV

Chapter 13

Somewhere, London

Detective Mulligan had been in that state for a while. Locked up. Starved. Tortured. He was about ready to give up on the fight. Since his last farewell with Sutton the traitor, Mulligan had lost all faith in humankind.

Lord Sutton had been a trusted advisor. A mentor. A wise man. A traitor. A murderer.

Detective Mulligan had unknowingly sent his one-time protégé right into Sutton's hands. He may as well have been handing Calcain a death sentence.

All this time, Calcain had been little more than a pawn. He'd been betrayed by Luke. By Sutton. And by Mulligan himself, though the detective wasn't sure if Calcain knew that or not. If he didn't, he'd piece it together soon enough.

The clock in the dingy shower room that had been Detective Mulligan's home for some time showed it was around nine forty-five p.m. Calcain must be dead; he was due to meet Sutton at one. Mulligan's last effort to overcome his initial failure hadn't worked. He'd lost. He was too tired to go on.

He'd been chained to the wall, left to starve to death, but he wished he could expedite the process. The chain was too short for Mulligan to hang himself. All he could do was wait, patiently or not, for death to come. He'd started hallucinating, reliving memories of a past long gone. Of chances missed. Of a lifetime of work lost on one single indiscretion. But it wasn't Hunter's death he was carrying the guilt of. It was how he'd missed his chance with Calcain. He could've turned the boy into a great detective, into a reliable officer of the law, into what Mulligan had always wanted to be.

But Mulligan had made one mistake, something he couldn't possibly have seen or have understood the ramifications of at the time. And it got a girl killed. And that was the moment when Calcain took the festering madness he felt about the Houses and truly became who Mulligan supposed he'd always, in some way, been. For six months, Calcain was missing, and for six months he was tortured. And when he came back, he wasn't the same. He was brutal. Violent. He wouldn't do things Mulligan's way any more. Not again. So he was banished. Forced to forfeit. Forced to break. And it all traced back to Mulligan.

It was too late to make amends now. The detective could feel death looming, stalking him, waiting. And then he heard a noise outside.

A door smashing. Things being thrown around. Shifting. Breaking. And finally, a familiar scream that sent the 'Great Detective's' heart racing: "*Mulligan!*"

It must have been another hallucination.

"Mulligan? Can you hear me?"

It wasn't real.

"Oh, come on," the familiar voice begged. "Mulligan?" The voice got distant. "Search everything, open every door. We're not leaving until we find him."

His one-time protégé. His one-time friend. The bright young star of Scotland Yard. Detective Calcain.

307

He couldn't control himself. Tears started running from his eyes. He thought maybe this was what death felt like. A final confrontation. Sad and happy at the same time.

As loud as he could, and through a dry, hoarse throat, he screamed, "*C-Cal... Calcain!*"

Voices followed.

"Did you hear that?"

"I think it came from down there."

"Where?"

"Behind that door."

Within seconds, the darkness was shattered with a loud smash and a light beaming through. A shadow stood in the doorway. The demon with the long coat.

"Fuck me," the shadow said before rushing towards Mulligan. "I need something to take these off."

The light was too bright for him to see. He heard the shuffling of feet. Then the chain around his hands was broken, and he was being carried away.

Maybe that was how he'd get to heaven. If it was, it reeked of petrol.

Water poured over his face, then gently down his throat. He could breathe again. He could speak. He could see. He wasn't in heaven. He was in a fucking garage.

"Wh-where?"

"Old Vic Tunnels. You remember? We cracked the Malone case around here?"

"Yes. Yes, I remember."

As the detective regained his composure, he slowly got to his feet. Holding him up was Calcain. Bloody. Bruised. It hurt Mulligan to see him looking so exhausted.

"Calcain, what happened?"

"I know everything. I know about Sutton. I know about Luke. They're both dead. But that doesn't stop the war. I need you, Mulligan."

The detective managed a nod. "I need a phone. And an escort to Scotland Yard."

Mulligan's knees felt weak.

Calcain turned. "Tanka, get us a car. A safe one. Tell Scotland Yard to have a medic ready."

"Okay, babes," replied a small, skinny Asian chap.

Detective Mulligan was in awe of Calcain's composure in spite of everything that had transpired.

"Have you got anything to eat?" the detective asked. "I'm dying here."

"Here, have a carbo-gel. That should sort you out for now."

The gel went into the detective's system like lightning. "I take it you know about Sutton's plans?"

"Seize power. Something about a Third House of Parliament."

"All the newspapers would have him as the lead candidate to run the country after the coalition breaks. The perfect guardian. A Lord Protector, like Cromwell, whom he hated, but also a conqueror of the streets. A bit like Richard the Lionheart. Hence his code name."

"Richard Oliver."

"Precisely."

Calcain briefed Mulligan on everything he'd missed. Mulligan was disgusted by Calcain's methods. Killings, explosions, multiple decapitations. It all reaffirmed Mulligan's decision to pull Calcain from the investigation into the Houses all those years ago. Still, Calcain was alive. He'd saved the detective. And for once, Mulligan chose to embrace Calcain as a friend and as a partner and as a brother.

And now, he would need to save the very thing he'd been trying to destroy. The Houses. He had to stop the war.

"Your car is ready," Tanka said.

"Thank you," the detective says. "Calcain, what is your plan now?"

"Going to go save Jimmy. He's too old to be fighting in this. You'll have to get this sorted out fast, though. Can you do that?"

"Let's hope so."

They left Calcain in the basement and let Tanka guide him upstairs.

Chapter 14

Whitechapel, London

Betrayal.

That was one feeling I'd gotten used to. It made me incredulous. But still, I let myself be fooled.

Fucked up on Dark Fire, I found myself in Whitechapel, not too far from the City. I was surrounded by countless corpses. Mulligan was supposed to end it before midnight. It was fifteen minutes past. The two Houses at war had outlawed guns.

"Play fair," they said. "Let's see who's really stronger."

But gunfire was still echoing through the City. People were desperate, and there I stood, stabbed twice but still powering ahead. Fighting people as though I was a fucking ancient soldier invading enemy territory. Punching, blocking, kicking stabbing. I tore people apart with the two knives I carried. I didn't go there to fight; I went to find Jimmy. But now I needed to fight my way out.

In the distance, I could see a captain commanding the wave of enemies before me. He was my target. If I got him, the rest would fall.

In my ear, She was singing.

I'm on the edge of glory…

I was bleeding. Heavily. I'd sprinted across London looking for Jimmy, but I was too late.

Russell had broken the initial barriers before midnight, so by the time I arrived, at five to, the war had already reached carnage levels. Charlie had planned to concede territory to get Russell deep into Whitechapel before launching his assault.

It was chaos.

Hundreds of people fought in the streets, but there was no sign of a police presence. It was humanity at its worst. I picked a side at random and fought alongside Russell's men, asking for Jimmy. It was hopeless. By the time I found him, he was long gone. At least six stab wounds to his chest. People were walking over him like they didn't know where the road ended and his body began.

Mulligan had failed to stop the war.

I lost it when I saw Jimmy dead. My brain cut out, and my body acted instinctively, fighting anyone and everyone within reach. If I was going to die, I wanted my death to be glorious.

I pushed and shoved my way to the captain. As I prepared to make a leap for him, he nearly deafened me with an airhorn. Before I could make my final stretch, I was being trampled on. I covered my head with my arms and waited for it to pass.

I blacked out. It felt like an instant, but when I came to, there was no one around. Suddenly, I was lifted up, carried, thrown into a car and driven away. I was too weak to move.

"Fuck me, mate, this is the second time I've saved your life in like three hours."

It was Ian.

"What the fuck happened?"

"War's over. The Houses called it off. It took Mulligan a while, but he got it done and negotiated a truce."

Thank Christ.

"Jimmy's dead."

Ian shook his head, disappointed. "That's too bad. Tanka

312

stayed at Scotland Yard. I think he knew what would happen."

"Russell's men moved before midnight. It was a trap."

"I know. When I showed up, I couldn't fucking believe it. It's the worst I've seen in London. Ah, there they are. Finally."

He pointed out the window at officers making their way past us.

"Showing up just as everything's finished. Fucking convenient."

"They were ordered to halt. By Sutton. Mulligan probably just managed to reach the commander of the Met."

"They're all cunts. I saw this officer once, and he was breaking up two chicks fighting. But I swear he was feeling them up when he was doing it. Like seriously getting a healthy dose of molestation in there. I mean, that's fucking excellent. I think it was Shakespeare who once said, 'Eat shit, copper, and let go of my balls'."

I smiled. Ian had a strange way of making me laugh even when I was at my worst.

I closed my eyes and let go. For the first time in a long time, I could lay still and savour the feeling of being at ease, thinking that, when I woke up, everything would be better.

I let Ian go to town with his stories. We both laughed. Like the old days.

The colours of London so close to Christmas were beautiful. I fell asleep knowing when I woke up, everything would be better.

Part V

Chapter 15

The Shard of Glass, London Bridge, London

Detective Mulligan was on top of the world. Literally. He stood at the very peak of Europe's largest building—the Shard of Glass. The view was amazing. All of London was laying at his feet.

It was a controversial building. It stood outside the City, far away from both the West End and the East End. This part of London was not controlled by one House but all three. Each had a stake in it. And the importance of the skyscraper couldn't be understated.

Hunter had gone to the Shard many times when it was being built. He was supposed be the one attending the meeting the detective was now attending. Mulligan had no idea what was to be discussed, only that it was very important and that Hunter's death had not only delayed the meeting but had sparked a war. Birthed a lunatic Lord. Saw a series of high-profile deaths come and go. And drew from banishment a detective only the most dangerous criminals knew and all of them feared.

The chaos had ended. The meeting was rescheduled. And Mulligan had been invited in Hunter's place. He brought with him Sutton's box, which contained information that may be valuable to the Houses and which he couldn't use to make a case against them. It wasn't enough, and the chain of evidence had been broken. So instead, he'd use it to his advantage. He'd make a deal with the people he wanted to take down. Calcain would hate him for it. But he had no choice.

It was eleven o'clock on the Friday before Christmas. The detective went to the meeting alone and stood encircled by bodyguards representing each of the Houses. He wasn't worried. He'd made arrangements with Calcain. If he arrived late to their agreed upon meeting place, Calcain would strike. And he would strike hard.

Mulligan heard footsteps, then the door in front of him opened. A person in a three-piece suit arrived, alongside two others, and he stood on the west side of the room. He was thin. He had a sharp face. He was probably in his late thirties and looked like a typical investment banker. He ignored Mulligan's presence as he whispered to his two advisors.

Shortly after, another person entered. This time, he was a tall, well-built Black man. His head was shaved, though he'd grown a long beard. He wore a white suit and red tie and looked to be of similar age to the first man, but with more worry lines around his eyes. He, too, entered with two advisors and stood on the east side of the room.

"It has been a little while, has it not, Charlie?" said the three-piece suit to the Black guy.

"I'm in no mood to be dealing with your bullshit, Elad." His accent was London Jamaican.

"Know your place and watch your tongue when you speak to me."

Charlie didn't look flustered by Elad's demand.

Charlie looked around the room. "Where's Russell?"

"Not here. Can you not see?"

Charlie ignored the comment.

A little while longer passed, and finally, the door opened a third time. The man who entered was wearing a dark brown jacket, a fitted pink shirt, light brown pants, and brown shoes. He had short, curly hair with a few grey patches and wore it combed back. He seemed athletic, like a swimmer or a rower. He and his two advisors took their place at the north side of the room.

"Right," Russell said softly. "Shall we begin?"

"I think that would be best," Elad said.

Without being told, all bodyguards and advisors exited the room. It made Mulligan curious.

Russell's voice demanded an audience.

"We've gathered here to participate in a meeting that should have been held months ago. But since then, things have changed. Quite a bit. We have all lost people we knew, cared about, loved. We all feel a deep, innate anger towards one another for those losses. But we can now all appreciate that no one here, enemy or not, was responsible for our suffering."

Charlie and Elad remained silent.

Russell took a deep breath before continuing.

"Gentlemen, I don't want to take up too much of Detective Mulligan's schedule. He's a busy man, and like us, he has been through a lot in the last few months. Detective Mulligan." He looked at me. "You know why you're here. We know why you're here. I suggest we take care of this business, so you may be on your way and the three of us can continue the rest of our meeting in private. Does everyone agree?"

Charlie and Elad nodded. It was time for the 'Great Detective' to become the 'Great Statesman'.

Speak carefully, Mulligan, the detective said to himself. *Let them do the talking.*

He cleared his throat. "I want to know why this meeting was

to be held in the first place."

Russell tilted his chin up. "This meeting was convened to discuss who would be in charge of the territory around the Shard. Put simply, we were going to give it to Hunter. It was to be agreed among all of the Houses that Hunter would be our mutual heir."

An enormous bomb was dropped right on Detective Mulligan's head.

"We didn't want our families involved in this work and are more than capable of understanding our disputes are bad for business. This was to be Hunter's first project. If he handled it well, he would have proven to us he was a capable leader, and in the years coming, we would have let him take more and more territory and business from us, granting the Houses a mutual, comfortable retirement. Does that answer your question?"

Detective Mulligan was gobsmacked. He and Hunter had done a better job than he had even realised. They hadn't just done well. They'd done very well. They'd done fucking well. They had been closer than he could've possibly imagined. Hunter was being groomed to take over as the leader of the underworld. Undisputed.

The detective's greed would have paid off.

He struggled to get his composure back.

"Yes, it does." He took a calming breath. "As you know, I have knowledge of relevant documentation about each of you. Rather than selling it to your opposites in this room, I elected to simply give it back to you. That way, peace will continue. I want to know what you can offer in exchange."

Charlie looked at the detective sharply. "Money. Women. Property. Power. We can give you anything you want."

Elad stepped in. "He's right. You can't ask us what we can give, that will get us nowhere. You need to tell us what you want."

"Not anything and everything, mind you," Russell said calmly. "An element of reasonableness must apply. But it's up to you to name your price, detective."

Mulligan pondered, then spoke in a measured tone. "Reduced operations."

"No," Charlie objected. "Sutton's war has cost us enough. We need to recover our losses."

"Fine." Mulligan shrugged. "Then I'll just give all the information to the highest bidder. Does that suit you better?"

He smiled.

"Detective, in this room, the Houses are entirely united," Russell said. "If Charlie will not reduce operations, then neither will I and neither will Elad."

Charlie looked surprised, and Mulligan's smile faltered. Just weeks ago, these men were massacring each other, and now they were supporting one another.

But the detective couldn't back down.

"Then I'll find a bidder outside this circle."

"We're getting carried away here." Elad stepped forward. "We have agreed to reduced operations with the government. Every year, we reduce activities by about one to three percent and instead receive government subsidies. So that's already granted. We can't give you more than that."

"That was an agreement with Sutton. Things are bound to change."

"I wouldn't bet on it."

Mulligan felt slightly outdone. He started again.

"You asked me my price, and this is it—further reduced operations. Money to cover the cost of the damage you and Sutton have inflicted on London and its infrastructure.

318

Information on at least the top thirty most wanted and finally…"

The detective hesitated. Maybe he shouldn't have intervened. But Calcain wouldn't be happy with him one way or another, whether he fought the man's battles or not.

"Calcain's redemption. I don't want him fearing for his life. I want his safety guaranteed."

Russell narrowed his eyes at Mulligan. Charlie and Elad move to speak, but Russell raised his right hand, silencing them.

"We agree to your terms."

Mulligan breathed a sigh of relief.

"Except Calcain."

The detective's relief flew out the window and fell down the Shard, crashing to the hard road underneath. He was furious.

"Why?"

"Calcain has demonstrated a great passion for our destruction, whether that fucks with the status quo or not. He won't stop. He is far too dangerous. And I don't have the energy nor the time to keep watch over him in Soho. Not any more. Our current objective, all three of us, is to eliminate all threats against us. That will mean a few deaths, but I assure you that they will not be bloody ones. That said, Calcain will be one of our targets. We cannot afford for him to roam freely. We cannot afford for him to live."

He was right. And Mulligan knew that. Calcain's thirst for the Houses had only grown. He was unpredictable. He could create carnage. But knowing he'd gotten Hunter so close to running all of the London underworld, the detective now had more confidence, more resolve to do things his way. Not Russell's or Charlie's or Elad's. Not even Calcain's.

Besides, Mulligan owed him.

"If you kill Calcain, I'll kill you. It doesn't matter who pulls the trigger; I'll take you all out. It's as simple as that."

Russell smiled. "I expected as much." He went silent, attempting to conjure a different solution. "How about this. We'll give you everything you asked for, but Calcain has to leave the country. And wherever he goes, he will be watched over from afar by a top member of each person in this room's team. Including you."

"Calcain will never leave England. He'll never leave fucking London."

"Then he'll die. That's the only offer I can give you. He must leave the country. And if he ever comes back, he will be killed on sight. You have my word on that."

Mulligan knew he wouldn't get a better deal. Especially once the Houses saw what Sutton had on them.

So be it.

"Deal."

Russell walked over to shake the detective's hand, then continued towards the window. He stared out over the City.

"I think about it a lot, you know. What we did to him. What we created. For days, we kept him captive. For weeks, he was tortured. And what did we gain? Nothing. He gave us nothing. We learned later that he didn't know anything that could've helped us at the time, but that didn't do much good in retrospect. Calcain changed so much, so quickly, during that time. We saw it happen right before us. As though the whole time, we were feeding some kind of creature inside him, hungry for hate. And we fed it well."

Russell turned and made eye contact with the detective. "We were wrong to do what we did."

He went back to the window, and Mulligan thought he looked uncomfortable.

"Detective, have you ever heard Calcain refer to himself as a monster?"

"Yes. Constantly."

"Well, that's a strange story really. My nephew, Luke—the one who freed him—often talked about the choice between man or monster. Calcain once said to him that the Houses, all of us, were like Dr. Frankenstein. We tore him to pieces, then tried to put him back together. And he came back as a monster. And like the monster in the book, Calcain will continue to pursue us until we are all dead. And then he will perish. That is how he sees matters progressing, and I am eager to prove him wrong."

Russell jutted out his chest and straightened his shoulders, levelling Mulligan with a sharp look. "He has thirty days. You are dismissed."

"Thank you." The detective stopped in the doorway as he was leaving. "If I can say one last thing…"

The room stayed quiet, granting him the floor to speak.

"You should speed up your retirement plans. For your sake."

He met eyes with each of the House leaders, lingering on Russell's.

Russell nodded once. "Noted."

Mulligan dropped three folders at his feet—the contents of Sutton's box—and took his leave. He tried to keep his composure as he left the building. But he was ecstatic. Thrilled beyond compare.

Because the 'Great Detective' still had one more hand to play. And he was confident the leaders would appease him.

*

Boxing Day

Detective Mulligan had a few surprisingly good days. But this meeting would not be a pleasant one.

The detective was at a cemetery near Watford, standing before the grave of an innocent soul. It was a few minutes before Calcain approached. He looked healthier. He'd bulked up a bit. Instead of thin and miserable, he looked toned and composed. But his eyes were still dark, and he was still pale.

"Thanks for coming," Mulligan said.

"Thanks for inviting me." Calcain stared down at the grave. "God bless her soul."

They both stood quiet. Mulligan broke the silence. "What sort of name is Leyli?"

"Persian. It's from a poem written in the twelve hundreds. A Romeo and Juliet style tragedy."

"But Shakespeare was—"

"Persians have been writing poetry for at least three thousand years, Mulligan."

He nodded. "Right you are. And now she's just another victim to add to London's body count."

"I would use the term 'victim' loosely, if I were you."

"I don't understand."

Calcain sighed, seeming almost annoyed that his one-time mentor didn't draw the same conclusion himself. "The only thing Leyli was a victim of was a broken heart."

"What?"

The gears of Mulligan's mind slowly started working, but Calcain was faster. He always was.

"I knew what had happened right away. I told you on the day, even. Do you remember?"

The Great Detective struggled to draw the specifics of his interactions with Calcain at the crime scene to mind. He'd been so overwhelmed by failure and by grief.

Calcain shoved his hands in his pockets.

"I'll break it down for you. Leyli fell in love with Hunter. So much so she was delusional over it. She saw this fantasy in her mind of the two of them together, getting married, having babies. She expected commitment and care. She became so obsessed with this concept that she lost everything, including relationships with her family. Then he did what famous footballers do. He cheated. She found out. And it tore her apart. A heated argument followed. Maybe she got the gun to protect herself. Maybe she got it as a threat. It doesn't matter. What matters is that she had no intention of shooting anyone. But there was that construction site next door. Some of those bricks came crashing down, startling her, and she pulled the trigger. She didn't mean to. It was an accident. But it happened. Hunter was dead. She was horrified, heartbroken and grief-stricken. She went mad. So she tossed the gun—if I were to guess, I'd say it got picked up with the trash and we'll find it in a dump somewhere—and then stabbed herself to death."

"But—"

"For her family. She couldn't bear for them to know what she'd done. She wanted it to look like it could've been someone, anyone else." Calcain paused. "If her crime was anything, it was loving Hunter too fiercely."

Calcain looked close to feeling something in that moment. Sadness or at least empathy. The detective thought there was hope for him yet. It had been two days since he had convinced Calcain to leave his beloved London. It wasn't an easy conversation. But Mulligan had promised him that once the Houses were dealt with, Calcain could come back. The detective's plans were already in motion. With his former student temporarily exiled, he could move forward without disruption.

"So," Mulligan said, smiling. "Have you made all your arrangements?"

"Yes. Tanka is finally back to form. He didn't take Jimmy's death particularly well."

"Understandable."

"Yeah. He and Ian will hold onto my possessions and look after my affairs."

"Well done. I promise you, Calcain, I will end this as quickly as I can. You'll be back in no time."

Calcain faced the detective. "You think being in a different country makes me any less dangerous? It just gives me time to think. To plot. And when I'm ready, I'll be back."

"And I'll be there to stop you. You can't have this your way. I won't allow it."

Calcain smiled. "Maybe before all of this is over, you and I will have a showdown of our own."

Detective Mulligan laughed. "Maybe so. You won't be quite so rusty next time around. I hear you've got a good private eye job somewhere."

"I do. It's the only job I'm suited for, really." Calcain straightened his jacket. "I've arranged for flowers to be delivered to Kimia. I'm glad Bell survived her car accident. I feared that, without her, the whole family would've torn itself apart."

"Car accident? Is that what you're calling it?"

Calcain shrugged. "It's easier that way. Safer." He tightened the scarf around his neck. "I'm going to take a quick walk around London before I leave. Take care, Mulligan. I mean that."

"You know," the Great Detective said as his friend began to leave, "despite everything, I think there's still some human left in you."

Those words went through Calcain like the many stab wounds he had suffered in the last few months. An old friend once told him he would one day have to choose between being human and being a monster. He couldn't live in both worlds forever.

So he finally made his choice.

He smiled as he looked at Mulligan, eye to eye. "You're wrong."

Calcain took out his phone and turned on Her song. His song.

Don't call me Gaga...Don't look at me like that / You amaze me / He ate my heart / He a-a-ate my heart / He ate my heart...Look at him, look at me / That boy is bad, and honestly / He's a wolf in disguise / But I can't stop staring in those evil eyes...That boy is a...

"I'm still a monster."

Monster. M-m-m-monster...

Calcain smiled and slowly left.

He ate my heart / He ate my heart...

Mulligan knew Calcain could not be stopped. Which meant the detective must work harder. And smarter. And faster.

Calcain disappeared slowly in the autumn winds, the orange and yellow and red leaves falling around him.

Detective Mulligan got up, looked at the beautiful blue sky, and thought to himself for a while. A few months ago, he believed everything was about to end. His career. His life. London. But things were different now. It would be a race to the Houses, and Calcain wouldn't stay contained for long.

But the Great Detective had a plan.

The End

Epilogue

Soho.

It just wasn't what it had been before. All the scum was cleaned up. The dirt was gone. The whores were expelled. There were far too many shops for my liking, and the whole neighbourhood overflowed with shoppers and tourists. The drug trade was all but dead. I blamed the artists. They wanted to make the area 'trendy'. But all they'd done was fuck it up.

It was late May, and the weather was beautiful. It eliminated my excuse to wear my long coat, but a bit of sun never hurt anyone. I listened to her sing 'I Like It Rough' in my ear. I'd loved Soho. But it just wasn't the same any more. Which is why I moved downtown and east, to a place full of life and full of colour.

By the time I got to my flat, it was totally dark. I decided a sneaky drink before bed was a good plan, so I popped down to my local bar and met Liam, the bartender. He was the closest thing I had to a friend at that point.

The serving stand was to the left, and there were plenty of empty tables around, including a few eight-seaters, but I took my usual place at the bar on the third stool down. Liam poured me a pint of Blue Moon without me having to ask.

"A shot of single malt as well, please."

"Long day?" he asked.

"No. Same old, really. Just finished a quick project, so I have a bit of cash. Need a pick-me-up."

"Which one? Oban?"

"Surprise me."

He went with the Oban and took a shot alongside me. The bar was quiet. It seemed he could spare a few minutes.

"Talk to me."

I smiled. "What about?"

"This project of yours. You seem fucked. Need me to hook you up with another chick?"

"No, thanks. I still haven't gotten over the last one."

"I thought you hated her."

"I do. But that doesn't mean I didn't like her. She ditched me."

"Remind you of Shelly?"

"Let's not talk about her."

"So this project…"

"Homicide. Woman found in the bathroom with her wrists cut. Uptown. Initial theory was suicide, but they couldn't find the knife. I found it, and I also found the husband's fingerprints all over it. Wanted her insurance money. This recession is a motherfucker."

"How long did it take you?"

"When did I leave this morning?"

"Ten, ten-thirty?"

"This long, plus time to walk around Soho a little."

"Fuck, man. You're fast."

"I've been doing this for a while. I get shit for it, but it pays the rent and buys me a few drinks. Some food. Keeps me in Dark Fire."

"You ain't gonna give that shit up?"

"Why should I?"

"It really fucks you up."

"Permanent effects?"

"Not yet, but there's still time."

"Until there's evidence of permanent brain damage, I think I'm good. Speaking of…"

I pulled some Dark Fire from my pocket and took a hit in the alley outside. I went back in for a few drinks, and before I knew it, it was four o'clock, there was a girl on my lap with her tongue down my throat, and Liam was closing up.

I took the girl home, no more than thirty seconds away, then took another hit. I was getting pretty fucked up, but that was the point. All I wanted to do was exist. Just exist. And wait. For the Houses to make a mistake. For Mulligan to make a mistake. Then I could strike.

Until then, I would wait. And I would plan.

*

Detective Mulligan was in Florida on semi-retirement. He'd taken leave early for his age, but that wasn't unusual in his line of work. It wore you down.

Florida was a predictable place to end up. He didn't need much: English speakers, good food, the beach, and sports. He'd made sure his bases were covered, but even now, he wasn't at peace. Even in death, he wouldn't be at peace.

Not as long as Calcain was alive and on the hunt.

His protégé had banished himself to New York City, away from the Houses and hidden enough to be missed by their franchises across the pond. Mulligan called up his friends at the NYPD on a regular basis to check on Calcain's movements, to see if his counterparts had any news of him or his whereabouts.

They never did.

They couldn't find him. Which wasn't surprising. Calcain couldn't be found unless he wanted to be found. So the detective spent half his time in London and half in Florida, determined to keep a safe distance but a close eye on his two most important subjects: The Houses of London and Calcain the Monster.

His plan was in motion, and he wouldn't fuck it up. Not like last time.

*

Stanton Street, Lower East Side, Manhattan

New York City, New York

I was at peace. In darkness. In silence. Fucked up on Dark Fire and wasted on alcohol from Donnybrooks, my local bar on Clinton Street. Greenwich Village, like Soho, had become too trendy. But in the lower east side, I got the odd investigative work from stumped cops in return for protection and total anonymity. For a small fee, I'd solve their cases for them. No matter how bad or how horrendous, I could solve it. I could solve anything.

But every now and then, I'd let myself fall into the Dark Fire abyss. Sometimes it took days to pull myself out. I sank into the pure darkness, unable to tell for sure whether my eyes were open or closed. I'd rest in my own world and my own zone. All I had to do was exist. I would listen to Her. I could feel Her. I could smell Her. I'd listen to Her voice, and I'd feel special.

Just give in, don't give up baby / Open up your heart and your mind to me / Just...

I missed London. New York City felt like a loving grandmother. But London reminded me of Mom. Because no matter how badly I fucked up or what evil shit I did, all I had to do was smile. And she would always smile back.

I never really woke up from Dark Fire. I only worked to feed my habit. But the work kept me sharp. Which is how I knew where Mulligan was: Miami, Ocean View Apartments, unit twenty-seven.

When I woke up—really woke up—I'd deal with him. And the Houses.

I'd strike hard.

But until then? Abyss.